About the Author

Mary-Anne O'Connor has a combined arts education degree with specialities in environment, music and literature. She works in marketing and co-wrote/edited *A Brush with Light* and *Secrets of the Brush* with Kevin Best.

Mary-Anne lives in a house overlooking her beloved bushland in northern Sydney with her husband Anthony, their two sons Jimmy and Jack, and their very spoilt dog Saxon. This is her second major novel; her first, *Gallipoli Street*, was published in 2015.

T0363196

Also by Mary-Anne O'Connor

Gallipoli Street

WORTH FIGHTING FOR

MARY-ANNE O'CONNOR

First Published 2016
Second Australian Paperback Edition 2017
ISBN 978 1 489 24141 2

WORTH FIGHTING FOR
© 2016 by Mary-Anne O'Connor
Australian Copyright 2016
New Zealand Copyright 2016

Published by
HQ Fiction
An imprint of Harlequin Enterprises (Australia) Pty Ltd.
Level 13, 201 Elizabeth St
SYDNEY NSW 2000
AUSTRALIA

® and TM are trademarks of Harlequin Enterprises Limited or its corporate affiliates. Trademarks indicated with ® are registered in Australia, New Zealand and in other countries.

Cataloguing-in-Publication details are available from the National Library of Australia
www.librariesaustralia.nla.gov.au

Printed and bound in Australia by McPherson's Printing Group

For Mum, Dad and my aunts and uncles.
The golden generation.

Sometimes, in order to find yourself,
you must first become truly and utterly lost.

Part One

Part One

One

November 1941
Braidwood, New South Wales, Australia

Junie Wallace was a smart girl. Smart enough to know that taking her cardigan off that afternoon was out of the question, despite the heat. Ernest Farthington's gaze bore down on her like a second sun and she pulled the buttons closer to the eyelets, hugging her arms tight; blocking every part of her person as best she could.

She forced herself to focus on the countryside instead. The aspect from the long, dark-bricked verandah was lofty and expansive, taking in the many hundreds of acres that made up the Farthington estate, but Junie had never felt the peacefulness of it. On the contrary, it had always felt as if she were awaiting sentence on behalf of the rest of the town here as the Farthingtons sat in judgement upon their high throne.

If the place itself lacked the serenity it deserved, the view was still unquestionably beautiful. Braidwood slept in a green and gold sea of soft-blanketed pastures, the cattle fat and lazy in the sun. The spring sky blazed with only distant tufts of clouds on its edges and a lone eagle glided against it in perfect, graceful arcs, rising to where the surrounding hills stood guard, shrouded in eucalypt haze. Junie breathed the hay-scented air deeply, envying the eagle, flying with it in her mind's eye. Over the stately house, the barn, the stables, the nursing paddock and milking sheds, out above the blue hills and far to the right where Michael Riley rode on horseback, rounding up yearlings beneath his wide-brimmed hat. She wished for some excuse to bring him closer, wondering if Mrs Constance Farthington, the mistress of the homestead and Ernest's mother, ever offered refreshments to their hardworking staff on hot Saturday afternoons. It was unlikely.

Henry Wallace was talking about the war, as usual, and well into his cups, which was also usual. Junie wished her father would stop. It was all he ever spoke about of late, mostly in comparison to his own experiences during the Great War.

'It's a simple matter of following formula: lead from the front, protect your flanks and make sure every man knows his duty.'

Generals can't win wars without soldiers who follow orders, and soldiers can't win wars without generals who know how to give them, Junie predicted.

'Generals can't win wars without soldiers who follow orders, and soldiers can't win wars without generals who know how to give them,' Henry declared.

'Quite right, quite right,' agreed Colonel Humphrey Farthington, who usually supported Henry's views so long as they promoted the ideals of 'the good old days'. He puffed on his pipe as he nodded and Junie wondered if his moustache would catch alight today. Watching the Colonel's grey handlebar whiskers begin to smoke was always the highlight of any social event for Junie and her brothers. The sight of him stomping about, red-faced and goggle-eyed until someone found some water and doused him made for great amusement. It usually left him resembling a bedraggled, astonished-looking house cat, and it certainly ruffled the feathers of the queen pigeon that was his wife, Constance.

The memories turned melancholy and Junie sighed, a familiar pain surfacing. How she missed her three older brothers. The youngest, Frankie, had been killed in Tobruk and the other two, Archie and Bill, were still away at war in Syria. Surely it would end soon. Surely that was enough for them to give.

'If every man knows his duty, plans can be executed and followed. Not this blind-leading-the-blind nonsense we're seeing now...and they can't keep using inexperience as an excuse any more,' Henry thundered on. Junie felt a pang of pity. Her father was far worse since Frankie was killed, blaming blundering leadership for the loss of his youngest son. She had stopped trying to ask him about the running of the farm or their finances – there was little point; it was as if he had retreated into a world of whisky, anger and grief and nothing else mattered, except the echoing pain in his wife, Lily's, eyes.

'Would the young lady care for a walk?'

Junie jumped at Ernest's request as he stood before her, lean and immaculate in his uniform. No desert warfare for him – Ernest's military career had been carefully plotted right from the start, when he'd made himself indispensable to his university professors and networked his way into the higher echelons of the AIF. Somehow Ernest Farthington had managed to make the war a stepping stone in his political career, spending his time far away from actual conflict and deep in the battles of the boardrooms.

'I, uh, have a slight headache I'm afraid,' she replied. 'Might just sit and finish my book.'

'Nonsense, my dear – the walk will do you good. You're spending too much time burying yourself in those damn books. Worst thing you ever did, letting her into our library,' the Colonel chastised Ernest, but in a good-natured way.

'Junie has a way of charming us with her clever mind, I'm afraid. Perhaps I should disallow it. She may leave us all for university at this rate,' Ernest said, smiling, his mouth thin in his otherwise handsome face, his black hair oiled and sleek. He gave Junie the unnerving impression of a snake.

'Bah! Women in universities. Absurd notion,' puffed the Colonel.

'Not so absurd for those who can afford it,' Mrs Constance Farthington said, overhearing as she came through the parlour doors with her twin daughters, Isabel and Ursula. She was followed by Junie's mother, Lily, who blushed at the thinly veiled reference to the Wallaces' currently precarious fiscal state. 'Both the girls are considering furthering their studies.'

'What would you study?' Junie asked Isabel, surprised. Neither Isabel nor Ursula were remotely academic.

'Books,' Isabel replied, appearing quite sincere in her answer.

'They have a very big library at the Sydney University,' Ursula added.

'Do they?' Junie said, trying not to smile.

'Perhaps we may even spend some length of time in the city,' Constance said smoothly. 'I do so miss Jane Chamberlain and the girls are simply dying to see Eliza.'

Junie scoffed internally. Constance was the biggest name dropper who ever lived and she sincerely doubted the queen of the social aristocracy in Sydney, Jane Chamberlain, gave two hoots about this snobby country nobody and her dim-witted daughters. As for Eliza Chamberlain, the lady in question's daughter, it was well known that she was the darling of the Sydney scene, witty and elegant, and surely far above socialising with the vapid Farthington twins from Braidwood.

'Can't see the point in educating females. Waste of money,' the Colonel said, banging his pipe on the rail.

'*Humphrey*, not on the white paint,' Constance admonished, barely concealing her customary impatience with her husband.

'A woman's place is in the home,' Henry agreed, ignoring Constance. 'What's the use in filling their heads with academic ambition when they'll never use it?'

'Some end up using it,' Junie said, bristling.

'Not many,' Ernest said in a tone that suggested he found the concept amusing.

Junie's face warmed. 'Well, we may not all be able to use it but that doesn't mean we should be denied the right to enjoy it. Besides, more and more women are taking on professional roles with so many of our men off at war.'

Henry muttered something about that being an unnatural state of affairs and Lily placed a hand on his arm. 'You forget how well Junie did at school. Your daughter has a wonderful mind, dear,' she said softly.

'Pity she wasn't born a boy then,' Henry said with a sigh, glancing at his wife, who was slim and pale in her black mourning clothes. His expression softened. 'Ah, she is a bright one, our Junie,' he said, bestowing a brief smile on his daughter. 'Her brothers could probably do with some of her nous but there it is. They'll do well enough...if these blasted fools in Syria can get their act together.'

'No university for either of them, then?' Constance asked, already knowing the answer. Neither Archie nor Bill was likely to pursue further studies, detesting any activity that deprived them of the outdoors. Of the three of them, only Frankie had shown any interest and there had been some talk of him pursuing a writing career after the war. Sadly, all that was left now were his letters – still too painful for Junie to re-read.

'My sons are farmers and fighters,' Henry proclaimed, pride and grief shooting across his features at the thought of the three that were now two. 'No shame in that.'

'No, no shame in that, sir.' The Colonel nodded. 'And damn good with the football too. Looking forward to the end of this blasted war so we can have our rugby champions back.'

What's left of them, Junie thought sadly, missing those halcyon days herself.

Constance arranged her skirt as she sat next to Lily, looking smug and unable to resist adding a few more boasts about Ernest's academic achievements. The twins had positioned themselves on the stairs to whisper and giggle and Ernest stood near Junie, ignoring his mother. Junie could feel his eyes upon her and she pulled her cardigan close once more, wishing she could shroud herself in a blanket and deny him any view whatsoever.

'Did I tell you Ernest has been persuaded to sit for parliament after the war? The general has great faith in him,' Constance said.

She had. About fourteen times in the past two weeks, by Junie's count. She continued her game of prediction: *I swear that boy was born to run the country.*

'I swear that boy was born to run the country,' Constance said in conspiratorial tones. 'Knew it from when he was a little fellow and he used to write his own declarations of independence and post them about the house. Little scamp!' She laughed.

Little troll more like, Junie thought. Ernest had spent a good part of their childhood ordering them all about, her brothers included. Not that he'd had any success there – the three Wallace boys had made short work of the scrawny, spoilt pest that was Ernest Farthington. Images of Ernest telling Frankie to fetch his horse and finding himself pushed straight into the manure pile caused her to smile.

Unfortunately, Ernest mistook her look of amusement and pressed again. 'The pups are coming along, Junie. Seriously, you must come and see them.' He offered his arm in anticipation.

'Such a charmer. Don't be too flattered, June,' Constance said. 'Half the girls on the Sydney scene have their cap set at him, including Miss Eliza Chamberlain.'

Junie sincerely doubted that too. 'Junie,' she corrected. Constance was the only person who ignored her preferred nickname.

'Of course, *Junie*,' Constance conceded with an icy smile. Junie knew that Constance disapproved of Ernest's interest in her. She would never consider Junie a suitable match for her wonderful son, the future Prime Minister of Australia. That would be a role for the Elizas of the world.

Ernest waited and Junie really couldn't think of a way to refuse him again, especially as everyone knew she adored animals, dogs in particular. They took off towards the barn as Henry's commentary on the war recommenced and she was glad to at least be spared that.

The feeling of reprieve didn't last long.

'You really should wear your hair up, Junie. It won't do to have it wild like a country bumpkin when you go to Sydney.' He flicked at a tangled brown curl and she shied away.

'I don't know for sure that I'm going –'

'Of course you do. Once we're married you will need to set up house in the city. It won't be logical to have you all the way down here once the war is over.'

'I thought you had changed your mind about State Parliament,' she said, avoiding the dreaded subject of marriage.

'No, as soon as the war ends, State is the logical first step, then maybe an overseas post before I pursue Federal in Canberra. I expect we'll have children by then and the country respects a family man.'

'Ernest, I haven't said yes…'

'You will.'

His confidence irked her. 'Your mother will object.'

'Then she will have to get used to it.'

'Ernest, I – I am not so sure I –'

'I saw a house in Mosman this week that should suit. No water views but the street is home to several respectable families – and it's near the ferry, which will be handy. The bathroom needs attention but it does have a decent-sized formal dining, which would seat a dozen or so quite comfortably…'

As he prattled on, Junie had a vision of hosting dinner parties with Ernest at the head of the table: the men discussing politics and the ladies in obliging costume, afraid to comment lest they appear unwomanly; the husbands looking down the necklines of other men's wives.

Suddenly it was unfathomable.

'Ernest, I can't marry you,' Junie blurted, shocked by her own admission, her heart racing.

Ernest slowed his steps and studied the horizon. 'And why not?'

'Because...I don't think I'm ready for marriage yet. Perhaps next year,' she said lamely, knowing that was weak defence against his store of artillery.

'Out of the question. I need to settle before the war ends and that's bound to be soon. Besides, you're eighteen now and I've waited long enough. We'll set up house this summer – that should give you enough time to get the wedding organised.' He slapped his hand against his thigh, killing a fly, and Junie felt her life as equally unimportant to this man. She fought an impulse to turn and run to the hills. To the man on horseback who offered the alternative she so craved.

'I'll have to think about it –'

'You won't be thinking about anything because there is nothing to consider.' Ernest's tone was still light but the set of his mouth betrayed his mounting temper. 'You seem to be forgetting your father's debt.'

She hadn't forgotten. Everyone in town knew the Farthingtons had bailed her father out in recent months – without them they would have lost the farm.

'I didn't do it to be neighbourly, Junie,' he said, stopping altogether as they reached the barn. 'I did it for you.' He turned her towards him, his fingers pressing into her flesh.

'Not *for* me. You did it to *own* me.'

He half-smiled at her words, pulling her towards him in a sudden movement and forcing his mouth on hers. She twisted in revulsion but it only dug his hands deeper into her arms.

'I do own you, Junie,' he said in quiet fury, shoving her back. 'Set the date for March. We'll announce it next weekend.' Then he turned and was gone.

Next weekend: the parish dance. The event she'd long been looking forward to was now something to dread as the future rolled towards her, like a dark storm menacing a summer's day. She rubbed absently at the imprints of Ernest's fingers on her skin as she looked towards the barn – straight into the eyes of Michael Riley.

꧁꧂

A little black body dived into Michael's lap, where two other silky pups rolled about, tumbling backwards, their tiny tails wagging. He gently picked one up and Junie watched his hands, tanned and work-callused, and so different to the ones that had bruised her moments ago. He hadn't said anything about what he'd witnessed and she didn't know what to say if he did.

One of the pups bounded over to her, and began to tug on her hair, pulling the last of the curls from their pins. The others seemed to think this a brilliant idea and she tried to disentangle herself in giggly objection as three small sets of teeth wrestled for the right to swing about on her long waves.

'Think we might have to call this one Curly-Locks,' Michael said, pulling one away and holding it in the air. It wiggled with excitement, back legs paddling.

'I'm sure they already have working-dog names like Bluey or Blackie or Red,' she replied. 'Mind you they're all black…'

'Well you can't exactly have three "Blackies",' Michael reasoned, helping her to untangle the other pups and cradling them as they climbed over each other to chew on his chin.

'Even so, I can't see them being given very creative names,' she said, wishing they could be pets instead of working dogs, but that wasn't how things worked around here. Everyone had a role to fulfil, including her.

'Let's give them secret names then,' Michael said. 'I stand by Curly-Locks for you,' he said holding the pup up again and grinning as it gave a high little bark of approval.

Junie hugged the large, fluffy male who'd made his way back to her and couldn't seem to stop wagging with joy. 'You can be called Hero,' she decided, cuddling him close.

'Why Hero?'

'Because he has a star on his chest, see?' Junie held him up for inspection and Michael tickled his neck.

'And what shall we call this cheeky fella?' Michael asked as the smallest, rumbliest pup nudged his way under his elbow.

'Well, he is rather plump…how about Georgie Porgie?' Her eyes met Michael's and they laughed again.

'Perfect.'

'You know, with the whole family off to Sydney soon maybe they'll forget and you can name the puppies in their absence. They won't really be able to object – a dog has to have a name.'

'And you'll be going too.' Michael's expression changed and Junie wished she hadn't mentioned it.

'How do you know that?'

'It's a small town, Junie.' He attempted a smile and she felt his sadness creep towards her, enveloping them both. Her conversation with Ernest hung between them and she forced herself to find a way to explain.

'Ernest…Ernest has loaned my father some money –'

'You don't have to tell me, Junie –'

'But I need to. I need you to know.'

'Everyone knows,' he said. It was a fact, not an insult. Michael too was feeling the brunt of her father's economic demise. The Farthington reach was wide.

One of the pups had managed to bury himself in the dirt and Junie bent to pull him out, smiling at his tiny, caked face, and he gave a surprised sneeze, showering her in earth.

'I don't know about Hero any more,' she said, laughing as she wiped his nose clean and he tried to lick her fingers. 'I think we may have to call you Digger.'

'Diggers are heroes,' Michael pointed out, laughing a little too, but there was wistfulness there. For some reason it prompted her to make a confession.

'I don't want to go to Sydney...' she said softly. *I want to run away with you...to somewhere safe in those blue hills.*

'Then why go?'

She cuddled Digger close and he nestled near her ear. Surely there was no reason good enough? Then Junie remembered the expression on her father's face as he looked at her mother today. 'Because we all have our jobs to do.'

'And it's your job to marry him, is it?' Michael's dark eyes held hers and there was anger and sadness in their depths.

'Yes,' she whispered. How she wished that answer was impossible.

He stood then, picking up the sleepy pups and putting them back in their stall. Junie stood too and they watched the exhausted little pile together.

'Michael –'

His hands gripped the wood of the stall and he lowered his head. 'Don't say anything, Junie. There's no point.'

'But I need to tell you that your friendship has been –'

'Just that,' he finished for her. He pushed away from the stall and strode out of the barn even as she looked for words that would stop him.

'It's – it's more than that,' she called, confessing the truth.

Michael paused, his tone odd in reply. 'You're not the only one with a job to do, Junie.'

Two

Mavis Riley squeezed the wet shirt through the ringer, her skin already puckered from an hour of laundry. It felt hard as always, a never-ending task that broke her back and cracked her skin, and she wiped her brow as her two daughters brought more baskets up from the creek.

'That's it, Mum,' Beryl said, huffing as she dropped the heavy load near the others.

'Did you get the stain out of Dad's shirt?'

'Mostly,' she said, picking it up to show her. 'I think there'll be a faint mark.'

Mavis frowned at the pale brown on the white of her husband's best Sunday shirt. That wouldn't do at all.

'Maybe we could dye the whole thing khaki. Say it's a troop support shirt,' Beryl suggested, wrinkling her nose as she studied it and pushing her blonde hair away from her face.

'Might become all the rage,' her sister Dorn agreed and they giggled, causing their mother to smile too.

'Keep it aside, Beryl. I'll try another soak. Here, Dorn, fetch a clean tub with her now.' Mavis hefted the one she'd just emptied and handed it to her youngest before they took off.

They were good girls, her two, uncomplaining and accepting of their lot and both blessed with good humour, much like herself when she could find the time to laugh. She allowed herself another smile now, imagining her husband, Rory, turning up at church tomorrow in a khaki-dyed shirt under his pressed jacket and tie. He was proud Irish, her man – Sunday best had to be just that, which made the image rather amusing.

Not so the Irish drinking that came with it though. No, there was nothing much to smile at there.

Mavis pulled a basket close to the line that hung between the great gum and the scribbly, pegging each of her husband's items carefully. A currawong sat nearby, watching her with yellow eyes before turning to call to her young. It was a strange, lamenting sound, Mavis had always thought; beautiful, yet sad too. Like a mother's love when she feared for her child.

Holding one of Michael's shirts now she felt the birdsong fill her, her instincts on alert. Something was up with that boy, something restless and unpredictable and it made her very nervous. Last time she had a son who wore that expression, he up and joined the army. It had been two long years of praying for Davey and Mavis didn't welcome the idea of adding a second son's name after each decade of the Rosary. She fingered the beads in her pocket absently. *Michael is only eighteen*, she reassured herself. It would be impossible for him to falsify his age and join up locally. They would just have to keep an eye on him and hope he didn't wander into another town's enrolment office when he was out droving.

The sound of the girls' chatter echoed and she squinted over at the house, tidy and well-tended but not much more than a shack really. The paddocks were overgrown and largely unused but the vegetable garden bore good return, thanks to the many hours of care she'd invested. The chicken coop was a blessing too, providing a regular supply of fresh eggs, but such luxuries couldn't make up for the cramped conditions within.

We need more room. It was a common thought, ever more so of late. Rory had promised he'd add extra space not long after they'd moved here from Tumut two years ago, but somehow it had never eventuated. It hadn't mattered so much when it was the girls sharing a room on one side of the kitchen and she and Rory in a room on the other, but now a two-bedroom home just wasn't working. Not since the stockmen's quarters had shut down at the Wallaces' and Michael had moved back home.

He wouldn't be with them for long, though. Especially when Rory kept coming home three sheets to the wind after handing over most of his sporadic earnings to the local publican. Despite her best efforts to stifle the grunts and creaks that came from their bed, she knew that Michael was well aware of what went on once her drunk, amorous husband fell alongside her.

Michael had taken to sleeping outside in a makeshift lean-to, backed up against the rough-hewn rocks that formed the house's chimney. But Braidwood was cold at night, even at this time of year. No, her youngest son wouldn't stand another winter at home now. Not with Rory the way he was.

It had been bad enough when the army had rejected her husband's enlistment at the beginning of the war. Despite wearing his Sunday best, Rory hadn't been able to hide the black eye he'd received the night before nor the after-stench of whisky. Nor could he hide the altercations on his service record that reinforced their opinion. Rory had been a decorated soldier in the Great War – infractions aside. He'd been many things before they'd hit hard times. When the army had accepted their son Davey it was another blow to Rory's pride, especially as he'd been teaching their boy to ride and shoot since he was a young fellow.

But the harshest blow had come this winter, when Henry Wallace had suddenly announced he was putting Rory off. These past few years Rory had fallen down, to be sure. He'd become a drunk, bad-tempered, even belligerent, but he wasn't a lazy man. He'd worked the farm for the Wallace family with as much care and dedication as if it were his own – more, she acknowledged, looking around her. He'd even taken his own sons to work alongside him. She knew he'd missed working with Davey once he'd left for war but at least Michael had still been with him each day. Now that was denied him too, and Mavis knew Rory resented not being able to spend time with his son even more than losing the regular wage.

Mavis still wondered at the coldness of Henry's decision; it was so unlike him. But of course Henry wasn't the one behind it – rumour had it he was in debt to the Farthingtons, because Ernest had taken control of the property. And Ernest had no room for an outspoken man like Rory on staff; he preferred lackeys to men with opinions, boys he could work like dogs and pay as little as possible. Boys like her son.

Her eyes pricked for poor Lily; she'd lost more than a child in this war. Henry was hitting the bottle hard too and they'd lost control of their staff and their home. Grief crippled people in so many ways, she reflected, sending a quick prayer to heaven for Davey.

And for Michael. Because he would soon leave, she knew it in her heart. It wasn't just his father's drinking, the cold nights or even Ernest Farthington that was driving him away. He was losing June Wallace too. The only person who had been keeping him here was set to be caught in the same net that held them all. Mavis could read the signs in Mass each week: Ernest was after that girl and what Ernest wanted he usually got, even if it meant standing up to his overbearing mother at last. Michael was about to taste the bitterness of a broken heart and she could no sooner prevent it than stop the sun from setting.

Mavis looked to the sky as that golden orb sank gloriously now, igniting the fields into a moving sea of light, shimmer and shadow, rippling and bowing to the breeze that cooled the day into night. The currawong continued her call and Mavis felt an aching maternal love move through her. It dipped and pulled, surpassing an old love and eclipsing it, the love she'd once felt for her man. Now as fallen and rusted as the gate on their drive.

Neither love gave her comfort any more. They just left her here, alone with the sky. To ache with the song of the currawong.

Sitting in the bay window of her bedroom, Junie Wallace watched the sun burnish the cream walls of the family homestead. The green pitched roof of the front parlour below was almost black now and the lawn was a dark carpet for the handful of rosellas in late search of grass seeds. She was running her fingers across the soft silk of her new dress, wondering how her mother had saved the coupons and put enough money away for it. Such items had been commonplace a few years back but now, with her father's debts and the Farthingtons' control of the estate, they were rare and treasured items. Especially when there was a special occasion to wear it to – like tomorrow night. Despite the dread she felt over Ernest's pending announcement, part of her couldn't help but feel excited by the idea of Michael Riley seeing her in this dress.

Suddenly she couldn't wait to try it on. Junie tore her cotton skirt and shirt off, pulling the soft fabric over her head and sliding it down her body before pausing to carefully zip it. Then she turned to stare into the oak-framed mirror that sat in the corner of her bedroom, admitting to herself that the girl she saw there was no longer a girl at all. The pale pink fabric clung to her curves where only last summer it would have fallen in straight lines. Junie, a late bloomer, had become a woman at long last, with accentuated hips and a rounded bust. Her best friend, Katie Burgess, said that Junie looked like the film star Gene Tierney, marvelling at the resemblance every time they passed the poster advertising the actress's latest movie *Belle Starr* at the theatre in town. Junie didn't know about that. Gene Tierney seemed to know what to do with her curves. Junie hadn't a clue.

She tried to practise some of the movie star's poses, lifting one shoulder and holding her hand at her hip. Maybe Michael would dance with her, his hand on her waist, his cheek against hers. She stroked the material absently. Maybe he would take her outside and kiss her in the cold moonlight, running his fingers across the silk, causing pleasures she could barely imagine. The thought made her stomach flutter and she took a deep breath, trying to calm her mind, but it went racing ahead regardless, darting into little tunnels and holes like a rabbit in a warren. Sometimes she hated the way her mind did that, always digging further, relentless, finding yet another tunnel when all she wanted to do was rest.

People had always dubbed her 'clever', in the almost pitying way they said such things about bookish girls, but the verdict had shifted somewhat with the arrival of her figure. Now she was viewed with discomforting interest by several of the men in the town, and expressions like 'good sort' and 'right little beauty' were tagged to her name. A few of the women were less effusive, marking the change in Junie with wariness or perhaps envy, using non-committal phrases such as 'grown up' and 'quite the young lady' at best, 'look out for that one' or 'up to no good' at worst – the last only whispered, of course, but Junie heard. Those who loved her were in turn apprehensive (her parents), teasing (her girlfriends), or frustratingly silent (Michael), but to those precious few she was still just Junie; clever, curvy or otherwise.

Michael's face came to mind again and the longing she'd read in his eyes today haunted her. It wasn't just her imagination – she knew he felt what she felt. But she needed him to turn that feeling into action or Ernest was about to close in and take any hope away.

He's going to anyway; it's too late, the rabbit in her mind warned, racing down an unwanted tunnel.

Junie stared at her reflection as the rabbit ran, twisting and searching for a way to stop this.

Maybe Michael is planning something. He said he had a job to do. Maybe he's lined up work for himself somewhere else.

Hope bounded with the rabbit.

I could leave with him! Then maybe we could make enough money to send home and I wouldn't have to marry Ernest – he wouldn't have any power over me. I could save the farm with Michael.

Then the rabbit hit a block and Junie paused.

But just how much money would be 'enough'?

There was no point in the rabbit running down any more tunnels until she knew that answer. The price of her freedom was really the price of her family's debt and she needed to find out just what that sum was.

Junie felt her resolve intensify. She was a woman grown, not a child to be bartered off. Forget her earlier resignation, she wasn't going to marry Ernest, not when her rabbit could tunnel its way to an answer. Not when the debt could be paid with a combined force of skill and wits from two instead of one.

And not while Michael Riley and pale pink silk dresses promised so much more.

⁘

The wireless was playing 'Somewhere Over the Rainbow' and Lily Wallace hummed along as she washed each glass carefully, spinning the crystal in the late sun and watching it make little

rainbows across her kitchen. It would have been a perfectly normal, cheerfully domestic moment if not for the fact that she was
also crying. She hardly even noticed it any more, it was just rain
on her face, matching the tears that rained every day in her heart,
ever since her boy had been taken from her.

Judy Garland's voice wrapped sweetly around her.

Frankie had drawn a picture of a rainbow for her once. He'd
given it to her for Christmas – or was it her birthday? Lily hated
that she couldn't remember, although she did remember that he'd
included a horse with three legs. She'd laughed and kissed his fair
little head, telling him he was an artist in the making. She wondered where it was now. Surely she'd kept it? Perhaps she'd look
for it later, after a little lie down.

'Mum.'

Lily started and hastily dabbed at her eyes. 'I'm in the kitchen,'
she called, wishing she had time to wash her face – Junie hated to
see her cry. She turned and gave a little gasp as Junie walked into
the kitchen in her new pink dress.

'Junie! You shouldn't wear it until tomorrow! Oh, but you do
look lovely,' Lily exclaimed softly. That girl grew more beautiful
by the day.

Junie glanced down at the dress in mild surprise. 'I tried it
on, then forgot I was wearing it,' she said. 'I'll take it off in a sec,
Mum, I just wanted to ask you something –'

'I think you should take it off now, don't you?' Lily said, wiping her hands on her apron and pointing to the stairs. 'Come on,
you can ask me whatever it is in your room.'

Junie huffed impatiently but did as she was told. She was a good
daughter like that, dutiful towards both her parents while her
brothers were away, despite her wilful nature.

Lily helped Junie out of her dress and hung it carefully on the
wardrobe.

'There. Now what was it that couldn't wait?'

Junie put her skirt and blouse back on and sat next to her mother on the bed, staring into the distance as she often did when deep in thought. Lily could almost hear the intelligent teenage mind at work.

'Ernest…' Junie began hesitantly. 'Ernest wants to announce the engagement at the dance.'

'Well, that's wonderful dear.'

'No. No, it isn't.'

Lily studied her daughter's face. 'You've changed your mind?'

'I didn't change it – I never wanted to marry him. I…don't want to now.'

'Oh.' Lily felt her world slip a little. 'But you said you wanted to marry him only last month –'

'I knew it was what you wanted to hear.'

Lily stared down at her hands. 'Oh, I see.'

'Mum, how much money do we owe him?'

'I'm not sure…I mean, your father –'

'Hundreds? Thousands?'

'I don't know…the house…the house has a mortgage, I think…and Ernest takes care of all the wages these days so…' Lily frowned, trying to remember what Henry had told her. Not much, she realised now.

'But how can you not know something like that?' Junie sounded exasperated and Lily felt ashamed. Once she would have known: she'd run this house like a well-oiled machine just as Henry and the boys had run the land. But that was before the war.

'I'm sorry.' It was all she could manage as the rain came again and she brushed at it, wishing she was far stronger than this, like she used to be. 'But whatever it is, I'm sure your father can work something out with the bank.' She tried to sound like her old self for Junie's sake but she was confused and her lungs were tight.

'If you don't want to marry him…yes, we could ask the bank… Ernest might know what to do. Oh dear.'

The cursed rain was falling harder now. Then Junie was taking her hands.

'It's all right, Mum. I'll talk to Dad. I'm sure everything will be fine.'

'But Ernest –'

'We just had a bit of a tiff today, about the debt and all,' Junie assured her and Lily hoped she was telling the truth.

'Are you sure…you seemed…?'

'Truly,' Junie said. 'Please Mum, don't worry about it. I just had a case of cold feet I think.'

Lily felt her breathing return to normal, relieved that more rainclouds were held at bay for now.

'Well, that can happen to the best of us.'

The wireless echoed up the stairs. Bing Crosby was singing 'You Are My Sunshine' and Lily felt every word as Junie's lovely face turned to hers.

'We'll have to start saving some coupons for the wedding,' she said, lifting one of her daughter's curls away from her cheek. 'You can wear your grandmother's pearl comb – now, where did I put that? Maybe it's in the attic near…' Her voice faltered.

Perhaps she wouldn't go up there looking for it, just yet.

'That sounds like a nice idea, Mum,' Junie said as Lily rose to leave.

'So beautiful,' she murmured as she went, little knowing her daughter stared at the door for a long while afterwards, wondering if that was a curse.

Three

Junie dared not turn on the light, igniting the kerosene lamp instead before scanning the shelves and cupboards, heart thudding. Her father's office had become Ernest's domain of late and she dreaded the idea of him finding her here, snooping around. In my own home, she thought with resentment. She cast the feeling aside; there was no time for it now. Ernest often turned up here after dinner to go through the books, probably preferring to do so away from his prying mother. The last thing Junie wanted was to be discovered trying to find out the truth about her family's debt – the situation was humiliating enough.

Junie searched through the book-laden shelves, disappointed to note many of her much-loved novels and encyclopaedias had been replaced by Ernest's university notes and texts. His framed graduation photo had been set front and centre and she was tempted to let it have an unfortunate accident. Then she noticed a photo of her three brothers in uniform behind it and drew it forwards, tracing their faces. She wished they were here to fix things.

But there was no time for wishing. Junie was a practical girl at heart; if things were up to her, then she would simply have to get on with it.

She paused, exasperated by the lack of progress, then moved across to go through each drawer of her father's timber desk, her favourite piece of furniture in the house with its hidden panels and compartments. It had been a forbidden zone when they were children but Junie and her brothers hadn't been able to resist its mysteries and she blessed their disobedience now as she continued investigating.

Junie seethed at the evidence of Ernest's full occupation of the great desk which spoke of his unpleasant, fastidious self: an expensive shoe brush; a silver cigarette case; photos of him with his boorish friends on hunting trips. She could only imagine what her brothers would have to say about it.

The deeper drawers were filled with pages and pages of legal documentation, neatly bound and ordered, tying local families into the Farthingtons' debt and service. Junie held a page up to the lamp, trying to decipher some of the complex language. *In due consequence and notwithstanding, this notice of understanding and intent and this claim of right by the lender henceforth commits and binds Mr Alfred Langron...* Junie scanned the strict terms that followed in disbelief, knowing full well the uneducated farmer involved would have little idea of just how damning a contract he had signed.

File after file revealed much of the same until she ran out of drawers and secrets and was left frowning. It had to be here somewhere. Junie knew Ernest would prize the power he held over her family above all others because it secured him this very farm and her own self into the bargain. A legal possession in human form, caught and chained with no choices left. No control.

Something sparked in the tunnels of her mind. *Chains.* Of course!

Junie reached under the desk, feeling her way along to the middle where she found a small button and pressed it. There was a click then a timber panel lowered itself on chains to reveal a slender box. A box that held a single ledger. She drew it out, relieved to have found it but apprehensive as she traced the Wallace name on the front. How much was she worth?

'Looking for some bedtime reading, are we?'

Junie jumped, her eyes blinking in the sudden light and her skin prickling at the sight of Ernest leaning against the doorway.

'Yes,' Junie said, trying to keep her voice as nonchalant as possible. 'A bit heavy looking, I'm afraid, but I'll get through.' She tapped at the book as she rose to hide her shaking fingers.

'Please,' he said, 'stay and have a nightcap with me. We have much to discuss, you and I.'

She waited, hating to stay, but knowing this conversation needed to happen now that she'd been caught. Perhaps this was a good thing. Perhaps it was time to reveal their cards – to see who was bluffing and who held the highest hand.

Ernest poured then sat in one of the two armchairs by the hearth, gesturing to the other with her drink. It seemed appropriate that an unlit fireplace would sit between them for this conversation. No heat, no heart.

She took her seat, accepting the drink and sipping at it. Her first whisky with him – actually her first whisky with anyone. It burnt her mouth and she was quite shocked by the horrible taste.

'I see you know your way around your father's desk,' he said, nodding at the ledger which sat in her lap.

'Yes, although I found its contents somewhat changed.'

Ernest examined his glass. 'You know he isn't up to it any more, Junie.'

She couldn't deny it, especially considering Henry was asleep upstairs as they spoke, passed out and beyond sense.

'Why do you want to know what they owe?'

'I want to know how to pay it.'

Ernest gave a derisive laugh. 'You can't possibly imagine –'

'Try me,' she said and he looked at her with a combination of amusement and annoyance.

'Turn to the last page. You'll see the running total as of this morning.'

He waited as she did so and Junie stared at the numbers in shock. They sat in a long cruel line of condemning ink and she felt the sudden need to be sick. All hope fled in their presence. All dreaming destroyed.

'But how?'

He shrugged. 'Well, we are in the middle of a war and it costs a lot of money to run cattle at the best of times. Besides, the year isn't out yet and we haven't gone to market. There's grain and hands – and what else can I say? Your father had lost control of things, Junie – wrote cheques to anyone who asked.' He sipped his whisky. 'You were overstocked and overstaffed.'

'Letting good staff go was a mistake –'

'What do you know about it?'

'I know Rory Riley tried to warn Dad. He tried to help –'

'Rory Riley is a drunk. I'm managing to get things back under control very nicely without him, as you would see if you looked at the whole picture. Mind you, there's a long road ahead – the Farthington money will be financing this farm for a good while yet.' He remained calm because he knew he had her. The money was piled in the centre between them and Junie had no way to match it. His cards were winning.

'My brothers…' But she lost her words. Even those experienced farmers wouldn't be able to overcome this.

'Would see I've done everything I can. Surely you can see that too, my dear?' he said, leaning towards her.

She shook her head, disbelief blurring the wretched sums before her. 'It's – it's so much more than I imagined.'

Ernest smiled. 'Not really. Not when something is worth the price.'

Tears began to fall then, despite her every effort to stay them, and he reached for her hand.

'I know you don't want to marry me, Junie. I know you think I am forcing you to do this but I am doing what's best for everyone, your parents and brothers included. Mother won't understand at first but she will come around when the grandchildren arrive. And what choice do you have other than to marry into money now? How many rich men are knocking on your door?'

She went to answer but the image of Michael flashed through her mind and she realised it was pointless. She didn't want anyone else, so what did it matter which man she chose? Hers would be a life of loneliness regardless.

'I…could earn money…'

'You'd never earn this money in a lifetime, especially as a woman. No profession would pay it.'

It was true. Even combining her potential earnings with the best wages Michael could hope to achieve, it was an impossible amount to find.

'Well, there is one profession – but that's what I'm doing anyway, isn't it?' she said, suddenly rebellious as she yanked her hand away.

His face turned hard. 'Don't be disgusting.'

'What would you call it then?'

'Quite the opposite. You're marrying a wealthy man and you will assume the role of a privileged woman in society. I'm offering you every woman's dream, Junie.'

Watching him closely, this man she had known her whole life, she knew he believed that. He truly thought he was offering her the greatest opportunity in the world: to be his wife.

'Mrs Ernest Farthington,' she said in disbelief.

'I'll make you proud to say it, you'll see.' He said it with arrogance, like he was raising the stakes while holding all the aces.

She stared at the ledger, wishing it would disappear. Then another thought dawned.

'I know what you're thinking,' he said quietly, following her every expression. 'I'm not offering you marriage just so you can divorce me later, Junie. There will be documents to sign, watertight ones, to ensure the farm goes to me if you do. And all monies owing would have to be paid back, among other things.'

Junie knew the likelihood of her ever having that kind of money was remote at best. The trap shut tight. 'I just don't understand why,' she whispered, 'why me?'

He touched her face, making her flinch, and Earnest sent her the slightest of frowns. 'Because you're like a beautiful wild brumby and I'm going to turn you into a racehorse.'

It was a decision, long-made and without question, and she felt the scope of his ambition defeat her.

Ernest stood and finished his drink and then, with a curt nod, he was gone. Not a word of love because there was none. He would get his pound of flesh and she would protect those she loved by letting him.

The book fell to the ashes as she rose and walked slowly from the room where once her father held reign. Ernest's victory was an immovable fact now.

Cast cold and final onto the grate.

Four

'God, I'm as thirsty as a dog with two tongues,' Katie Burgess said, tipping champagne into their glasses behind a pot plant in St Bede's Parish Hall. Junie's best friend had picked up quite her fair share of colourful language working as a barmaid at her father's pub, to her mother's chagrin. She'd also picked up a fondness for having a tipple or two, on the sly, of course. 'Here. Quick – while the pigeon isn't looking.' Katie thrust the extra champagne glass into Junie's hand and they turned to the wall and drank in one go, hiding the evidence in the foliage before moving away and nodding at people politely.

'You'll go straight to hell one day, Burgess,' Junie said, deciding that champagne was far preferable to whisky. It was the third time Katie had snuck her some and she was pretty confident it wouldn't be the last.

'Even Jesus drank wine, Genie-Junie,' Katie replied.

Junie giggled, despite her mood. 'Stop calling me that.'

'You look exactly like her. I think you could alert the press and people would believe Miss Tierney is living in Braidwood. Especially tonight.' Katie flicked her eyes at Junie's pink silk dress, still incredulous. 'You should negotiate your terms with Ernest now. Tell him if he wants to marry a movie star, you have a few conditions.'

'One: no legal marriage.'

'Two: you get all his dosh,' Katie added, getting them each a slice of cake and taking up position near the stage, ready to dance when the band began.

'Three: the pigeon is sent to Timbuctoo.'

'Four: Michael Riley gets to kiss the bride.'

'Shh, Dorn and Beryl might overhear,' Junie hissed, looking out for Michael's sisters, who were two of their closest friends.

'Five: Michael Riley gets the wedding night honours.'

Junie choked on her cake and a piece flew out of her mouth and straight onto Constance Farthington's expensive white sleeve. Constance flicked it off disdainfully, glaring at Junie.

'Good evening, Katie. I hope you aren't overindulging in the refreshments before the dancing begins,' Constance said stiffly.

Katie gave her a cake-filled grin in response. 'Certainly am, Mrs Farthington.'

Constance's face was a mask of disapproval that melted as she saw Ernest approach, missing the small pigeon noise Katie made in the background.

'There you are, Ernest! Father Holloway has asked you to make a speech.'

'Done up like a dog's dinner tonight,' mumbled Katie in Junie's ear, forcing her to stifle another giggle. He certainly was, with hair so slick it looked set to slide off his scalp.

'Yes, Mother, I know. All ready, are we, Junie?' Ernest spoke like a man conducting a minor bank transaction rather than one who was about to announce his own engagement. Constance looked perplexed and Junie felt it was almost worth the horrible business of getting engaged to Ernest just to see the look of outrage that was about to dawn on his snobby mother's face. That smug little thought died as Ernest took to the shallow timber stage and the Colonel tapped his glass, silencing the hall.

Junie felt her despair rise and looked across to the door, praying that Michael would arrive, then praying he wouldn't. As hopeless as it all was, she still wanted him to see her in this dress. To dance with him, just this once, on the night she became engaged to someone else.

Michael was late – far later than he had intended – and he adjusted his new jacket nervously, the khaki stiff and uncomfortable after years of moleskins and flannel.

He'd debated this decision to see them all one last time before he left: his parents might dob him in and stop him from going. It would have been wiser to enlist in Sydney but the trip to Orange to deliver stock had proved fateful. By the time he'd stumbled out of the pub with Jake and Cliffy, his two droving mates, the temptation to join up with them had been too great. One in, all in.

His favourite stock horse, Barney, led him on through the night, up the near-empty main street, past the pub and the post office to turn at the cenotaph towards the hall. The monument was silver in the half light and Michael tipped his hat to the Anzac statue which seemed to speak to him as he passed.

Say your goodbyes, lad. Hope to God they aren't your last.

That I will, he promised the stone soldier. Whatever this night held there was one goodbye he was bloody sure he would make – and he'd be sealing it with a kiss if he could.

And, with war on his horizon, Michael figured Ernest Farthington could stick his objections to that where the sun don't shine.

Ernest cleared his throat. 'Ladies and gentlemen.'

Junie tensed and Katie squeezed her hand briefly as the room quietened to a whisper. So this was it. No last-minute reprieve. No Michael arriving on his faithful steed to cry out his objection, profess his love and steal her away from this wretched fate.

Ernest welcomed the most important people, thanked the organisers and said all the right things in his best politician's voice. Half the town were scornful, she knew, but some of the clergy and quite a few of the ladies on the committee seemed impressed with the town's budding politician. Ernest seemed to swell beneath the approving murmurs and applause and Junie glimpsed what the future held as his wife – spending her days sitting in the shadow of his ego.

She looked at her parents, standing alongside, and wanted to feel resentful, but only pity remained. Lily held on tightly to Henry, dreamy and vague in her grief. Henry Wallace just looked old and, as he met his daughter's gaze, somewhat ashamed. She comforted that shame as best she could by sending him a smile, nearly crying herself as she watched his eyes fill.

Henry leant over and spoke in her ear. 'You don't have to do this if it isn't what you want, love.'

The last-minute offer of reprieve was genuine, she knew, despite the devastating position they were in. But there, in her father's eyes, lay a spirit shattered by sorrow. He could no longer care for himself, let alone his family, not because he didn't love, but because he had loved too much. She wished she could tell him the truth, hide in his shoulder and ask him to make it all go away, like she used to when the thunder frightened her as a child. But those shoulders were slumped now and it was she who had to protect him from the storm.

Right then she knew she was doing the only thing she could do. She had to protect these broken, cherished people and she had to give her brothers a home to return to. They deserved that much.

It's what Frankie would have wanted.

Michael tethered Barney and walked to the hall's doors, opening them just in time to see Junie walk on stage to stand next to Ernest. The first thing he thought was that she had never looked lovelier: she had a dress on that made her look like a movie star, emphasising a figure he had only imagined until now, and her face was so filled with compassion as she looked at her parents he wanted to push through the crowd just to hold her. But Ernest was holding her now; his hand was around that silky waist, the other brushing her hair casually off her shoulder. Like he owned her. Michael felt a terrible wave of jealousy crash through his being.

'And so it is with great pleasure,' Ernest said, 'that I announce my engagement to Miss Junie Wallace.'

Junie's smile was fixed amid the applause, faltering slightly as Constance slammed her way out of the side doors in undisguised fury, silencing the hall in her wake. It was then Junie's eyes found Michael's and for a second he saw her heart in there, regret burning in their depths.

'Michael,' she said, and the crowd followed her gaze to him. Ernest noticed him too, looking at his uniform with surprise then satisfaction. Then Michael's parents and sisters rushed over and he lost sight of Junie as people began shaking his hand. His mother was arguing, telling him they wouldn't let him go and his father was drunk, lost as to what to do, save tell his wife they'd talk about it when they got home. His sisters were crying and the Colonel was slapping Michael on the back, stating he was a credit to his country. That he and Ernest would be heroes together now.

Then the band played 'Waltzing Matilda' and the whole absurd scene became too much.

The cold air embraced him as he went back to his horse, ignoring the calls and confusion behind him. His mother, his father, his sisters, this town; Junie and the goddam Farthingtons. A stiff breeze swept across the park as he galloped past the statue and out into the night.

'I didn't say my goodbyes,' he told the Anzac that stared sightlessly into the night. 'But God knows, for some, they would have been my last.'

Five

Mavis gazed out at the glorious heavens – she had called many country towns home since she'd married Rory Riley, but the night sky was more brilliant here than anywhere else they had lived. Seas of constellations, brilliant diamond planets and the occasional shooting star invited her wonder and awe but she wouldn't give it to them. Not when another son was going to war. And not when he could still be stopped.

'You'll catch yer death,' Rory warned, swaying slightly as he approached her. He was drunk, but not as drunk as usual. 'Here.' He took off his coat and placed it on her shoulders, something he'd not done for many years, and she looked at him in mild surprise. She'd have been touched if she wasn't so angry – with him, with Michael.

'I'm angry with God,' she finished the thought out loud.

'I've been angry with Him for some time,' Rory admitted.

They watched the sky together as the moon began to rise over the hill, a brilliant, slowly revealing globe to grace the beautiful night.

'I want you to do something.' She said it firmly, no trepidation for a change. She was too heartsick for that.

'I know you do.' Rory lit a cigarette and she breathed it in. It was sweet against the cold night air and it seemed to comfort him, making her half-wish she smoked herself.

'It's only been a week. You could go to Sydney. Tell them his real age. Or you could let me go.'

Rory shook his head. 'We have to let him be the man he wants to be. You know we'd never stop him now – he'd still find a way. I did when I was his age.'

Mavis knew that was true but would never agree – even if they had to hunt Michael down a hundred times, she'd still try to stop him from going to war.

Rory dragged on his cigarette and the orange light illuminated the sad resignation of his features. 'You know, I could see it coming. I could tell he liked that Wallace girl and with that bastard Farthington having his way...' He threw his butt on the ground in disgust. 'Anyway, I'm heading into town for a nightcap.'

She watched him leave, disappointed to see the familiar hunch return to his back. The shadow of the man she married was fading into this beautiful, hopeless night and she nearly called after him but then she saw him reach into his pocket and take out his hip flask. She hunched over then too, hugging her arms about herself to stem the loneliness that rose at that simple act.

Raising her eyes to look at the sky once more, she watched a shooting star blaze then fade and knew that was all she'd witnessed tonight; a brief glimpse of her husband and now he was gone once more.

And without Rory's support her Michael was well gone too.

Junie tugged at the collar of her dress. She hated the scratchy material but she'd outgrown all her others. The only other good dress she owned that fitted was the one she wore last Saturday night and she figured the St Bede's parishioners wouldn't take kindly to the pink silk making an appearance at Sunday Mass. She smiled a little to herself at the idea then sank back into her brooding, leaning against the stone wall in the sun, around the corner and away from well-wishers and critical eyes.

'Come on Genie-Junie,' Katie said, finding her. 'Cheer up a bit, for Pete's sake! You've just come out of church – didn't you pray for a miracle?'

'I don't think praying is going to get me out of this.'

'Well, if we have to sell you off to the pigeon's son we can at least let you leave the nest in style. Beryl, Dorn!' Katie ushered the Riley girls over. 'Snakes alive, you look as mopey as this one.'

'Hi Junie,' Dorn mumbled and Beryl gave her a brief hug.

'Come on, come on, enough of all that,' Katie said, flapping her hands. 'I've got an idea to cheer everyone up.'

'With another brother run off to war? Good luck there,' Beryl replied, looking slightly hopeful just the same. Katie Burgess was an expert at fun.

'How many times have I told you? The secret to life is having something to look forward to.'

'Three words for you: Mrs Ernest Farthington,' Junie said.

'Not yet, you're not,' Katie told her. 'Listen up. You know how men are always so secretive about bachelor parties?'

'Don't tell me we are having a bridal shower tea with the pigeon. I couldn't take it,' Beryl protested, groaning.

'I said *cheer* everyone up, not torture them.' Katie dropped her voice. 'Remember I told you my uncle has a little shack down by the ocean near Sydney?'

'Burning Palms, isn't it?' Dorn asked, and they all nodded. None of them had forgotten that exotic-sounding name.

'That's the one. I've been working on Dad to let us go there for a bit of a holiday when they go on their next fishing trip –'

'But how would we be able to go to Sydney? I have to work,' Beryl said.

'Me too,' said Dorn. Both sisters were cleaners at the hospital and they all knew the Rileys needed their modest incomes, especially now.

'Minor details!' Katie dismissed the objection. 'Uncle Ernie and Dad will be going up to the city for one of the nights which leaves the place all to ourselves. Soo-o,' she drew the word out dramatically, 'how would you girls feel about a *spinster* party?'

Dorn screwed up her nose. 'Ugh! Spinster. I hate that term.'

'How about the bride's funeral?' said Junie with a sigh.

'It doesn't matter what we bloody well call it,' Katie said, exasperated, 'the point is that we get to go on an actual holiday by the seaside *and* I've got a few things planned, special party things. Really do this in style, if you know what I mean.' She opened her handbag to reveal a bottle of champagne and grinned widely.

The others exchanged glances. Katie's enthusiasm was contagious.

'Style, you say,' Beryl said.

'We could call it the Hollywood Holiday,' Katie suggested.

There was a pause as they all looked to Junie, who rewarded them slowly with her best Gene Tierney smile.

'Roll out the red carpet.'

Mavis didn't know what Katie Burgess was up to this time but she couldn't help but feel a little warmed to see the girls excited about something after the worry their brother had caused them this past week. All the whispering was beginning to wear thin though.

'All right, what's going on with you two? I saw you plotting with that Katie over something after Mass.'

'Nothing really,' Dorn said, by far the worse liar of the two. Beryl nudged her and Mavis waited, resting the potato she'd been peeling on the bench.

'Out with it,' she said.

Dorn looked uncomfortable and Mavis pinned her with the raising of an eyebrow.

'Just an…idea Katie had. To cheer us all up.' Dorn was cracking under the pressure of that eyebrow and Beryl nudged her again.

Mavis switched her scrutiny. 'Beryl?'

Her eldest daughter gave a little guilty jump and Mavis was a little intrigued despite herself. 'It's just…uh, you know how Bob Burgess has a brother who lives in Sydney? Well he has this holiday house down on the coast.'

'House, is it?' Mavis well knew the makeshift destination they were referring to.

'Well, shack, I suppose. But Katie has invited us…she's going with Junie.'

'It's the Hollywood Holiday!' Dorn burst out.

Mavis now had both eyebrows up.

Beryl quickly went into persuasion mode, pushing Dorn slightly behind her. 'That's just a bit of a joke name we came up with. It's actually perfectly sedate, Mum. Mr Burgess will be there the whole time, well except one night, and Katie's uncle and aunt –'

'I wouldn't imagine an aunt of Katie Burgess would want to go to a fishing shack with her husband and brother-in-law.'

'Well, perhaps not. But we do!' The normally reserved little Dorn couldn't seem to contain herself and Mavis had to hide a smile as Beryl made wild eyes at her sister.

'Hmm…I'm not sure your father would approve. Besides, what about getting time off work? Have you given any thought to that?' Mavis was inclined to let them go even as she said it.

'We've got it all worked out. We'll work extra shifts the next few weeks. Matron said we could help her sort out the kitchen cupboards. Plus we can go in Mr Burgess's car – there's plenty of room,' Beryl said. 'We've organised Gladys Woods and Iris Corby to cover our shifts on Monday and Dot McKenzie will do Tuesday night…'

She continued her sales campaign but Mavis had stopped listening. A humming had begun in her ears at the sight of a car coming over the rise and down the dirt drive.

'…and then Gladys can do Wednesday but not Thursday…'

It was a black car. A very familiar one, with two figures inside.

Beryl's voice faded as Mavis moved slowly to the window, touching the pane as if to stop the vision of the approaching tyres disturbing the dust.

'What is it, Mum?'

Mavis had no voice. It had been replaced by a choking fear that heated her heart, her insides. She shook her head. 'No.'

It was Dorn who opened the door to let the priest and the postmaster in as Mavis fell into a chair.

'Is Rory in, Mrs Riley?' Father Holloway had his sombre tone on. The one he used for funerals.

Mavis couldn't reply, still unable to speak past the fear.

'He's – he's gone over to the Langrons' for work,' Beryl said, staring at the telegram in the postmaster's hand and slowly sitting next to her mother.

'Oh dear, that's a problem, I'm afraid.' The postmaster frowned at the telegram worriedly then over at the priest. 'This telegram is clearly addressed to Mr Rory Riley. I can't legally give it to anyone else.'

Father Holloway looked taken aback. 'Surely under the circumstances –'

'We don't know the circumstances, though, do we?' The postmaster was trying to whisper and Mavis looked at him in desperation.

'Give it to me – please,' she managed to say. The only thing possibly worse than the telegram's existence was not knowing its contents.

'I'm afraid I can't,' the postmaster said, shaking his head. 'You will have to send for Mr Riley.'

They all stared at him, varying degrees of disbelief, worry and anger sweeping the room. Everyone knew what it could contain.

'My son…my son is fighting overseas…'

'I understand, Mrs Riley, and I'm sorry.' He didn't look sorry. He looked like the cruellest fool in the world and she wondered if she could seize the telegram from him, but he was a big man and he held it tight.

Father Holloway cleared his throat and Mavis placed her hope in him as he spoke in a reasoning tone, his funeral voice modified, she noted with faint hope.

'Mrs Riley can't be expected to wait at a time like this. I know you are new to the area, Mr Curtis, but I can vouch for this lady that her husband would certainly want her to open it in his stead. They are my parishioners, as you know.'

Still the man didn't budge.

'Mr Curtis, is it?' Beryl said, her face as sweet and charming as she could make it. 'Perhaps you would like a cup of tea as we sit and read the contents together? Might make us all feel a little more prepared.'

Mr Curtis looked tempted but shook his head yet again. 'It is addressed to the master of the house.'

Mavis began to cry in silent streams and Dorn moved forwards to hold her shoulders.

'I'll go,' Beryl said, grabbing her coat and running out the door but not before casting the postmaster the most scathing look Mavis had ever seen. His face was red and he looked uncomfortable but he didn't move the hand that held the fate of her maternal heart.

There was no more discussion now, the only voice that of a distant currawong as Mavis closed her eyes against the wait.

Rory was chopping wood when he spied Beryl riding across the field on Barney, reminding him he had to return the damn beast to Farthington when he got the chance. Michael had left him at the train station with a note and Rory cursed its short, angry contents yet again. Damn women and damn the war.

Beryl was riding awfully fast and he paused to watch, the axe slipping from his hand as he saw her expression.

'You have…to come home…telegram…' she panted. 'Mum needs you.'

The Rileys borrowed a second horse that day and no-one asked for it back for weeks to come.

Amazing grace!
How sweet the sound
That saved a wretch like me!
I once was lost
But now am found
Was blind but now
I see

The singer delivered the last note and all that remained was the rain. It pattered against the red, blue and gold of the stained glass and Junie stared at the saints who were frozen there, promising them all that God would take care of them in the next life. But not so much in this one it seems, she thought bitterly, as Mavis was helped to her feet by an ashen-faced, sober Rory.

No casket, no flowers, no burial. Just black dresses and his mother's choking tears. David James Riley had only been in town a few short months when he joined up, so none of them really knew him all that well. But Junie knew that pain. It was written in the lines of grief on her mother's face and etched deep into her father's soul. She pitied Beryl and Dorn as they followed their parents down the aisle, grieving one brother and fearing for the other. *It will never leave you*, she wanted to warn them. *And things will never be quite the same.* But of course she would say quite the opposite, as people do.

The rabbit sat still within her mind. It knew there was no point running today. There was no answer to death, save faith.

༻❀༺

Rory watched as she stood outside, this time under a leaden dawn sky, her breath misting in the early cold. When would that woman ever remember her coat?

He went out to join her, draping his own about her shoulders as he'd taken to doing of late. Mavis ignored him and he couldn't say he blamed her – he'd woken up on the floor and didn't remember how he'd got home last night.

'Should come inside, love, looks like rain.'

She shrugged. 'Doesn't matter.'

'You shouldn't have let the girls go,' he said.

Mavis shook her head. 'No, there's not much happiness in this life. They should grab it while they can.'

Rory nodded, lighting a cigarette. 'Aye, that's true enough.' Funny how his father's brogue made an appearance every now and then, especially when he was pensive. Mavis used to laugh at it.

They watched the clouds roll by in heavy grey, allowing them torn glimpses of daybreak.

'We've not been alone for twenty-three years,' she said. Rory felt the truth of it keenly. He hadn't noticed how much he valued the noise and rhythm of their home until now. It was as if death had settled its ash upon everything they'd ever loved.

'It's only been a day. The girls will be back in a week and things will seem a bit more normal.'

'Life will never seem normal again. It can't – it all just means nothing now...' Her voice cracked and he felt his own grief overflow as she cried those slow, terrible tears that always cut him. He wished he had something to drink.

She took a handkerchief out of her pocket, dabbing at her tears. 'Going into town again this afternoon?'

'No...no,' he said. 'I'll stay here with you, love.'

She sniffed. 'Calling me love again? Giving me your coat?' She took one of his cigarettes and he watched with surprise as she lit it. 'Just go. I'm all right.'

For the first time in a very long while, Rory saw her as the girl he remembered. Not because she was young again, or vibrant and hopeful as she once had been – he'd destroyed much of that. But because she was strong somehow, despite this shattering blow. Bitter, yes, but strong nevertheless. He'd forgotten about that Mavis. He hadn't even noticed she wasn't around. But now that he needed her, now that life was desolate and the pain wouldn't leave him, he wanted that Mavis to care again.

'No pub. Not tonight.' He knew there was nothing there for him, save the drink. The only thing he wanted to do was stand here with Mavis, now that the war had taken their boy.

'It doesn't bother me. Do what you want,' she said.

He searched for something to say, to charm her back to him as he'd always been able to do. Silver Tongue, she used to call him, back in the days before.

'I – I know I've been a no-good husband to you these past few years –' He stopped, hearing the cheapness of his own words.

'It's not even that so much...you've not been much of a father lately. That's far worse.'

Rory lit a cigarette too. He couldn't deny it but it pained his heart, especially now.

A currawong landed on the fence and Mavis looked at it, straightening to all of her five and a half feet. 'I'm going to Sydney, to find Michael and tell him about Davey. And to take his birth certificate and hold him from going to war – for now at least,' she said firmly. 'I'm fighting this time, Rory. Don't try to stop me.'

'No, you're not going.' There was thunder in the far distance and the rumble ran between them. 'I am,' he said, making up his mind.

She stared at him for a moment then walked past him back into the house, one word carrying on the wind as the rain found the earth.

'Good.'

Six

The man was beginning to bother her. Michael could see it in the way she tapped on her cigarette packet and shifted her legs around. He was a burly bloke, his biceps bulging from his shirt and hair hanging over the thick meat of neck at his collar. The brute bent in, closer than the girl wanted, breathing what could only be a putrid cocktail of rum and cigarettes into her face as she leant back as far as she could from him. Michael had been watching her since she'd arrived, a small, dark-haired girl with large eyes, trying to look older with her painted lips and tight dress. He supposed he was just missing his sisters and Junie but he instantly wanted to protect the girl and now he just might have to. If he could hold his own after – how many beers had he had, anyway?

'Whoever that girl is you're moping about from home that ain't her,' Jake noted, following his gaze. 'Don't poke the bear, Mick.'

Jake Loadsman had been droving and sharing in stockman duties with Michael for the best part of two years. He and his other droving mate, James Clifford – or 'Cliffy' as everyone knew him – had falsified their birth certificates together and were now locked in each other's company, day in, day out. Training had been easy enough, they were used to shooting and hard, physical labour, but they'd missed having a drink.

And Michael missed seeing Junie.

He hadn't realised just how much he'd looked forward to Sundays at church purely because she would be sitting there, mere feet away. Or occasions in town when she could be glimpsed through shop windows or chatting to her friends on the footpath. Without those prized moments to look forward to and revisit each night, life was dull – a chore to be borne – and he was pained in the knowledge she was too far away to be seen. Nor his to look for any more.

And so he watched this girl as she tried to stand and leave, clenching his glass as the man pulled her back down by the arm. She was beginning to look frightened and searched the pub, probably for the woman she'd arrived with, an older, more hardened type who had already exited through the back door with a sodden-looking private.

His attention shifted as Cliffy came waltzing across the bar, singing 'I'm in the Money' in a very loud voice.

'Shh, y'bloody idiot. Why don't you just put a sign around your neck while you're at it?' Jake hissed at him. Michael watched the big thug to see if he had noticed. He hadn't, busy as he still was harassing the girl, but his equally brutish friend had, finishing his drink in a gulp and moving away from the bar to circle in on Cliffy.

'Twenty quid,' Cliffy announced happily, brandishing it under their noses. 'None of them city boys know a thing about throwing darts.'

'Some of them may know a thing or two about killing,' muttered Jake as the big man moved closer.

'Well…we might need some pointers, all things considered,' Michael muttered back. 'Don't know how much use he's going to be.'

He nodded at Cliffy, who was busy counting his money through one eye and swaying in his seat.

'About as useful as a one-legged man in an arse-kicking contest,' Jake agreed under his breath, smiling widely at the arrival of the brute. 'How are you today, my good man?' he asked cheerfully, leaning back in his chair to stretch towards the pool cue rack.

The beefy man smiled back, displaying an alarming absence of teeth. 'A bit low on funds actually.' The first man had noticed the scene now and joined his mate; they presented an unnerving wall of muscle. Then a third one arrived, similar in girth and with a large scar running down the side of his face.

'Times are tough during wars,' Michael said amiably, sizing up what weaknesses he could and finding none. 'What happened to your face?' he asked the third man.

There was no smile from him. 'Had a disagreement with somebody a few days ago.' He looked at Cliffy's pocket. 'He thought he could beat me at something. I disagreed.'

'Let's play darts in Parramatta,' Jake mumbled under his breath to Cliffy. 'Good plan, mate.'

'Give us the dough and we might let you live,' the first man said, growing impatient as he noticed the girl with the dark hair make her way to the door.

'Tell you what,' Michael said, stalling as long as he could as he noticed her too. 'How about you walk away now and we won't add to your list of reasons?'

'What reasons?'

Michael grinned at him. 'Reasons why women can't stand your repulsive self.'

Cliffy pointed at the one he'd beaten in darts. 'Reasons why you couldn't hit a – hic – dartboard if someone stuck a dart in y'mouth and threw it at ya.'

'And reasons why *your* ancestors obviously remained Neander-thals,' Jake finished, winking at the third.

'Arrrgh!' The Neanderthal in question took sizeable offence to that and Jake met his lurching attack with a swift blow across the head from a pool cue.

The pub must have been ready to ignite because bodies came from everywhere, all stinging for a fight. Michael met the first man's swinging arms with a small table but it was instantly smashed into pieces and he was left holding the leg in amazement. It proved to work well as a weapon, however, which was fortunate, considering the man had picked up a chair arm. They sparred with them like swords.

Meanwhile Cliffy was busy utilising his talented aim as a dart player by hiding behind the bar and launching anything he could find at his opponent. Jake had managed to outrun the Neander-thal, making use of his fence-balancing skills as he moved along the benchtops, ducking the odd stray missile from Cliffy before one connected and he slipped and fell straight into a bunch of uniforms. He managed to crawl away under the remaining tables, leaving the soldiers he'd landed on to tangle with his pursuer.

'Retreat!' Michael yelled as his table leg was snapped in half against the big man's face and his opponent gave him a bloodied grin.

'Leg it!' Cliffy called to Jake and the three took off out the doors and down the street just as the sirens arrived.

Michael looked back to see the three thugs pause outside the front door as the police drew close, then they took off in the other direction.

'This ain't over!' The first man called after them, spitting out blood and looking murderous.

'Tell it running, Ugly!' Jake called and they struggled to keep going for laughter.

Michael figured they wouldn't be risking the seedier pubs in Parramatta again any time soon.

Cliffy was singing, something he wasn't doing too bad a job of considering he had a fat lip and a half-empty bottle of rum in his hand.

'Bollocks! was all the band could play.'

They were lying on their bunks, still talking about the brawl and comparing stories for the entertainment of their bunkmates.

'Seven feet in his socks, he was,' Jake was telling Wally Simpson, a young fellow from Yamba whose eyes were round in their glasses.

'Seems to be growing taller with each telling,' said Tommy Hawkens, Wally's mate. 'Sure he wasn't standing in manure?'

'He smelt like it,' Michael said, laughing.

Footsteps sounded down the hall and bottles were quickly hidden under blankets and beds as the men stood to attention.

'At ease, gentlemen,' said the sergeant, turning a blind eye to their inebriated states. 'Riley, Captain Marren wants to see you.'

Michael looked up in surprise. 'Me?'

'Yes you, y'great galoot. Look sharp.'

Michael walked the halls across to the office, straightening his uniform as he knocked on Captain Marren's door, wondering what news lay within.

Whatever it was, he hadn't expected it to be delivered by the figure that rose from the chair in front.

'What did he want?' Jake asked as Michael made his slow way in to the room a while later.

He said nothing until he lay down and stared at the ceiling. 'It's…it's my dad. He found me. He's here.'

The others went very quiet then Jake sat forwards. 'Did he dob you in?'

'Worse…much worse. My brother Davey…' He couldn't finish the sentence, his throat tightening as his chest began to heave.

'Mate,' said Cliffy.

None of them seemed able to find any other words so they sat with him a while, listening to the painful sobs that held no shame here; in a room full of young men, watching their friend lose his only brother to the same war they were about to enter. Pub fights seemed like child's play now. There would be no police sirens to break things up over there – it was fight to the actual death – something that no longer seemed a distant, possible fate.

For death brushed close now, touching them all.

❧

'Drink?' Captain Marren was pouring, probably wishing he hadn't witnessed what had just transpired. 'Think you deserve one tonight.'

Rory hesitated, but took it. 'Just the one.'

The captain studied him. 'Served yourself, did you?'

'Yes,' Rory said, 'the Somme and Palestine. Did three years in the end.'

'No thought to re-joining? Army's looking for experience.'

'It crossed my mind.'

Captain Marren looked thoughtful. 'My brother was in France. Gas still affects him, poor sod, but it was Turkey that got to him first. Lost his best mate,' he said, sipping his drink. 'Least you missed out on that.'

'I was underage when I went to France as it was,' Rory said.

'Many were back then.'

'Many still are.' Rory put down his drink and took out a piece of paper from his pocket. 'I've come here for more than one reason.'

Captain Marren frowned, scanning the birth certificate Rory had placed on the desk. 'Eighteen?'

'Yes. Only just.'

'They've put it down from twenty to nineteen now, as I'm sure you've heard. We need men.'

Rory held fast. 'Even so, a year's a year. Besides, he needs parental permission under twenty-one, and I haven't given it.'

The captain walked over to the window, staring out at the lights of the barracks. 'Best shot in the outfit. Natural leader...I had my eye on him. He'll make a damn good soldier.'

'He's a damn good son.'

Captain Marren nodded. 'I can see that.'

Rory took another sip of his drink, eyes wet.

'I can't keep an eighteen-year-old lad,' the captain conceded. 'I'll see to it.'

'You may need to see to a few others too. Clifford and Loadsman are only eighteen as well.'

'Bloody hell.' Captain Marren frowned.

Rory drained his glass. 'I think you may be surprised just how many of the country lads are; it's quite easy to forge dates and notes from parents out our way – just ride far enough until no-one knows you.'

'So it seems,' the captain replied, obviously rattled, and he finished his own glass. 'Thank you, Mr Riley. Where will you be staying so I can reach you?'

'The sergeant has given me a bunk.'

'Excellent. Forgive me, I'm forgetting my manners. Again, I am so sorry for your loss. We'll talk again tomorrow and I'll arrange things.'

Rory stood, holding his hat. 'I know he needs to be a man, but his mother needs her boy right now.'

'Of course,' the captain said, but as he left Rory couldn't help but feel this wasn't quite over.

The sun was high as Rory sat in the captain's office next day, wondering why he was waiting. The sense of uneasiness returned. Surely it was just a matter of telling Michael to pack his things and they could head back home?

He stood and moved over to look out on the empty parade ground, thinking about Davey. He'd trained here too, before he went. The dark buildings stared at him in stony disregard and he imagined his son marching past them, handling his gun with ease and experience as he'd been taught on the land. *Taught by me,* Rory thought bitterly.

Davey was as skilled as any man Rory had seen, but all the skill in the world hadn't saved him in the end. He wondered how he had died. There were no details in the telegram, only the stark words that he'd been killed in action. Every imagining of what that entailed was as bad as the first, because they all ended with his body falling, his voice being silenced forever; that cheerful, practical sound that rang out across fields as they mustered together. Rory knew it would haunt him always. *Round 'em in.*

Country through and through, that boy. Rory took his handkerchief out of his pocket and absently wiped his cheeks.

It was another ten minutes before he heard footsteps and the captain opened the door and entered – not with Michael, Rory noted warily, but with a major.

'Sorry to keep you waiting. Mr Riley, may I present Major Reynolds. Major, this is Rory Riley.'

'Mr Riley.' The major nodded, taking a seat.

Rory did the same. 'Is – is anything wrong with Michael?'

'No, no, not at all,' the major assured him. 'On the contrary, actually. Your son is one of the finest we've had through in quite some time. Crack shot. Where did he learn that? From you?'

'Yes,' Rory said, feeling pained rather than proud. He'd prepared Davey to shoot and look where that had got him.

'Smart too,' Major Reynolds said, taking out a cigarette case and offering it around. 'Takes the lead like a natural.'

Rory took his time lighting his smoke, waiting for them to come to the point. He knew an army pitch when he smelt one.

'Truth is, we don't want to lose him. Or Clifford, or Loadsman,' the major said. 'Or the other dozen or so outstanding underage men we've been discovering in our ranks over these past few hours. Definitely need to keep a tighter rein on some of these remote enlistment personnel,' he conceded, flicking at the ash tray. 'Must thank you for bringing it to our attention.'

Rory wondered what kind of thank you they had in mind.

'Seems a shame to send them all home – I mean, here they are, some of our finest lads, drilled and fit and eager to serve. God knows their country needs them,' the major continued, 'Japan looks set to declare war any day now.'

'Pity they're underage then,' Rory said carefully.

'Yes, pity,' the major agreed. 'Unless…we encourage them to stay.'

Rory looked at him, confused.

'The captain here tells me you were an underage recruit yourself – so was I.' He smiled. 'I'm sure you remember the reasons why we joined up: a bit of excitement; the women liking the uniform; overseas travel. Of course we had no idea what war really was. Truth was, we weren't prepared.' He leant towards Rory. 'What if we did that for these boys? What if we prepared them properly?'

'By keeping them here?'

'No, not here,' the captain said, joining in. 'Liverpool. There's an empty set of barracks, a parade ground. Plenty of room to set up a special squad of elite recruits.'

'*Underage* elite recruits,' Rory reminded him.

'Who receive more training, more preparation, than any men in the Australian Army.'

The major nodded. 'And who do so under the guidance of an experienced soldier. Someone who understands exactly what they need to know...someone with a particularly strong motivation to protect them.' He paused, looking at Rory meaningfully.

Rory stared at them. '*Me?*'

'Who better?' the major said. 'I've checked your records. Plenty of brave action and a promotion to colonel in Palestine. Few bust-ups and wild nights, but didn't we all?' He shrugged. 'You could teach them how to survive, Mr Riley.'

'I – I don't know...'

'Rory,' the captain said, dropping the pretence of formality, 'you know Michael will just go home and try to join again anyway. This way you are guaranteeing him another year away from fighting until he turns nineteen.'

'You won't stop him going to war.' The major spoke with finality and Rory knew it was true. 'But you can possibly stop him from never coming back.'

'Aye,' Rory said, nodding slowly, his father's voice echoing through him. He knew what he would say: *God helps those who help themselves.*

Davey entered his thoughts, rounding up the yearlings on horseback, innocent of the horrors before him. Rory knew he would have given anything to help his elder son in this way. A whole year of training. Maybe it would have saved him.

'Shall we call Michael in?'

Rory looked at the major. 'Aye,' he said again.

'Wait,' the captain said, 'I think this calls for a toast.' He poured from his decanter and they raised their glasses. 'Gentlemen, to the Elite.'

'The Elite,' said the major.

'The Elite,' Rory echoed, looking at his glass and sending a promise to Mavis. *This time I'll try to be a better father. I'll try not to hit the bottle and be a soldier once more.*

And I'll do everything I can to save our boy.

Seven

December 1941
Burning Palms, New South Wales, Australia

Junie walked along the ocean's edge, marvelling at the feel of sinking sand under her soles for the first time and looking back at her dissolving footsteps in fascination. She stopped and let her feet be buried in golden swirls, wiggling until she was ankle deep then lifting their heavy weight out to run from the waves. A frothy wall chased her, finding her bare legs and splashing her swimsuit – but she was already wet so she didn't care. Surely she couldn't care about anything much today.

Junie had never been to the beach before this holiday and it felt as if the waves were literally washing across her mind to soothe her. She'd spent much of her time so far rambling through the bush and along the hillsides to just watch and breathe it all in. But today she wanted to immerse herself in the sea on her own, to be part of this magnificent southern lady as she flung her foamy petticoats across the sand.

Junie had never known anything so intoxicating, having only seen the sea twice before, each time resting in Sydney Harbour during the brief visits she'd made there. She'd thought it beautiful then, but now she realised viewing the sea in a harbour was like meeting the great lady glittering in a parlour, well-mannered and calm. Now she'd witnessed her wildness and her power as she lashed the cliffs, her anger when the storm came and she'd turned green. Junie had watched her be calmed by the blue sky afterwards, and display her glorious love for the sun as she welcomed and farewelled it each day in a million jewelled colours.

And each day Junie welcomed and farewelled the one she loved too, sending out pieces of herself to wherever Michael was now, under that same sun. No-one could deny her that right; she could still love. It was her heart.

The thought offered comfort if not cure.

The girls were waving and calling out from the shack and she saw Bob Burgess's brother Ernie emerging from the steep bushland, awkwardly trying to negotiate his way with a range of building materials strapped to his back. Everything had to be carried down the thickly vegetated hillside on foot as the huts on the beach at Burning Palms were inaccessible any other way. The contents of Ernie's shack, which boasted an icebox, four bunk beds and a cast-iron stove, were a wonder of perseverance and optimism. There was even an actual kitchen sink with taps that ran water from a small rainwater tank.

She watched Ernie unpack as she approached, noticing a door handle and quite a bit of timber, and thinking the only thing missing from this shack was some privacy for – Junie burst out laughing as Bob Burgess stumbled from the scrub. He was very red in the face and no wonder, as he lugged a toilet. He set it down then collapsed in the sand.

'Dad, how the blazes?' Katie said, incredulous.

'A mate…had a spare one. Can't have…the young Hollywood starlets without…a powder room.'

Ernie grinned proudly, reaching into his pocket and holding up a gold wooden star. The girls thought it a great joke, making Junie hold it, and she did so gladly, happy to see Beryl and Dorn smiling for a change. Maybe the ocean was healing them a little too.

As the men set to work digging a very deep hole, the girls started making lunch, ham sandwiches and orange juice squeezed fresh from the fruit off the tree behind the shack. Junie loved how sweet it was, seeming even more so when sipped in the open, salty air.

The hole was halfway dug by the time the group sat on blankets on the sand to eat and Katie quizzed her father on his plans for his trip to Sydney the following day.

'Will you still go overnight?'

'Should do.'

'But will you have it all done by the time you leave?' she asked, nodding at the hole. 'What if it rains and it fills up with water?'

'It's gonna have water anyway. Ocean runs under the sand, you know – soaks in,' Ernie told her. Junie was curious, wondering at the fact.

'Ernie'll build the frame this afternoon and I'll finish digging. Just a matter of sticking the fibro on then,' Bob said between mouthfuls. All the shacks were mostly made of fibro and the men had a good stack of it leaning against the back wall. It was the lightest building material to carry down the hill. 'Should all be done by tomorrow morning, then our young stars can have all the privacy in the world while we're away.'

'You might even get Mum and Aunty Maureen here at this rate.'

'Think they'd expect one that flushed,' Ernie said doubtfully.

The afternoon stretched beneath sunny skies and the girls passed the time exploring the spectacular rock pools at the end of the beach. Sparkling in shades of pale green and blue, the water in each was so clear they could make out schools of tiny fish darting at the bottom where chains of seaweed swayed, casting intricate shadows on the light-patterned floors. Little starfish clung to the walls and Junie held one in her hand very gently, the sun glistening on the delicate markings on its back.

Each pool was like a treasure chest and Junie and the girls made slow, happy progress across rocks that were warm beneath bare feet, avoiding the sharp periwinkles and patches of algae, slippery where it lay in bright green carpets. It was warm but the breeze cooled their faces and the occasional sea spray found their skin.

Then Dorn made the discovery of the day.

'Mr Burgess! Mr Burgess! Look at this!' she called out, pointing beneath a rock shelf. The men came over to investigate and Ernie pulled out a massive crab, claws snapping in protest.

'Dinner!' he announced happily, holding it in the air.

'What a beaut!' Bob exclaimed. 'Let's get him in the bucket.'

Junie felt sorry for the unfortunate creature as they placed it inside, perhaps because she understood how it felt to be trapped. She wondered how much trouble she'd get in if she let it go. 'Poor fella,' she said.

'You won't say that when you eat him,' Bob promised. 'Crab's damn good tucker – I couldn't let you miss out on this experience, young lady.'

Junie frowned doubtfully as the crab tried in vain to climb the sides of the bucket. 'But I'll never know the difference if I never try it. Why don't we let him go and I'll make you something else?' she said as coaxingly as she could.

'Nuh, crab's on the menu tonight – nothing better,' Bob announced as he moved back to his digging.

Junie tried again, following him. 'But there's not that much meat to go around. How about I help with the digging while you go fishing and hook us some nice flathead instead?' Somehow the thought of eating a fish didn't seem half as cruel as letting this magnificent animal suffer in a bucket all day before it was boiled alive.

'Huh! This is man's work. Go and enjoy yourself,' Bob said, picking up his shovel.

Junie watched him, thinking hard. 'Pipis would be just as good, wouldn't they? They're also crustaceans so surely they have a similar taste to crab? What if I collect enough to make you a big, delicious batch – then will you let him go?'

Bob stopped his digging in exasperation. 'Strike a light! You really don't give up easily, do you?'

'Pipis are good eating,' Ernie said from his makeshift workbench. 'Stubborn as a mule that one,' he said, nodding at Junie. 'I'd give in if I were you.'

'Ever caught a pipi before?' Bob asked.

'No. But I can figure it out.'

'All right,' he said, looking at the shoreline with a knowing grin. 'You catch me a bucket of pipis and I'll let him go. I think you've got Buckley's, though.'

Junie lifted her chin. 'Well, we'll have to see about that.'

⋰⋰⋰

A few hours later the girls were all ready to give up on helping Junie. In fact, Katie was making them rather hungry for crab, describing the taste in rapturous detail.

'A delicate flavour, a bit like lobster, and with butter and salt…'

'What was it you said about using your toe like this?' Junie interrupted, tracing wide semicircles in the wet sand.

'That only works for beach worms. I told you, you're flogging a dead horse. Speaking of which, did I ever tell you girls I ate horse once? Rubbishy stuff…not at all like crabmeat which is light and juicy…'

'They must be here somewhere,' Junie said. 'It's just a matter of thinking it through.'

'Oh God, it's school all over again,' Beryl said.

'Come on, Junie, you'll never find any,' Dorn moaned. 'It's been hours.'

Junie looked at the three of them, tired and despondent, then studied the shore yet again. 'Must be some.'

'That's it, I'm heading back,' Katie said and the other girls followed her. The wind had come up, blowing their hats and flapping at their shirts, and Junie watched the movement, realising the wind seemed to come most afternoons – she'd noticed it when Ernie was teaching her about the tides yesterday. Her mind-rabbit stopped in its tracks. The tide. Of course!

She ran down to the rocks, back to where they had been when the tide was high on the sand. The water had receded quite a bit by now and there were little arrows in the shallow water as it ran away from the shore. Junie began picking her way through the patterns, discarding shells and rocks until she found her first prize.

Then her mind slipped over to its far larger relative in the bucket across the sand and she felt a wave of satisfaction wash over her.

It shouldn't matter so much, she supposed. She was still as trapped as she'd been when she woke up this morning – and as trapped as she'd still be when she went to sleep tonight, but she'd won a tiny victory for freedom today.

It didn't alter a thing, but the thought made her smile.

Eight

'When do we start?'

'Monday. You're on leave until then.'

Michael nodded at his father as he got his head around the fact that he was still in the army, though wouldn't be going to war for some time. That and the fact that his father was his drill sergeant.

His father wasn't really drinking, sitting on the one, almost untouched, beer the whole hour they'd been here. Michael wanted to ask why. He wanted to ask a lot of things – questions about his mother and questions about Davey – but he supposed they would answer themselves eventually. Besides, right now he felt too numb to ask them. However, there was one question he did feel compelled to ask now, although the answer was bound to be painful.

'How are the girls doing?'

Rory almost smiled. 'They're on a Hollywood Holiday, apparently.'

'A what?'

'Katie Burgess has taken them to her uncle's shack at Burning Palms. Bob and Ernie are there for most of the time. I wasn't sure about your mother being on her own but she wanted them to go.' Rory shrugged. 'Said there's not much happiness in life, they should grab it while they can.'

'True enough.' Michael struggled to ask the next. 'Are you… is she…'

'She's a good woman and I've let her down,' Rory said in a quiet voice. Tears formed in his father's eyes and Michael watched him blink them away, unable to absolve the guilt that caused them. 'But never again.'

There was something in his tone that Michael recognised from earlier years and, for the first time since Rory's arrival, he reached out to shake his father's hand. 'I'll hold you to it.'

'Make sure you do,' Rory said, and there was so much promise in his words, Michael believed him.

Rory rose to leave. 'Best be off. Train leaves in ten.'

Michael nodded and stood to watch as his father made his way to the door. 'Dad,' he called. Rory turned and Michael hesitated before blurting, 'I'm glad you're going to be here.'

Rory rewarded him with a fleeting smile, the first he'd worn these past few days. 'Aye,' he said. 'Get those mates of yours and have a good break. I'm not going to be soft on you lot come Monday.'

'I'd better grab some happiness while I can then.'

Rory smiled again, then he was gone, and, as he watched his father disappear onto the city streets, Michael wondered exactly where on earth that could be found.

❧

Beryl was halfway down the beach but even so, Junie could tell she was crying. She wanted to comfort her but there really was nothing she could say to make it better – losing a brother was a pain that couldn't be cured. Besides, Beryl probably needed a good cry. Dorn had done so earlier, when Katie said something about Anzac biscuits; they were always Davey's favourite. Seemed they all needed time to mourn and what better place than here, at the great lady's side?

Junie had to hand it to Katie, she was certainly doing her best to make everything as much fun as humanly possible. Bob and Ernie had left an hour ago and already she was rummaging around inside, planning some kind of party for tonight when it would be just the four girls on their own.

There was a loud thump and Junie raised her eyes at Dorn across the card table they had set up outside.

'Sure you don't want any help?' Junie called.

'I'm fine! Oh bugger...' came the reply.

Dorn giggled, picking up a card. It was hot but the afternoon breeze was picking up once more. Ernie had told Junie it was to do with the air over the water heating differently to the air over the land. He knew a lot of interesting things about the ocean and had piqued her interest to the point that she was looking forward to devouring whatever information she could find on the subject in Ernest's library.

Thinking of her fiancé made her feel depressed, and she let out a deep sigh.

'Penny for your thoughts,' Dorn said.

'Owing the pennies is the whole problem. That's what's got me in this mess.'

'Ah.' Dorn nodded in understanding. 'Still, if you don't mind me saying so...well, if you have to marry him, at least it's some small comfort to have money and be able to help your family. I wish I could. I've lived without it my whole life and it's a hard road.'

Junie didn't like to consider that. She didn't like to consider there was anything redeemable about the whole nightmarish situation. 'Can't see what difference it really makes in the end,' she said.

'It's actually very different. You don't know what being poor is like, Junie. Not really. Having to save coupons for dresses isn't real poverty. It's…it's watching your friend be allowed to finish school when you have to go to work and…having to ask the butcher for the ham bone to make a soup to feed the family. And keeping the peel on the potatoes to stretch a stew – or just going hungry. I've watched Mum – it's hard, like I said. You don't want it believe me.' She was almost crying and Junie's annoyance faded to be replaced by a sense of shame. She'd been vaguely aware of what the Rileys had been through over the years but now it seemed she'd also been far too indifferent.

'I don't really know, that's true. I'm sorry Dorn, I should have…'

'No, no, it's fine,' Dorn said, holding up her hand. 'I didn't mean to say so much. I'm just missing Mum I think – never been away from her before.' Dorn wiped at her face and Junie found a handkerchief, passing it to her.

There was a crash from the shack and a very unladylike exclamation that changed the mood, causing them both to laugh a little, but as they continued playing, Junie couldn't quite shake the feeling of being ashamed. After all, God had provided. She just didn't want to pay the price.

⁂

'Slow down!' Michael yelled, rolling to the side with the luggage as they turned another hairpin bend. 'Bloody hell – floorboard!' He grabbed the piece of timber as it bounced into the back of the car and handed it to Jake, who placed it back under Cliffy's feet, but not before all of them had copped a lungful of dust from the road.

'I told you we should have gone to the Blue Mountains,' Jake spluttered, coughing over the straining engine. 'At least there's sealed roads.'

'You said your cousin only works as a waiter at the Hydro Majestic. There's no way he would have got us a room for free,' Michael yelled back.

'Well, at least it's a fine hotel. Even if we slept in the bloody kitchen. This is Woop Woop!' Jake called with disgust as they passed a bunch of fishermen whose truck looked almost as dilapidated as the car they were driving, an old Austin borrowed from Cliffy's uncle.

'You're a drover, for chrissakes!'

'Not on holidays. A man likes a few comforts then.'

'I told you,' Michael said, 'there's a shack –'

'Probably the Fibro Majestic by the sounds of it.'

Michael and Cliffy laughed.

'Very funny. You should be in show business,' Cliffy said, turning to look at him.

'Watch the road!' Jake and Michael yelled in unison.

The little car narrowly missed a tree and bounced back onto the track, losing its floor once more. 'Floorboard!'

There was a minute of madness as Michael saved Jake's bag from falling under the car and they replaced the timber.

'Least we might have lived through a trip to the mountains,' Jake complained.

'Same driver,' Michael pointed out.

Cliffy turned around to object. 'Hey, at least I've got my licence –'

'Watch the road!'

'No appreciation,' Cliffy said, changing gears before swerving out of the way of a dead wallaby.

Michael fell into the corner holding his nose while Jake held on to the door, straightening the floor again with his feet.

'Corr, that stinks!'

'Just quit your bellyaching. You're going on a holiday to the beach, for God's sake,' Michael reminded him as they turned the corner and saw the sign for the parking area at last, glimpsing the ocean through the trees.

'And I'll get to see Katie Burgess. I remember meeting her once. Nice assets, if you know what I mean,' Jake said, nudging Cliffy.

Michael was less than impressed. 'Just watch yourself. Bob Burgess is a big fella.'

'Killjoy,' Cliffy muttered, parking the car. 'All I can say is these sisters of his better be worth it.'

'I heard that,' Michael warned. 'Off limits, you hear? You can fish, drink beer and – fish. That's it.'

They were silent as they started to unpack, but the tension was soon broken by Jake. 'Dart throwing in Parramatta is starting to look like a bloody good idea.'

It was hot, sweaty work making their way down through the bush, and there really wasn't any kind of actual track to speak of, but the sight of the beach and the ocean drew them on. Their packs were heavy, stuffed as they were with beer and food, but it wasn't far now. Michael guessed Cliffy and Jake felt the same relief he did at being away from the city and back in nature, especially the novelty of having both the bush and ocean to enjoy. They'd all been to the beach a few times, mostly due to some coastal droving work, but never for a holiday. Now Michael couldn't wait to get down there, to throw himself into the water and battle some of the scars of the past few weeks; see what he could wash away.

'Look,' Jake called out, and they peered down to see a few haphazard fibro constructions edging the sand.

'Told ya,' mumbled Jake. 'Bloody Fibro Majestic.'

'Better view over there,' Cliffy said and they turned to see girls lying in the dappled sun in front of the last shack.

'Beer and fishing,' Michael reminded them.

❦

'Waves look nice and small. Think I might go for a swim,' Junie said, stretching and putting down the book she'd been reading, *Lost Horizon*. It had been her favourite movie a few summers back when it was on constant replay at the local cinema, in fact on the day she first met Michael and his sisters she was on the way out of one such viewing. Even then she'd felt drawn to him, despite barely mumbling two words in his direction, skinny and shy as she'd been.

As much as she'd loved the film, the book was even better, and she truly had been lost in it; the perfect distraction as she, Beryl and Dorn had a lie down on blankets in the mottled shade beneath the palms. Katie, meanwhile, was continuing her mysterious preparations in the shack.

'Have fun,' said Beryl, half asleep.

'Hmm,' mumbled Dorn.

The salted breeze was fresh on Junie's face as she stripped down to her bathers and ran into the water, which embraced her in a sudden cold that soon warmed to just right. She dived under waves as Katie had taught her, careful not to go in past her waist. Fortunately the small break only reached her hips, so she could relax into the rhythm of the tides, the push and pull, the dance.

Floating on her back, she thought about Shangri-La, the fictional, heavenly place in *Lost Horizon* where people didn't grow old and everything remained perfect. Where happiness was a permanent state of being, never to change unless you left. She knew she was a long way from that kind of happiness because change was the only thing giving her hope. She needed it like air, welcoming it like the cool of the sea on this hot afternoon.

Junie closed her eyes, taking this little taste of happiness anyway, immersing herself in the lady who was as unpredictable as the future. The sun touched her face and she smiled, feeling its warmth, safe in the knowledge that Michael still felt that too. And while that remained true, she'd take her chances on change. It was the last piece of reassurance she had.

'Junie!'

Katie was calling her.

She thought about ignoring her for a while, keen to float in that rare happiness a little while longer, but that wouldn't be fair. Katie was obviously in a state of excitement about whatever plans she'd made so Junie reluctantly made her way back to the beach, waves crashing against her legs.

As she stood on the shore, shaking the water from her hair, the breeze carried her name once more, only this time it wasn't Katie's voice. It was a man's.

❦

He'd run out on to the beach, throwing his pack down to have a swim straight away, ripping off his sweat-soaked shirt, not seeing her as she floated just beyond the break. He still hadn't seen her as he kicked off his shoes and threw himself into the water, the cool incredibly refreshing after the hot track. Even when he did see her, walking past him only a few feet away, he had a moment of pure shock and didn't quite register that the vision was real. How could it be?

Junie Wallace emerged from the ocean, swimsuit clinging to every part of her body, the dark blue material glistening against golden limbs. She shook her hair and the curls stuck against her upper arms and back, mesmerising him. Then he called her name and she turned, the blue of the ocean in her startled eyes as she recognised him. She spoke his name too, then she was moving towards him and he was moving towards her and the ocean was drawing her so close he couldn't help but reach out his arms.

And then she was in them. In that skin, with that hair tangled in his fingers, and he was kissing her.

And then every single rational thought was gone.

Junie was on fire. It spread across her damp skin to every part of her being, especially where Michael's body was warm against hers. Never had she imagined it could feel like this, and she'd imagined it a lot. His burning kisses drugged her like an elixir from the gods that she had to drink. Soft yet strong. *More, more*, she begged him silently. She craved him, wanting whatever it was that happened next to happen now. Then he pulled back, running his hand along her arm and holding her chin.

'Don't stop,' she whispered and so he kissed her again and pressed her close, wet skin meeting wet skin.

Michael pulled back once more and smiled with happiness so great her eyes stung with tears as she traced his face with her hand.

'I love you,' she said softly.

'I love you,' he replied and she could feel the actual force of it.

The sun shone in warm approval as they continued to make their bond at the feet of the great lady, uncaring of what might happen in the future. Because whatever happened now, nothing could ever wash this moment away.

Nine

'Knock knock.'

Katie turned around, startled to see a soldier at the shack door and almost dropping the icing bowl she was holding.

'Hi, I'm Jake, you must be Katie Burgess. I think we might have met once...back in Braidwood...'

She peered at his face, remembering. 'Oh yes. Hello...you're a long way from home.' She walked over cautiously, very much aware that her father and uncle were away and she was in charge of looking after three rather vulnerable girls in their absence.

'Yeah, I'm here with my friend Cliffy...'

'Nice to meet you,' said another soldier from behind Jake. He was grinning from ear to ear but Katie just glared at his naked chest.

'...and...uh...Mick is here of course. Michael Riley. Sorry, should have said. He's just having a quick swim.' Jake pointed at the ocean.

'Michael's here?' Dorn said, sitting up from her nap under the trees, eyes suddenly wide open.

Beryl yawned next to her. 'Who's here?'

'Michael!' Dorn said, jumping up.

'What? Where?' Beryl did likewise and Katie joined them in searching for him in the water.

'Is that? Oh bugger me,' Katie said, missing Jake's look of surprised approval at her language. She was too busy staring at the sight of Michael kissing Junie, right there in broad daylight, while she was engaged to another man.

'Saints alive,' said Dorn, looking faint as Beryl's mouth dropped into a perfect O.

The boys turned to follow their line of vision in confusion then found themselves in similar states.

'Bloody hell…' said Cliffy.

'Well,' said Jake, 'so much for just beer and fishing.'

'Do something,' Katie hissed at him.

'What do you want me to do?' he said, starting to laugh.

'She's engaged!' Dorn said, scandalised.

'Really?' he said thoughtfully. 'Well that explains a few things. She wouldn't by any chance be from Braidwood would she?'

'We're all from Braidwood you nong!' Katie exploded.

Jake grinned at her. 'You know I really do love a girl with spirit…'

'Don't get any funny ideas prawn-face.'

Jake looked taken aback then grinned even more.

They all stood watching the couple in the water in awkward silence which Jake decided to break with the sound of a beer bottle being opened.

'What do you think you're doing?' Katie said, staring as he plonked himself on a chair.

'What Mick instructed.'

She looked back at the water then shook her head. 'Better give us one then too.'

⚜

The laughter was floating down the beach by the time Junie and Michael arrived at the shack, Jake's voice carrying.

'Then Mick said, "Reasons why no woman can stand yer repulsive self!"'

Katie could be heard laughing very hard at that.

'He didn't!' said Dorn.

'He certainly did, then Cliffy said – hold on here's our lad at last. Hey, Romeo.'

Beryl and Dorn stood and ran to their brother and there was a minute of fierce hugs.

'It's all right, Dornie,' Michael crooned as she wept against his chest. 'There, now.' Beryl held his other arm tight and neither let him go as they moved to the blankets and chairs.

'Way to hog the women, Lothario,' Jake said, grinning. 'Speaking of which, the name's Jake.' He stood up and gave Junie a bow, followed by a low whistle.

'Junie,' she replied, a little shy.

Cliffy knocked over his chair as he stood, his face a picture of awe. 'I'm…uh…' They all waited as he simply gawked.

'Cliffy. Your name is Cliffy,' Jake reminded him.

Cliffy nodded, his mouth still hanging open, and the others laughed.

'Entertainment over already?' Jake asked Michael.

'I see you've settled yourself in,' Michael said, ignoring his question. 'How are you, Katie?' he said, kissing her on the cheek. She gave him a knowing look but refrained from her usual outspokenness.

'How on earth did you know we were here?' she asked instead.

'Dad told me you and the girls were having a holiday, although I didn't know Junie was here too. That was, uh, until I –'

'Received a nice jolt to the arteries?' Jake suggested.

'Pretty much,' Michael conceded, rubbing his neck, embarrassed. 'Anyway we were given some leave because –'

'Why was Dad with you? What was he doing in Sydney?' Beryl interrupted.

'Why wasn't he with Mum?' Dorn added.

Michael looked at them and decided to tell the whole story from beginning to end. By the time he was finished, they were all silent, digesting it. Then Junie found her voice.

'You mean to say you are going to be in Sydney for the next year? Training with this Elite squad?'

'Yes,' Michael said.

There were a few uncomfortable glances exchanged before Katie said, 'And the girls and your mum are moving up too?'

'Looks like it.'

'Bloody hell. What am I supposed to do with myself?' she exclaimed.

'Come join the party!' Jake suggested and Katie looked him up and down sceptically.

'Oh, speaking of parties,' she said, suddenly remembering, 'I've organised one for Junie tonight! A Hollywood Holiday party to celebrate – um, to say a farewell of sorts...' she fumbled, 'but I didn't cater for three more and I don't have anywhere to really put you that is...appropriate.'

'We'll crash on the sand in our sleeping bags, don't worry,' Michael reassured her, 'and we have plenty of food of our own. But maybe we could make a fire and sit together out here?' He looked at Junie tenderly. 'That might be nice.'

Junie smiled at him and took his hand. 'I'd like that.'

'Ahem,' Katie said, and they let go to the obvious relief of his sisters, who were still gaping at them in shock. 'Let's just get organised shall we? How about you boys get some firewood and I'll see about combining some of this food into a meal? I've got some lamb and bread rolls and I made a cake...'

'I do love a girl with appetites,' Jake said, following her.

'And I like a man who can control his. Firewood!' she instructed, pointing to the bush.

'I don't understand women,' Jake confessed to Cliffy as she bustled off.

'Hey, I'm still trying to figure out why they put a gold star on the dunny door.'

❀

The fire was crackling and beginning to blaze by the time Junie and Dorn had finished setting up the picnic. Only Beryl had been allowed inside with Katie and the hostess herself came out now, waving as they all gathered around.

'Ladies and gentlemen, on behalf of Miss Genie-Junie the movie star, welcome to Hollywood,' she announced as Beryl rolled out an actual red carpet across the grass and sand towards the picnic. 'Your outfit selection can be made herein.'

'Bloody hell,' said Jake as they all walked to the door and stared at what was now an Aladdin's Cave of fancy dress costumes and accessories.

'I knew that bag was suspiciously large when your dad lugged it down here,' Junie said, both awed and amused.

'But it's all for women!' Cliffy exclaimed, holding up a gold sequinned scarf.

'Invite yourself to a women-only party and pay the consequences,' Katie said airily. 'Get a move on. We've movie charades after dinner.'

By the time the girls had selected a variety of ridiculous props and dresses for the boys, they barely had time to throw things on themselves before dinner but the overall effect they'd achieved had them all in peals of laughter. Jake was dressed as some kind of belly dancer in a spangled skirt, gold brassiere and a curly black wig and Cliffy had been given a red sheath dress with a plunging neckline that revealed quite a bit of hairy chest. He also wore make-up courtesy of Beryl, although the lipstick had gotten out of control and he looked a bit like a freakish clown, a fact that had her in a constant state of teary giggles. Then there was Michael who, with his long legs and tanned face, almost carried off the yellow evening frock, but it clashed somewhat with his army boots and orange turban.

Fortunately the girls had managed to be a bit more tasteful, although Katie's gold dress was a little tight around the bust and rear – something Jake had to be reminded to stop staring at – and Dorn's fake fur dragged in the sand on her diminutive frame.

'She looks like a little bear!' Michael chuckled, patting her head fondly.

Beryl was definitely pulling off the Spanish gown and lace fan, despite bits of lace falling off every time she waved it, but it was Junie who stole the show. Everyone went quiet when she stepped out of the powder room in a crimson twenties-style flapper dress and feathered crown – an outfit she'd actually chosen to look a bit silly and have fun. Instead she looked quite stunning, prompting Jake to comment that Cliffy would never be able to remember his name at this rate.

Junie figured even Hollywood couldn't have produced a more perfect evening. They ate and drank and played charades, and danced in the sand to the wireless. Then Cliffy played a little ukulele he'd brought along and Dorn was persuaded to sing in her sweet soprano. The others listened as they lay on blankets around the fire, mesmerised as she sang 'Cheek to Cheek (I'm in Heaven)', sparks breaking and flying off into the night.

Junie looked over at her copy of *Lost Horizon*, lying in the sand, and wished she could crawl into its pages with Michael, taking this feeling with them to stay there together, forever. Change had arrived and she never wanted another, because life at this moment really was heaven. Junie refused to consider what lay beyond it or even what had gone before it. All she knew was the same feelings were echoing in Michael's eyes and that, in the quietest hours before the dawn, she would not be able to resist coming to find him; to let him take her down to the shadowed shoreline.

❧

The moon was full, casting a silvered pathway across the great lady, who shimmered in her black evening skirts. There, by the sea, Michael's kisses of the day grew unrestrained in the cloak of night and they fell to the sand, clinging together. It was the first time for both of them and he traced her naked form, fingers trailing in worship across her breasts and stomach and thighs until he found places that made her gasp and strain against him. She held onto his back as he moved on top of her, marvelling at the strength beneath his skin and wondering how he knew what to do. There was pain, but it was soon gone and she was moving with him until he found his release and cried out her name, falling to the side to bury himself in her neck and kiss her long and slowly in wonder.

She knew it was this that she would remember most, the perfect moment when she lost herself to him completely. Finding her own Shangri-La, there in Michael's arms.

Holding onto him was the only thing she'd ever really wanted.

And it was the only thing she just couldn't have.

Part Two

Ten

Slim Baxter was laughing harder than Marlon Stone had ever seen him laugh. But little wonder – Joe Henry Jr was shaking his hips like there was no tomorrow and even the dancing Hawaiian girls couldn't hold it together, doubling up with their graceful hands across their flat stomachs, tears pouring down their pretty faces. No-one ever had a chance with any of them but God how the men loved to watch the girls move and sway. Marlon stood and clapped with the rest of the crowd as Joe finally fell in a heap on the sandy bar floor and crawled back to their table.

'Think you need to fix your nuts,' Marlon said, pointing at the makeshift bra Joe had made from the coconut husks their cocktails had come in.

'Or find them,' Slim said, still laughing.

'Oh a wise guy, eh?' Joe said, swaying. 'Hey, I think I got it now...'

'Keep practising, sweetheart. Hey barkeep – 'nother round. We need some more nuts,' Slim yelled.

Marlon decided he'd better find some room for that and made his way to the Men's, pushing past an array of drunken US personnel dressed mostly in Hawaiian shirts, shaking hands and slapping backs as he went. It was turning into a wild old party, as per usual for a Saturday night at the Grand Tiki Bar, and a far preferable scene to Marlon than the officers' party he was supposed to attend. Just because he'd been promoted didn't mean he was about to turn around, demote his buddies and become a snob. He'd had enough of those types back in his Harvard days. This was much more his thing, although as he returned, he made a mental note to stop drinking at midnight. He and Slim had planned an early morning flight, more for sightseeing than anything else, although it was officially under the guise of combat practice. Not that any of them were particularly worried about England's war. It seemed a long way off from here.

He had almost reached his table when he saw her, the same beautiful woman he'd been flirting with the last few Saturday nights. A six-foot, killer-curved paradigm of blonde womanhood, surrounded by a throng of drunken men all dying to see what lay underneath that tight red dress of hers. He managed to catch her eye and an unspoken message passed between them. Maybe tonight would finally be the night but Marlon knew a girl like that needed to come to him, not the other way around, so he went back to the guys and continued drinking. Not too difficult, considering the fine form they were in.

The band started up and the drumming got Joe dancing again, a wide circle around him as the throng cheered.

'Wooh! Give it to 'em, Joe!' Slim shouted as Joe put his hands behind his head and did some very enthusiastic gyrations before tripping over his boots and falling into the crowd. They pushed him back into the circle and urged him on and Marlon clapped and cheered too, laughing.

'I'm thirsty,' someone said in his ear and he glanced over his shoulder, playing it cool at the sight of the blonde behind him, hand on her hip, trying to look bored. He turned slowly, taking his time, and placed a second straw in his coconut cocktail. Then the woman leant forwards and took a long sip from his drink as he took the other straw, their faces inches apart. He could smell her musky perfume and read the daring in her eyes, but still he waited.

Joe flew past and landed on the ground next to Marlon and he and the woman both glanced down but continued drinking, this time each with a smile at the corners of their mouths. Then she lifted her lips away from the straw, saying the words he'd been waiting for: 'I want you.'

Maybe she'd chosen him because he was the only guy taller than her in the bar, or maybe it was because he'd learnt long ago that the hottest broads needed the least attention to find a man challenging, but, looking at her mouth, he didn't care. He wanted her too. And that feeling exploded into hot desire as she bit her lip, her expression darkening with all sorts of secrets before she mouthed another word.

'Now.'

He put down the drink and steered her deftly through the crowd, barely making it outside before she pulled on his tie and they fell against the wall around the corner. She kissed him urgently as he tore his way through her clothes to where he wanted to go. Then he took her hard against the concrete wall and she was crying out and panting and her breasts were falling out of her dress but he didn't care if anyone heard them or saw them. What man would at a time like this? The sight of her abandon was the end of him and they climaxed together.

Inside the crowd was chanting 'Go, Joe! Go, Joe! Go, Joe!' and they began to laugh.

'Sure that isn't your name?' the woman said.

'I think it is tonight,' he replied and kissed her beautiful mouth once more. She returned the kiss with a pleasured sigh then patted his chest, pulling her dress back into place.

'I'd better go home. My husband thinks I'm in bed with a headache.'

Marlon tried to hide his surprise, which was difficult, considering how drunk he was. 'Where is he?'

'At some boring work function. I can't stand those types of things.'

Marlon had a bad feeling as he asked, 'What does he do?'

'Runs armies.' She shrugged, blowing him one last kiss before hailing a taxi and getting in.

Marlon stared after her, realising who she was as the car's lights receded down the road. Looking towards his base, he made a mental note to avoid any contact with Major Hamlin. Now that he'd slept with his wife.

༺✿༻

'Aloha-aaa-ee…aloha-aaa-eee…' Joe was singing as they hitched their way home. He was still wearing the coconut bra and they were receiving some ribald comments from other revellers as they went.

'You're gonna have to see her again. She sure is the swell – hic – swellest-looking gal I've ever seen. *Ever*,' Slim repeated for emphasis.

'She's also the major's wife,' Marlon reminded him, dragging on his cigarette and trying to walk in a straight line, both activities proving challenging in his current state.

'Damn, I'd heard she was hot but this mama was smokin'! Can't figure why she'd take such a risk on a bum like you! 'Specially when she coulda had a talented fella like me!' Joe bowed in front of them and they laughed as his coconuts finally fell off. 'Nuts,' he said, retrieving them on wobbly legs.

'Hard to fathom,' said Marlon.

'A dame like that would never go for the likes of us,' Slim slurred, stopping to light a cigarette. 'Marlon here, he's got that whole Tyrone Power thing going on. Sits back and lets the gals chase him.'

'It's that Injun blood. He's a good hunter.'

Marlon just laughed, although once it would have bothered him to be called an 'Injun' by a white man. Here, it didn't matter. His buddies said it with a kind of pride and he suspected they thought his mother's family lived some kind of noble native life back in Sausalito. Truth was they were just hanging on to pieces of the old culture like his wealthy father's family held on to Christianity: a picture on the wall here, a carving on the shelf there; tokens of past faiths. His mother's relatives pretty much led modern, conservative lives, their skin paler with each generation, Marlon included. All except his grandmother. Marlon smiled at the thought of her crinkled, nutmeg face with its chin tattoos. No-one would ever bleed the Coast Miwok out of Liwa, who held on to her native name with pride.

'Yeah, well, he sure hunted some nice-looking prey tonight. Come on, spill the beans, did you make a home run?' It was Joe who asked but they both looked at him hopefully.

'A gentleman never tells,' Marlon said as a truck slowed and they clambered awkwardly onto the back.

'Aw, come on!'

The ribbing went on most of the way back to Hickam Field, where they alighted, yelling their thanks over the engine to the driver, before stopping to sit near the runway for one last smoke. Their barracks, nicknamed the Hickam Hotel due to the size and amenities, were quiet and Marlon wondered how they would get

Joe in and up to the third floor without waking anyone – he was still humming Hawaiian tunes to himself as he lay on his back next to them.

'Here she comes,' Slim noted, pointing at an approaching B-17D. The bomber glided in and Marlon figured the pilot was doing a pretty good job as it landed quite gracefully.

'Not bad for a flying monkey,' he said and Joe changed his humming to 'Follow the Yellow Brick Road'. *The Wizard of Oz* had been playing in town and they'd seen it several times over the past few weeks.

'Yeah, well that monkey's better at flying in the dark than me. Need to get more hours up,' Slim said, yawning. Marlon had done plenty of night flights back in San Francisco, where he'd worked as a domestic pilot for a year before joining the air force. Liwa still couldn't understand why he would want to serve a country that had decimated his people and he couldn't really explain to her that he was a modern American too – that wouldn't be something she would want to hear.

'Don't spill your Miwok blood for white war,' she'd said.

'There won't be any war, Liwa. I'm just getting in a bit of travel while I'm young,' he remembered telling her.

'You just keep your head down and stay that way,' she'd replied, wagging a bony brown finger at him. Marlon smiled at the memory.

The night was quiet now and moonlight outlined the mass of American military power that lay here: planes, buildings, runways, hangars. All ordered and waiting – a long way from any real war. They looked to Marlon as though a child had lined them up in perfect formation for imaginary games to begin. A soft breeze whispered against that weaponry and the moon touched the tips of the swaying palms and hibiscus trees nearby, their red flowers bowing in a dark, delicate dance.

'Wonder why they called it Pearl Harbor?' Slim said, watching the night too.

'Wai Momi,' Marlon said. 'That's the Hawaiian name. It means "water of pearl". Used to have a lot of oysters out there back in the day.'

'Reckon there's some still there? I got a gal back home who likes pearls. Her name's Pearl.' Joe laughed to himself, still lying down, but now with his eyes closed. Marlon had thought he was asleep.

'Doubtful. Mostly been farmed. Lots of the locals aren't too happy about that. Aren't too happy 'bout all this either.' Marlon gestured at the buildings around them, thinking about the long conversations he'd had with Kalani, a bartender at the Grand Tiki Bar.

'Should be happy we've come to protect 'em,' Slim said, lighting another cigarette.

'Nah, some believe they already had protection from the gods but we've made them angry by wrecking their land. Blame the quakes on it every time.' Marlon paused, trying to remember what Kalani had told him. 'They say the shark goddess...what was her name again? Ka'ahu pahau, I think, and her brother Kahi... something –' Marlon stopped again, frowning against the alcohol in his brain. 'Kahi'uka! Yes, that's it. They guard the locals from trouble...especially man-eating sharks. They're supposed to live in a cave at the entrance to the bay.'

'How the hell d'you remember stuff like that?' Joe mumbled.

Marlon had never really thought about his knack for remembering interesting cultural facts. He guessed he got it from listening to Liwa all these years. He was surprised he was remembering them now, though, and said so.

'Yeah, well, here's hoping the gods want to protect us too. Not too fond of sharks meself,' Slim said. 'Wouldn't want to be greeted by a bunch of fins if I land one of those in the drink.' He nodded at the A20-As lined up in a row, the planes they'd been training in, and Marlon looked too, remembering their flight in the morning. He stood up, yawning, and reached down to haul Joe to his feet.

'Time to hit the hay.'

'Why, whaddid the hay ever – hic – do to you?'

Marlon chuckled, telling him to shush as they made their unsteady way to the barracks. But as he looked back at the A20-As, he had to agree with Slim. He wouldn't want to meet any sharks in the water either, so for what it was worth, he offered up a little apology to Ka'ahu pahau and her brother before turning in.

That night he dreamt of Liwa, singing beneath the palm trees and chanting in the old ways. He watched as she grew fins and dived into the bay, swimming out to meet with the Hawaiian gods. To tell them that she was Liwa, a daughter of the Miwok, and that her name meant 'water'. That she too was from a coastal tribe and that her blood ran with the tides. And to ask that they protect her grandson, Marlon, named for the great fish. Not really a white man.

To keep him from the man-eating sharks too.

Eleven

The church bells were ringing when Marlon woke, caught up in his sheets and head thumping. He wished they would shut the hell up. Slim was groaning and Marlon joined him as he sat slowly and began to get dressed, wishing he could sleep in like Joe, who was passed out like a starfish, coconuts on the ground next to his bunk.

'Ready to fly, monkey?'

Slim groaned again but sat up too, pulling his undershirt off and finding a fresh one. 'Don't know how I'm gonna fly. Can't even see,' he mumbled.

It was even harder to do so when they walked outside into the dazzling morning sunshine. They both reeled from the glare.

'Sweet mother of God,' Slim said, clutching the side of the building and finding his sunglasses in his pocket. Marlon cursed the fact he'd lost his a few days ago; it was physically painful waiting for his eyes to grow accustomed to the brilliance of the day.

They walked to the hangars, each lighting a cigarette. Despite his hangover, a familiar excitement began to build in Marlon, the same feeling that had arrived the first day he'd ever felt wheels leave tarmac. That cruel sun was relaxing and settling into morning, dazzling in a sky that was clear Hawaiian blue, and it was calling to them to find wings and rise too. Suddenly Marlon couldn't wait to get up there and he began to sing.

'One more line about that goddam wizard and I may have to kill you, buddy. Man, I definitely need a coffee. Want one?' Slim asked, looking over at the mess.

A few officers and their wives were on their way to church and Marlon and Slim paused to salute them.

'God, we must look a sight,' Marlon muttered as they passed, feeling shabby in his crushed gear against the crisp shirts and dresses on parade. He kept an especially wary eye out for a tall blonde on a major's arm.

'Coffee?' Slim repeated.

Marlon went to reply in the affirmative but was stopped by something he heard.

'Hello? Marlon?' Slim asked, waiting.

'Yeah, I just…hold on,' he said, searching the skies as the distant humming increased. He wondered if some new Flying Fortresses were arriving today – rumour had it they were due.

Then he heard it, a sudden rumble.

'Look,' said Slim, pointing to a trail of black smoke rising into the air from the harbour. 'Boy, somebody sure fouled up.'

They stood and watched and a few of the churchgoers did the same.

'Could be a gas explosion,' Marlon said. But the humming was getting louder.

'There they are,' said Slim, pointing at black dots in the sky. 'Maybe it's the Japs,' he joked. 'Say, they're really going places.'

The black dots were fast emerging in plane form. Marlon was about to reply when he noticed something that ran his blood cold: they were diving. Fast.

'Say, slow down, buddy,' Slim said, confused as one approached, low. 'Holy shit! Is that…?'

'Meatballs!' someone yelled nearby, pointing.

Marlon stared in shock at the red dot on the wing, realising it was, unbelievably, a Japanese dive bomber. They ran and pressed themselves against the hangar wall as the enemy plane powered over the ground, seeing clearly that it was a two seater with a gun in the rear cockpit. Both pilot and gunner were goggled and helmeted, and Marlon had a second of mad wonder that they were real people, this mystery half-enemy. Then any delusion of non-reality was blasted into a million pieces as gunfire began to hail down on them and glass shattered from the windows.

Large numbers of planes were now heading to the harbour and they watched the stubby, pencil-like bombs sail down, that glorious sun reflecting off them in innocent Hawaiian welcome. Explosions shook the earth and Marlon watched the rising plumes of black clouds in disbelief. Japan had awoken the sleeping American navy by introducing them to hell.

But before they could really comprehend what horrors were unfolding on the water, the pencils were coming towards them and Slim yelled 'Cover!' grabbing Marlon's shirt as they hauled themselves towards the sandbags.

This time the earth didn't just shake, it bucked like a giant mule, kicking the wind out of them as they landed. The deafening roar of bomb blasts and gunfire was all around and Marlon saw hell first-hand as the hangars exploded and the planes were fired upon like ducks in a row. Flashes of how he'd thought their neat arrangement almost childlike last night interrupted his panic momentarily before they burst in masses of splinters, falling against each other, consumed by flame.

Noise – the *rat-a-tat*, crashing, whirring cacophony of war – assailed him for the first time in his life, a terrifying soundtrack to the scene playing out before them as they crouched in horrified audience, helpless to stop it. The planes kept coming, like vicious dogs; attack, attack, attack. Menacing and relentless, they dropped their bombs and sent America's air force back into the sacred Hawaiian soil in a deranged mass of twisting fire, too fast for anyone to comprehend. Then one bomb fell on the mess hall, where Marlon and Slim knew so many of their buddies would be. There were screams in the cacophony now as the pride of the US military, the million-dollar Hickam Hotel, ignited in a series of massive, mighty fireballs.

Joe.

Marlon stood to find him but Slim held his arm fast as a soldier fell right in front of them, red pock marks lining his torso. *Rat-a-tat.*

Marlon had never seen a man die before.

The smoke came in thick choking waves then, and the death planes seemed to leave but explosions continued as oil found fire. Marlon and Slim grabbed the opportunity to run to the barracks and mess hall, now a scene of apocalyptic destruction, destroyed buildings shedding into the heat. All was chaos and confusion: men covered in blood trying to lift others out; torn, maimed bodies. A severed leg lay near a book in the rubble. *Of Mice and Men.* Marlon would never forget the title for the rest of his life.

'Marlon!' he heard Slim yell over the cries of pain and roaring fires. Joe was in his arms, eyes closed and chest stained a deep claret. Marlon ran, helping Slim to drag him over to where the wounded were being gathered, placing Joe on the ground and searching for a pulse. He found one and took a shaking breath.

'Alive.'

Slim nodded, pale and shaking too. They could see many weren't so lucky. The dead and dying were being lain in a sickening line and Marlon wished the fire could burn the images from his mind.

'You men,' he heard Major Hamlin shout at some mechanics. 'Get over to the flight line! Get some goddam planes ready!'

Marlon stared at the major, vaguely registering something about his tall, blonde wife in the back of his cluttered mind.

The major pointed. 'Stone, get yourself up there.'

'Yes, sir,' he said. He took one last look at Joe and ran off, Slim following.

Finding a plane that wasn't on fire or damaged took some time, and all Marlon could think was that it was like playing blind man's bluff with all that smoke – they couldn't see a damn thing. The mechanics managed to find a B-17D but had to get it combat ready, and Marlon and Slim helped them carry a machine gun on board and set it in place.

'Need some more ammo. Oh shit, look out!' Slim shouted as the whirring returned. Marlon decided this time he wasn't going to sit idly by.

'Come on!' he yelled at Slim as he lifted the machine gun back out.

'You gotta be kidding!' But Slim helped him all the same and they hauled the gun across the road just as a Japanese pilot rounded in and fired, hitting the dirt behind them and finding the B-17D. The tail was obliterated and the right side crashed into the ground as it caught fire. One of the mechanics caught fire too and the sight enraged Marlon, prompting him to ram the ammo into the gun and begin firing with a mighty roar.

This time the *rat-a-tat* was from him as he hurled death back at the enemy. He missed. But then another plane came, and another. He and Slim fed that gun as hard as they could until they caught one of those meatballs right in the heart.

'Yeah! Cop that from Milwaukee!' shouted Slim, punching the air. Then a bullet flew through his chest and Slim looked at

Marlon, his eyes filled with surprise before emptying as he fell, lifeless, to the ground.

'Slim! No – oh God...' Marlon dropped to the ground too, blinded by tears.

❧

Eventually he found the gun again, and fed it with ammo until every plane was gone. But nothing would ever erase the fact that Slim's life had been ripped away and, no matter how many meat-balls he found, Marlon couldn't shoot down the moment that stole it.

Marlon would later hear many things about that day. How the Japanese had never declared war, just snuck up like thieves to snatch their prize, one sunny morning in paradise. The American President would call it an act of infamy. Overnight the nation would rally and declare war themselves and the whole country would seek revenge for the loss of 2,403 American lives, and for the 1,178 wounded. Half their air force planes had been destroyed and all eight battleships in the harbour were hit. The *Arizona* would never be raised again, nor the thousand souls who per-ished, some days later, trapped forever in an iron coffin under the waters of Pearl Harbor.

The Hawaiian gods never came as the iron Japanese sharks sent their torpedoes into Wai Momi. They never came as the might of America's fleet sank into her sandy depths. But they did protect the grandson of Liwa, whose tribal name means water. He who was Miwok, with the tide running in his veins.

Only they couldn't protect him from the new dreams that came in the black of night, where dots in the sky turned into sharks too, circling their prey with blood on their fins. Sinking their teeth through Slim's white-man heart.

And where Joe writhed in the nets, caught and beached, only to die a slow death as the claret ran dry.

And part of Marlon's soul that had never known death perished too, sinking into the sand to wash away, abandoned. Lost forever as it blended with the remains of his countrymen, left now to flow in Hawaii's blood-soaked sea.

Twelve

January 1942
Braidwood, New South Wales, Australia

The double doors opened and there she stood, raised on a pedestal like a queen in front of the windows. The sunlight was in brilliant caress and it lit the silk and lace to a shimmering white, the fabric hugging her narrow waist and long silhouette, causing her to appear almost ethereal. Junie's curls had been lifted to the nape of her neck where her grandmother's pearl comb clasped them in an elegant twist and the effect drew the eye to her face, even more exquisite than the rest of her; all cheekbones and large, blue eyes.

'Junie,' Lily said in a breath. 'Oh, my dearest girl.'

'As long as I live I will never see a more beautiful bride,' said Marguerite, the seamstress, who stood nearby, her eyes brimming with proud tears.

Junie turned to look in the mirror, the long veil trailing the floor like angels' wings at rest and saw a bride too, only not a beautiful one. She saw an actress wrapped up in finery; an elaborate white lie.

'Ernest is a lucky man,' said Marguerite, wiping her face and then her hands before she gathered the train to spread it across the floor for them to admire.

Junie's heart weighed heavily at those words. Oh, for it to be Michael she came to as a bride, for him to take her hand so she could promise him her life.

Katie stood to the side, silent, and Junie knew she was reading her mind.

'Look at the lace – so intricate! Marguerite, you've done a wonderful job,' Lily told her, and they went on to discuss the finer points of the woman's handiwork. It was good to see her mother engaged in something, even if it was this.

Junie watched as Katie skirted around to the drinks cabinet and mimed the pouring and gulping of some of its contents. It made Junie smile and Katie returned it as the secret passed between them. If nothing else, at least Katie knew the truth; she, Dorn and Beryl. Without that, Junie didn't know how she would have withstood these past few weeks.

There was a scratching at the door and Junie smiled again. There was another little friend giving her comfort too.

A bundle of black fur peered over the timber at the base and pawed at the glass of the front parlour's door.

'Oh no, you don't! I don't know what Ernest was thinking, giving her that puppy,' Marguerite scolded, shooing him away from the door. 'Go on, back to your blanket. She's spoiling him,' she said to Lily.

Lily smiled indulgently. Truth be told, they all were. Even though Ernest had only given him to Junie as part of his act as the doting husband-to-be, she did adore that pup.

'As long as he doesn't spoil this lace,' Lily said, and they gathered it gently to take off Junie's veil.

Junie bent her knees, accommodating, but she was busy watching Katie sneak out to the verandah to play with Digger. She'd kept the name from that day in the barn with Michael. Had it really only been in November? So much had happened since then. Another death, her own engagement. Michael joining the army, only to now stay in Sydney with the Elite until the end of the year. The declaration of war against Japan after the shock of Pearl Harbor. More and more things to worry about as everything they knew sat beneath the chilling threat of invasion. Junie could only cling to the hope that America's might and force would recover and help them defeat the rampaging Japanese.

But overriding all the worry there was something else, something that eclipsed even the war: the ever-present obsession she had with matters of the heart as her own impending battle loomed before her. It was easier to look backwards instead, back to that place of comfort where a brief armistice had been called. A pause in time for happiness.

Burning Palms.

Her mind flooded with the intoxication of the name, and her own palms seemed to burn at the memory of Michael holding her hands tight in his. That final moment before he went and the plea left his mouth; those impossible, longed-for words: 'Don't marry him, Junie. Marry me instead.'

Her response had plagued her every waking hour since.

Marguerite and her mother helped Junie out of the dress and she was careful not to ruin the woman's work. It wasn't Marguerite's fault it felt more like a shroud than a bridal gown. She put on a blouse and a pair of trousers, thinking a nice walk with Digger and Katie might help her cope with the pain of the afternoon, but Lily's voice stopped her as she reached the door.

'Wait for a minute, Junie, I need to speak to you.'

Even though she knew her mother couldn't possibly know what had transpired this summer, Junie still felt the guilt clamp in her stomach. 'Yes, Mum?'

'Come, sit.' Lily patted the settee and Junie sat slowly, wondering what else this day would ask of her.

'Ernest came to see me. He…he says he thinks it may be best if we don't come to Sydney.'

'But Mum, the wedding…'

'Oh, we will be there for that, don't worry. Of course,' she said frowning. 'Yes, at St Mary's. Saturday the twenty-first.'

Junie waited. It still took her mother some time to remember certain things. She wondered if that would ever change.

'You'll be such a beautiful bride – we just won't be there before. Ernest says we need to stay to supervise things here with the new cattle arriving and…everything…'

'But, Mum, you haven't really been –' she searched for the right word, '– involved with that side of things much lately. Surely someone else can take care of it for you?'

'Ernest says we're not to come,' Lily said quietly.

Junie watched her thoughtfully, wondering at her true motives. 'Mum,' she said, after a pause, 'Ernest isn't your boss, you know. And I am your daughter. I need you to help me set up house and prepare –'

'Constance said she will do that,' Lily said, twisting her handkerchief in her lap.

So that was it. Already the bars of the prison cell were forming and she wouldn't even get to choose the colour.

'I'll have a talk with Ernest,' Junie said.

'No, no, don't do that.' Lily looked very distressed now and Junie became more concerned.

'Mum, what is it? Tell me.'

'I just…don't want any stress on your father. He hasn't been well, what with the news about Japan. He's…he's very worried about the boys…and about you being in Sydney. But I suppose Ernest knows best.'

Junie felt concern slide into fear. The doctor had been earlier in the week. 'Is Dad – is he sick?'

'I can't – you don't need to know anything just yet –'

'Mum,' she pleaded.

Lily's eyes were watery and she raised them to the door where Henry was approaching. He walked past them, unseeing, and headed for the cabinet, helping himself to a scotch.

'Dad.'

Henry jumped, then turned to the two of them. 'Good Lord, don't do that to a man.' He finished pouring his drink, some of which was now on the floor, and sat down heavily on the chair opposite. 'Terribly hot, isn't it?'

'Not bad, considering yesterday,' Junie said distractedly, looking at him closely for the first time in weeks. His face was mottled pink and she noticed the red dots on his cheeks were very pronounced today. He looked tired, his eyes bloodshot, and the weight had grown around his belly. It was as though someone had blown air into him, like the puffer fish Junie had seen washed up on the beach.

Lily was composing herself for her husband's benefit and forcing a light tone. 'Perhaps we'll have a nice salad for tea. And some river trout. Bob Burgess caught some this morning and sent it over.'

Henry coughed, taking a minute to recover. 'Sounds good, love.'

She took his hand and Junie saw the concern on her face. There was love there still between the two of them, despite their individual sorrows.

'Mum…Mum said you won't be coming to Sydney until the wedding. She says you're not well,' Junie said haltingly, afraid of the answer.

'Bah, doctors,' Henry said, finishing his drink. 'They want to run some blasted tests in Canberra, so we'll be delayed. But don't you worry, my beauty. We'll be there on the day. Wild horses couldn't keep me from my little girl's wedding.' He gave her a reassuring smile and she tried to smile back but her eyes filled instead.

'There now,' he said, frowning. 'Don't tell me you're having second thoughts? I could see you weren't happy about marrying the man at first but then you seemed right as rain at Christmas.'

Christmas. The biggest performance of her life. Sometimes she wondered if she really was channelling that Gene Tierney, so convincing had become the lie.

'No, no…I'm just worried about you.' Junie began to cry at the hopelessness of it all and the new shadow upon them. 'The doctor –'

Henry held out his arm and she buried herself against him for a rare hug. 'What's all this eh? I'm going to be fine. Just fine.'

So they sat for a stolen moment, just the three of them, and Junie knew it was one she would remember, like a photograph framed in her mind.

But gilded cells and wedding dresses and big city society drew steadily towards her, and she could no sooner freeze time in a frame than stop her heart from still wanting to move forwards, despite it all.

Because Sydney held so much more than all those things. It held her other fiancé too.

Thirteen

It was stinking hot. So hot Michael could feel the sweat trickle down to the already damp part of his shirt that was clinging to his lower back. But that was the least of his problems. Cliffy and Jake had disappeared well over an hour ago, along with the others, and he was isolated in this piece of scrub near the beach, unable to move. He eyed the blue patches on the two 'enemy' soldiers in front, new members of the Elite who had been allocated to one of the opposing groups today. They were having a smoko in the grass and chatting about the barmaid in the village. Michael tried not to listen to their descriptions of her generous endowments – he didn't need more images of women's bodies in his head right now. As it was, five minutes didn't go by without some thought of Junie: Junie combing her hair with her fingers after a swim; Junie eating an orange and licking the juice from her fingers; Junie wearing a crimson, feathered crown and lying naked with the moon reflected in her eyes.

Michael cleared his head, forcing the thoughts away before they consumed his ability to focus. He'd have time enough with his love once she became his wife but right now he needed to get out of these bushes, and with these two jokers preoccupied with their own witty exchange, the time was probably now. Shouldering his gun as carefully as he could, he crept along behind them, wondering what his chances were of taking them prisoner.

Actually pretty good, he surmised, as one of them lay down and put his hat over his head.

'Bugger this, I'm taking a kip,' he heard him say.

The other man sat down next to him and started rolling another cigarette. 'Wonder what the poor people are doing,' he said, rather contentedly.

Michael couldn't blame him. The beach was like a postcard, all turquoise water and white sand, and Tomaree Headland reached towards the cloudless sky in a steep, forested slope of green. Michael had counted seven dolphins while he waited, their silvered backs glistening in the sun as they sliced up and out of the water, then dived to make their playful, rolling way along. Idyllic spot for a picnic, really.

But today was no picnic. Today they were playing at war.

Michael took off his shoes and carefully placed his foot on the sandy, scrub-littered earth, remembering what Daku, an Aboriginal drover mate, had taught him once about hunting: *Ease your weight gently. You weigh nothing at all, you are part of the earth, the air. Easy now, boy. Slow steps, light of foot.*

Flick. The soldier's lighter found its mark.

Michael paused, frozen like a wallaby raising its ears at the snap of a twig. *Lightly, lightly. You are the earth.*

'Reckon we should just stay here until they give up,' said the one lying on the ground.

'Yeah, bloody code word. Who gives a –'

Click.

'Captain does actually. Captured, gents, let's go.'

The two soldiers gave a rather comical performance of scrambling and gaping before looking at Michael's gun and realising they were well and truly caught out.

'Bugger,' said one. 'Nearly made me swallow my ciggie.'

'Look lively,' Michael said, grinning and pointing back to the scrub. The two soldiers walked in front, grumbling about the unfairness of being ambushed as Michael stuck his boots on with one hand and held the weapon with the other.

'We were on smoko,' complained the man who had been lying down.

'Japs'll still shoot you when you're lying down. Saves them a bit of time actually,' Michael replied. 'Come on.'

❧

Nigel 'Nige' Rollings was fiddling with the radio when Michael lobbed a she-oak cone at his neck and the sudden yelping made the others stare in bewilderment.

'What the hell are you doing?' Cliffy asked.

'Think there's some bloody drop bears around,' Nige said nervously, looking up at the trees.

'I told you, they only come out at night. When everyone's asleep. Easier to get fresh meat that way,' Jake said, biting into an apple as the others hid their grins.

'No way to run a war,' Nige muttered, putting his glasses back on and peering at the branches above him. Cliffy had warned city-raised Nige only too well about the vicious cousin of the koala, the drop bear, which hunted men by dropping from the trees, clawing at their faces with sharp, deadly claws. The only thing Nigel Rollings didn't know about drop bears was that they were entirely fictitious.

'Anyway, as I was saying,' Cliffy said, 'soon as we find Mick, I reckon we go back up along the beach and –'

Another cone arrived, smack on Nige's nose, and he jumped up, grabbing his gun.

'Who goes there?'

The others looked at him in amusement, only to jump up themselves at the sound of approach.

''Tis I, Sir Michael of Braidwood.' Michael laughed, emerging from the scrub. 'And I come bearing gifts.' He shoved the two captured soldiers forwards, now gagged and with their hands on their heads. The squad all looked relieved to see him and more than a little impressed with his 'gifts'.

'Mick, you sneaky bastard!'

'Where'd you go?'

'Had to wait for these two galahs to finish their smoko before I could persuade them to join us,' he told them. 'Do the honours for me, will you, Cliffy?'

'I'd be delighted, Sir Mick,' Cliffy said, jumping up. 'Give us a hand, Tommy. Plan K, is it?'

'I think that might work for these two,' Michael said.

There was a distinctly uncomfortable look in the prisoners' eyes as Cliffy and Tommy tied the two men between some trees, arms stretched to the sides, leaving front and back exposed.

'Might be time to hear their lovely voices. What do y'reckon, Mick?'

'Be my guest, Cliffy,' he said, sitting down and taking a long drink from his canteen. 'Ah, thirsty work, that.'

The two men stared at the water longingly as Cliffy ungagged them.

'It's –' one began, then coughed a little. 'It's in the rules you have to give us water.'

Jake smiled at him, peeling another apple with a long knife. 'Don't really care for rules much in Red Group. Get in the way of having a bit of fun.'

'Oh, come on now, Jake,' said Cliffy. 'This one looks as dry as a dead dingo's donger.'

'A dead dingo's donger,' Nige repeated, chuckling. 'Now I've heard everything.'

'Country lads,' Wally said.

'Never know what we might say.' Cliffy came up close to one of the soldiers. 'Never know what we might do neither. What's your name, mate? That's in the rules ain't it? Have to tell us your name and rank.'

'O'Connell. Private Jason O'Connell,' he said, holding his chin out with bravado.

'Jason O'Connell, eh? JOC. I bet they call you Jocco, do they?'

'My mates do, yes.'

'Ah, well we could be mates. Couldn't we, fellas?'

The rest of Red Group nodded.

'Sure,' said Jake. 'Good mates.' He was cleaning his knife and pointed at the unlit fire. 'Light that up for me will ya, Wally?'

'No – no fires. Sarge said,' stammered the second soldier.

'Hello, who do we have here?' asked Cliffy.

'Smith. Private...Kevin Smith.' This one didn't even try to look brave. He was too busy staring at the fire that was beginning to crackle. Wally threw some sticks on it and gave it a fan.

'Ah, Smitty is your handle, I reckon, yeah?'

The private nodded, eyes wide.

'What's a little fire among mates, eh, Smitty? Keeps things all cosy like.'

Jake stood up and walked over to the flames. 'Nice work, Wally.' The two prisoners watched in growing fear as Jake crouched down next to it and placed his knife at the base of the coals.

'What – what is he doing?' asked Smitty. There were beads of sweat on his forehead now and Michael felt a bit sorry for him. Or he would do, if he didn't know what was about to happen next.

He bit his lip to stop himself from smiling and took out a cigarette instead.

'Never mind about Jake. Just likes to play with knives and fires from time to time,' said Cliffy as he came close to the prisoners once more. 'He doesn't really like secrets, though. None of us in Red Group do. You've got a secret, haven't ya, boys?'

'We gave you our name and rank,' said Smitty.

'Yes, but you see, we don't really care about that much. We just want to know that little word of yours.'

Jake pulled the knife out of the fire and examined it before replacing it and adding more wood.

'What's the code, lads?' Michael said, breaking his silence. 'You'll never get out of here any other way.'

'*Vouloir, c'est pouvoir,*' Jocco announced defiantly.

'Bloody hell,' Cliffy said in surprise.

'I think he just asked to call his mum,' guessed Tommy, as the others laughed.

'What's your mate saying there, Smitty?'

'It's – it's French. It means "Where there's a will, there's a way." He likes to speak it. From time to time.'

'Very nice to have an educated man in our midst but I'm afraid it won't impress this lot,' Michael told them. 'Come on, make it easy on yourselves and we can all sit down and have some nice cold water.'

'Can't be too cold if you've kept it out here,' said Jocco.

Cliffy chuckled. 'Ah, very true, Jocco. Very true. It's hot today, ain't it?'

Jake took the knife out again and wandered close. 'Very bloody hot,' he agreed, grinning.

'What's the code word?' Cliffy said, right in Jocco's face now.

'I'll never tell.'

'You'll tell me, won't you, Smitty? You'll tell me that code word and then we can all relax.'

Smitty looked set to faint.

'He doesn't know it,' blurted Jocco. 'Leave him alone.'

Michael was impressed with that. Loyalty wouldn't be too easy for any man right about now.

'Well, that just leaves you then, doesn't it?' Jake said. 'Drop his trousers, boys.'

'What?' Jocco yelped. 'You can't be serious! You...you – hey!' Wally and Nige dropped the man's pants and Jake held the hot knife close to his face.

'Last chance.'

'I said I'll never tell!'

Jake walked around behind him, knife raised.

'Tell us the code word!' yelled Cliffy.

'No!' cried Jocco, eyes squeezed shut.

Jake dropped the knife to the ground and took out a spare one from his belt and in one swift action lay the cool blade on Jocco's backside.

'Mayflower!'

It was some time before Jocco stopped shaking but he eventually did, after some water and ciggies and quite a few back slaps and apologies.

Two things changed for Private Jason O'Connell that day. He won the respect of other members of the Elite for his loyalty to his mate Smitty, but he lost his nickname Jocco. From that day forward he was only ever referred to as Mayflower.

Fourteen

Junie lifted her hair away from her neck and patted Digger, who had fallen asleep in her lap, his tired puppy face resting between his paws, his snores soft from his velvety black snout. He'd been very good on the car ride from Braidwood and Junie was glad – Ernest barely tolerated him and Digger seemed to watch her fiancé with a kind of wariness, shrinking under Junie's chair whenever he showed up. The pup had slept in his basket in the car and entertained himself by chewing on one of her father's socks, his favourite activity. In fact, by the time they'd left, Henry had claimed he needed Digger out of the house or he'd have to start going about the place barefoot. Despite his protestations, Junie knew he hated to see her puppy go. Digger had found a way to comfort them all somehow and she knew both her parents would miss him.

She was sitting on the porch of her new home, or home-to-be, a half-read book about the history of Sydney on the chair next to her. Living with Constance and the twins while Ernest stayed in officers' quarters on the headland was, of course, extremely uncomfortable.

She felt more like an inconvenient servant than a future part of the family, let alone the lady of the house. The only reprieve would come in the form of Ernest moving in when they were married and his mother and sisters moving out, a dismal prospect that weighed on her with increasingly leaden inevitability each day.

Constance, on the other hand, seemed to be enjoying a holiday away from the Colonel, who far preferred country life. She'd taken to the task of creating Ernest's Sydney abode with relish, despite her continued disapproval of his bride.

'Yellow just won't do at *all*,' Junie heard her voice carry from the parlour. 'I want something that is subtle enough that it doesn't offend the eye, yet bright enough to feel fresh and modern. What have you got in orange?'

'Something quite ravishing,' the decorator said, 'mandarin!'

'Oh, I could simply eat it up!' gushed Constance. 'And we could plant fruit trees outside the windows.'

'Inspired suggestion, madam. You really do have *exquisite* taste.'

'Well, one tries to help where one can. Now, what on earth shall we do about this ghastly wallpaper?'

Yes, her mother-in-law was the true mistress of this house, and Junie doubted she would ever feel it was otherwise.

It sat elevated on Cowles Road in Mosman, near enough to buses and shops but without water views, as Ernest had said. Junie supposed if she could live here with Michael and decorate it herself, she would probably love it. It was classic Federation style with stained glass in the windows, moulded ceilings and tiled fireplaces in most rooms and polished floorboards throughout. A sandstone fence ran along the front and it was lined by neatly pruned rose bushes and camellias which extended down the sides and around to this shaded verandah out back.

Nothing could change the fact that she now lived in a crammed city but she was saved from feeling confined by the proximal location of the ferry, not to mention Balmoral Beach and the harbour foreshores. The country girl in Junie was able to shake off the constraints of suburban life down there and stand beneath open vistas and the wide expanse of sky. Best of all, she could visit the great lady once more who listened to the secrets of her heart in quiet reception. Even the presence of warships, planes and soldiers couldn't detract from the harbour's calming beauty. It was as if the lady was protecting them all as she hugged Sydney's shores and carried the converted ferries, now equipped with guns. This was her parlour, her domain, and she threw her claim at the headlands in crashing deterrent as they stood guard at the gates to this: the reputed safest harbour in the world.

Junie's thoughts drifted to Michael, here somewhere too and training hard. The Riley girls had sent word a few times from their new home in Hurstville to the city's south, all settled in now with their mum and working shifts at St Margaret's Hospital in Darlinghurst. Apparently Rory Riley was a very tough sergeant because they hadn't even seen Michael yet, but he had leave this Sunday and, after he'd visited his family, he was meeting Junie at Manly. All the agony of waiting while trapped in the world of the Farthingtons was about to be relieved by one sweet afternoon. The knowledge had kept the wedding farce bearable although what to say to Michael was causing her to lie awake and stare at the patterned cornices on her ceiling. She'd counted one hundred and twenty plaster roses last night.

Digger stirred and licked her fingers before sleeping again, and Junie stroked his ears absently, listening to the wireless. It was playing 'They Can't Take That Away from Me' and she found herself reliving the last moment she'd shared with Michael before they'd parted. The palms in the backyard swayed in the summer breeze and she could almost hear the waves crashing as she'd uttered the words of acquiescence he'd begged for: 'Yes, I will marry you. *I will.*'

She couldn't regret them. How could she, when to be his wife was everything she dreamt of? But she did regret giving him false hope, because the truth was she couldn't possibly marry him. The practical part of her brain knew that as fact. Her parents couldn't be turned out on the streets and the idea of renting some small place and squeezing them all in had too many flaws. Michael's modest army wages would barely cover the lowest of rents and her earning prospects were hardly auspicious. And even if, by some small miracle, she could make that work, what of the monies they owed? And her father's inevitable medical bills? And what of her brothers, Archie and Bill? Heaven only knew if and when they would return, or if they would be able bodied when they did.

Yes, Junie knew all of this and her practical mind accepted it, but the tunnelling rabbit in her mind wasn't listening to her brain right now – it was listening to her eighteen-year-old heart. And so it continued to run and she continued to walk alongside the great lady or sit with Digger while it did, praying for her rabbit to find a way out. Because to believe her wedding day to Ernest would truly eventuate was like believing someone could invade the great southern lady in her harbour.

Surely such violations were impossible. Surely God could never really let such things come to pass.

Not far away, Marlon Stone stood on George's Head, trying not to imagine Sydney's waters and skies suffering the same fate as Pearl Harbor. It looked vulnerable from up here, despite the growing American presence that was combining with the Australians' and building each day. Memories of the Japanese attack assaulted him but he pushed them away.

The Australians seemed a friendly lot so far, open and welcoming, yet very much on the alert. Japan wouldn't be catching them unawares, but it could well catch them unprepared. Converted ferries didn't make very impressive warships but the Australian Navy was small and, with a good chunk of the American fleet decimated at Pearl Harbor, they were all scrambling to make do.

They did have one main reassurance: US aircraft carriers had been at sea during the attack. As a pilot Marlon knew this could prove crucial; the war in the Pacific was likely to come down to air dominance. Hence his part in some of the planning.

He was still trying to become accustomed to his new role as captain and being consulted in such matters. Ironically, his being promoted again was largely due to Major Hamlin, whose wife he'd been intimate with the night before the bombing. The major had been impressed when witnessing Marlon's quick thinking in hauling the machine gun out of the plane to shoot down the enemy. He said a man who can act like that under pressure, even when his buddy dies alongside him in battle, deserves a promotion. It didn't hurt that Marlon had more experience flying than most and that he'd gone to Harvard, although no-one seemed aware that he had Native American blood. He wondered if he would be quite so welcomed into the prestigious world of these officers if they did.

Marlon heard his name being called and turned to salute the major as he approached, customary cup of coffee in hand.

'Thought I'd find you here,' the major said. 'Looks a bit like home doesn't it?'

They gazed out at the vast panorama before them and Marlon had to agree that it wasn't unlike San Francisco, with its waterways and prominent bridge. But this city was something else again. The afternoon sun was burnishing the sandstone cliffs along North Head and the deep blue water formed a vast, rippling ribbon across the mouth of the harbour then all the way down towards the city. It moved in liquid satin past glowing beaches, bushland, rocky edges and sprawling suburbs to find the heart of Sydney: a divided, splendid metropolis on either edge of the great bridge.

'Yes and no,' Marlon replied, thinking of Liwa. There was only one place that was truly home, but she would say it ran in his veins wherever he went, so long as the ocean could find him.

The major shrugged. 'This is the third Pacific harbour I've been to in recent weeks and they're all the same to me. Places I have to help stop the Japs blowing up.'

Marlon nodded in understanding and they stood together watching the sunset blaze. He found himself thinking about the major's wife, whose name he now knew was Samantha. He probably shouldn't have gone near her that night in Hawaii, but how was he supposed to know she was married? The second and third nights back home he couldn't excuse so easily, except to admit he wanted some respite from the sleeplessness and nightmares that had followed him to California. Besides, Samantha had sought him out in San Francisco and taken him to bed, not the other way around.

He could hardly be blamed for their brief affair. But he felt guilty all the same. Hamlin had turned out to be a pretty decent guy and Marlon was spending a great deal of time with him since they'd arrived in Sydney. He was just grateful Samantha wouldn't be joining them.

'Pity we didn't get a bit more leave back home,' the major said thoughtfully and Marlon knew he was thinking about his wife too. The guilt twisted a little tighter.

'Yes, still, it was nice to see family again,' Marlon said lightly, hiding it. That much was true. Liwa had been so relieved he'd survived she'd made him sit through an entire ritual up in the hills, insisting he allow her to tattoo him to thank the gods, marking a fish on his inside wrist. Despite the pain it did make him feel better somehow, like Slim and Joe had been with him in spirit. Even though he still couldn't quite accept that they were gone, he was now able to feel grateful for the times he'd spent with them. And that was a start, as Liwa liked to say.

Marlon wasn't about to share that memory with the major, of course, because the truth was, at times like that, he knew he was really more Miwok than white man. But when it came down to it, essentially it mattered nil, because this wasn't just a white man's war. Liwa was wrong about that.

The major offered him a cigarette and he took one, lighting it.

'I don't like the look of things in Singapore. They've underestimated things over there.'

Marlon had to agree. The Japanese would be going hell for leather to take the northern strong-hold and the Americans had just seen what that meant first-hand. 'They have the numbers.'

'But not the air power.'

'Exactly.'

They stood together, considering what that could mean here.

'Seems logical they'll strike the Northern Territory first.'

Hamlin nodded. 'Makes sense. I'm thinking I might send you up to Darwin soon – you'd be valuable to me up there.'

'Yes, sir.'

Hamlin threw his cigarette on the ground. 'Good man. Anyway, enough war talk for today. Coming to the party tomorrow?'

Marlon shrugged. 'Not sure, sir.' Officers' affairs still weren't really his style but the booze would help him sleep, he supposed.

'Do you good, Stone. You can't look back in war, son,' Major Hamlin said, understanding underscoring his words. 'Come and have a drink and forget about things for a few hours. That's an order.'

'Yes, sir.'

'Getting merry might be the easiest order I ever give you,' the major called over his shoulder as he walked away.

'I'm sure it will be, sir,' Marlon said. He looked back at the fading blue and apricot of Sydney's skies and scanned for dots that turned into sharks.

I'm sure it will be.

Below Georges Head the Elite were in training. If that's what you could call it, Michael thought grimly as he felt his way along the walls. Every sense was on high alert and he wished he could locate himself in the dark like the fruit bats that were hanging in the trees outside. Endless hours with no sleep were beginning to sit hard upon his nerves and it took everything not to call into the black ink that he gave up, that he didn't care any more; that he just wanted to get out of here and breathe the fresh air again, in the light.

'We know you're in there, Aussie. We're going to find you and then we are going to hurt you.'

The Asian voice echoed around him and he focused on what Rory had taught them: *They're only words. They've got nothing until they've actually got you. Until then you are free men. Fight for it, lads.*

Michael crept closer to what he was still hoping was the east and fresher air. The tunnels twisted beneath the headland seemingly forever and he wondered if anyone actually got lost here permanently. But that was ridiculous – the army wasn't trying to kill him, especially not his own father. He wondered how long it had been. It seemed like weeks, and exhaustion was starting to make him lose his usual level-headed composure. Michael struggled not to panic and breathed long, quiet breaths instead.

'I've got a knife, Aussie. A big knife just for you.'

He moved away from the voice, figuring about twenty feet separated them, wondering who the man was they'd been using to psyche them out. Where he was from. He was hardly likely to be Japanese.

There wasn't any real objective to this exercise, save not getting caught, which meant you could never really rest. The voice taunted and the footsteps and mysterious clangs and crashes came at sporadic intervals, jarring at his fraying nerves. He and Mayflower were the only ones left, with poor Smitty giving up quite early in the piece, a shrieking mess until Michael heard someone find him. Everyone knew Smitty suffered badly from claustrophobia. After that, Michael had counted each capture: Jake, Cliffy and the twin brothers from Parkes, Jack and Des Richards (nicknamed 'Liquorice' and 'Allsorts' by Cliffy due to their startlingly thick black hair) and, one by one, the rest of the Elite. Michael knew Mayflower was determined to live down his nickname and prove himself tough. For his part, Michael never gave up easily and knew the day might come when he would remember this training and need it.

Because the only thing that really mattered was surviving this war and making it back home to Junie.

He closed his eyes and leant against the wall, envisaging her face. It floated there, lifting him out of the dark, calming him. The Asian voice called again but he rejected whatever it said now. Stay with me, my love. And she did.

Minutes slid past but he surrendered to the wait. Perhaps it was the sheer exhaustion, but he had moved past fear now and into this dream. He supposed he was hallucinating. Crimson feathers above blue eyes; eyes that read deep into his soul. Junie.

'We are going to kill you, Aussie.'

The voice was close but he stayed very still as Junie melted into him and he held her light within.

'Captured!'

Michael's eyes flew open, but it wasn't to see a captor. He saw a faint light around the bend instead and heard Mayflower's voice giving his name and rank in defeat.

He stumbled towards both as the whistle announced the end of the exercise and arms reached out for him among the flashlights.

'Here now, mate, it's all over,' Jake said in his ear, taking his arm over his shoulder and helping him from the labyrinth, out, at last, into the air. 'Stand tall.'

Michael couldn't see a thing save a warm glow that he assumed was the sunset. He was blinded by the glare after so much darkness but he could hear the cheers from his mates and Captain Marren's voice as he made the announcement.

'Gentlemen, you are looking at the winner of this exercise and, as the overall most outstanding recruit of this training period, your new leader: Corporal Michael Riley.'

The glare began to recede, giving Michael just enough time to see the pride on his father's face before he passed out in Jake's arms.

Fifteen

The water cascaded down the fountain, making sweet, tinkling music as it patterned into the pond where the lilies floated, their delicate faces pale in the sunshine. Junie had thought Government House impressive enough in the black and white photo in her book but now, in the full splendour of a summer's day, she could only gaze in wonder. It was magnificent, more like a castle from a fairy tale than a government building, and, with the bridge and the harbour's sparkling blue waters serving as a backdrop, the overall effect was quite breath-taking.

And then there were the people, milling about on lawns that looked like they'd been tended with nail scissors and stopping to converse under shadowed archways. The soft strains of a string quartet flowed towards her and Junie had to swallow unexpected nerves. She'd never been intimidated by affluence before but this party was filled with the top echelon of the upper crust, resplendent in crisp uniforms and starched summer frocks, and she felt quite self-conscious. Fortunately her pale blue linen was holding its own, as it would want to, considering what it had cost. Even though Constance disapproved of the marriage, Junie had to hand it to her – she'd spared no expense in making her look the part of Ernest's fiancée. The new wardrobe, the house furnishings, even her up-to-the-minute, sleeker hairstyle looked straight out of the pages of *Vogue* magazine. Which was probably where most of the inspiration came from – Constance didn't really have a creative bone in her body.

For all the fear over the war, Sydney's aristocracy wasn't about to let the Japanese deprive them of welcoming the American officers in style. Heavy silver trays were circulating, filled with chilled champagne and fancy seafood wrapped in elaborate little pastries or mounted on miniature breaded platforms like trophies. Junie didn't even know what half of the food was, still trying to hide her distaste for the tiny black balls that Constance had loftily informed her was caviar.

'Shoulders back and watch your manners,' her future mother-in-law hissed. The much revered Eliza Chamberlain and her mother Jane were approaching, and Junie would have been insulted if it wasn't actually quite amusing to watch Constance perform one of her unwitting pigeon impersonations.

Junie smoothed her dress down as the ladies arrived. Just get through this. Tomorrow you're seeing Michael, she reminded herself, and felt a wave of excitement wash through her.

'Jane, how marvellous to see you,' crooned Constance, bobbing forwards to kiss the air on each side of the socialite's coiffed hair in a theatrical imitation of the French way. She missed slightly, her lipstick landing on the woman's ear, and Junie felt compelled to laugh but swallowed it.

'Constance, so glad you could make it,' said Jane, and Junie immediately heard the false sincerity of the welcome.

'How are you, Eliza? The girls send their regrets but sadly they've both succumbed to a cold this week.'

'Such a shame,' Eliza said, masking her relief rather poorly, in Junie's opinion.

Junie studied her, struck by the young woman's beauty. Eliza Chamberlain was every bit as glamorous as her reputation would have it with her fine golden waves and slender frame. She was dressed in white, her long arms ending in lace gloves and a sparkle of diamond bracelet, and the word 'elegant' occurred to Junie in perfect summary.

'Ernest is here somewhere, making himself available to the general, of course. Poor darling is always working.' Constance craned her neck, trying to find him.

'Yes, I saw him earlier. I don't believe I've had the pleasure?' Eliza said, turning to Junie.

'Oh, yes, this is June Wallace, Ernest's fiancée,' said Constance, not entirely hiding her disapproval but probably thinking she had, Junie guessed. None of these women were very good actresses.

'Junie,' she corrected automatically. 'How lovely to meet you both at last. I've heard so many nice things about you.' Junie spoke in her best society voice. Braidwood girls could be charming too.

'My goodness, how did Ernest manage to snag a doll like you?' Eliza said, looking her up and down in surprise. That straightened Constance's spine from her craning quick smart.

'They grew up together,' Constance said with a forced smile.

'So, a country girl?' Jane asked, pencilled eyebrows raised, and a more superior expression Junie couldn't remember witnessing. She focused on the lipstick on Jane's ear to bring the woman down a peg or two in her mind. 'How quaint. You mustn't feel too overwhelmed about mixing in proper society, my dear.'

'As opposed to living in a bark hut, I'm sure.' Eliza laughed, winking at Junie.

'Yes, I'm pleased I remembered to wear shoes,' Junie said, smiling back and forgetting her nerves. She was rather liking this Eliza Chamberlain.

Jane's eyebrows rose further up into her pale forehead. 'Quite.'

'Come with me and we'll see what I can shock you with,' Eliza said, linking arms with Junie and leading her away, whispering in her ear as they went, 'although I can't imagine anything more shocking than having Constance Farthington as a mother-in-law.'

'Quite,' said Junie and they both giggled. Despite her earlier misgivings, Junie had to admit this party was starting to look up.

The view was undeniably stunning from the end of the verandah, but Marlon was bored. This society do felt more upper-class English than Australian, and he was missing the easy-going culture he'd admired so far. It reminded him of the time he'd gone with his father to London on a business trip, back before he'd decided to become a pilot. He'd loved the backstreet pubs where the 'common' Londoners entertained him with their colourful banter and he'd been touched by the generosity they'd shown when most didn't have much to give. Not unlike the Aussies he'd met so far in Sydney. But the aristocracy over there had left him cold with their small talk and affectation and it seemed Sydney had a similar scene at play.

'I've heard some of these Japanese actually eat fish raw. Can you imagine?' drawled Miles Harrington, an officer whose family connections had landed him a nice, safe, desk job. Marlon decided he had the most affected English accent he had ever heard outside of England.

'Primitive race,' scoffed George Fellowes, Miles's equally ridiculous companion.

How were they supposed to win the war with inbred politicians and officers like these at the helm?

'I say,' said Miles. 'Who's that with Eliza?'

Marlon turned and saw two women cross the lawn, a blonde and a brunette. No-one seemed to be able to answer Miles and Marlon was grateful that something had silenced these bores at last as they all stood and watched. They were a pretty sight, that's for sure. The blonde was very beautiful, shaking her head at something the other girl was saying, her fair hair catching the sun, but it seemed a rather practised gesture to Marlon's eye. He'd met many a debutante and she was a prize exhibit, top shelf but on show at all times.

The brunette, however, was something else altogether. There was an untamed air about her, despite the modern dress and styled hair. She looked as if she would be more comfortable riding a horse along the beach, wild and barefoot, than at a garden party in heels. He stopped, wondering where on earth that thought came from as Miles called out to them. The blonde waved, and the women approached. So the mystery woman was the brunette. Marlon's interest was piqued, even more so as he got a closer look.

Her cheekbones were high and covered in skin that obviously soaked up the sun easily. It ran in a light tan across her face and down her throat and her arms, coating every other delicious bit of flesh he could glimpse. Like a perfect cup of coffee with a generous dash of cream. The colour made her blue eyes striking, the contrast further enhanced by frames of thick black lashes that lowered shyly then lifted defiantly as she fought to appear poised. Society girl she may be, but Marlon suspected this level was all new to her.

'And who is this beautiful young lady you've graced us with?' Miles asked, after greeting Eliza.

'Gentlemen, may I present Miss Junie Wallace,' Eliza said, looking slightly amused at their stares.

'Miles Harrington at your service.'

'George Fellowes, but please, call me anything your heart desires, my dear.'

'A-Angus Peabody.' The third officer had no wit or charm to embellish his introduction but, considering the preceding greetings on offer, Marlon supposed him at the advantage so far.

'Marlon Stone,' he said, bowing his head slightly to each woman in turn. The blonde smiled at him, a brief message in her eyes, but the brunette only glanced at Marlon before looking away. He felt a little disappointed, and decided to try harder. 'I don't think we have anything quite this beautiful back in the States.' He glanced at the view, letting the women wonder if it was a compliment to them or to the city.

'And whereabouts in the States are you from?' Eliza asked.

'San Francisco, well, Sausalito actually. Across the bay.'

'A man from the other side of the Pacific. You've swum a long way.'

'Well, I am part fish.'

'Ah yes, the *marlin*. Quite an impressive fish too,' Eliza said in easy flirtation.

'I went to San Francisco once, with Father. You'll pardon me for saying so, but a few too many Mexicans and half-breeds for me. Not really my thing,' Miles said dismissively as he sipped on his champagne. He reminded Marlon of a nasty little lap dog, jealous over a biscuit.

'Come now, Miles, you'll have our American friend think us dreadful snobs at this rate,' Eliza said, laughing. 'I've always longed to go to California. It seems terribly glamorous in the movies.'

Marlon shrugged. 'Depends which part you visit, although I imagine wherever *you* go the glamour would surely arrive with you.'

Eliza gave a pleased little gasp. 'My goodness, how charming you Americans are.'

Miles frowned at him, lighting a cigar.

'How about you, Junie,' asked George, entering the fray. 'Have you travelled terribly much?'

'No, I'm afraid my travelling days are ahead of me.' Deftly manoeuvred, Marlon thought.

'You must come to England when the war ends. Our family holds an annual hunt and I'm sure you would look quite ravishing in riding attire,' Miles said with what he probably thought was an admiring look, but it appeared to Marlon as a rather revolting leer. There was also a bit of champagne spittle on his chin and his cheeks were beginning to flush, neither fact likely to improve his chances.

'Look out there, Junie,' Eliza drawled, 'he'll hold you to it and give you a devilish time if you go. I wasn't sure what was worse, the hounds or the hunters.'

'What do you hunt?' Junie asked, smiling.

'Women, usually,' Eliza said, and they all laughed.

'Foxes, my dear,' Miles answered.

Junie frowned. 'Goodness, what point is there in that?'

'To provide me with a lovely fur stole,' Eliza whispered loudly, linking her arm in Junie's.

Miles looked at Junie almost pityingly. 'The *point* is to win, my dear. Have you never been on a hunt before?'

'Well, back home, my brothers shot the crows but that was mostly because they attacked the new-born lambs. It was necessary.'

Marlon was curious. 'And home is?'

'Braidwood, not too far from Canberra.'

Miles gave a snort of derision. 'Ah, well that explains it. My dear girl, that is not *hunting*, that is *farming*. There is a very wide world of difference between an Australian farm and an English estate.'

Junie's eyes were beginning to flash at the tone in Miles's voice and Marlon wondered how she would respond.

'Yes, it seems we kill predatory animals to protect our stock and you kill defenceless animals for sport,' she said almost nonchalantly.

Bravo, thought Marlon as Eliza disengaged herself from Junie's side and took another champagne from a passing tray. Miles opened his mouth to retaliate but Angus Peabody finally spoke up.

'S-so long as those f-farmers keep joining up, we all stand a chance anyway.'

Marlon realised it was a stutter, not nerves, that kept the man mostly quiet.

'B-b-best shots I've seen so far are the country lads. Keep shooting those crows, I-I say.'

Marlon decided there was one less fool standing with them today. 'I've heard that,' he agreed. 'God knows we'll need them against these Japs.'

'Bah, ridiculous bringing our men away from Europe. Our first allegiance is to the Motherland,' Miles muttered dismissively.

Junie placed her glass on the table and faced him, fury in those beautiful eyes now, but her voice was light and calm. 'I had three brothers fighting for England: Archie, Bill and Frankie – only Frankie is lying dead in a desert now. He went willingly to help our British friends, but I hate to think what he'd make of us sacrificing Australia to the Japanese for this Motherland of yours.' Her composure was admirable as she stared at Miles and added quietly, 'What of *my* mother? What about her?'

A very uncomfortable silence followed before Miles seemed to realise an apology was necessary. 'Forgive me. You must think me insensitive –'

'I'd have to care enough to have an opinion of you to think that. Excuse me.'

As she walked away, Marlon had to hand it to her – country she may be, but Miss Junie Wallace had just given the biggest snob at this city party a lesson in class.

꧁❦꧂

She was in trouble. Anyone could see it, even from a distance, as private as he was obviously trying to be.

'Ernest Farthington,' Eliza explained, coming to stand next to Marlon as he watched the arguing couple down by the fence line. 'He won't be pleased with that little display. Nasty rumour mongers in this set, I'm afraid.'

'What business is it of his?'

'Miles is one of Ernest's chums, although she obviously didn't know that.'

'And he cares because?'

'She's marrying him next month.'

Marlon swallowed his disappointment with his champagne.

'Sorry, old chap,' she said, reading his expression.

'Wouldn't have thought she was old enough to be getting married.' Marlon was usually better at hiding his feelings but he was feeling a little drunk and for some reason this girl had gotten right under his skin. 'Why didn't you introduce her as Ernest's fiancée?' he asked as an afterthought, wondering at her motivations.

'Thought it might be a bit of fun to see what they made of each other, to be honest. Besides, I only met her today,' Eliza replied, pushing her hair back in the afternoon breeze. 'Only met a dashing American pilot today too but he doesn't seem too adept at reading a girl's mind.'

Marlon studied her pretty face. 'And what's on your mind, Miss Eliza?'

She grinned at him and twirled once. 'Dancing.'

Marlon looked back over at the couple, still in heated discussion, and decided he didn't need to be involved in any of that. Putting on his hat, he offered Eliza his arm. 'Let's say we blow this malt shop.'

She laughed, putting one glove around his elbow. 'Now *that's* the most sensible thing I've heard all day.'

Sixteen

The bus was airless and Junie felt her legs begin to stick to the seat through her cotton skirt. It didn't help that she felt slightly hungover from the champagne she'd consumed yesterday, or maybe it was the fight with Ernest that had left her nauseated this morning. Either way, this was no place to feel the need to vomit, and she took out a mint, trying to think about something else.

But the argument stayed.

She hadn't meant to be hostile towards Miles Harrington but that comment about not bringing the troops home had really rattled her. Pompous ass. It seemed everyone associated with Ernest's world was absurd in some way; none of these idle rich seemed to have any idea about the rest of the country or the realities of the war. A bunch of pen-pushers with their heads in the sand, her father would say. With the possible exception of Eliza Chamberlain. That woman had definite friendship potential.

The driver swerved and Junie clutched at the seat in front, counting down the minutes until she would see Michael – fifty-three by her watch. She sighed as she stared at it, a gift from Ernest's parents at Christmas, ornate and rather garish, but she'd needed a watch today and it was the only one she had. Just another trapping inside the trap, she thought, watching the ocean come into sight as they began to descend the hill. It was a deep blue today, and the Norfolk pines lining Manly Beach held out their feathered arms before it, stretching between sea and sky.

The view disappeared behind buildings as she alighted at the bus terminal and she made her way down the Corso, eager to see more. It was quite an experience, with a swathe of American and Australian servicemen dipping their hats and sending her admiring looks and comments. The mall was alive with buskers and vendors and she was exhilarated by the atmosphere of it all as Sydney showed off its beach culture with cosmopolitan flair. The wafting scent of hot fish and chips vied for the soldiers' money, in competition with colourful mounds of ice cream in milk bar windows and flapping beachwear on shopfront walls. It was all very enticing but Junie rushed on by, impatient now. There was only one thing on her mind today: her rendezvous with Michael outside the Steyne Hotel.

She arrived at the corner where the old pub sat overlooking the beach and the full force of Manly welcomed her in an extended expanse of gold sand, curling blue water and clear skies. It was crowded, unsurprisingly, and there was a sense of peaceful rebellion here as she took in the beachgoers lying on their towels and being buffeted by the waves, intent on escaping the war for a day.

She was intent on that idea too.

Junie perched herself on the sandstone ledge that ran beneath the giant pines to drink it all in and wait for Michael, memories of Burning Palms assailing her on the salt wind. Taking off her shoes, she let that breeze tickle her feet and it was easy to fall into a sensual place of anticipation until he materialised in the flesh. She felt no guilt in doing so, nor did she feel guilty in the knowledge that she would be in Michael's arms again today. Ernest would soon have everything else of her, and judging by yesterday's argument, it was going to be far harder to have any kind of freedom after they were married. He had threatened her with all sorts of restrictions if she didn't toe the line and start acting the part of the perfect politician's soon-to-be wife.

'Just tell me now if you want out of this, Junie. I can cut your parents off whenever you say.'

Junie had wanted to fling words back, shout that he could go to hell, but he had silenced her with that threat. It was his unbeatable ace and they both knew it.

Only the white lie of spending the day with Katie, visiting from home, had got her out of the house today. And they had arranged to meet, late in the afternoon, when Katie would accompany Junie home and make an appearance for the Farthingtons' sake – so it wasn't a complete untruth.

No, she felt no guilt at all over deceiving Ernest. But she couldn't get past the stone that dropped sharply into her gut whenever she tried to face her deception of Michael. The truth would have to come out soon but, please God, not today.

A seagull landed nearby, tilting its head at her quizzically, and she mirrored it, tilting her head back too as it hopped closer. Lucky she hadn't thought to bring Digger. He would have been beside himself in puppy delight trying to chase it. She reached into her bag and gave the bird a bit of the sandwich she'd packed and found herself immediately inundated with a dozen more gulls.

'Bugger,' she muttered, taking another bit and attempting to throw it far enough away to get rid of them. It was a poor throw and the birds doubled in number again. This time one landed on her head and she jumped up with a squeal.

'Junie?'

She had imagined the moment they saw each other again many times, but never would she have thought he'd find her screaming, hair upside down with a flapping seagull stuck in the tangle and about twenty other birds squawking in alarm around her.

'Bloody hell, get out! Ouch!' Michael was trying valiantly to help her but the bird was quite panicked and to be honest, so was Junie. It took several attempts and quite a few finger pecks before it was released and Junie could stand up, hair in God knows what kind of state, to look at him with wild eyes as the birds flew away around her.

'It got stuck,' she said unnecessarily.

'Yes, I noticed,' he replied, his mouth beginning to twitch. Suddenly they were doubled up with laughter, tears streaming down their faces as onlookers who had paused to watch gave them a round of applause. They took their bows comically. 'Come on,' he said, putting his arm around her and leading her over to the front parlour of the Steyne. 'Powder room for you, I think. Let's find a door with a gold star.'

❧

Michael was still smiling when she emerged and crossed the room to a booth he'd secured near the wall.

'You know, you can't blame the seagull. He just has good taste,' he said as he patted the seat next to him and she sat alongside.

'To think how long I thought about what to wear so you'd see me sitting there all demure and ladylike,' she confessed, brushing at the pretty blue flowered cotton skirt and white blouse that now sported several dubious marks. 'I don't even want to know what that is,' she said, pulling a face.

'I wouldn't care if you came wrapped in brown paper,' Michael said, and she met his gaze, her hands stilling. He leant forwards, capturing her mouth in a kiss. There was no hesitation, just a sudden rush of heat that had built up for too long. Desire erupted into urgency and Junie pulled back to still her racing pulse, drugged by him.

'Do you want a drink?' he asked, curling her hair around his finger to hold her face close.

'No,' she said, staring at his lips with longing. 'I just want you.'

'I could…get a room,' he said, tugging at the curl to draw her lips in once more.

'Yes, please.'

'So polite.'

'Not always.'

Michael tore himself away to pay for a room and Junie waited at the door, aware of several interested stares but uncaring, then Michael returned and they went upstairs, hands held fast. Once inside the room, they barely even registered anything about it save for the bed, which they fell on in desperate need. He pushed the cotton skirt to her thighs and kissed his way up.

'God, you've been driving me crazy.'

She unbuttoned his shirt, almost tearing it, and he flung it from his arm impatiently, ripping his singlet over his head and pulling at her blouse and under things until she was bare against his chest.

'Take them off,' she panted, pulling at his trousers and soon they were both naked.

He entered her quickly. It was hot in the room and Junie felt as if she would explode from the intensity of each thrust, urging him on until they both cried out. At that moment he held her so close and so tightly, she felt they'd become one person and she clung tightly back.

'Oh God, I love you,' he said, kissing her. 'I love you so god-dam much.'

'I love you too,' she gasped, holding his head against her breasts in the steamy, shadowed room.

She stroked his hair as they lay, listening to the great lady dance in rhythmic waves outside the window as their heartbeats calmed to her tune.

'I love you too.'

❦

The bus rumbled its way along and Katie watched Junie in silence, something she'd been doing for a good minute, and it was getting on her nerves.

'What?'

'You're going to have to tell Ernest. It's no use pretending you're going ahead with it.'

'I am going ahead with it.'

Katie stared at her, shocked. 'You can't possibly mean it.'

'I don't have any choice,' Junie said, desolation settling in with each mile that separated Michael from her once more. 'What would you have me do? Let Mum and Dad be destitute?'

'You can't be responsible –'

'Yes, I can. I have to be.'

Katie folded her arms and gave Junie the look she reserved for when she was really fired up. 'Junie Wallace, your parents would not let you do this if you were bloody well honest with them.'

'That's why I'm lying.'

'I saw the way you looked at Michael today, the way he looks at you – you can't break his heart like this.'

Junie stared out the window, the trees and houses blurring. 'Dad's sick, Katie.'

There was a pause. 'How sick?'

Junie shrugged. 'Mum won't tell me, but I know he isn't good. You can tell. I've known for a long time I suppose…it's the drink, I think.' Tears welled in her throat and she stopped talking to swallow. 'It just takes away the last piece of hope, you see. It's impossible now…'

'Oh, Genie-Junie,' Katie whispered, putting her arm around her and Junie's head came to rest on her shoulder. 'Oh, my poor girl.'

They sat for a while, each searching for any kind of answer.

'You have to tell Michael then. You owe him that,' Katie finally said.

'I know I do. I just couldn't today, it was too perfect,' Junie replied as she straightened up. 'I'll tell him next week. We're meeting again, hopefully.'

Katie frowned, looking like she wanted to say something else.

'What is it?' Junie asked, wiping her eyes with a handkerchief.

'Junie, have you…er…and Michael…you know?'

Junie looked down, blushing, and nodded. 'Yes. Why?'

'Well, it's just…how are you going to hide that from Ernest on your wedding night?'

'What do you mean? He doesn't know. How could he?'

'You do realise that men can tell…if a woman is a, um, you know, a virgin or not.'

'What? How?' Junie's mouth had dropped open and she looked at Katie in disbelief. The expression was mutual.

'How the hell can you not know that?'

'How the hell *do* you know that?'

'My mother, of course.' They stared at each other, each digesting the fact that Junie's mother was too much in her own clouded world to have thought about telling her such things.

'How can he tell?' Junie was pale now, and more than a little afraid.

'Well, the first time it's apparently a bit harder for the woman because there's some kind of barrier and then there's some blood,' Katie told her. 'Maybe you could just…act like it hurts.'

Junie nodded, remembering that night on the beach at Burning Palms. It had hurt briefly.

'And maybe, I don't know, pour some blood on the sheets afterwards? Make sure he's good and drunk so he doesn't notice?'

'How much blood?'

'Bloody hell, how should I know?' Katie said, exasperated. 'We need to look it up somewhere.'

'The library,' Junie said faintly. 'Yes, I'll go to the library.'

'There you go,' Katie said, trying to sound confident. 'It should all be fine.'

Only it isn't fine, Junie thought as the bus continued to Mosman. Every single part of this is horribly and terribly wrong.

Seventeen

It was an ordinary kind of Wednesday night, with Constance and Ernest discussing the wedding guest list that was growing out of control under Constance's social ambition – although Ernest was hardly one to criticise. He had half the politicians in New South Wales on it, even ones he didn't know. He was particularly irritable tonight, and restless, seeming to only half listen to his mother and going outside to look across to the city at least half-a-dozen times. The doors had been left open due to the heat and Junie was managing to sneak Digger some pats as he sat near the door in his basket.

The wireless played in the background, on almost permanently since the invasion of Singapore had come to pass, all fears confirmed, and the Japanese were on the advance.

There were an estimated eighty-five thousand Allied troops ready to defend the island and confidence was fairly high that the enemy would be held at bay. But since the attack on Pearl Harbor, such confidence was always tainted. Without Singapore, there was no other major fortress of defence between Japan and Australia and everyone was nervous. No-one liked to consider life under the rule of the reputedly ruthless Japanese, and each news broadcast sent the room into immediate strained silence, even more so than usual, from Junie's point of view. The Farthingtons were emotionally involved now, with Ernest's old university chum Cecil Hayman in Singapore at High Command Headquarters, and Junie was worrying about her brothers. They were on their way home with the 6th Division from the Middle East and she was praying they hadn't been diverted.

The household had settled into a routine by now. Constance ordered everyone about and organised their calendars, the newly arrived Colonel puffed on his pipe and generally agreed with the radio commentator and Isabel and Ursula played cards, flicked through magazines and whispered as they'd always done. Meanwhile, Ernest got on with the self-importance of being Ernest, as Katie liked to term it.

And Junie read. In truth, she might as well have been invisible in the household if not for an occasional attempt by Ernest to kiss her when he came to visit, which she tolerated but did not respond to. He made light of this, probably to protect his own ego, dismissing it by saying she was an innocent, but that would soon change. She hoped he wouldn't see through the ruse she'd play on their wedding night and learn just how wrong he was. Life with Ernest desiring her was unbearable enough – life with him despising her would be far worse.

There was a knock at the door and Junie looked up from her book in mild curiosity. Probably one of Ernest's horrible friends. Hopefully not Miles Harrington.

'Eliza,' said Constance, beaming as Maria, the maid, let her in. 'What a pleasant surprise. I'm afraid you've caught us quite unprepared for visitors.'

'Yes, forgive me. I was in the neighbourhood and I'm just popping in for a minute.'

Digger erupted into an excited flurry of barking and Constance hissed at him to be quiet.

'Oh, who is this little fellow?' Eliza took off a glove and tried to pat him, laughing as he tumbled over backwards in his excitement.

'That's Junie's dog,' Constance said, not masking her disapproval. 'Get down, Digger!'

'Well, hello!' Eliza crooned, holding Digger's happy little face as his tail pumped excitedly. 'Aren't you just gorgeous?'

'Tea?' Constance asked smoothly, already waving a hand at Maria, who scuttled off to do her bidding. Eliza pulled at her other glove, taking up the offer of a seat on the best chair in the room, the velvet settee by the fireplace. She was dressed in a lemon-coloured suit and looked rather perfect in Junie's eyes, from the tip of her French twist to her white patent leather shoes.

'Nice to see you, Eliza,' said Ursula.

'Hello again,' mumbled Isabel.

'Hello, girls,' Eliza said. 'How are you, Ernest?' She offered him her cheek for a kiss.

'In excellent health, thank you. You're looking very well yourself.'

'Thank you kindly, although you're in terrible trouble with me. How dare you keep this delightful girl hidden out of sight for so long?' Eliza pouted, reaching out for Junie's hand, which she surrendered in surprise.

Ernest looked uncomfortable. 'My sincere apologies, I'm afraid I've been rather selfish on that account. Besides, we've all been a bit preoccupied,' he said as he turned down the wireless.

'Well, no more. Poor darling needs to have a bit of fun in these dreary times. Come down for luncheon on Friday. I'm getting a few of the girls together so you can meet some of the gang.'

'That sounds wonderful, thank you,' Junie said, touched.

'Sure you won't lead her astray and take her out afterwards? I know what you're like with that dance hall, you and your friends,' Ernest said, lighting a cigarette at the door.

Eliza took one herself from a thin gold case, feigning innocence as she leant forwards for him to light it. 'I promise not to do anything you wouldn't do.'

'I'm sure the girls would *love* to see the family home,' Constance said, looking fit to burst at the idea of such a social coup but Eliza seemed determined to ignore those two elephants in the room (as she confessed to Junie with a giggle much later).

'Don't dress too formal, just a nice frock you can wear to the club afterwards,' Eliza said with a wink at Ernest.

'Minx,' he said, smiling, but he looked a little worried.

Junie wasn't. She was excited. A Friday night away from the Farthingtons! She wondered if Michael could meet her somehow, away from prying eyes, of course.

'Right, well, I'd best be off,' Eliza said. 'Don't like to stay out too late at night.'

'But what about tea?' Constance asked as Maria arrived with the best china.

'No, she should probably go. I don't mean to alarm you, Eliza, but they are running a blackout test tonight, so you'd best get home,' Ernest said.

'You kept that very quiet,' Constance objected.

'I've told you before, Mother, top secret is top secret. Not for running home and telling Mummy.'

Eliza laughed, turning to Junie as she left. 'Don't forget your dancing shoes.'

Junie made a mental note to buy some as they all went outside and watched Eliza get into her very flash-looking car then drive off with a wave.

'Oh, a silver Mercedes,' breathed Isabel, awestruck. Personally Junie was more impressed with the idea of having a driver's licence and wondered if she could talk her way into getting herself one.

'You'd think she could have invited the twins,' Constance said, sniffing.

'I don't want to go. Wouldn't know what to say to those girls,' Ursula admitted.

'Me neither,' Isabel agreed.

'For goodness' sake – they've got a hothouse! Even an imbecile can talk about flowers!' Constance said in disgust, striding back inside.

Junie had to stifle a giggle at Ursula's confused whisper to her sister: 'Why is the house hot?'

'I don't know,' Isabel whispered back. 'You'd think rich people like that could afford some fans.'

༄

Constance had insisted she take a gift but Junie had considered dumping it quite a few times on the two bus rides and the hot walk it took to get to the Chamberlains' harbour-front residence at Point Piper. It was quite a feat to see past the enormous orchid in its blue pot and avoid falling, but she finally arrived, pushing the buzzer and staring at the plaque on the stone wall, which read *Aqua Majestique*. It made her smile, thinking of the little sign Cliffy and Jake had nailed on a tree at Burning Palms that read *Fibro Majestic*, with an arrow pointing at the shack, but her amusement faded as the gates opened in response to her ring.

There, in all its privileged glory, sat the most beautiful house Junie had ever seen: Jane Chamberlain's home. And in front of it stood the most intimidating butler she had ever seen. He was eyeing both herself and the plant with glacial disapproval.

'Can I help you?'

'Er, yes, Miss Junie Wallace here to see Miss Eliza Chamberlain.'

That melted him a fraction but he looked down at her new black dancing shoes with suspicion before they moved.

'Mind the lawns, miss.'

Junie navigated her way carefully, managing to stay on the wide flagstones and away from the grass somehow, and making it all the way up the front steps to the entrance hall.

'Good Lord, she's brought a tree with her!' exclaimed Eliza, gliding in, a vision in pale pink.

'Constance,' Junie explained from within the foliage and Eliza laughed.

'Well, it could have been worse, I suppose. Mother does love her flowers. Come in, come in. Alfred, find this a spot somewhere – mind you don't block the view,' she instructed and the reluctant butler relieved Junie of her awkward load, allowing her to follow Eliza through to the guests.

It was difficult not to gawk now that she had a clear view of the place. Everything was exquisite, from the towering columns to the polished marble bannister on the circular stairwell. An actual waterfall ran soothingly in the corner and masses of flowers adorned side tables in artful arrangement, possibly the work of Jane Chamberlain. But all flashes of elegance paled in comparison to the view that greeted her from the balcony.

'Wow,' was all she managed as the harbour was unveiled in brilliant, sun-soaked magnificence. It seemed the home was, in fact, very well named. A swimming pool met the shallow gold beach that hosted several expensive yachts just offshore, and they bobbed gently in the pale blue. Behind this stretched a harbour preparing for war with its gunships and cranes, but almost as a sideshow compared to the dazzle of sun on water leading to the span of the bridge.

'Still with us?' Eliza said, watching her with a grin. 'A lot of people say "wow". Daddy threatened to call the house that when they built it but Mother wouldn't allow it, of course. Come, meet the girls.'

Junie followed a little nervously, conscious of the seam of her green dress sitting just right and hoping she'd hit the mark. She had – the ladies all wore similar styles in an array of colours, one even in red, and she was relieved. All that shopping with Constance had paid off, as excruciating as it had been.

'Ladies, allow me to introduce Junie Wallace. Junie, this is Maree Thornton, Margaret McKinnon, Patricia Fairfax and Eugenie Hayman.'

Junie nodded at each in turn. She already knew that Eugenie was Cecil Hayman's wife, Ernest's friend in Singapore. The others looked familiar from the lawn party at Government House but she hadn't stayed long enough that day to be introduced. Or inspected, more to the point. She was certainly under inspection now – all the way down to the tips of her new shoes, which were happily grass free. Fortunately she seemed to pass and found herself seated between Patricia and Eugenie.

'Goodness, have you walked in this heat?' asked Eugenie, fanning her own, very red face.

'Yes, it isn't far from the bus-stop.'

'It is when the mercury's nudging a hundred, although the papers say it will cool off tonight, so that's welcome news.'

'Do you like mint juleps?' asked Patricia.

Junie said yes, even though she had no idea if it was a drink, an appetiser or possibly some kind of flower from the enormous hothouse nearby. As it turned out it came in a glass, and was very refreshing after lugging the plant all the way here. Even better than champagne.

The afternoon turned out to be a rather pleasant one from then on, and Junie found the company entertaining enough, despite the conversation centring around places she'd never been and people she didn't know. And what the chances were of rain, courtesy of Eugenie. As it turned out, the woman stuck to only two topics of conversation all day: the current weather and the impending weather. At least it wasn't about Cecil and Singapore, which would have made things rather sombre. Nobody seemed particularly keen to discuss their husbands or beaus at all, or Ernest for that matter, but they all knew him anyway, so what to tell?

They did ask about the wedding, after all they were at that age. Apparently they were all attending, which Junie managed to pretend she was aware of.

She had supposed the whole afternoon would pass by in idle chit-chat and gossip, and that expectation turned out to be well founded, but she hadn't expected the women to be so nice to her. Junie wondered if Eliza had instructed them to be so, and why. She certainly hadn't expected them to be quite so risqué, as revealed when Eliza's friend Eddie sailed by on a manned ferry with his troop. The radio blasted from the boat – 'Chattanooga Choo Choo' – and there was much waving and catcalling across the water.

'Give us something worth fighting for, gals,' yelled Eddie as he swung from the top deck.

'You heard the man. Come on!' called a slightly inebriated Eliza. She climbed onto her chair and raised her skirt, showing off some impressive legs, and the others clambered to do the same. Junie joined them, giggling, and soon six pairs of pins flashed across the harbour to the enthusiastic reception of some very lucky marines.

There was much laughter after that but by far the best part of the day for Junie came when the big clock inside struck five. At last they could freshen up to go out dancing at the Trocadero. Junie had sent a note to Katie, who was staying with the Rileys, and her friends from Braidwood would meet them there. She prayed that Michael had received her note too and she would get to see him again after six long days apart. The thought filled her with both joy and dread, because as much as she longed to see him, she also knew that tonight could herald the end. Time was closing in on the inevitable truth.

Junie piled into the cab with the others, her mind swirling in a cocktail of excitement and trepidation, but also hope, however nonsensical that was. That youthful brand of it that grasped at the happy stuff beyond logic, now left to bubble along with the mint juleps in Junie's head.

It was an impossible thing to ignore as the car carried her to George Street, the city's heart, to dance with the pulse of a country at war. To whatever changes were heralded upon the warm breeze, whatever fate awaited, this late summer's night.

Eighteen

The Trocadero was full, despite the tension that had settled over the city, or perhaps because of it. It seemed every young person in Sydney had turned up determined to defy the Japanese threat. Junie gaped at the sight of girls being twirled about and even flipped upside down as Dick Freeman's orchestra played 'In the Mood'.

The American and Australian military presence was high; marines, soldiers, pilots, servicemen, nurses and officers – there were khaki, blue and white uniforms from one end of the hall to the other. And then there were the civilians, a kaleidoscope of girls in dresses and skirts. The music pumped in their blood and filled the room with a frenzied recklessness that only war could produce. Tomorrow they may all face invasion, combat or even death, but tonight was all about that music and how much it matched their youth and passion.

Junie spied Katie, Beryl and Dorn at a far table and took Eliza's hand, leading the other women over to them. After some enthusiastic hugging, mostly from Katie, Junie made the introductions. They were yelled rather than spoken over the band but even so, Junie noticed the condescending looks the Sydney girls cast her Braidwood friends. Looking at them herself, strictly from a society viewpoint, she couldn't help but cringe inwardly at their home-made cotton skirts and blouses. Then she felt ashamed.

'Genie-Junie! How good is this place?' Katie yelled to Junie happily. 'And look!' She held up a bottle of wine and poured her a glass. 'Managed to sneak some of Dad's stuff in. Want some?' she asked Eliza.

'Er, no, thank you. I've a tab here.' Eliza gestured to a waiter who nodded back at her in recognition and made his hasty way to the bar. Patricia Fairfax gave a derisive little laugh, which Katie didn't seem to notice but it made Junie blush.

'Look at the size of the band, Junie!' Beryl exclaimed.

'And the dancing! Those two are amazing,' Dorn said, pointing at a couple who were in full jitterbug, and Junie had to agree, although she wished her friends would look less wide eyed at it all.

'Don't you have dancing in that country town of yours?' Eliza asked Dorn.

'Not like that,' Dorn said, her mouth falling open as the girl hung upside down.

'Perhaps I could ask my friend Eddie to give you a lesson,' Eliza suggested, waving at the marine they'd flashed their legs at earlier that day.

'Nice gams!' he yelled as he spun an equally talented dancer about.

'Must be all the jitterbugging,' Eliza called back. 'That's him. He's very flash.'

'Oh no, I think I'll just dance with our boys, when they arrive,' Dorn replied, looking suddenly nervous and moving closer to Beryl.

'You needn't feel intimidated. The city boys won't bite,' Eliza said and the other girls laughed.

'And they don't really care what you wear as long as you can keep up,' added Margaret McKinnon, glancing at Dorn's polished but worn shoes.

Katie paused mid-drink, lowering her glass to the table. 'City boys might not bite, but it seems the city girls do.'

'Oh, here comes the champagne,' Eliza said smoothly as two waiters arrived with several bottles on ice. Junie felt a momentary relief from the tension that was further broken by the arrival of the boys.

'They're here!' cried Beryl, waving.

They all turned to watch Cliffy and Jake make their way through the crowd, a few others in tow.

'Katie!' Jake exclaimed, grinning widely as he arrived. 'You look beaut!'

'Knock it off,' she said, but with a pleased smile. The others were mixing and saying hello but one important party was missing.

'Where's Michael?' Junie asked Cliffy, trying to hide the eagerness in her voice.

'On his way. Had some officers' meeting.'

Junie breathed out, both relieved and nervous.

'Who's Michael?' Eliza asked, watching her.

'Oh, uh, one of our friends. Excuse me,' Junie said. 'Might just visit the Ladies.' She made her getaway, deciding that she didn't want anyone to see her greet Michael when he showed up – it would give too much away.

The powder room was hot as she reapplied her lipstick, and she stared at her reflection, ordering herself to calm down. The right words would come when she needed them. The rabbit would find something for her to say.

She went back out and moved along the wall to search the crowd for him. So many uniforms, so many men, but only one who mattered. The music was beating hard as her gaze fell on the awkward mix of her old and new friends. Then Cliffy was shaking someone's hand and the figure turned. Michael.

Junie drank in his face, her stomach filling with butterflies, her heart almost hurting at the sight of him. She waited for him to feel the love that seared through her and across the chaos of the dance hall, and so he did, finding her and sending her an intimate message with his eyes that was so strong it was as if he had actually touched her. It seemed impossible that they were not alone as the rest of the world faded into nothing and he made his way across.

But then she saw something else, something that rammed into her throat, stopping her breath. Ernest. He was here and he was approaching from the left, two drinks in hand, his eyes on her too. Junie was trapped, a victim of her own making but a victim all the same. The truth would be impossible to hide now; Michael would know she hadn't broken her engagement to Ernest and Ernest would know she was having an affair with Michael. That was the only possible outcome. The room began to spin and she fought to find the air that refused to fill her lungs. Lies, lies, lies. She was filled with them and about to explode. Junie felt her world crumbling into the floor as her legs gave way.

But then she was dancing. Someone had caught her and was spinning her away into the crowd. She stared at her rescuer's face in shock, recognising it as belonging to that American captain from the party at Government House. The one named after a fish.

'Remember me?' His white teeth flashed and she blinked at him.

'Marlon?'

'Got it in one.' He held her strongly, steering her away from Michael and Ernest and losing them deep in the throng.

'What – why?'

'Next time you go out dancing, you should check to see if your fiancé is in the room before you send another man a look like that,' he said in her ear, nodding politely at another dancer as they bumped their way through.

'I don't know what you – what you mean.'

'That man you just melted and who obviously melted you right back. That scene was hot enough to fry eggs. Not a stranger, I take it?'

'No.'

He nodded, the crowd now a protective wall around them. 'Thought as much. Is he your lover?'

Junie gasped. 'That is…none of your business.'

'No, I don't suppose it is. Should I take you back?'

'No!' She stopped dancing, looking over her shoulder, her mind scrambling. 'Just – oh God, I need to get out of here.'

'Might be difficult to explain if you just disappear, last seen with a Yank,' Marlon said. 'I think you have enough complications in your life. But of course, it's none of my business…'

'No, it isn't,' she said, then realised how rude she sounded. 'I, uh, thank you for your assistance but I think I should perhaps find my fiancé.' She frowned. How would that work? Michael was sure to still approach her.

Marlon observed her procrastination and rolled his eyes. 'How about I stall for you? I'll keep your fiancé occupied while you have a quick chat and get rid of lover boy.'

Junie thought about that. It seemed the best idea. 'What will you talk about?'

'What's he interested in?'

'Himself.'

Marlon smiled at that answer. 'Then it should be easy.'

Junie began to move away then turned. 'Why are you helping me?'

'Never enjoyed watching hunting – can't stand cruelty to animals myself.'

She looked at him in surprise, almost returning his smile before resigning herself to being prey.

❧

'Corporal Farthington, isn't it?'

Ernest paused in his search to find Junie, who'd disappeared in the sea of uniforms, to respond to the tall American captain who had materialised in front of him. 'Yes, sir,' he said, saluting.

'No formalities needed here, Farthington, relax,' the man assured him, waving his salute away. 'You're the general's main man, I hear. Captain Marlon Stone, but you can call me Marlon.'

'Ernest,' he said, shaking the man's hand. 'Marlon Stone. Aren't you attached to Major Hamlin's lot?'

'Yes, I'm one of the team there, although I'm off to Darwin in a week for, uh – certain reasons. Bit hush-hush, to be honest, but I don't suppose there's too many secrets kept from the general.' Marlon looked at his empty drink, appearing disappointed.

Ernest was intrigued. There were plenty of cards being played close to the Americans' chests and a bit of insider information never went astray. 'No, not much gets past him. You know who else they're sending up, I suppose?'

'Well, it's not so much who but what, of course...' the captain said, looking at the bar.

'That's true,' Ernest bluffed. 'Here,' he said, handing him Junie's drink. 'Allow me.'

The American seemed pleased and clinked their glasses together.

'To Darwin!' he said.

'Yes, to Darwin,' Ernest agreed.

'And to the major's plan,' the captain added, swaying slightly.

Let Junie jitterbug with whomever she liked, Ernest decided. He had his own dance underway.

❧

The look on his face when he saw her outside was one of relief.

'Oh God, you had me worried. I thought that Yank had kidnapped you,' Michael said, pulling her into his arms and holding her tight. 'Where is he, cheeky bastard? Didn't even ask you to dance, by the looks of things.'

'No, he, uh…he was a bit fresh,' Junie mumbled against his chest, breathing him in, trying to find the strength to pull away and say what needed to be said. But oh, the familiar feel of him. The safety of this place, next to his heart.

'I saw Ernest, by the way. We might need to hightail it outta here. Could get pretty uncomfortable.'

The words were muffled against her ear, like they came from inside the drum of his chest, and she had a mad moment of wishing she could crawl in there.

'Michael,' she began, forcing herself to look at his face. 'We have to talk.'

He looked back at her cautiously. 'All right.'

They moved down the street and around the corner to stand beneath the shadowed stone walls of Town Hall.

'What's wrong, my love?' he asked, pushing her hair back from her face. 'Are you worried about Singapore? Don't listen to gossip. I'm sure they'll hold.'

'Yes,' she admitted. 'I am worried about it. I'm worried about you and the boys.' She felt heartsick at the thought of her brothers. 'And the Japs coming here…'

'We've got the Americans – thousands coming and more planes and boats every day,' he reassured her. 'And I'm here for a while yet. Why don't we just elope and get married right now?' He kissed her neck. 'Forget planning a wedding and all that rot. Anything to be with you sooner.' He kissed her on the mouth then, longingly, and she felt great tears well at the cruelty of resistance.

'I – I am planning a wedding…it's all done.'

He looked confused. 'Weren't you going to discuss things with the groom?'

She hated herself and the words that followed. 'I have been.'

Michael stared at her for a long minute, comprehension descending like a terrible bomb. 'You – you're still going to marry Ernest?'

'Yes.'

The final word ripped and the explosion ignited, shattering in his eyes.

'But I love you. And you love me. I know you do.'

'I love my parents too. And my brothers. I can't be selfish –'

'Yes, you can!' he said with anguish and she started to cry.

'No, I can't! Dad is sick and Mum is – isn't herself. You know this, Michael. You *know*…'

'But you said yes to me,' he said, incredulous. 'How could you do that?'

She slumped against him, grasping at his shirt. 'How could I not?'

He held her close, his cheek against her hair. 'Be selfish for me, Junie. I'll be going to war…I – I'll need you.'

'We can still be together…we don't know what the future holds.'

'I don't want you as my *mistress*. I want you as my *wife*.'

'Then that's the difference between you and me, because I would take you any way I could get you.' She reached up to cup his face but he shook her hand away.

'But we couldn't live together, we couldn't raise a family – you'd be with him. In his bed.'

'I'll never really be married to Ernest. I'll be married to you in my heart. Always.' She was choking on her tears now, clinging to him.

'Then that's the difference between you and me,' he replied brokenly, taking her hands in his, 'because I could never ask you to settle for that.'

He dropped them and walked away, his shoulders hunched against the night, and Junie collapsed against the wall, closing her eyes. The rabbit had run and the battle had been lost.

And she was left to marry the enemy, more alone against that unforgiving stone than she'd ever felt in her life.

Far away to the north other battles were being waged as the great fortress of Singapore began to fall, taking many thousands of lives with it. The Allies surrendered the territory two days later and Japan proved to be a merciless victor, slaughtering men in their hospital beds, nurses doing their rounds, civilians in their escape boats. The much feared invaders took almost fifteen thousand Australians prisoner with little compassion for those who 'shamed themselves' with defeat, and began to march them towards death.

Then, on a clear Thursday morning, Australia's greatest fear came to pass when the Northern Territory town of Darwin was bombed. Another harbour, another surprise attack, another devastating blow.

Australia was on her knees and America knelt with her as February faded, taking summer away at last. The long hot autumn to the north was met by those who now walked and worked, starving and bleeding their way through Asian hells of man's making. Limbs would soon wither to bones, beaten and tortured until many prisoners of war would eventually fall, half dead, only to meet their maker soon after. Most would be left without burial, without ceremony or pause, only the tears of their mates to bless them as they passed.

Wasted lives granted no mercy, despite the love that would pour each day from the land to the south.

And one Sunday early in March, a bride took her slow walk too, down the aisle to her own enemy in her white wedding shroud. A vial of blood hidden beneath, to fool the fool who had cheated her of love.

Something had died in Junie that summer, but something had been born too.

She held her stomach as she looked in the mirror on her wedding night, delaying the inevitable task of lying with her new husband. Then she allowed herself a small smile, for she had her victory too. Because whatever blood had been – and would be – shed, some small amount was now blending inside her womb, and she would fight a war of her own to protect it.

No, Ernest would never fully take her Michael away. Not when his child would fill her days.

Part Three

Nineteen

Marlon read the newspaper with disgust, tossing it away and finishing his coffee. Another air raid, this time in Broome in Western Australia. More lives lost, although with censorship heavily at play it was hard to guess how many. He blocked the memories that tapped on his mind, far worse since he'd arrived here in the aftermath of another Japanese victory. Scorched earth, obliterated planes, sunken boats, chaos. Death. The memories wanted to replay his own nightmare at Pearl Harbor, something he kept refusing to allow them to do during the day, but at night he had no control and they won. They burnt him in his sheets, the tropical air taking him back to the fire and flames, and the image of a single slicing bullet beneath the black, roiling clouds made him cry out as he woke, soaked in sweat and shaking.

He turned the paper over, not wanting to invite any more comparisons, and lit a cigarette. It was unbearably hot of course. It may be fall, or autumn as the Aussies liked to call it, but no-one seemed to have told the Northern Territory, which was still as humid as hell. Looking at his watch, he noted that he had a good fifteen minutes to wait for Major Hamlin's flight from Brisbane to arrive and he tapped his fingers, wondering how to pass the time. People-watching, he supposed.

He studied those around him, noting the few women were all Aboriginal. Most of the white civilians had been evacuated long before the bombings, but no-one had bothered enforcing the evacuation of the coloured women and children. Apparently it was all right to give a black man a gun and a uniform now, but not protection for his family. It seemed racism ran deep on both sides of the Pacific.

Everyone looked wary, the horror fresh on their faces, and it was quiet, save for the murmur of muted conversation. Their home had been annihilated, then looting and crime had poisoned the city before order was somehow restored, and now the locals mostly seemed to wander rather than actually achieve anything. But it would be hard to know where to begin – something he well knew.

Marlon recognised one young woman who had worked near him these past few days. They'd been down at the railroads mostly, sorting through debris and salvaging supplies for the base. Many personnel had been temporarily relocated but they had left Marlon to supervise some of the clean-up and he'd been impressed with how hard the girl worked. He had tried talking to her a few times but she was a bit of an enigma. Quiet and shy, she let her black hair fall over her eyes rather than meet his and spoke softly when asked a question. But she could surprise him too. When he asked her which direction the planes had come from, she'd simply said, 'Hell.' And when he asked her for her name she'd told him he would have to guess, so they had a little game every now and then.

'Kate?'

'Keep guessing.'

'Edith?'

'Keep guessing.'

Once he'd added, 'Don't you want to know my name?' to which she had responded, 'No.'

Today she was wearing a bright yellow dress and looked very nervous as she peered at the sky then at the clock on the wall. He waved at her and she lowered her eyes, raising one palm quickly before hiding it in her skirt.

Marlon chuckled. She was completely refreshing, especially compared to the women he'd had in his life lately.

Samantha, who just wanted to cheat on the decent man who was her husband, Major Hamlin.

Eliza, who'd made out with him the night before he'd left only to tell him she'd just agreed to marry that pompous idiot Miles Harrington come spring, but would he like to continue this new arrangement anyway?

And then there was Junie, the most disappointing of all. A girl he could really have fallen for if she hadn't been engaged to someone else – and busy with a lover on the side.

He gave a short laugh as he tallied it up, realising just how shallow they all sounded. He'd really been interested in the wrong kind of women since he left home – but war was like that: you didn't have much time to think, just act.

The girl walked outside and Marlon followed her, stopping nearby to smoke, waiting for her to say something. She didn't. She just looked at the sky, waiting.

'Do you have someone coming?' he asked, rather needlessly.

She nodded, fiddling with the yellow skirt of her dress. She had shoes on today, black ones that looked uncomfortable. He wanted to tease her and ask if it was her sweetheart arriving but figured she'd never speak to him again if he did.

'Daisy?' he asked instead.

She smiled, her teeth white against her skin. 'Keep guessing.'

The drone of an approaching plane began and everyone looked up nervously; no-one trusted the skies any more. Marlon watched the clumsy landing on the only narrow bit of airstrip that was still operational and waited for the passengers to alight, curious to see who it was the girl waited for. Two soldiers and a medico came down the stairs, followed by the familiar sight of Major Hamlin carrying his coffee cup. Cold or not, that black water was always his companion. The girl waited and looked worried as the plane emptied, then, at the very last, a tall, elderly, black man in a loud Hawaiian shirt appeared. The girl ran across the runway to greet him, throwing herself into his arms and weeping. Marlon smiled. After so much grief it was good to see a reunion here.

'Friend of yours?' Major Hamlin asked as he approached.

'Nah, she won't even tell me her name.'

'Smart gal,' the major said, as they walked towards to the waiting jeep.

Marlon gave one last glance back and saw the young woman take off her shoes and stuff them in her bag before gently escorting the old man away. He figured then that the major was probably right.

༶ঞ্জৎ৹

'How many injured, really?' Major Hamlin asked as he stared out at the pouring rain from their meeting room. 'Curtin said there were only thirty-five on the wireless but of course…'

'I heard the chief officer on the *Manunda* say he had two hundred casualties on board when they berthed at Fremantle,' said an Australian corporal called McCauley, or 'Macca' by most. 'Tom Minto's his name. He'd know.'

His pilot mate, Corporal 'Johnno' Johnson, added his estimate. 'We reckon at least a thousand. People tend to forget the blackfellas.'

The major had paled at the figure but defended the Australian Prime Minister. 'Curtin has to keep the public calm.'

'He also said the raid wouldn't give any satisfaction to the enemy,' Marlon remarked dryly.

'Yeah, we heard that too,' Macca said. 'Tom said they must be hard to please.'

Marlon gave them a grim kind of smile, stubbing out his cigarette. 'Twenty aircraft, eight ships at anchor, airfield a mess and most of the town gone. I don't think the Japs are sitting around crying.'

'And neither are we,' Johnno said pointedly. 'I know you lot have heard there's been some desertions, and there have been a few, but that was mostly confusion. People thought it was a full scale invasion. The men are itching to rebuild and give it back to 'em. Trust me.'

The phone rang and Major Hamlin took the call. 'No casualties? I see. Thank you, Corporal.'

They waited as he hung up. 'Flying boat attacked the PK-AFV again. No damage or casualties, thankfully.' Major Hamlin looked around at the other three faces and sighed. 'Looks like this isn't a one-off raid, invasion or not. Gentlemen, we need to get this town operational again. How long will it take?'

Macca shrugged. 'Depends how much you want to rebuild. Runway's got more holes in it than a machine-gunned crumpet.'

The major appeared momentarily amused before his face fell to seriousness once more. 'The 49th Fighter Group are on their way, so we need to repair it.'

'If they make it. Mate said if you want to follow the Brereton Line to Darwin just look for the crashed Kittyhawks. No offence.'

Marlon sent Johnno a look, not offended but worried at the truth of his words. The loss of life in simply getting the US airmen to this remote part of the world was a serious concern. But they had to come. As predicted, this was going to be a war of the skies.

'I'd look to putting them in Batchelor for now,' Macca said.

Batchelor airfield was fifty miles south but Marlon had to agree with Macca. 'I don't think we have any other choice.'

'Right, let's move on it then. Who's started a list of basic needs?'

'I've got one,' Johnno said, scribbling something down then holding up a piece of paper that said, *The rest of our bloody army.*

The major looked at the page with a wry smile. 'I think Curtin's taking that little issue up with Churchill as we speak.'

'Yeah, well, bugger the delays, I say,' Johnno said, screwing up the paper. 'Don't get me wrong, Major. I've got British mates too. Hell, I've got a stack of cousins in Yorkshire. But we need our blokes home to protect their own bloody country.'

'Couldn't agree more, fellas, but let's just get on with the job of having a country for them to protect first, eh? Stone,' the major said firmly, pointing at a pad and pen, 'start a list.'

Marlon took up the pen, half tempted to write the same thing at the top as Johnno's, and for some reason Junie's comments about her brothers went through his mind. The Motherland would just have to take care of itself for now. Australia needed her sons.

Marlon was tired but he craved the comfort of the ocean more than sleep and so he headed off to find a quiet spot along the water to lean against a tree and ponder. If you discounted the presence of war and the destruction of the raid, the harbour itself was very beautiful, he observed as he walked along. He perched himself on a sandy cliff that looked straight out over the mirror-like water and relaxed, drawing the air into his lungs in a deep draught.

It wasn't much of a tree that he leant against but it did provide a little shade from the hot afternoon sunlight, and propped his back up enough for him to enjoy watching the view, particularly the spectacular birdlife. There were too many species to count but he'd heard there were over four hundred in Darwin and they were making a good representation of their numbers today. The sun was setting in a ball of gold, inviting a red glow to surround it, and the silhouettes of the birds turned black against the backdrop. Marlon wished he knew the names of the wide-winged water birds that hung in the air like gliders or the noisy black parrots that watched him curiously as they lumbered along the whispering casuarina trees nearby. Regardless, it was an incredible display, and he felt his spirit lift as the parrots took flight, rising before him in deafening song, suddenly graceful as they made their voyage across the harbour.

Then he noticed another silhouette, a girl with bare feet, the hem of her dress tucked into her waist, walking slowly through the water and holding a line. Her limbs were long and thin, her hair falling forwards in twisting, tight waves that caught the gold of the sun on their ends. She looked as at home here as the birds and the trees and, to Marlon, she was even more wild and beautiful than the harbour itself.

'Mary,' he called.

The girl stopped and he saw a brief flash of white as she smiled at him for the second time that day. Making her way over, she stood beneath him in the shallows and looked up.

'Marri,' she confessed. 'You close enough.'

'Marlon Stone, very nice to meet you,' he replied, surprised at just how pleased he was.

'We a match,' she said, looking happy at the discovery.

'Almost.'

She cocked her head, observing him. 'You a big fish.'

'So I'm told,' he replied. 'What are you hunting?'

She shrugged. 'Whatever I find.'

'Such as?'

She seemed to consider his words then climbed the hill, remarkably quickly in Marlon's opinion, and sat nearby, winding the line and the hook and putting it in her pocket.

'Get barramundi 'round here. Good eating. My people call 'em damabila'

'Damabila,' Marlon said slowly, tasting the word. 'Don't you use a spear for them? I saw a man with one further down.'

'Nah, men's business.'

'Oh,' he said, nodding. 'What else can you catch?'

'Madla. Big mud crab. I want one for Uncle.'

'Is that who arrived today?'

She nodded. 'He went down to Alice but now he back to check on me.' Marri pulled at the grass absently.

'Are you alone?'

'Nah, you right here,' she said with a giggle.

He smiled at the lovely sound of it. 'I meant do you have family here?'

She shrugged, serious again. 'Some. Sister got taken away. They say she got white blood in her so she can't live with us. Mum's gone south with the others. She scared of them bombs but I don' wanna leave.'

Marlon was appalled. 'Hold on, they took your sister away? Where?'

'Somewhere,' Marri said softly, her eyes wet. She wiped them with the back of her hand. 'Not here. She belongs here. We been here since the Dreaming began and she one of us.'

'What's the Dreaming?'

'Hard to explain.' She shrugged. 'The story, I guess.'

Marlon nodded, liking that. 'What's the name of your tribe?'

'Larrakia the big mob. Not a tribe though, we a people. The Saltwater People.'

'I'm a saltwater person too.'

She cocked her head, studying him. 'You got black man's blood?'

'Kind of...well, brown at least.'

She looked curious but didn't ask any more questions. They stared out at the water as the sky blazed pink-red and she pointed at the arrival of a sea eagle. '*Garngarn*,' she said, grinning widely with excitement. 'Good sign from ancestors...from spirit.'

'How do you know?'

She looked thoughtful before answering. 'How it make me feel, I s'pose.'

Marlon watched contentment slide over her face once more. 'Then you must be a good sign for me.'

She was gone then, her hair sliding forwards, her long limbs running into the bush, but not before she gave him one more of those smiles. Marlon let it rest in his mind as he looked back at the burning sky. The Japanese might bomb them and the white people might steal their family but he had a feeling no-one would ever take this saltwater from her people. Not while their ancestors sent the *garngarn*.

And not while they were still dreaming.

Twenty

Junie had counted on being bored but she'd obviously underestimated Eliza Chamberlain's ability to turn on a show. There was
nothing tedious about the party 'celebrating' Eliza's engagement
to the boorish Miles Harrington.

Eliza had chosen to hold the event on a Sunday, an unusual
enough choice in itself, but it was the risqué theme that would
keep Sydney society gossiping for weeks to come: The Fall of
Rome. The party was saved from scandal by being held in the
daytime – Junie supposed it was the only way Eliza could get
her mother to agree to it. Anyway, most guests wouldn't understand the pun but Junie knew Eliza considered this a marriage
of convenience – the joining of two extremely wealthy families
by law – and the theme was a metaphor for the bride's surrender. Secretly, Junie thought it was ridiculously decadent but she
couldn't help but relate to the sentiment.

The magnificent garden already rather resembled something
from Roman times with its statues and abundant foliage so the

addition of heavily laden trestle tables along the pool, long swathes of silk curtains, and chaise longues strewn with luxurious cushions somehow didn't look out of place. It would probably be said that the champagne fountain was a bit over the top but Junie just wished the alcohol wasn't making her nauseous so she could drink more, especially when there were fine gold goblets being passed around to do so. Yet another drawback of pregnancy.

Junie pulled up the toga that she'd worn over her dress, glad that the costume disguised her stomach, which had finally begun to pop out in recent weeks. By her own estimate she was over five months gone although Ernest thought it not quite three, the amount of time that had passed since their wedding night. Fortunately, she was hiding it well. Another thing to add to the list of pretences.

Junie felt a familiar hollowness as she thought about their cold marriage bed where sex had become something she detested instead of a wondrous, sublime event. Ernest didn't seem to notice, happy as he was to have her at last, and she'd learnt to fake enough enjoyment for him to achieve his climax.

Seemed she was a good actress after all.

But those performances had a terrible price. The acts were far more loathsome than she'd ever imagined because she knew what it could be when you loved rather than despised. She almost wished she'd never known Michael's touch now that she had to bear the clammy hands of Ernest. He took her in lust, not love; in triumph, never reverence; and there were no words, only grunts. There was nothing left to say. And there was nothing left to do, save lay there and pay.

Michael was wrong. Far better to be asked to live as an adulteress than as a whore. At least as an adulteress it would be a fall of her own choosing. At least then she would still have the sweetness of love's touch on her body for stolen moments of her life. She could bear the penance if she were only allowed the sin.

Ernest, of course, seemed to notice nothing at all unless it was directly affecting him and it astounded her how insensitive he was to her true feelings. Or perhaps he did know but didn't care – she was merely an accessory to his career – although he'd been genuinely pleased about the baby. Being a family man was a political necessity. He'd decided today was the perfect occasion to tell people and she felt like one of the garden statues as people came to pay their respects before moving on. Small acts of worship at the altar of her fertility, she mused. She wished the Braidwood girls were here to hear that little witticism, although she imagined Katie could come up with far more amusing comments about this farcical world.

Junie was grateful for Eliza though, because, despite her sometimes snooty ways, she did make her laugh. She needed a friend, and what a friend Eliza was.

The lady herself approached in her rather fabulous Roman gown and gold-heeled sandals. 'Come on, cheer up,' she whispered, coming to stand alongside. 'If I can't pout, neither can you. Have another champagne, for God's sake.'

'Can't,' Junie reminded her, pointing at her stomach. 'It makes me feel sick.'

'Oh, that's right. How perfectly dull.'

Junie shrugged. 'It's not for all that long. I'll be done by Christmas.' Actually, quite a bit sooner but she had to get used to the lie.

'Thank God. Hopefully this ridiculous war will be over by then too,' Eliza said, sipping her champagne and surveying the crowd, who were rather subdued considering the setting and the theme. 'Lord, it's all they can talk about. The battle in the Pacific this, the threat of invasion that. The bloody Nazis and the bloody Japanese. Haven't they got anything better to do than try to take over the world?' She pushed her stack of gold bracelets further up her arm to stop them from tinkling against her glass. 'I'm sick to death of the gloom and doom in this city – can't wait for summer. You simply have to come to the beach house, you know. It would be so tedious just with Miles and Cecil and their crowd.'

Ernest and Miles's friend Cecil Hayman had managed to escape Singapore and avoid capture along with a few other officers, something Junie found rather suspicious considering how many Australians had been taken as prisoners of war. Still, she tried to pretend to be happy to see Cecil each time he turned up, despite the sloppy kisses he always landed on her cheek, lingering just that bit too long.

'I don't think I could bear a whole month with just Eugenie for company. Why is that woman so concerned about the bloody state of the weather?' Eliza said, nodding towards Eugenie, who was deep in conversation, pointing continually at the sky.

Junie had to agree but changed the subject for the sake of politeness. 'How are the wedding plans coming along?'

'Disastrous. Mother has me trussed up in a nightmare of froth. I look like the bloody cake!'

Junie giggled. Jane Chamberlain had let Eliza have her way with the engagement party but the wedding was firmly under her rigid control.

'Then we have seven bridesmaids looking like stuffed pastries, *and* none of them you. We should give people spoons at the door.'

Junie giggled some more. 'I'll probably look like a stuffed pastry by then anyway.'

'Never. You'll be one of those glowing, gorgeous types, unlike that Patricia. Honestly, she looks like an overripe tomato and only two months ahead of you!' she whispered behind her hand. Junie tried not to smile at the sight of poor Patricia Fairfax, who was very bloated, and, with her red hair and pink complexion, an overripe tomato wasn't an unrealistic comparison, if rather unkind.

'You really are awful.'

'I know. And getting nastier every day in preparation.' She nodded over at Miles, finishing her drink. 'Mum's the word, lovely.'

Watching her walk away, Junie envied her honesty. She'd grown used to being Eliza's confidante, something that probably had quite a bit to do with her being an outsider. She only wished she could confirm Eliza's assumption that she too had a marriage of convenience and not love, but something always stopped her from doing so. Perhaps it was pride. Perhaps it was shame.

Wandering down to the balcony's edge, Junie stared out at the harbour, a sparkling jewel in the May sunshine. She wondered what Michael was doing right now, whether he would ever forgive her. Whether he had moved on to love someone else. She doubted that. Katie had seen him at the movies with the others last week and said he hardly spoke a word all afternoon. The Burning Palms gang met up regularly these days and Junie ached to join them, but she couldn't face him like this.

The girls were sworn to secrecy regarding her pregnancy – and the truth about the child's parentage. Junie wanted Michael to hear about the baby from her as soon as she could find the courage to do so, which didn't feel any time soon. Maybe when they sent him to war. Maybe then. It might convince him that somehow they would always be connected, that fate would be kind and the Allies would win and they'd end up together because they truly were meant to be. That this child was a sign from God to confirm it. Maybe.

She searched the skies, wondering what the future really had in store for her; if she would ever find true happiness again, as happy as she'd been at Burning Palms, on a stolen night on the sand, when it was just she, Michael, the great southern lady and the moon.

It seemed hard to believe.

Watching two planes approach from the west, she thought about the Japanese. They were close now, so close they were bombing the north and said to be moving south. Many thousands of her countrymen were enslaved in prisoner of war camps and she could barely stand the thought of what the future might truly hold. Maybe Michael would be taken too. Maybe he would die. Maybe they all would, she realised, imagining the bombs raining down on this beautiful city.

The two planes were low and they banked left and headed down the Parramatta River, causing the crowd at the party to pause. Then they gasped and pointed in wonder as the Kittyhawks flew towards them, straight under the great arch of the Sydney Harbour Bridge. It was a breath-taking sight as they passed – near enough that the guests could see the airmen wave – and everyone cheered and waved back, boats in the harbour and cars on the streets sounding their horns. In a single rash act, those two American pilots were sending Sydney a message of hope: Whatever Japan threw at them, they weren't about to lie down and take it. This was their way of life too and they would protect it with courage and daring – no matter how many bombs were hurled from above.

Just then the baby inside her moved for the first time in the slightest of flutters and Junie felt a rush of pure wonder. Tears sprang to her eyes as she rested her hand against her stomach, love infusing her for this little life within. Maybe it was all a divine test and she had to find courage too; courage for this tiny soul and for herself. Because life was unpredictable. Planes flew under bridges and babies moved in response and maybe one day she would find happiness once more – a place of pure contentment.

Perhaps she would even figure out a way to stay there; to hold on to Shangri-La. Maybe.

Twenty-one

The ferry was minimally lit, as all vessels necessarily were now, and Michael pulled his jacket close, staring at the black and silver water.

She hadn't turned up. Again. He supposed he should have been relieved but, despite every piece of common sense telling him it was for the best, it had cut like a blade into his chest when the other girls had arrived without her. It made him feel desperate, as though he should just rush to her somehow, find her wherever she was and kiss all the terrible aching away. Give in to that forbidden affair and take whatever was left. But that kind of illicit love would never be enough for either of them and he wasn't sure he could bear the thought that she felt another man's touch.

Manly had been cold today and barbed wire now lined the beach; vicious and stark, an abomination on the beauty of the place. All day the others had chatted and laughed, trying to forget about the war, and all day he'd fought memories, trying to forget about her. He was imprisoned by those images, as if someone had wrapped the barbed wire around his mind too, and nothing else could get in or out. Michael had battled against visions of the last time he'd been there, staring at the fortifications as if they had been placed just to remind him that Junie was now off limits.

Everything about Manly had added to the desolation he felt: the seagulls, the Steyne Hotel, the sound of the ocean. They all sent the same message in stark refrain: She'd known that summer's day. She'd known she wouldn't marry him, that it was all they would have. And she hadn't said anything, except that she loved him. Without that memory, without those wretched words spoken from deep in her heart as he lay against her breast, perhaps he could accept losing her. But because of them he was as empty as the beach had been on this lonely, autumn day.

Cliffy and Jake were murmuring nearby and the breeze sent the occasional waft of tobacco his way. Michael took out his pouch, intending to have one himself as they rounded Bradley's Head, when he was surprised by the sight of searchlights. He looked back at the USS *Chicago*. Nothing seemed out of the ordinary there. Then he noticed the lights were focused on the approaching boom gate that marked where the nets lay beneath.

'Never seen that before,' said Jake, coming to stand next to him with Cliffy. They were all aware that an enemy plane had been spotted over the harbour the night before.

'Maybe they're just a bit nervous,' Cliffy said.

The ferry from Circular Quay moved through, then it was their turn and they scanned the waters closely. Suddenly Jake nudged them.

'Look!'

'What?' said Cliffy.

'I thought I saw a periscope.'

'Where?' Michael asked, craning to see.

'Just there.'

They all stared into the swirling black ink behind the boat.

'Are you certain?' Michael asked.

'Not completely. But it bloody looked like it.'

'Maybe you should tell the captain.'

'Do you reckon?' Jake asked.

None of them were sure so he decided not to, but they continued to watch in nervous silence.

Michael's heart was thumping hard in his chest and he silently urged the ferry to get to the quay faster. The dark waters looked ominous now with the idea of an enemy submarine lurking beneath them, armed to kill. His imagination raced. Was this it? Would planes arrive now? Would the invasion of Sydney be tonight? He stared across at Mosman, praying for Junie. God keep her safe. Just give me that much. Then his thoughts went to his family over at Hurstville and he wished he could get word to them to get in that damn bomb shelter his father had insisted they build. Filled with redbacks and water no doubt, but at least it would protect them if this really was a raid.

Hurry man, hurry, he mentally implored the captain as the ferry continued its slow progress, stopping repeatedly, searchlights sweeping across them. Michael would have worried they were a sitting duck if he didn't figure they were likely to be low on the priority list for the Japanese.

The ferry finally arrived with a dull clunk and they jumped off, walking swiftly away from the wharf.

'What should we do?' Cliffy asked Michael.

'I don't know.'

'You're the bloody officer!' Jake reminded him.

'Right,' Michael said, gathering his wits. 'How sure are you really?'

Jake rubbed his face. 'I'm pretty sure –'

He was cut off by the sound of explosions.

'What the hell was that?'

The noise seemed to be coming from Rose Bay and lights flashed in that section of the harbour. Then the enormous bridge was illuminated in an eerie orange light and Michael felt a rush of protectiveness for his country consume him.

'Come on!' he yelled, running towards the Botanic Gardens.

'What are you doing?' Cliffy shouted behind him.

'Looking for a gun!' he said. They all ran then, searching for defensive posts, but then the explosions stopped and they stood on the street, confused, as the air raid sirens began to wail. Searchlights now scanned the sky and people were running in every direction.

They were lost in the chaos, not sure which way to go until they saw a group of soldiers pass with two machine guns on the back of a truck. Michael gave the signal to follow them and, as they rounded the corner, the harbour came into full view. For the first time in history it was alive with war. Gunfire pounded from all sides as the lights criss-crossed the water, momentarily blinding them, and it was frightening and deafening in equal parts.

'Come on!' Michael yelled.

They reached the truck at a sprint and helped the men haul sandbags around the guns and set up ammo. Cliffy took the honours on one – he was getting to be an expert at handling a machine gun – and the other soldiers didn't argue as they watched him in action. No-one knew exactly what they were shooting at but if Pearl Harbor was anything to go by, they couldn't pour enough firepower into the water where the searchlights landed.

It seemed to last forever, like an endless, terrible cracker night, then an almighty explosion took out one of the converted ferries as it sat near Garden Island. Michael watched in horror as sure death hit the air, knowing the men within had almost certainly been killed. Great flames leapt into the sky and Michael closed his eyes against the image, but it remained, burning against the grey inside his lids.

The fireworks continued into the night until the battle finally petered out and someone turned the sirens back on to tell the city it was over for now.

Then Michael, Jake and Cliffy walked slowly back to the quay, shaken by their first experience of real combat and solemn in the knowledge that the battles were no longer in someone else's backyard.

They weren't playing war games any more.

They would wake in the morning to discover three subs had entered the harbour that night, one tight on the heels of a Manly ferry, and that twenty-one men had died in their beds near Garden Island, aboard the HMAS *Kuttabul*.

Over the next few weeks, Sydney would be shelled again, as would Newcastle, and by July, sixty-two crewmen would be dead and seven ships destroyed off the New South Wales coast at the hands of the Japanese.

❧

With the coming of the cold winds the great lady mourned, restless now as the weaponry of May littered her harbour depths. The dark war had visited her gentle parlour and she carried the lives of the dead with her now, forever the mark of their watery grave.

But her people worshipped her still. They mourned with her and looked to her for comfort as she continued to guard their home, crowned by the great bridge like a queen.

And, as winter arrived to add chill to the wind and the rain, they prepared for battle along with their allies, gathering their collective armies to leave her safe waters. To fight for their freedom in the jungles to the north and again on her wide blue skirts.

This time they sent their own boats armed with black dots towards Hawaii, to a place known as Midway, to meet the enemy in swarms and surprise them with new forms of attack and defence. Developments that could turn the fate of the war.

Weapons of intelligence.

Twenty-two

June 1942
Darwin, Northern Territory, Australia

Marlon watched in awe as she pulled the snake from the reeds and snapped its neck.

'Dinner!' Marri said happily, holding it up for him to admire.

'I think I'll pass,' he said and she grinned at him.

'Chicken.'

'Yes, that would be better.'

Marri laughed and brought her prize over. 'Him's good tucker,' she said. 'This a real big one.'

That he was and Marlon recoiled as she shoved it in his face. 'Finished now?' he asked, trying not to show his fear.

'Never finished,' she reminded him. Marri was always hunting, or not. Gathering food was part of her everyday life, necessary but more a casual eventuality than a conscious activity. Unless she was fishing. That gained her full attention.

They strolled along and he felt that easy feeling that always came over him whenever she was around. Maybe this was the day he would finally kiss her, he considered, observing her brown legs where her wet skirt clung. Then he looked at the slimy snake dangling from her hand and figured maybe not. They chatted pretty much every afternoon, going for twilight walks and learning about each other. Marlon hadn't shared the native side of his life with anyone before. He told Marri stories about Liwa and she shared some of her family history in turn, including a little background about that uncle of hers. Seems he went walkabout once for ten whole years. Marlon was still hoping for an introduction so he could hear some of that tale.

They paused at the turn of the bay and she pointed across the water.

'*Dungalaba*,' she said casually.

Marlon felt slightly sick as a massive crocodile made its slow way across the sand. 'Should we, uh, get out of here?'

'Nah, he not bothered with us today.'

Marlon hoped she was right, noting the ancient reptile's massive jaws. Flocks of wading birds lined the waterway and he tried to remember the Larrakia words for each but failed. He was at the point of recognising some animal names but not recalling them easily, especially birds, of which there were endless varieties. Marri tended to rattle off their identities very fast. To his eyes they were long-legged adventurers, sand-hugging families, flocks in great patterns against the sky, solo gliders on the wind. Like the *garngarn*, he thought, pleased to remember that one name at least.

Darwin may be slowly rebuilding itself but its wildlife seemed to be ignoring the war completely, damaged in parts of course, but still resilient and thriving. He was starting to feel the rhythm of it, recognising something he'd only ever found back home: the patterns of nature, the blend of her relationships. He had tapped into the calls of the birds, the movement of the tides, the tiny details that made up this rich environment, teeming with life.

This tip of Northern Australia was lush and green, still carrying the bounty leftover from 'the big wet', although Marri said it would turn 'brown like the madla' by September, when the land waited for those monsoonal rains to return. The hail of bombs could not halt the ancient patterns, they remained timeless and unbroken and Marri was the essence of it all, as much a part of it as the water that gave it all life. Abundant, free, joyful.

Woman.

She was the perfect foil against the job of war he performed each day, the balance that kept him clear-headed and calm as they prepared the base and withstood repeated air attacks, smaller now, but consistent. By day he was a white warrior, but at twilight he was Saltwater People, with her.

Marri chased the birds in a sudden rush of laughter and her face turned back to his, open, trusting and filled with a timeless beauty, and Marlon knew he was hers now, if she wanted him. She was in his native soul.

❧

'Defeated?'

Marlon was the one who spoke but it was the word they were all clinging to.

'Seems they had no idea we were on to them. Intelligence did its job – broke the codes so we knew what they were up to, and of course radar gave us an advantage,' Major Hamlin said. 'Basically, it was a reverse ambush. It's a big victory, gentlemen – we've knocked out a huge chunk of their navy now.'

They all stared at him, hardly daring to believe it. The arm wrestle in the Coral Sea had given them hope but to actually defeat the Japanese for the first time seemed too good to be true. Midway was about to become everyone's favourite word, except for those who had lost someone in the battle.

They had been enjoying some success with intelligence themselves, especially radar, and Marlon was back at home in the skies
now that the airfield was once again operational. Sections of the
49th Fighter Group were under his tutelage and he'd had the
mixed experience of shooting down three Japanese attackers. It felt
satisfying to prevent a bomb from landing on Marri's home, but
it was still a sobering sight to send lives screaming into the ocean,
to perish in fire or water. Which way he would never know. But
there were many more lives missing than these in the Pacific now.

'They lost four aircraft carriers?' repeated Johnno, echoing the
major's earlier summation.

'That's right, four out of the six that were responsible for Pearl
and the first attack here.'

'Bloody ripper!' said Macca, slapping his thigh.

'And a heavy cruiser. We lost the *Yorktown* and one destroyer.'

'Casualties?' asked Marlon.

The major picked up his hastily scrawled notes. 'Estimates have
it at about three hundred to us and – who knows? Maybe ten
times that to them?'

Marlon shuddered to think how well the sharks near Hawaii
would feed today. The gods had certainly left man to his own fate
this time.

'So what now?' Macca asked.

'They'll rebuild, or try to. We seem to have a big advantage
over them on the home front. Quite frankly, I think they'll put
all their efforts back this way, probably PNG, but they won't be
able to attack by sea for a while. They'll remain in the air and on
the ground.' He lit a cigar, offering them around, and sipped at his
cold coffee. 'They'll still be hitting us, no doubt there.'

'Bring the buggers on,' Johnno said, grinning widely.

Marlon lit his cigar. Yes, bring it on and bring it to an end, and
take this goddam war far away from this land and her Saltwater

People. White man was already trying to erase them from the earth, they didn't need the Japanese to keep trying to do the same.

He was almost too tired to go but the pull of her was strong, so Marlon dragged his battle-weary body to the little cliff where they often met and sat, a bottle of whisky in his hand. It had been a tough couple of days with the Japanese flinging their fury at Darwin once more, this time with over two dozen bombers and at least twenty fighters. Radar was doing its job but they had suffered some casualties and it weighed on him.

A few buildings were still burning and he watched the smoke as he drank. It all still felt like distorted children's games to him, like some mad version of tag, only being caught meant an instant grave.

'Dinner.'

He turned to see Marri holding a good-sized barramundi.

'Now this I will eat,' Marlon said.

She sat next to him, noticing the bottle. 'You drinking?' she asked in surprise as he took a swig.

'Yeah, I am tonight. Tough day at the office,' he said, pointing at the sky.

She peered up, a large flock of birds moving across above them. 'Better to fly like birds. They don't have to worry 'bout them Japs.'

'No,' he agreed. 'Want some?' She looked doubtful but tried it anyway.

'Ugh,' she gasped. 'No good.' Her face contorted as she coughed a little.

'Try again,' he dared. She did, not coughing this time but still pulling a face.

'Better than snake, surely?'

'You don't know. You chicken.'

Marlon laughed and she smiled back. The wind was blowing her hair away from her face and he could see her big brown eyes clearly, filled with that radiant spirit of hers, and suddenly he couldn't wait.

He leant forwards and kissed her.

She pulled back a bit, taken by surprise, then let him gently try again. There was nothing practised about her, no artful, flirtatious games, but there was a raw feminine sexuality and Marlon felt the power of it seduce him. This was more than desire. It was primal.

'I never done this before,' she whispered.

'I've never felt like this before,' he admitted in turn.

Her eyes watched him as he leant down again and she met his lips with a shy eagerness. His blood was pumping hard then as he kissed her throat.

'I want you.'

'I want you too Marlon.'

Her gaze was trusting and he felt like he was moving into the wilderness within her, deep into those eyes that reflected the colour of the water. Marlon guided her down onto the sandy grass gently, running his hand along her brown leg and finding her stomach, which was warm and soft on her thin frame.

She pulled at her dress and he helped her remove it, uncovering her like a beautiful gift; the most precious this land could offer. She pulled at his clothes too and then they were naked together, the breeze caressing their skin as they ran their hands along each other's flesh and tasted one another, a slight blend of whisky mixing with the lust in their blood.

'Do you want to?' he asked.

'Yes,' she said.

He moved into her and the land seemed to welcome them as a fierce passion took over, sudden and burning. There, on the shores of the saltwater, their entwined bodies found a mutual rhythm. The wild birds called in an eclectic chorus and the life-giving water mirrored the orange skies above as that passion took flight and they shared an ultimate, intense surrender.

Lying in each other's arms afterwards, they watched the sunset fade to red and indigo, neither wanting to let this moment go.

Until the insects came.

'Them buggers know how to wreck a good time,' Marri said, slapping at them.

'Only good?' He laughed, pulling her dress closer and finding his shirt.

She dipped her head shyly as she drew the cotton fabric over it. 'No.'

'Perfect?'

'Yes,' she said, white smile flashing.

He reached up and held her chin, entranced by her dark, beautiful gaze once more. 'I'm yours if you'll have me.'

'Yes,' she agreed, tracing the tattoo of the fish on his bare wrist, 'and I'm yours, Marlon.'

He let the sound of her saying his name settle like the night over the land, deep into his being, then reached over to seal their vow with a kiss.

The *garngarn* sailed above them, carrying the spirit of her ancestors, and Marlon knew then it truly was a sign. It was just how it made him feel.

❦

It was brilliantly sunny, like most days in the dry season here, and Marlon made his way across the base feeling as if the whole world was rolling over, almost ready to wake up from the terrors of war at last. Hopefully the Japanese wouldn't come today.

They couldn't surely, not after last night, when everything had come full circle and life finally made perfect sense. Surely the gods could feel it too.

'Marlon.'

He turned towards the sound, his heart leaping as he spied Marri near the sheds, wearing her best yellow dress. She never usually came near the airstrip, saying once she was afraid if she watched him leave she would never see him come down again.

He ran to her and lifted her up, pressing her body against his as he kissed her, seeing his own happiness reflected back in her expression.

'Hello,' he said.

'Hello.'

'Hunting for snakes?'

'Don't hunt snakes, just find 'em,' she said. 'Have to watch out, though – case they bite.'

'I won't bite,' he said, kissing her again. 'Promise.'

'You need to go fly.'

'Why are you watching today?'

''Cos I'm goin' with you,' she said, placing her hand on his chest shyly. 'Here.'

'Is that where you'll be?' he said, nuzzling her neck and loving the saltwater smell on her skin.

'Always now,' she said, holding his head and stroking his hair.

The others were calling him and sending a few strange looks his way, and he put her down reluctantly.

'I can't wait until the sun sets,' he said.

'I'll wait at them railroads,' she promised. 'Where you first ask my name.'

'And you didn't want to know mine,' he reminded her.

She smiled, walking backwards. 'If I knew your name then I had a word for you.'

'What'd be so wrong about that?'

'Then you real.'

And, in her usual flash of brown legs, she was gone and Marlon was left to wonder the same about her as he made his way over to the plane.

'Getting to know the locals?' asked Johnno.

Marlon put on his headgear, ignoring the question. 'Ready to fly, monkeys?' he called. Better to make light of things and defuse any rumours. Let them think Marri was a distraction, just a bit of fun. It worked for now and the others got ready for take-off without any further comments, although there was plenty of smirking.

Fortunately, the art of flying was soon occupying his mind but unfortunately the enemy was soon detected on the radar. It seemed the gods had decided they were staying well out of the war today – no matter how much one man's world had changed overnight.

The black dots approached and the engagement was vicious and swift. Marlon flew for his life, a life that meant so much more now than it did before, and soon burning planes were falling to the Timor Sea, death streams in their wake. He followed one bomber closely, trying to get it in his sights to clean it up too, but the pilot seemed pretty determined not to die today either. As the Japanese bomber got closer and closer to shore, Marlon felt the pressure to take it out steadily increase. Then it became critical as the bomber descended towards land, ready to let hell fall on Darwin once more. Marlon tried to get to it in a frantic dive of his own before the bombs were released, but he was too late and the shiny pencils fell.

He chased the bomber with desperate flying, sweat pouring until the hell-makers were sent to their deaths. But not before the bombs had found earth and oil. And pieces of the railway were turned to fire and dust.

❦

He took off at a run, tearing at his goggles and straining against gravity to get him there faster. The clouds were black from cumulous explosions, the gritty air blinding. A rat ran past and the image of a book lying on the ground on another such day flashed through his mind. *Of Mice and Men. Of Mice and Men.* For some reason his brain repeated the words until he got to the railroads and tried to find his bearings in the smoking debris. He searched frantically for a flash of white smile. Brown legs running. But there was nothing. Only hell.

Then there was a man, a tall dark man in a loud Hawaiian shirt, carrying a girl in a yellow dress. Those brown legs were no longer running, they hung limp from the man's arms, and the white smile was gone, blood trailing from still lips instead.

And then the gods turned their back on Liwa's grandson, he who was Miwok, not really a white man. Saltwater tribe from the other side of the ocean.

The black clouds closed in and Marlon's spirit fell deep into their darkness as he collapsed to the ground and wept for the girl who didn't want to know his name. And he wished now that he didn't know hers.

Because then this was real.

Twenty-three

Junie wrapped the blanket around her shoulders, poking at the fire. She'd forgotten just how cold it got back home in winter. Even Digger was subdued, his breaths coming in little misted puffs as he watched her from the glass doors. He whined and Lily took pity on him from her knitting chair.

'Let him in, Junie, poor fellow.'

Junie did so gladly and Digger wagged his whole body with happiness, licking every part of them he could get to and bounding about.

'Cheeky,' Junie crooned. 'Yes, you are! Mr Cheeky,' she said, hugging him awkwardly over her stomach.

'Careful, Junie,' her mother warned. 'The doctor said you're moving along too fast as it is.'

'Bah, doctors,' Henry huffed as he joined them, giving Digger a quick pat. It was his favourite saying of late. It was usually followed by 'half of them wouldn't know if their arses were on fire' to which her mother would always respond, 'Henry, please.'

'Half of them wouldn't know if their arses were on fire,' he said, right on cue.

'Henry, please.'

Junie laughed to herself, stroking Digger's ears and the dog seemed to laugh too, tongue lolling and tail thumping.

'Ah, now, what's going on in the world today then?' Henry asked his paper as he sat down near the blazing fire with his cup of tea. It made Junie almost teary every time he did that. The heart medication he was on was doing its job and, aside from some ongoing issues with arthritis, Henry was practically a new man. Cups of tea had replaced glasses of scotch and there were no afternoon drinks in this house any more, just a little wine with dinner. Doctor's orders were being strictly adhered to – knowledge regarding the state of their arses notwithstanding. They had brought life back to her father, perhaps literally, and a spark back to her mother, who now bossed Henry about quite like the old days. For all her sacrifices there were rewards here, at least, and it gave Junie a break from her 'captivity', as she viewed life with Ernest. She could almost pretend it didn't exist while back in her parents' world.

And her husband wouldn't be here for another two glorious weeks. She smiled contentedly, sipping on her own tea and enjoying what she considered her true home while she could.

There was a knock at the door and Digger barked importantly as their new maid, Louisa, went to open it. Having a servant was another comfort returned to the family now.

'Ouch,' said Junie, stretching her rib cage as the baby kicked against it. 'She's sticking her feet up there again. Move down if you want some room.'

'I don't think she can hear you,' Lily said.

'Might be a boy,' Henry reminded them both from behind his paper.

'Excuse me, ma'am' Louisa said, entering, 'but there are two men at the door.'

Three pairs of eyes flew to the maid and Junie held her stomach in fear.

Henry's newspaper dropped to the floor as he stood. 'Are they... are they clergymen?'

'No, but they are in uniform,' said a booming voice.

'Archie!' Lily cried, her hand flying to her mouth as her son stepped into the room.

'Bill!' Henry said, his face crumpling with tears. 'My boys!'

Junie could hardly see, blinded as she was by her own crying, but her brothers found her and dragged her up, holding her in their safe arms at last.

'Oh, little one,' Bill said, patting her tummy. 'Not so little any more, eh?'

'I trust you'll be calling him Archie?' said the same, with a grin so familiar and so missed she started crying harder.

'It's a girl, apparently,' Henry said, giving a helpless shrug, and they all laughed.

'Well, Junie would be smart enough to know!' Archie said, holding her shoulders tight.

'Why didn't you tell us? We would have come to the station,' Lily admonished Bill as he hugged her again.

'And miss the looks on your faces? Not bloody likely!' he exclaimed. 'Wouldn't swap that for all the tea in China.'

'Or Ceylon,' Archie added.

'Yes, yes, Ceylon. What's that like then?' Henry said, sitting down and wiping his eyes.

'It's pretty hot, I tell you – hold on, I think I'd better make this fella's acquaintance. Who are you, eh? What a beaut!' Bill exclaimed, hauling up a now deliriously excited Digger into his lap.

'Digger,' Junie and their parents told him simultaneously.

He looked at them in surprise. 'Well, I reckon he could be at that. Could have used these at Tobruk,' he said, laughing at the pup's big paws.

'He could have chewed some trenches for you, let me tell you,' Henry declared as Digger wagged his tail madly, now upside down between the two brothers. 'Right, cups of tea all round, Louisa. See what you've got from Ceylon and keep them coming. We want to hear absolutely *everything*.'

'Bloody hell, that's a tall order,' Archie said jokingly, but there were shadows on her brothers' faces and Junie knew then they would never hear the whole story. Not all of it. She shook that knowledge off. They were here. They were alive. And whatever stories they had, the only thing that really mattered was that they had survived them, even if Frankie had never seen this day.

Two out of three happy endings were better than none.

It was many hours later, when the rain had settled in with the silvered dusk, that Bill found her in the kitchen, beating at a cake to welcome them home.

'So,' he said, 'Ernest Farthington, eh? Wouldn't have thought he was your type. Last I remember, he was a skinny little weasel trying to order you about and you were usually trying to kick him in the shins for trying.'

'He still is, and I still would if I could reach,' she replied, gesturing at her stomach with the spoon.

'What gives, Junie?'

He was serious now and she felt a tightness in her throat that words couldn't get past. It was all very well to lie to her parents, but her brothers were another matter.

'Did you – did you have to marry him?' he asked, looking from her stomach to her face.

She found her voice then. 'No, no, it wasn't like that.' If only she'd had to marry the baby's father, she thought sadly.

'Mum and Dad sounded different in their letters…after Frankie,' he said.

'They were,' she admitted.

'Seems Ernest has taken over Dad's office. That's different too.'

Her expression probably said it all so she didn't bother to respond.

'I've looked at the ledger,' he said, throwing it on the table.

Junie opened her mouth and closed it again, tears in her eyes for the second time that day.

'Bloody hell, Junie, what did you do?'

She wiped at her eyes and lifted her chin. 'I gave you something to come home to, Bill. Just leave it alone.'

'But we don't want you to sacrifice yourself for us. Frankie wouldn't have wanted that either.'

'You didn't see them; you don't know how bad things were –'

'Yes, but to marry that ridiculous man – for God's sake, Junie, you detest him. I know you do.'

'What's all this?' Archie said as he came in carrying the cups.

'It seems that rat-face Ernest blackmailed her into this bloody marriage.'

'What?'

'The farm was in debt because Mum and Dad weren't coping… after Frankie. That's the truth of it, isn't it, Junie?'

She could only nod.

'We would have lost the lot,' Bill said, opening a page in the ledger and pointing. He lit a cigarette, throwing the match on the hearth in disgust.

'Why didn't you write to us?' Archie said, staring at Ernest's neat rows of figures, aghast. 'Wait till I get my hands on him, filthy little worm.'

'No, Archie. Let it go. It's…it's all just too late. Anyway, Mum and Dad are a lot better now and Ernest paid the debts out, so all's well that ends well.'

'I'll kill him,' Archie spat, slamming the book shut.

'No, don't be angry, I'm fine. Really. I mean, he did nothing wrong when you think about it – we owe him.' She sat down heavily on a kitchen chair, feeling suddenly weak in the legs.

'Bullshit,' Archie said, and she flinched, arms going protectively around the baby. 'He probably orchestrated the whole thing, overstocking and over-extending the farm. Just how much is in his name now? Wouldn't mind knowing that too.'

'No, it's in our name but…well, there was a document I had to sign.'

'Let me guess – if you divorce him he takes the farm and the debt stands again?'

'Yes. And the baby will…ugh…'

'Bloody hell,' Bill swore, not really listening any more as he paced the room. 'How dare he do this to our family while we're off fighting?'

'Low-life bastard,' Archie agreed. 'He was always sniffing around after you! I swear, I'm gonna make him sorry he ever –'

'Arrrgh,' Junie grunted again, doubling over in pain.

'What's going on in here? Junie!' cried Lily, rushing in with Henry.

'The baby –' she gasped, pain searing through her.

'But it's far too early,' Lily said worriedly, rubbing her back. 'What have you two been arguing with her about? You know you can't upset an expectant mother.'

'We just –'
'We only –'
'Arrrgh!'

Whatever else would have been said and whatever confessions may have surfaced that day, no-one would ever know. Francesca Katherine Farthington had decided to announce her arrival the same day as her uncles' returns, and whatever issues they had with her parents' marriage mattered nil to a baby supposedly very early, but actually past full term. Francesca held that secret for her mother by arriving a petite little thing, but there was nothing diminutive in her strong cries and determined stare. Her mother's blood ran through her, her proud uncle Bill declared, as she very cleverly held his finger that night, and her namesake would watch over her. Archie said he hoped she'd prefer being called 'Frankie' instead of the fancy Italian version of the name her mother had come up with.

But she was Francesca Farthington for now and, as her perfect little face closed in sleep, her charm fell upon the Wallace family. For whatever reasons, and for better or worse, Ernest Farthington was the father she'd been given.

And all the adults in her life now realised they were just going to have to deal with that.

Twenty-four

November 1942
Sydney, New South Wales, Australia

'Over sexed, over paid and over here,' Cliffy declared. 'Bloody Yanks.'

'You said it, mate,' Michael agreed, although he was watching Jake who was glaring at the sight of Katie dancing with yet another marine. The man was jitterbugging like there was no tomorrow and, like all the other girls in the hall, Katie seemed to be loving it.

The Americans had been welcomed at first but with their better pay, skilled dancing and sweet-talking ways, they'd been welcomed by the Australian girls a bit too much in the local fellas' opinions. The Elite had just spent a six-week stint in the humid rainforest around Cairns practising guerrilla warfare and they were exhausted, thirsty and starved for female company. Compounding that, their year of hard training was just about up and it was nearly time for them to ship out. With the Japanese on their country's doorstep their nerves were already wearing thin and the last thing these Aussies needed was for anyone to mess with their women.

But right now that's exactly what was going on at the Trocadero.

'Forget the Japs, we've already been invaded,' Mayflower observed drily. 'Why don't you just cut in?'

''Cos she's mad at me again,' Jack said.

Mayflower shrugged. 'Faint heart never won fair lady.'

'What's she mad at you for this time?' asked Smitty.

'I told her she had nice curves and somehow that means I told her she was fat.'

'Women,' said Cliffy.

Just then the marine grabbed Katie on the behind and Jake slammed his hand on the table.

'Don't do anything hasty,' Michael warned, too late.

Jake strode over and the other members of the Elite hurried behind him. Liquorice and Allsorts had come out tonight along with two new members of the group, Jaffa and Nugget.

Jaffa was from Tamworth and had been so named by Cliffy for his rather bulbous red nose. He was an excellent athlete, especially at running, and Cliffy had gone as far as to suggest the red nose was really a red light reminding his body to stop when he'd reached his destination. Nugget had joined the squad with his mate, Jaffa, and he so closely resembled an actual gold nugget with his yellow hair, thick neck and large shoulders it made Michael smile every time someone said it. Cliffy had christened him with it on sight, adding he was 'so huge he'd have muscles on his shit'.

Jake tapped the marine on the shoulder. 'Being a bit too friendly there, mate,' he said over the music.

'Bugger off, Jake,' said Katie, grabbing his drink and taking a deep swig.

'You heard the lady, buddy,' the marine said, putting his arm back around her.

'Maybe I'm not making myself clear, *buddy*.'

'Don't get y'knickers in a twist, it's just a little dancing,' Katie said. 'Get a – hold of yourself.'

'It's what *he's* holding I'm not too happy about.'

'Well, maybe he doesn't think it's too much to handle,' she said, slightly unsteady. Quite a lot of people had stopped dancing now and uniforms were building up on each side.

'Yeah, I sure do like a woman with curves,' the American said, grinning at Katie's backside.

Jake glared at him then turned to Katie. 'Oh, so it's all right if a Yank says it but not an Aussie.'

'*He* meant it as a compliment.'

'You know, I give up,' Jake said, throwing his hands in the air. 'Dance with this pelican if that's what you want. I'm getting a beer.'

The marine laughed, as did his mate nearby.

'That figures. Typical Aussies.'

'What do y'mean by "typical"?' asked Liquorice.

'And I'd be real careful about my answer if I were you,' added Allsorts.

'Well, maybe if you took more interest in your women folk than your beer they wouldn't be so starved for attention.'

'Who says I'm starved?' Katie objected, turning to face him.

'No-one would be saying that about you, ma'am.'

'Don't you bloody talk to her like that!' Jake exploded, lunging forwards.

'Not too bright, are you?' Michael said to the marine, restraining Jake with difficulty.

'Dumb as a hammer,' agreed Cliffy. 'Think you lot better hightail it outta here while y'can.'

'I think I know why they drink so much,' said the marine, ignoring the warnings, 'they need it to make their partners look better.'

'Who?' the other one said, laughing. 'The women or the men?'

'Well, based on this ugly guy here, I'd say it's the women.'

That comment was met by a fist, but not a man's. It seemed Katie drew the line at insults to Jake.

The Trocadero erupted into a sea of fighting and the band stopped playing in the chaos. Fists were flying on all sides now and the two marines were being buried in a blur of Australian khaki as the Elite boys fell on them as one. American and Australian uniforms swarmed into the fray and soon Nugget was delivering single punches that felled three marines on impact. Meanwhile Liquorice and Allsorts were somehow managing to fight in perfect unison.

'Incoming!' yelled Cliffy, launching himself from a table and knocking over several soldiers like skittles.

'Come on,' called Michael, pulling Jake away after he'd delivered the man who'd insulted Katie a few well-aimed punches. The whistles of the military police could be heard and it was definitely time to make an exit.

'In a minute!'

'Now!' Michael said, grabbing his shirt.

'You're going to hell in a handbag, mate!' Jake yelled, still swinging as he went. 'Bloody hide of 'em.'

'Stop grouching,' Katie ordered catching his hand and pulling him along.

He looked down at it, surprised. 'What's this?'

'Well, I don't wanna lose you now,' she replied, stumbling a bit as they landed on George Street and Michael hung back, pretending not to listen.

'Why? What's changed?' he asked, turning her around as the police rushed by.

Katie's dimples appeared in her cheeks. 'You seem to have learnt how to – hic – pay a girl a compliment.'

'By starting an all-in brawl?'

'Well,' she said, placing her hand on his chest, 'it was in defence of my curves.'

A slow smile spread across Jake's face. 'I hope this isn't just the beer talking.'

'Better kiss me just in case.'

And so Jake won Katie over at last and Michael could only applaud his mate's luck as he stood to the side, trying not to think back to the time when he too held a girl, on this very same spot, little knowing it was all about to end. Grabbing what happiness he could find.

But not every heart won fair maiden, faint or strong – it just came down to fate. It played with their hearts as it would play with their lives and there was no way of predicting who'd win and who'd lose.

Nothing fair in love nor war.

Twenty-five

She was lying on a blanket in the shade, her very blue eyes focused on the sky above her. Or so it seemed – people said she was too young to really notice very much, but Junie knew her baby was taking everything in like a wonderful little sponge, absorbing the world as it passed on by. Archie had said Francesca was 'an old soul', something Junie could well believe. She wished he and Bill could have spent longer at home before being shipped out once more. They'd barely had any time with their family, however their leaving had logistically prevented a confrontation with Ernest – undoubtedly a blessing.

'That's about it,' Ernest said, standing on the porch, his bag alongside. 'I'm off then.'

Junie nodded. He seemed to hesitate before walking over and looking down at the infant, whose stare turned towards him. She offered no smile, just gazed at him with curiosity.

'Bye-bye, Francesca,' he said. He was still very awkward with her, not taking to fatherhood naturally at all. In fact, he rarely had anything to do with her, save having some level of pride that she existed and insisting she be put on display in the expensive dresses his mother kept buying. Junie tended to take them off as soon as Constance left from her lengthy and excruciating visits. It seemed bragging about her grandchild had superseded bragging about her son.

'Bye, Junie,' he said, equally as awkward as he kissed her cheek. 'I'll call you in a few days.'

She nodded again, not really bothering to hide how glad she was that he was going. Brisbane and his new idol General MacArthur could have him for as long as they wanted. Let Ernest pay homage to the hierarchy, so long as she didn't have to go too.

Digger watched Ernest leave without interest and Junie marvelled at how cold her husband's world really was, yet he didn't seem to notice. Ernest was only ever concerned with Ernest.

She stood and stretched her back, glad she wasn't breastfeeding any more. It hadn't come easily and the baby was sleeping through the night now that she was on the bottle. Junie felt like a new person with the extra sleep and was enjoying wine again, courtesy largely of Katie who dropped over regularly with various additions for their cellar. Junie loved her visits – her friend's commentary on her recent marriage to Jake proving very comedic indeed.

'No-one told me men had hair on their bottoms,' she remarked casually one day. 'Do all men fart in their sleep?' she asked on another occasion.

In fact, every visit had been great fun up until yesterday when Katie had dropped the bombshell Junie had been dreading: 'The boys are shipping out.'

No, she hadn't delivered that piece of news casually at all. Nor the announcement that there would be a farewell party this Saturday night at the Manly cottage she and Jake had been renting. Junie had decided to go, which had her in a state of terror. What to say to the man she loved as he left for war? 'You have a baby but I'm raising her as another man's child; hope that's something worth fighting for'?

Junie smiled at Francesca and the baby instantly returned it. Oh, how she looked like Michael when she did that. It warmed Junie's heart every time, to have this part of him; something no-one could deny her. But it was tainted in the knowledge that Michael was denied such sweet parental joys. Perhaps it would be better if he didn't know. Her rabbit couldn't decide and Junie had given up asking it to. It may well turn out to be a decision it just couldn't make and God only knew what would end up happening – because then the decision would have to be made by her heart.

'Attention.'

They lined up in perfect formation these days, as well drilled and professional as any top level unit.

'Gentlemen, it's been a tough year, but you haven't let us down,' began the major.

The Elite lived up to the name: fit, skilled and prepared for a wide range of combat possibilities, but it was more than physical readiness that made them so special. The games of war had sent them deep into caves, jungles and scrub. They'd been hungry, they'd been filthy, they'd been sore. Sergeant Rory Riley knew a thing or two about frontline conditions and he'd made them feel it. For their own good, they'd grudgingly admit if you'd asked them, although Cliffy would have chosen a few colourful phrases to describe it; 'hungry enough to eat the arse out of a low-flying duck' being one of them.

They knew war would be a shock no matter how prepared they were. Facing death square in the eye had its inevitable terrors but at least they faced it together, with their Elite brothers. Men they'd bunked with in cabins, under stars and in the rain nearly every night for a year, men they'd eaten with, drunk with and laughed with. Even shed tears with. The Elite were in each other's blood now and each had individually honed skills essential to the squad:

Smitty – Mr Fix Anything.
Tommy – the crack shot.
Nugget – the strong man.
Jaffa – the runner.
Liquorice and Allsorts – the explosive experts.
Nige – the communications whiz.
Wally – the technician.
Mayflower – the interpreter.
Cliffy – the machine gunner.
Jake – the tracker.
And Michael – the leader.

A specialised bunch to be sure, each complementing the other. But more importantly, they were mates. A bond had been forged, something their sergeant knew would be more important to their protection than anything else, and they were as ready for war now as they'd ever be.

They shouldn't really be going, men weren't supposed to see first-hand combat until they were older, but the Army was in dire need of specialist forces. The jungles to the north were still seeing fierce battle, despite victories along the Kokoda Track, and with Japan still occupying large sections of New Guinea, Australia needed infiltrators. Men who knew how to steal the advantage.

And so it was time.

As the major finished his speech, Rory watched his son stand tall in front of his mates. Yes, Michael was a man now, far more so than he'd been that long year ago. But he was still a boy in so

many ways. The years hadn't had time yet to give him all the les-
sons he needed to balance experience against that youthful mettle.

But even so, it was time.

Thinking of Mavis deep in prayer at church, he sent one to
Davey himself, asking for forgiveness yet again, and hoping with
a father's heart he'd done enough to save this second precious life,
his youngest son.

That God would be merciful, now that it was time.

The great southern lady was in a powerful mood today, stirring
uneasily in her open sea. It was windy and hot and Junie was glad
she'd worn so light a summer dress, more to hide what was left of
her pregnancy belly than anything else, but it also had deep side
pockets that conveniently held her purse and a small Christmas
gift. They could hold her sandals too, which made it easier to
walk in the heavy wet sand near the Manly Beach shoreline.

Funny, really, how each aspect of the lady's disposition today so
perfectly matched her own. She seemed emotional and flighty, as
if barely holding her own form. Waves flung themselves in giant
fanning sprays against the rocky outcrops ahead and distant Mona
Vale was misty in the residual veils, mysterious and unknown to
Junie, much like this day. The sets almost galloped in their impatience to find the shore, manes falling behind them in the wind
as they ran in green, tightly-wound spirals; tense, expectant and
restless.

Her rabbit was restless too, it bounded from one side of her
mind to the other but couldn't find a way to make this all turn
out fine. What words could it find? What choices could it really
give her?

It was almost five by Junie's watch and she made her way
back for the party, aching to see the lover who'd held her in this

beautiful place but aching more because there was no returning to that perfect day. The higher sands were soft as she broke into a jog, her heart taking over from the rabbit with each step. Maybe she would tell him, maybe she wouldn't. Maybe she would hold him, maybe she would leave. Too many maybes now; they were throwing themselves onto the sand and out of control.

But there was only one maybe that counted now and it was saturated in that youthful hope that hadn't quite died. Because maybe, when she saw him, she'd somehow just know what to do.

༜

Katie was swearing as Junie walked in, red-faced and annoyed at a big pile of twisted, knotted tinsel.

'What are you up to now?'

'Well, they're – ugh – shipping out before Christmas, so I just figured – ow – bloody thing…'

'Don't even try to talk sense to her,' Beryl said, appearing with Dorn, each carrying plates and napkins and cutlery. 'Hello, lovely.' She gave Junie a kiss. Dorn did the same but failed to hide the look of concern that accompanied it and Junie knew they were nervous of an impending scene involving their brother.

'Where is –' Dorn began, before stopping herself.

'With Constance and the Colonel. I know, poor little thing,' Junie said softly, watching the door.

'Blast and all blast!' Katie said, pulling hard on a piece of tinsel then banging her elbow. 'Of all the stupid, bloody, flamin' –'

'Ah, there's the sweet sound of my bride,' said Jake, walking in and giving her a kiss. 'Hello, Dimples.'

He was followed by his Elite mates and a bunch of other friends, all 'fresh off the ferry and feeling merry' according to Cliffy. One by one they filed into the little cottage, doffing hats, cracking jokes, handing over bottles of beer and other assorted offerings.

Then the last man arrived and stood back to the side. His eyes met Junie's for an agony of seconds before moving to anywhere else he could find to rest them, but not before she read ten months of pain in their depths.

'Michael,' said Beryl and Dorn, and Junie felt a jolt at the sound of his name, every inch of her on high alert. The room was filling with party-goers but she felt like one of those radar machines, searching for an approaching enemy ship. A destroyer, fully armed. Wherever he was in the room her radar followed, even when she was looking the opposite way.

'Nice to meet you,' said someone she didn't know.

'You must be Junie,' said another.

'Strike a light, here's a sight for sore eyes,' said Jake.

'Hello,' said the voice that haunted her every day.

There was nowhere else to look but at his face, so handsome above his uniform she could have cried. She smiled instead.

'Michael.' Her mouth was somehow forming words. 'How are you?'

'How are you?' he said at the same time. 'Good,' he added.

Then people pushed between them and there was a drink in her hand and food on her plate, and someone turned on the music. Junie drank and ate and danced and did all the things people expected of a young woman at a party. But there was no escaping the fact that three months ago there had been a baby in her womb and that the father was ten feet away, unaware the child existed.

Then there were more drinks and it was dark and people spilt out onto the beach or sang around the wireless and Michael was on his own at last, no-one else around. And she knew he was waiting for her.

'Walk?' she asked.

'All right.'

His silence felt cold as they made their way towards the Corso, but when he spoke, she wished he hadn't.

'Last time you asked me to take a walk I wished later I'd said no. Might not have buggered up my life.'

She opened her mouth to reply but she had no response to that.

'What did you want to tell me this time, Junie?'

'I – I wanted to tell you –'

'That you're getting a divorce?'

'No,' she said. 'No…I can't.'

'Used to living the high life now, are you?' He stopped to roll a cigarette and she flinched at his words.

'No, it's just there's family involved and there are…legal complications –'

'And if you divorce him he closes in and takes it all away like the dog he is? I get it, Junie.' There was venom in his tone and Junie felt a stab of regret that she'd made this beautiful man so bitter.

'It's not just that.'

'Yes, I know, it's the security of having a nice house in Mosman too and friends like that socialite, whatshername Chamberlain – and having a husband who won't have to fight, so he won't die on you, I guess.'

'That's so unfair,' she whispered, tears scratching at her throat.

'Don't give me unfair!' His voice was strained and he stopped to calm himself, rolling the cigarette with shaking hands now.

'Michael, I need to tell you something…'

'No, no more words – you shouldn't have told me anything in the first place. We should have left it in Braidwood where it belonged.' He gave up on the cigarette, throwing it into the wind. 'It's over, Junie. He wins. I'm going to war on Monday. You're Mrs goddam Farthington and may you have many little Farthingtons to warm your lonely bloody days.'

Now, the rabbit said. *Tell him now.* But her heart cried and she fell against him instead, heaving with the painful sobs that accompany futility. For a second he resisted, then the rigid anger gave way and he held her tight, just for one desperate, sweet moment.

'I can't do this any more, Junie,' he whispered, his voice breaking.

Then he was gone from her once more, off at a run, wanting distance, she knew. Distance from her.

In a swirl of emotion, Junie found her voice too late. The words had to pour forth; they had to be heard, so she said them to the great lady instead.

'We have a child...'

But the lady could only hold her words and take them deep into her glittering depths, just another secret to lie in her seas.

Twenty-six

Central Station was crowded as the Elite made their farewells.

A new bride clung to her husband, trying to send him off with a glimpse of the dimples he was so fond of, and a final press of her curves against his lanky frame. She pressed a bottle of rum against him too, a last-minute farewell gift.

'Courtesy of Dad's bar. I was saving it for Christmas.'

'I do love a woman with appetites.'

And so her dimples faded and were covered in tears, after all.

A father stood to the side, wishing he could be their sergeant overseas as well, but wishing most of all for them to make it back home. They'd all become like sons to him now: young, courageous, *funny*, he added, watching Cliffy dip kiss Mayflower's mum goodbye in dramatic style. But ultimately his eyes were drawn to their leader who held his sisters and his mother close as they said their farewells, putting a brave face on things as he always tried to do. Rory Riley was not an emotional man but tears escaped now as his blood son clasped him close too before boarding the train. They slid down his face and soaked into his uniform. *Bring him home Davey. Dear God, bring him home.*

And so the sweethearts and the mothers and the fathers said goodbye, and families and friends raised their hands and blew kisses to the air around these young men, surrounding them with love, with luck, with prayer.

And their leader leant out the train window only to notice a small Christmas gift his sister had put in his pocket, something from her friend. Supposed to give him comfort but it only broke his heart further when he opened it.

And a woman rushed down the platform, looking for that man, holding a child in her arms, searching every face on every uniform until she found the one that echoed in her baby's smile. But he was looking at something in his hand. She called his name but the train sounded, drowning her out, then the man turned away and disappeared in the smoke. And then he was gone. This time too far to be found if she needed him.

Perhaps never to be found again.

Part Four

Twenty-seven

January 1943
Wau, New Guinea

He'd thought it an easy enough flight until now but as he looked down at the steep, narrow strip on the top of the rise, Marlon felt the sweat build on his palms. 'You've got to be kidding me.'

It was almost comical, like someone had put a piece of sticking plaster on a knee and called it a runway. Built by the Aussies, he could almost feel their humour in its design, imagining Johnno or Macca back in Darwin telling him it 'does the job, though' and was 'better than a poke in the eye with a blunt stick'. He smiled wryly at that thought, loosening his grip a little.

He was escorting a supply mission and hoped to God there wouldn't be any Japanese raids today. Marlon had run dozens of sorties with the 49th of late and seen enough flying debris from ships, men running from strafing and spiralling Japanese planes to fill a movie. It had driven him to the bar most nights and he knew he was getting frayed, but of course there was little time to recover in this Pacific war. Ironically, this task of supporting the 7th in a P-40 was something he'd been asked by the major to do as a kind of break, a reprieve of sorts if you didn't count the recent Japanese bombings of the town, the hazardous airstrip, the unpredictable weather and the high percentage of crashes around this ridge. Of course, the major was also keen for him to be his 'eyes and ears', stay a night or two and 'check out the lie of the land'. In other words, something big was about to go down and Marlon was important enough to be entrusted with finding out the facts but dispensable enough to risk doing so.

He had to admit the lie of the land was quite something to behold. They were circling around the aerodrome at fifteen thousand feet and the beauty of Wau was impressive. Gold miners and timber cutters had tried in vain to tame this wild outpost and the reasons for their limited success were obvious from the air. New Guinea was so thickly vegetated it looked as if worn sheepskin rugs had been thrown over the mountains, only of course they were green, then bluish where they met the horizon. The sky was clear for now and Marlon relaxed into the flight, enjoying the freedom of flying without the enemy biting at his heels. The sky was one of only two places he felt at home – the other being the sea.

Memories of being a child of the shores, of idyllic times lying in the salt water, being infused by it, happy, had always calmed Marlon. But now thinking of the sea also made him think about streaming planes and sleeping harbours he'd seen rudely awakened. A girl with the sun touching her hair as she held a fishing line. Marri's face came to him then and he pushed it away forcefully, unwilling to spend his waking hours suffering the same torment that haunted his nights.

He forced himself to focus on the sky. It looked as though it wanted to be part of the land here as low clouds walked slowly across the mountain ridges and valleys, constantly resting and in no hurry to free themselves from the earth's rugged embrace. This was a sky that gave life, as the water gods fed the gushing streams, sending their bounty down gullies and crevices to eventually find the ocean at the end of a wilderness journey. Home to the Papuan harpy eagle and the brilliantly coloured bird of paradise. And now home to war and the black dots.

Just like the ones coming his way.

He squeezed his eyes shut and opened them again but no, he wasn't imagining them – three black dots, turning into planes, now in clear view. And looking below, there were many more, bombers and Zeros, too many to count.

Marlon dived for the bombers, trying to halt their release, but he was too late. He fired at one anyway, the rear gunner firing back, then banked to chase a Zero. *Rat-a-tat.* The familiar sound pelted at the enemy and vice versa. They both missed, then Marlon noticed a Zero chasing a supply plane and found himself belly up in pursuit. He fired again. This time he connected and watched as the Japanese plane lost altitude in a whine then exploded into the mountainside.

The chase continued, enemy planes occasionally falling, but no Allies went down and Marlon was finally able to breathe more normally as the Japanese melted away and he could land at last. No mean feat – it had to be spot on or he'd go crashing into mountains on either side. The sticking-plaster runway met his wheels in ludicrous greeting and he bumped his way upwards – and at one point almost sideways – then quickly moved out of the way to allow the next plane in. Most were landing uphill, unloading and taking off downhill pretty quickly. Marlon watched them do so, still scanning the skies nervously for the enemy's possible return.

Then the drop-off was complete, the damage from the bombings minimal, and he decided to look for whoever was in charge of this crazy excuse for an aerodrome and see what his 'eyes and ears' could discern. And whether or not they served coffee in this upside-down corner of the war.

⚜

'That's correct, sir. They should be the equivalent of about two companies, all up, but a lot of them are sick.'

'What's that?'

'I said a lot of men are sick in Kanga Force. Mostly malaria. They're not full strength.'

'Japs have been sighted coming your way, so get as strong as you can.'

'Yes, sir,' Marlon responded, wondering just how he was supposed to achieve that.

'Any sight of the enemy up there?'

'Only in the air.'

'What's that?'

'I said, we can't sight them on the ground but plenty of air attacks.'

'The 17th are being sent but it's a matter –'

Marlon swore at the mouthpiece impatiently as the major's voice dissolved into crackling.

'Sorry, major, I didn't get that.'

'Having enough planes –' *Crackle.*

'Landings are still hazardous – we almost lost another one this morning. Did you get that, Major? Major?'

Crackle. '– keep at it –'

'Yes, sir.'

'– special force – want you to take them under your wing –' *Crackle.*

'Who?'

Crackle. '– Elite.'

'Major? Major?' Marlon swore again, banging the mouthpiece.

'No, not "shit",' the major's voice came through, and Marlon could hear the amusement through the breaking line. 'The Elite.'

'Sorry, sir. When are they coming?'

Crackle crackle. The line was pure static now and Marlon sighed, putting the mouthpiece down. So much for a break from combat. Looking out at the mountains, he wondered which direction they would attack from, because an attack was imminent; he could feel it. Any airman could tell that the Japanese were serious about preventing reinforcements up here and that could mean only one thing. He just hoped these 'elite' men they were sending weren't as green as the hills around them. And that they survived the bloody landings.

❦

'Bloody hell,' Mayflower cried as he slid along the plane floor into Nugget, who tried to hold him up with one giant hand. There were no seats in these American 'Biscuits' and, with plenty of banking left and right, Michael wondered if the poor fella would make it off without throwing up. He looked pretty pale.

Cliffy held onto his helmet and yelled to Michael, 'We're like bloody sardines in a tin.'

He couldn't agree more. There was regular gunfire and he could hear their fighters savagely protecting them, but he'd never felt more vulnerable in his life than sitting in this steel cylinder in the sky. It was the first time he had ever flown and so far he was thinking it was the most unnatural state of being known to man, especially when Japanese Zeros were busy trying to shoot them down. But he was the officer in charge no matter where they were – water, land or sky – and it was up to him to reassure the men.

'Easy does it, mates. All over in a minute.'

They began to descend and Michael decided the Elite needed further distraction from what was going on around them.

'What do we do when we land?'

'Run for cover, heads down,' they said automatically.

'When do you return fire?'

'When you're out of sight.'

'Because what's hard to shoot?'

'A snake in long grass.'

'Again.'

They groaned but Michael made them repeat it three times, as much to occupy them as to reassure them. It was one of many drills his father had made them recite over and again, and today they would turn it into reality.

But saying and doing are two very, very different things.

They braced themselves as the big plane came in and Michael wondered fleetingly how it would be possible for it to land anywhere up in the New Guinean mountains. He was glad he didn't have to watch.

But he did have to feel it.

The plane jolted at an unnatural angle, crashing them against each other, the landing an absurd, terrifying affair until somehow they finally came to a halt.

Then the door was released and Michael saw immediately there was fighting underway. Firepower could be heard on the ground and in the sky and they would have to follow his father's words exactly to avoid flying bullets.

'Behind me,' he yelled, jumping out.

The scenery was a blur of greens and browns and the racket from the planes and anti-aircraft artillery challenged his ability to listen for the direction of snipers or otherwise. He kept his head down and made for whatever cover he could find, hoping the others were doing the same, and found safety behind a mound of sandbags and old machinery. There were snipers around all right – a bullet hit the bag behind him and he crouched lower, dropping his pack. Hoisting himself up, he tried to find the source of the shooting, discovering that it came from a nearby rise. He shouldered his gun, glad to see Jake land next to him. Soon they were both firing and Michael squinted at the sky, noticing a thick shroud of mist moving over the aerodrome.

Maybe that would deter them.

It did. The enemy seemed to retreat once they couldn't see and Michael was soon able to sound the whistle and pull his men together.

They turned up, one by one, from whatever hiding places they'd found, and he felt his heightened senses begin to settle as each face appeared.

'Where's Mayflower?'

'Relieving himself of his breakfast,' said Nugget.

'Brilliant,' Cliffy said, grinning.

Mayflower emerged to a fair dose of ribbing. Then Michael heaved his pack on, and the others followed suit.

'Right, let's head over to Command and see what's next.'

'Yes, sir,' said Jake, and Michael looked at him quizzically. 'Reckon we better start calling you that now we're finally at war. Otherwise they might shoot the good-looking fellas first instead.'

Michael laughed as they started to walk. 'And why would they do that?'

'Pure jealousy. Japs are only human too.'

They found Command soon enough and Michael went in to talk to the officers in charge while the others sat down for a well-earned smoko.

There was only one man inside, an American officer who seemed to be having trouble with the radio.

'Sniper activity,' he yelled at it before banging the top.

'Corporal Riley and the Elite squad reporting, sir,' Michael said, saluting.

'I'd lose the mantle to anyone but yourselves round here, buddy,' the captain said, squinting at the machine. 'Goddam useless things,' he mumbled.

'Yes, sir.'

The man stood, checking Michael over and flicking his eyes to the patch on his shoulder that contained a gold capital E. He walked over to the window to look at the rest of them.

'How much combat have you boys actually had?'

'About half an hour,' Michael admitted. 'Just then.'

'You're joking.'

'No, sir. But we've had special forces training for the past year and we've been well drilled in –'

'Training isn't combat.'

'Yes, sir.'

'Green as the hills,' the American muttered to himself. 'Oh well, let's see what we can do with you. I'm Captain Marlon Stone, and – sorry, Riley, was it?'

'Corporal Riley. Michael.'

Captain Stone nodded at him, looking thoughtful. 'You know you look familiar for some reason…'

'Might be the uniform?'

The captain seemed taken aback, then amused. 'Come on, let's get you settled in before you try any more of that Aussie humour on me. Don't think I can survive much more of it after Darwin.'

'In that case, you may want to avoid any conversations with Private Clifford.'

৩৩৩

They were waiting, each passing the time in their own way. Jake was writing to Katie, sending her quite an essay by the looks of things, and Tommy was picking up little rocks and pegging them lightly at the back of Nige's neck. Nige looked up at the trees nervously each time; the others had told him drop bears were common in this part of the world too. Mayflower was studying Japanese and Cliffy was singing quietly to himself, a rude little ditty he'd picked up in Port Moresby to the tune of 'My Home in Tennessee':

A map of Germany was where I'd never been,
And up and down her hips was a line of battleships,
And on her kidney, on her kidney,
Was a bird's-eye view of Sydney...

Michael checked his watch impatiently. It was almost midday and they'd been sitting here since breakfast. He had already decided this was the part about real war he hated the most – time wasted was time to overthink things: impending danger, his responsibility for the others. Junie. He made a futile attempt to resist walking into that painful part of his mind.

Reaching into his pocket, he pulled out the Christmas gift yet again, running his hand over the silver lighter, reading its inscription: *Burning Palms, December 1941.* A strange choice, he thought for the hundredth time. Did she really think he would ever forget that night? Her face came to him, eyes dark in the moonlight as she lay on the sand, crimson feathers soft on her brow. He needed no reminder of it; he could never erase that image, reckoning it would be the last thing he thought of before he died.

Michael lit a cigarette then shoved the lighter back into his pocket, trying to shove thoughts of her away too. Surely it was enough to focus on the approaching enemy without worrying about his foolish heart and what it might choose to envisage if death came their way.

'You know, I'm not too sure about calling ourselves the Elite up here. People might think we've got tickets on ourselves,' Jake said.

'I was thinking the same thing,' said Cliffy. 'How about the Eventually Got Heres?'

'The Egotists?' said Tommy.

'Empty-Noggins?' continued Cliffy. 'Actually, looking at Mayflower, how about the Eggheads?'

He was obviously enjoying this game but the distant shelling was intensifying and Michael held up his hand. Cliffy immediately fell silent. The sound of machine guns echoed and Michael wondered just how long they would be kept away from the action. At least they'd got this far – quite a few planes had crashed, visibility and air raids proving hazardous, and with the mist now settling into a still layer of fog any kind of landings were deemed impossible. Captain Stone was in quite a state about it. He'd been wrangling with poor communication in the radio room all day and Nige had been in there trying to help them get better reception.

Apparently Kanga Force, the collective name for the Australian soldiers up here, had been involved in a lengthy arm wrestle with the Japanese for control of these ridges. Decimated and disease ridden, the Australians were nonetheless currently engaged in intense fighting. The battle they could hear was only a few hours' walk away and the Allies were desperate for the weather to clear so they could land fresh troops.

It was frustrating for the newly arrived Elite who were itching to get to the Aussie captain, Bill Sherlock, and help stall the advance, but so far they'd been told to wait.

'We'll need you here if they break through,' was Captain Stone's curt reply when asked if they could move out.

Michael stood and paced, restless as the sounds of combat continued. They knew Sherlock only had a hundred or so men, including reinforcements from 9 Platoon. God only knew how many Japanese were out there. Spying the American captain walking towards the radio room once more, he decided to try again.

'Captain,' he called, running after him.

'Not now, Riley,' Marlon said, striding fast.

'Sir,' Michael insisted. 'The men are stinging to go down. All this waiting –'

'I don't care if you're bored, Riley. I told you before, this is war, not training. I'm not sending you boys in there without numbers.'

'Yes sir, but it sounds to me like numbers are falling,' Michael replied, 'and you've got Buckley's of landing reinforcements in that.' He pointed at the white haze surrounding them. 'Would you rather we just waited here like sitting ducks?'

The captain paused, then turned to face him with a sigh. 'Better than dead ducks.'

'We'd rather go to it than wait, Captain. It's what we're trained for.'

Marlon stared at him as the sounds of muffled explosions reached them both.

'Captain,' called one of the men from the communications room as he ran towards them. 'They still can't get past from Black Cat.'

'Damn!'

Michael knew Marlon was wavering so he waited as the captain scratched his head and stared down the hill.

'All right, Riley, get down there, but for God's sake, keep your heads down.'

'Yes, sir!'

The Elite were up and off almost as quickly as Michael gave the order.

'Ready?' he asked Jake as he stuffed his letter away.

'Rather fight than wait,' Jake said, grinning. But behind that grin Michael knew he was scared. They all were. The American captain was right about one thing: training isn't combat.

⁂

They arrived amid ferocious fighting.

'Corporal Riley, Elite squad,' Michael panted, not saluting Captain Sherlock. Green he may be, stupid he wasn't.

'Some kind of commandos, I take it,' the captain said briefly, glancing at the patches on their shoulders as he moved along the lines.

'Yes, sir,' Michael responded. 'Some kind.'

'Well, you've walked into hell here, son, I don't mind telling you,' Sherlock said, checking one writhing man's injuries.

'Yes, sir.' Michael tried not to stare at the wounded man but it was difficult. Half his insides were spilling out.

'Least he's alive. Japs don't take prisoners no more,' said a soldier nearby and Michael turned to look at him in shock.

'Are you serious?'

'Couldn't feed us anyway,' the man shrugged, kicking at an enemy corpse as he moved on. Michael took in the dead man's skeletal frame. Maybe it was true.

'Send this,' Sherlock ordered the private standing nearby, handing him a hastily scrawled message then crouching low as machine gun fire exploded to the left.

'Some of the 9th are trapped over there sir,' a nearby soldier yelled.

Sherlock swore then checked his ammo, calling out to his men. 'On my signal.'

Michael watched as he shouldered his gun. 'Cover me,' he said, and Michael nodded, signalling to the others.

'Hold on mates,' he heard one man say. 'We're coming.'

❦

'"Cut off as of 1455 hours",' Bates read the message from Command, the radio on the blink again. 'Hold on, here's another one. Sherlock says any help sent may be too late. "9 Platoon overrun and countering now". That was half an hour ago.'

Marlon stared at the jungle outside where a wall of cloud still frustrated any effort to land troops, and found himself praying to the gods – not his own – to the gods of the Saltwater People in Darwin, for whatever help they would be willing to give the white men of their country this day. But up here the water ran in the mountains and the clouds, not the seas, and Marlon wondered if those faraway gods could find them.

'Pull them out! Pull them out!'

Michael obeyed, grabbing whatever bodies he could as the Elite and the newly arrived 2/5th worked desperately to pull survivors away from enemy fire. 9 Platoon had fallen in terrible numbers and the forest floor was littered with bodies. There was blood and noise and maiming and death and an endless supply of Japanese soldiers. They poured like insects over the rise, seemingly in their hundreds.

'Grab him!' the captain yelled, pointing, then ran to do so himself as one man struggled to claw his way back.

'Good God,' Michael muttered as the man's leg hung in grue-some tatters.

And still the Japs came.

'Get whoever else you have left down there!' The voice came through the radio clearly this time.

'I've sent the Elite…'

'We need more than a dozen men for God's sake…'

'Yes sir. Any news on Duffy?'

'Yes – the 2/5th should be there by now but…' the rare radio clarity struggled against static once more and Marlon strained to hear.

'What was that sir?'

His mind raced as he waited. Duffy's 2/5th Battalion might have got there in time to save some. And then the weather might clear and troops could be landed. Perhaps all wasn't lost.

'…only forty…still standing.'

Marlon stared at the radio, the crackling deafening in its finality. 'Yes, sir,' he said after a pause. 'Yes, I understand.'

It was a ragged, exhausted lot that retreated back to Wau; a slow-moving trek hampered by the amount of wounded. They were crossing a log bridge, boots slipping and muscles straining, and the thick air of the jungle was in their lungs. Michael wondered if there was any place less suitable for warfare in the world, having to agree with Kanga Force's unofficial name for it: Bloody Ridges. They were bloody, all right. He could only guess how many lives had been lost in this battle, having seen plenty of it today. His first sight of death.

He looked around as he reached the other side of the stream, thinking it wasn't the forest's fault – it would be beautiful here without man. Then there was a flutter of colour and he paused.

Maybe it would have been different if he hadn't noticed that bird of paradise land nearby at that precise moment, perhaps the most beautiful animal he had ever seen, glowing in crimson plumage – exactly the same colour as a feathered crown he'd once seen framing a woman's face. Maybe if he hadn't been looking at that wondrous creature he would have noticed the enemy nearby. He may have seen the movement that gave the Japanese away as they repositioned their machine gun. And he may have moved his own gun in time to stop them.

Michael missed that much, but he didn't miss the deafening crack of sudden fire, nor the sight of a man jerking in response and falling off a log. He didn't miss watching Captain Sherlock run to kill the machine gunner and protect his countrymen.

And he didn't miss seeing that brave 34-year-old Australian captain meet gunfire and die, right in front of his men, there among the Bloody Ridges.

No, he didn't miss seeing that, and the shock would cause that bridge to haunt his dreams for the rest of his days. The birth of a memory that Michael Riley would never fully block out.

The Elite would later learn that during the 36-hour battle on that ridge at Wadumi Captain Bill Sherlock and just over one hundred men had held position against an estimated two thousand starving Japanese soldiers. Because of their stand there was enough time for the skies to finally clear so fresh troops could land at last, saving the town of Wau and turning this corner of the war back in the Allies' favour. But it was not without cost.

Over one and a half thousand Japanese soldiers died and one hundred Australians also gave their lives for the small town of Wau.

An aerodrome set on the side of a woolly hill in the remote New Guinean mountains, often lost in seas of moving clouds. Home now to the souls of lost soldiers.

Visible only to the gods.

Twenty-eight

February 1943
Sydney, New South Wales, Australia

The elephant dipped his trunk then sprayed water over his enormous form and Junie gazed at him in admiration.

'Gah!' said Francesca, seemingly impressed too.

Junie smiled at her daughter, although she had to admit coming to Taronga Zoo on a regular basis was as much for her own pleasure as it was an outing for Francesca. Watching the bull elephant, she had to admit something else: despite the beauty of the animals, the panoramic view of the harbour and the great privilege of seeing nature's vast species on display, the whole place left her feeling slightly outraged. This incredible animal shouldn't be standing on concrete in front of a man-made pool, he should be in the wild, on the foreshores of some mighty river, king of the jungle. Not an exhibit. The feeling had been intensifying recently, feeding an idea that was growing each day, something she had decided she would be voicing as soon as Ernest came home tomorrow. She wasn't worried he wouldn't agree – quite the contrary. She was worried about what he would want in return.

'Junie!' Eliza called, waving as she arrived. She was impeccable as usual, clad in a white and navy dress with a polka dot scarf casually trailing from her handbag, as chic as a fashion model, rounded stomach notwithstanding. 'My goodness, back to Africa today,' she observed, taking in the soft jungle print on Junie's dress.

'It seemed fitting,' Junie replied, smiling. 'How's the morning sickness?'

'Gone mostly, although I still have to stomach Miles each day. New boyfriend?' Eliza asked, nodding at the elephant.

'I think I'm in love.'

They laughed as the elephant bowed at them and Eliza blew him a kiss. 'There, you cheeky fella, now I'm stealing her for lunch. Come on.'

They meandered towards the ferry in easy conversation and Junie realised just how lonely she'd been while Eliza had been visiting family in Brisbane. With the Riley girls busy at work and Katie back in Braidwood for now, spending all day, every day with only a baby for company was a very quiet existence. And it gave her rabbit way too much time to tunnel.

'I met MacArthur's wife at luncheon. Scandalously young!'

'Pretty?'

'I suppose. He's completely devoted to her, possibly even more so than he is to himself!'

Junie giggled. 'Don't they have a son too?'

'Yes. Are you ready for this?' she said dramatically, pausing on the pathway for effect. 'Arthur MacArthur!'

'Oh dear,' Junie said, giggling more.

'I know. Honestly, if you are going to be that limited in your imagination you shouldn't be allowed to name your children.'

'Perhaps it's some kind of family name?'

'You are too bloody nice for your own good, Junie Farthington. Oh, did I mention I saw Ernest and your mother-in-law?'

'No, you didn't.' Junie was surprised. She'd thought Constance was in Braidwood with the family.

'Apparently she felt the need to go and check on Ernest's health in person, although it was perfectly obvious she was there to add to the names she can now drop. Even "Arthur MacArthur" might impress that woman.'

'I'm sure it would.' It was cool near the water while they waited for the ferry and she tucked the blanket around the now sleeping Francesca.

'How's everything been in Sydney?' Eliza asked, studying her.

'Bit boring to be honest,' Junie admitted. 'I think I got too used to having company after two weeks in Palm Beach with you.'

'Thank God you came. I think I would have gone mad if Eugenie had been the only other woman there. Honestly, who reads the weather report out loud over breakfast every single day? Who?'

'Poor girl. She is a bit unfortunate.'

'Unfortunate?'

'My mother taught me that's the only polite way to describe someone who is…well, lacking in some way.' Junie sipped at a bottle of lemonade.

'Lord, I think I'd rather be called homely or boring or…or *something*. Unfortunate? As if to say, "This woman has been born without *any* good fortune. Whatsoever. Unfortunate. She who fortune has forsaken." It's actually the worst insult of all time.'

Junie refrained from replying, mostly because she'd choked on her drink from laughter.

'It's tragic because it's true. The girl has hair like a coconut husk.'

'Stop it,' Junie gasped, wiping her eyes. 'You're too wicked.'

'I know. It's most unfortunate. Now, tell me what's going on.'

'What do you mean?' Junie asked, taking out her handkerchief to pat her cheeks dry.

'You're cooking something up. I can tell.'

'Don't be silly, I just said I was bored, not plotting.'

'Most plotting stems from boredom, or so my father says. Come on, spill it. You looked positively wistful when I arrived.'

'I did not,' Junie protested.

'Yes, you did. Almost makes me wonder if you've got a lover hidden away, even though you'd never admit it.'

Junie fussed with her bag to hide her blush. 'Don't be ridiculous. One man's enough.'

'Depends on the man,' Eliza said, so dryly Junie had to smile.

'It's nothing like that. I just – I had an idea, but I'm not sure what Ernest will say.'

'Since when do you care what Ernest says?'

'It costs money.'

'Oh, I see. Extending the house?'

'No,' Junie said, rising to meet the ferry. They boarded as Eliza made an assortment of amusing suggestions as to what Junie's idea could be.

'You want to go shopping in Paris?'

'War might get in the way there.'

'True, true. I know, you want to be a racing car driver?'

'I can't drive.'

'Yet,' Eliza reminded her.

'Yet.'

'Hmm, a bit of a dampener on things there. I know! You want to buy that elephant.'

'Yes,' Junie admitted. 'But that isn't really it.'

'What do you mean, really?' Eliza said with a laugh. 'Come on, now – tell me or I'll just get worse.'

'Oh, all right,' Junie said, collapsing on the bench inside the ferry, sunshine on the water reflecting across the walls. 'I suppose it does come down to boredom, really, but it's more than that. Truth is, I do want to save elephants – I want to fight any injustice.'

'What on earth are you talking about?'

'I want to study law.'

Eliza's jaw dropped and Junie felt she may have been less shocked if she had said she was becoming a racing car driver.

'For animals?'

'Well, that's one of many possible areas I could work in…'

'You want to be an animal lawyer?' Eliza clarified, lips twitching.

'No, no, not necessarily. I just think it would really be something if I could address suffering…in all its forms. There's nothing worse than having no say in what happens to you.'

'Like a caged elephant,' Eliza said, and a look passed between them.

'Yes.'

Eliza shook her head in wonder. 'Well, I must say, few people in this world surprise me but you sure are one of them. Studying law – what next?'

'Well, you could teach me to drive.'

'I don't know…are you going to fill my car with outraged clients? I'm not having baboon hair on my upholstery. Actually, what am I talking about? I drive Miles around in it all the time.'

Junie laughed again, in fact she found herself laughing most of the day, partly because Eliza's amusement at her ambition made for a constant stream of witticisms and partly because saying her idea out loud to someone else made it plausible. Why not make her life mean more than a loveless marriage and a child to another man? She wasn't yet twenty years old – she had her whole life ahead of her. Let the true Junie rise, the bookish girl; let the rabbit loose and see what it could find in the halls of Sydney University.

After all, she'd been Junie Wallace long before she was ever made to be Junie Farthington.

And Junie Wallace was, supposedly, a smart girl.

❧

Ernest was considering it, she could see that much. Considering what he could get out of it too, no doubt.

'I can't see when you'll use it. As a man, it made sense for me to do law, but as a woman...'

'I just want to study, not necessarily to practise.'

'But surely, when more children arrive...'

'Then I will take time off to look after them. Honestly, I don't care if this takes ten years to complete, I just love learning. You know that about me, Ernest.'

'Yes, I know, I know. I suppose I shouldn't really disallow it. Especially if it makes you happy.'

Junie was surprised at those words. 'I didn't think –'

'That I care if you're happy or not? Come now, Junie, I'm not the monster you make me out to be. Of course I care. A happy wife means a happy life.'

Miles and Cecil often said the same words and they grated on her. These men had their own interpretation on the theme. To them it meant 'just shut them up and you can get away with anything you want'.

'And if you're happy, then maybe more children will come,' Ernest finished meaningfully.

So that was it, she realised. The inevitable price. Keep giving him what he wanted in their cold, loveless bedroom and he didn't really care what she did. But she was still surprised he would pay for a woman's education.

'You're sure you don't mind the money?'

'It can come out of your parents' estate – that seems only fair. Of course you'll have to get them to agree to it.'

Ah, yet another twist – selfish to the last. He probably thought she'd give up now and her parents would be to blame. Well, Ernest Farthington had made a habit of underestimating her. Let's just see whose cards would win this time around.

'Bit less on the pedal, darling! Baby in the back remember. And in front,' Eliza said, patting her stomach. 'Saints alive, you could have been a racing car driver!'

Junie grinned widely. 'Anything's possible!'

'Oh, that's how it is now. She owns the world.'

'Who knows what I can do?' Junie said happily, and she meant it. The green fields flew by in a blur and the sun was shining in a perfect sky, as though God was making a deal with her. It was one of those magical days, a rare memory in the making, because today there was hope once more. Change had arrived, her old unpredictable friend, and maybe now she could make life count again; to be one step closer to grasping on to that happiness that always seemed to elude her.

'Good Lord, what have we done?' Eliza said, putting on sunglasses against the glare.

'The impossible!' Junie shouted, holding the memory of when her father said yes in her mind, loving her mother with her entire being for her part in the final decision.

'Without Junie's support I doubt we'd have anything left to give her,' Lily had said to Henry.

'Ernest was the one –'

'Yes, but who did he do it for?'

The only thing better than them funding her degree was the fact her mother was slowly coming back to reality, enough to even recognise that Junie's 'support' had saved the farm. In truth it was more 'sacrifice', but Junie was happy for her mother not to have that much knowledge. In fact she hoped she never would.

'"There's a track, winding back, to that old-fashioned shack",' sang Junie as they passed the turn-off to Gundagai, her heart lighter than it had felt in years.

Digger barked, Francesca cooed and Eliza laughed, joining in. '"Along the road to Gundagai!"'

The silver Mercedes flew along the highway, carrying with it two young women, a dog and a baby celebrating a victory in their own little corner of the world. Not a battle in mortar and guns but a battle just the same, because Junie's war of words had just been declared.

Twenty-nine

February 1943
Wau, New Guinea

'Our Father, who art in heaven...'

Michael was paying lip service to Father Patrick Kilkelly's Mass, but in truth he was more interested in watching the two native carriers Ovuru and Semu as they sat nearby, listening. Ovuru had holes in his ears and both had tattoos on their faces that Michael found himself staring at, wondering at their meaning. The two men seemed like they were from another planet, so different did they appear to the Australians, and Michael felt himself very much a gawking country boy – but he couldn't help it. They intrigued him.

It had started after the battle in Wadumi when the locals began to show up to help them carry out the wounded. Michael had been struck by their care of each man that day and continued to grow more and more fascinated with these gentle men of the forest. The company was journeying towards Mabu and the two New Guineans were carrying heavy supply packs without complaint. They'd brought with them Patrick, the missionary, who'd been living under Japanese occupation in a native village for some time and couldn't seem to stop praying in thanks since their liberation – hence regular Mass along the track. The Elite didn't really mind – a bit of prayer couldn't go astray after the hell they'd witnessed.

Patrick Kilkelly was almost as interesting as the natives, a very tall man from Tenterfield who'd followed a life of service after losing his young wife many years ago. With no children to care for, Patrick had decided he'd dedicate the rest of his days to the Lord, taking the Gospel into the wild lands of New Guinea like a prophet entering the Garden of Eden itself. Michael was fascinated by his story, which Patrick shared quietly on the side of the track each night, and he wondered at the courage of the man. Without the war, Michael doubted he ever would have left Australia. To take off into these almost impassable mountains armed only with a Bible, and live among people who still wore grass skirts and lived in huts on stilts seemed incredible.

'Weren't you afraid of cannibals?'

'Yes,' said Patrick, 'although there aren't many in this part of the country.'

'Didn't you worry about malaria?'

'Not after the third time I contracted it.'

'Don't you miss home?'

'This is home.'

Michael's curiosity grew, and he asked not only the obvious questions, but the not so obvious ones, the reflective ones that had begun to underscore his recent experiences.

'Don't they have their own gods?'

'That's not the point, is it? God doesn't discriminate, Michael. He has us all.'

'But they don't believe in our God, do they?'

'It doesn't change the fact He is there.'

Michael often went quiet after Patrick said things like that. He didn't know what to believe any more, not after witnessing good men die in the prime of their lives. What divine purpose was there in that?

'What does it matter whose God it really is if He lets bad things happen?' he eventually asked Patrick.

'Maybe He doesn't let bad things happen. Maybe they are planned.'

'What, just to torture us?'

'To test.'

Some nights Michael would roll over and swear to stop talking to this frustrating, strangely calm man. But once the others went to sleep and there were no further distractions save the forest, the rain and the occasional distant rumble of war, he found himself continuing the conversation despite himself.

'What a godless place to talk about God,' Michael said, after one such discussion was interrupted by an intense downpour.

'If you think that then you're not paying attention.'

That night Michael dreamt he was in Eden and it was being bombed. The jungle floor fell away behind him with each explosion, and he ran in fear only to find there was but one way out: logs over black torrents. He took a step but it was slippery and he saw then the logs were covered in blood. Too late to pull back, he stumbled and fell, deep into the black, the thunder of guns around him, and he screamed his terror.

Then something caught him and he was safe once more on the forest floor, trying to open his eyes to see his rescuer before they disappeared. But all he saw was a flash of crimson feathers that faded into light.

'Here y'go, sport,' Cliffy said, tossing some biscuits to Ovuru, who immediately shared them with Semu. They never asked for the same rations as the Australians and weren't supposed to receive them, but the Elite – or the Eggheads, as Cliffy now liked to call the squad – were having none of that. Equal share for equal effort was the unanimous consensus.

Cliffy's were the first words spoken for some time, the track being particularly steep today, leaving no room for wasted breath, but they were rewarded with an impressive view across a buckling carpet of hills and ridges, and their favourite pastime: smoko. Cliffy and Liquorice were doing the honours and the billy was boiling away by the time Michael had checked his compass and map. It was still a fair walk but they were making progress, despite the mud. Better still, Nige had managed to get through on the radio at last and they'd got an update from Wau.

'Captain Stone's flown back to Port. Something's definitely going down.'

That didn't surprise anyone. The Japanese were bound to make another move since their recent defeat and Michael had figured it would be sooner rather than later. He just wondered how much it would affect what greeted them at the end of this trek.

'Anything else to report?'

'A few skirmishes down your way. Nothing too serious but some natives were saying there were Jap raids –' *crackle* '– villages.'

Again, that didn't surprise them. The dead they came across were all skin and bone. It was obvious the Japanese were still starved for supplies but it was telling that they would steal from the locals. What few they had on their side would quickly turn on them at this rate and native loyalty was a big thing to sacrifice in this part of the world.

They were beginning to lose the line to familiar grainy noises and Jake leant over.

'Any mail?'

'Not yet.'

After the communication ended, Michael left a dejected Jake to check the mud for any tracks and walked over to sit next to Patrick and Mayflower. The priest was chatting to Ovuru and Semu in a few words of native language, which Mayflower was trying to learn.

'Do you speak much of their lingo?' Michael asked as Mayflower wandered off to scribble some notes.

'No, not really,' Patrick said. 'There are hundreds of languages up in these parts.'

'Really? I thought they would all speak a common one.'

'Well, there is Tok Pisin, but not everyone speaks it. New Guinean people are...let's say very tribal. Each tribe owns their own land, each has their own customs and yes, dialect or language, and each are very protective of what's theirs.'

'And their own religions?'

Patrick smiled. 'Yes, Michael, their own gods too. I think we've covered this, have we not?'

'Just checking you were paying attention.'

They sat in companionable silence, punctuated by the chatter of the birds and, less idyllically, Cliffy's singing further down the track.

'Hitler had only one brass ball...'

Michael laughed. 'Don't bother trying to translate that one, Father.'

'No, I don't think I will,' he agreed, laughing too.

Semu and Ovuru were watching them and Michael wondered how they felt about this war that had arrived in their backyard. It must seem as alien to them as this primeval landscape was to him.

'Do they fight?' Michael asked.

'Not like this, sir,' Semu said, pointing at Michael's gun.

Michael looked at him in surprise. 'Oh, I'm sorry. I didn't realise you could, er, understand me. I mean, speak English.'

'Bit,' he said with a sheepish grin. 'Not good.'

'He didn't want you to know – bit embarrassed he isn't better at it,' Patrick explained.

'Better than my effort at his language.'

Semu's grin widened.

Michael pointed at the weapon. 'You don't know how to shoot a gun?'

'Never try, sir. But can…uh…' He finished his explanation by imitating what looked like spear throwing. 'Ovuru better.'

'That he is. He's a well-known warrior among his people,' Patrick said.

Michael looked at Ovuru's proud, tattooed face and felt a bit ashamed he'd let them carry the heaviest load. Suddenly giving them biscuits didn't seem a very adequate amount of respect. Semu must have noticed Michael's frown at the packs and he held up the pale palm of his hand.

'We carry, you shoot.'

Ovuru nodded in agreement and Michael decided he'd leave it for now. Maybe that was their way of feeling valuable. And truth be told, their strong muscles and stamina were of immense value in this steep, difficult terrain. They made the Elite look rather average in comparison.

'Okello,' Ovuru said, nodding pointedly at Patrick then Michael.

'What does that mean?' Michael asked Patrick.

'That's his brother's name. I think he wants me to tell you about him.' Patrick and Ovuru exchanged a few words in native language before he continued. 'He's a spy. Been with the Japs at Salamaua for some time, leaking out messages and so forth. Quite a character, by the sounds of things.'

'Salamaua,' Ovuru confirmed, pointing in the general direction of the town.

'Is that why you're here? To find your brother?' Michael asked.

Ovuru shook his head but there was a suspicious amount of emotion in his eyes just the same.

'I understand,' Michael said. 'Believe me.' He reached for a stick and drew two figures in the dirt. 'Me – Michael,' he said, pointing at himself then pointing at the first figure.

'Sir,' Ovuru said, pointing at him.

'Yes, all right, sir. That's me. That's my brother, Davey,' he said, pointing at the other. Then he wiped the second figure away. 'My brother will never come home.'

They all sat, staring at the blank earth, and there was pain in that silence.

Then Ovuru leant forwards, offering his hand. They shook and Michael was surprised when the New Guinean placed their joined hands on his chest briefly before releasing it.

'*Wantok*,' said Ovuru.

Michael looked to Patrick who smiled before translating.

'Friend.'

Thirty

'How many times have I told you – not straight and not level!' Marlon yelled at Marty Harris, his newest charge.

'And never for longer than thirty seconds when in combat. Yes, sir,' Marty's reply came through.

'Then do it, for God's sake!'

'Yes, sir.'

Marlon knew he was being hard on the younger man but there was no room for niceties in the air, despite their stunning victories so far. The dark blue water below was littered with sinking, smoking ships, like macabre toys in a bathtub, testament that all the drills and rehearsing had been worth it. In Marlon's opinion, the pilots under his charge were the best prepared of the war so far, including Harris. If nothing else, the Allies were getting better at killing the enemy, a necessary eventuality if this war was ever going to end.

And there had been plenty of killing today.

'To your left,' Marlon warned and young Harris was quick to react, sending the Zero into the ocean in the space of a few minutes.

Yes, they were well drilled all right. Professional killers.

The call came to return to base and he turned them back with relief. Another day over, another bunch of men sent to their deaths at his hands. Another night to try to sleep with that knowledge while the faceless men became part of the sea. The same sea that flowed in his saltwater veins. Now forever a part of him, too.

⚜

He was slow to move the next day, revolted by the prospect of what lay ahead. The enemy had been devastated with the loss of only a handful of Allied planes. All twelve Japanese troop transport ships and destroyers had been sunk and the gruesome job of picking off survivors trying to make for shore was underway. A 'terrible yet essential finale', according to Command.

'Where to, Ace?'

Marlon looked at Harris, ashamed of the nickname that glorified how many men he'd killed but even more ashamed of what he would be asking this boy to do.

'Finishing off,' he said.

'Sure thing,' Harris replied cheerfully and Marlon wondered if he'd ever been that naïve.

Marlon didn't say his customary 'Ready to fly, monkeys?' and a few of the longer-serving men looked at him questioningly. There would be no humour on offer today.

The Bismarck Sea was beautiful and brilliant, too pristine to be a graveyard in the morning sunlight, and it drew them on, closer to the task of killing once more. Only today it would be pure massacre.

The sunlit water stayed with them that morning, each mile of it taking them closer until finally they were in view of a barge filled with what must be a hundred men.

'Strafe them,' Marlon ordered, dragging the words unwillingly from his throat.

'Yes, sir.'

And so they flew down, pulling their triggers, and terrified men were running, falling, diving. It was well known many Japanese soldiers couldn't swim.

Then they were gone and the planes rose once more.

'Poor fellas,' said one pilot.

'Yeah, well, they can take that for Changi,' said an Aussie.

'One less Jap is one less gun on our guys,' said a third.

Harris was silent.

Marlon felt sick.

Then there was another barge. It couldn't even be called that really, more like a battered raft with half-a-dozen wretched souls on board. One didn't even have a helmet, just a small face staring up at them, fear evident even from a distance.

A pilot's voice came through: 'Ace?'

That was when Marlon realised he couldn't do it any more. No more enemy blood in his veins. Not today.

'Ace?'

He gave the order. 'Turn back.'

'But Captain –'

He ignored the voice. He ignored the ocean, the raft, the sea. He only had one objective now: to fly that plane as fast as it would take him, away from the battle, away from the death.

Away from the goddam war.

'You know I could have you court-martialled.'

'You could,' Marlon agreed, past caring as he downed another whisky.

Major Hamlin took out his wallet with a sigh, ordering a drink himself. 'They should never have asked you men to do that,' he admitted, 'but that's war, Stone. Kill or be killed.'

'I know that,' Marlon said, feeling the burn of whisky relaxing him and wanting more. 'I just – I couldn't do it any more. Unarmed men like that. It's murder.'

'That's what this war has become.'

'Yeah, but what have I become in the process?' Marlon muttered, staring into his drink.

The major didn't try to answer that, he just swirled the contents of his own glass thoughtfully. 'When's the last time you had leave?'

Marlon had to think hard, not easy when your brain was clouded by half a bottle of spirits. 'A year or so, I guess. Same as you, though, isn't it?'

'Yes, but I'm not the one in the air,' the major reminded him. 'Take a week or two. Fly down to Brisbane or Sydney and get some headspace, or whatever it is the doctors call it these days.'

'Is that an order?' Marlon asked him, gesturing at the bartender for two more drinks.

'One of my easier ones.'

'S'pose it's better than a poke in the eye with a blunt stick.'

'If you're going to come back talking like the locals, I'd say stay away from Darwin.'

'Yes, Major,' Marlon agreed as the new drinks were poured and he took a sip. 'No fear on that score.'

But the truth was he couldn't stay away from Darwin. It followed his every day and haunted him at night, and with every mission the violent suddenness of death poisoned him further, polluting his saltwater blood, which he diluted with alcohol to numb his reality.

He couldn't leave Darwin any more than he could leave Hawaii or New Guinea, because they were etched into the map of his mind, tattooed there forever; a garish gallery of war. Adventures once undertaken so lightly were now experiences he could not erase, no matter how diluted his blood became.

But yes, he would go to Sydney all the same. Find a bar and work on that dilution.

However he knew the war would follow him wherever he chose to go. There was no taking leave from that.

Thirty-one

March 1943
Sydney, New South Wales, Australia

Junie's slightly sweaty palms clenched and unclenched around the strap of her handbag as she tried to adopt a cool and composed expression.

'Perhaps you should try a smaller course of studies at first. Have you considered teaching?' asked Professor Rickard, looking over her letter with little enthusiasm.

'No, law is definitely my preferred choice,' she said carefully. It seemed her first battle had commenced even before she'd attended a single lecture.

It was raining outside in a cool, half-misted drizzle and Junie had experienced the full impact of the university's grandeur as she'd made her way to the main quad. It was both beautiful and intimidating: Gothic spires pointed to the sky as if daring those who entered to achieve and the lawns were immaculate green carpets – a sumptuous welcome to those worthy enough to be here. She'd had vague notions of Brontë novels as she watched a single crow circling the turrets, and it was the thought of those wonderful sisters that had pulled her shoulders back and propelled her forwards. This is not a man's domain. Intellect belongs to us all.

But that defiance had been immediately challenged as she'd crossed the quad and noticed she was, in fact, the only woman around. And there were many men in uniform; they'd spoken in murmurs, sending her wary looks, and Junie had felt the ambiguity of university politics surround her. Sydney University may be a modern place in terms of the war but tradition still underlined every other aspect. By the time she'd sat in Professor Rickard's visitor's chair she knew an opinion of her had already been formed, and not a favourable one. She was a married woman with a baby at home, wealthier than most and without the 'need' for an education. She may have won her case with Ernest and her parents but this was a bigger hurdle – if she wanted to study law she'd need to show this man something more than what her papers confirmed.

'Law is heavily dominated by male students – in fact, I think we only have a handful of women in the entire school and most not quite as, er, young as yourself. You may find it uncomfortable being around so many men.'

'Please, professor, I am a married lady and I've grown up with three brothers. I am quite *comfortable*, I assure you.'

He looked over his glasses at her very fashionable – and now much regretted – bright yellow hat and cleared his throat. 'It is a very heavy workload. I'm not sure you understand the magnitude of what you'd be undertaking,' he warned her, gesturing at the rows of heavy tomes that lined his office walls.

'My husband studied law, so I am well aware of what it entails; besides I'm no stranger to study. I read almost constantly anyway so I might as well find some reward for the habit.' She tried a charming smile on him but it failed to crack his stony expression.

'How did you do in your leaving certificate again?' he asked, flipping through the paperwork almost dismissively.

'I came first.'

'And in which school was that?'

Junie pinned him with her most determined look. 'I came first in the state.'

Professor Rickard stopped his paper shuffling and there were a few seconds of surprised silence, filled only with the soft patter of rain and the tick of the grandfather clock in the corner.

'You won't receive any special treatment.'

She met his stare with another attempt at composure, abandoning charming smiles altogether as the clock continued its metred journey. 'I don't expect any.'

'Well, I suppose we could let you try a semester then. See how you go.'

'Yes, sir,' Junie responded calmly but her heart raced and it was pounding hard against her ribcage by the time she stepped out into the still grey but now seemingly spectacular day. Along the magnificent stone corridors and out into that magical rain, Junie walked then ran, tossing her hat high and twirling in the silvery world around her, arms wide to embrace this wondrous place, this font of precious knowledge. A world of learning – hers for the taking.

'Excuse me, miss,' said a voice nearby and she stopped her twirling, pushing her damp hair back from her face.

'You seemed to have dropped this rather extraordinary hat,' a young man in uniform said. He had an engaging grin that distracted the eye from the metal frame on his leg and Junie took her hat from him, a little embarrassed.

'I, er, just got accepted into law,' she explained, feeling rather silly.

'Ah. A perfectly valid reason to throw one's headwear to the elements. Harry's the name, victim of law studies too, I'm afraid.'

Junie shook his hand, deciding she liked him immediately. 'Perhaps I'll see you around here,' Junie said, putting her hat back on.

'Not likely, I'm afraid. I'm, uh, just visiting a friend today. The School of Law is actually in the city, near the law courts. Hasn't anyone told you?'

'Oh. Is it?' She felt naïve and quite a bit disappointed. How she'd longed to sit on this grass and stare at the graceful old buildings of the main campus. But nothing could spoil this day and she found her smile again. 'Goodness, you must think me a very unlikely candidate for a lawyer so far. I've done nothing but look ridiculous.'

'On the contrary, Miss…?'

'Farthington. Junie Farthington.'

'I don't think I've seen a more refreshing sight in this stuffy place since I arrived.'

Junie blushed, adjusting her hat. 'Well, thank you for your assistance, Harry. Hopefully I'll still see you around at the actual School of Law.'

'I'm sure you will.'

Harry said goodbye by throwing his own hat in the air, making her laugh. A university enrolment and a possible friend already, she congratulated herself. Not a bad start to academic life.

A week later, Junie wasn't anywhere near as confident as she sat in the classroom awaiting the first lesson. She hadn't seen Harry about as yet and was feeling very lonely as the only woman in her class. Quite a few of the students were in uniform and Junie was trying to figure out how they attended as part of the army, eavesdropping on every conversation she could. Unfortunately, this also allowed her to hear their comments about her and she was now wishing she had worn a less fitted blouse. At least she had left the extraordinary hat at home.

'Morning,' said Professor Rickard, entering, and the room immediately went silent. 'Welcome to Legal History. I trust you all brought your text books.'

Junie picked hers up and placed it in her lap. She had only read through *Lectures in Legal History* once so far and hoped she wouldn't be called upon for any answers to questions.

'In the first few lectures we will be covering the origins of Norman Law through to the Magna Carta. Can anyone outline the latter in a few brief words?' Professor Rickard held the chalk expectantly and looked around the half-filled lecture theatre. No-one volunteered as he wrote *Magna Carta* in large letters across the top of the board and turned to wait again.

'What does it mean?' he said with a sigh.

'Great Charter,' said one man, not in uniform, who sported thick glasses on the end of his long nose.

'Correct, Bartholomew, however a Latin major doesn't make one an instant historian.'

'Doesn't hurt,' said Bartholomew and there were several chuckles around the room.

'No, it doesn't hurt. Neither does knowing the most basic facts about this subject prior to classes commencing. Come now gentlemen, the Magna Carta.'

'Excuse me, sir, there is a lady present,' one man in a corporal's uniform reminded him and Junie thought his smile more of a smirk than anything else.

'Indeed. Apologies, Mrs Farthington. I see you have your book with you. Had a glance through it yet, have you?' Professor Rickard moved towards her, not seeming too interested in the answer.

'Yes, sir.'

'Perhaps you can enlighten us then?' dared the smirking man.

'Oh, I don't think we need apply too much pressure to the lady on her first day,' Professor Rickard said.

Junie's eyes narrowed at the smirker and she found her voice. 'Please, sir, the Magna Carta was established in 1215 under King John of England to form a peace treaty between himself and rogue barons at Runnymede. It effectively states that everybody, including the king, is bound to adhere to English Common Law.'

The professor raised his eyebrows. 'And the relevance to us being?'

'Well, it's considered the founding document for English constitutional development and thereby modern Australian law.'

The smirker was no longer smirking. In fact, the whole room was staring at her in stunned silence and Junie couldn't help but feel slightly smug.

'The lady is quite correct,' the professor said after a pause. 'Write that down. Magna Carta: the founding document for English constitutional development. I want one thousand words on it by tomorrow.'

The lecture moved on without further event but Junie knew she'd won another battle in her war of words that morning, because despite the fact she was the only woman in a room full of men, everyone in it was bound by the same common law. She had the suffragettes to thank for that.

And after over seven hundred years, common law was, still, a great charter.

꧁꧂

'I hear you caused quite a stir today,' said a voice nearby.

Junie turned, pleased to see Harry at last as she sat alone in the cafeteria eating her lunch.

'Well, at least he picked something I had read about.'

'I'm sure that is quite an extensive knowledge base to draw from. Do you mind?' he asked, pointing at the seat opposite.

'Not at all. Be my guest,' she invited and he sat smoothly, despite his leg brace. 'I think quite a few of them resent my being here.'

'You're always going to have turkeys on the farm,' Harry said cheerfully. 'Just think how wonderfully you'll be able to stuff them once you're done.'

Junie laughed. 'I think I will be happy just to pass one day.'

'Just pass? I think you'll do better than that. What's this I hear about you topping the state in your leaving certificate?'

'Oh well, that was a few years ago now...'

'How many?'

'Well, two.'

'Goodness me, I'm surprised you can still read.'

Junie laughed again. 'It feels a lot longer.'

'Yes, marriage and a child too.'

Junie looked at him quizzically.

'Professor Rickard is my father,' he confessed.

'Oh,' Junie said. 'That explains why you were over at the main campus.'

'Yes, among other things. My father's office is there. I don't know why he doesn't just move it over here to where all the action is, but still.'

'Are many of the lecturers based here?'

Harry nodded. 'Most are practising. There's a lot of double career work going on in the School of Law – pays to stay near the courts.'

'As long as you're on the right side of the room.'

'Yes, indeed,' he said, picking up the menu. 'What's good today?'

'The chicken was nice. Why are so many students in uniform?' she asked, diverted by the arrival of the smirker, among others.

Harry shrugged. 'Army needs lawyers too. Especially when the war ends and everyone starts fighting for the leftovers. Speaking of which, do you want that bread roll?'

'No, have it,' she said, eyes widening as he tore at it hungrily. 'Doesn't the professor feed you?'

'Mrs Professor does but I'm never full,' he said between mouthfuls. 'Chicken,' he managed to say to the waitress, pointing at the menu.

'Why weren't you in class today?' she asked.

'I'm only doing it part time. Besides, I'm in second year. Second degree too, actually.'

'But you're so young!'

'I'm twenty-six,' he said, 'and it was only a maths degree.'

'*Only*. I can just imagine. But why do another?'

Harry gave a bread-filled grin. 'I'm a masochist. Hello, here's trouble,' he said as Bartholomew joined them. 'Bartholomew Frewe, may I present Mrs Junie Farthington...'

'No need. She will forever be Magna Carta to me,' Bartholomew said with a haughty wave but there was amusement in his expression as he lowered his long, skinny frame to sit with them. 'What's that? Bread?'

'Get the chicken,' Harry suggested.

Bartholomew gestured to the waitress for a second serve then and turned to Junie. 'So, what's a good-looking sort like you doing in a dreary place like this?' he asked, pushing at his ever-falling glasses.

'Enjoying the common law.'

'Hmm,' he said. 'Enjoyment might be a stretch. Can't believe you've already been browsing this bloody thing,' he said, examining her copy of *Lectures in Legal History*.

'It's actually quite fascinating –'

'I find it difficult to imagine anything remotely fascinating associated with it,' Bartholomew said sceptically.

'You don't sound very enthusiastic. Bored already?' Junie asked.

'I'm a Latin major, which leaves me two choices: medicine or law. And I can't stand the sight of blood.'

'That why you're not in uniform?' asked the smirker as he walked past, wearing his now expected derisive expression.

'Brian Chester,' Harry told Junie. 'Just ignore him, Bart. It's not like he's going to last very long anyway. Wouldn't know his arse from his elbow, as my granddad used to say.'

Bartholomew cleared his throat, slightly red-faced. 'I suppose you're wondering –'

'None of my business,' Junie said. 'You were saying about the text?'

There was a flicker of gratitude over the wire rims but he was prevented from responding by Harry.

'Actually, there is one very interesting fact about it: it's written by one of my father's friends, Victor Windeyer. Ignore the initials. He prefers Victor to William,' Harry said as Junie looked at the author's name, WJV Windeyer. 'Quite a serious type of fellow, I thought, but Dad says he's a good man. He's in the military right now, a commander.'

Something clicked in Junie's memory. 'Wasn't he in Tobruk?'

'Certainly was. Had some important victories, although he lost his brother there –'

'I lost my brother in Tobruk too,' Junie said quietly, the old pain surfacing.

'I am sorry,' Harry said, pausing. Bartholomew looked uncomfortable and she moved the conversation on to spare them.

'Quite an exceptional man this Windeyer, by the sounds of things.'

'Yes, and now in charge of an entire brigade. Not sure if he'll pursue a military or academic career on his return, but he's sure to excel in either.'

'Or both,' suggested Bartholomew.

'He obviously deserves it,' Junie said. 'I have to say, based on some of his writing, I can well believe he's a natural commander.'

'A leader that combines theory with a good dose of first-hand experience they say. "A page of history is worth a volume of logic,"' Harry quoted. 'That's actually Holmes but I know Windeyer likes it.'

'Depends what history you're involved in,' Bartholomew said. 'Speaking of which, has Harry been letting you in on his top-secret secrets?'

'No.' Junie looked at Harry, who had buried his face in the book.

'He's the man of the moment over on campus. Come on, tell the pretty lady how you're winning the war for us.'

'Name, rank and serial number,' came the mumbled reply.

'Maths genius,' Bartholomew whispered to Junie. 'Secretive stuff to do with code breaking. MacArthur loves him – might adopt him at this rate.'

'You really shouldn't tell people,' said the voice behind the book.

'Aw, come on. It's the best chance you've got with a girl like this!'

Junie felt her cheeks go pink for the second time in front of Harry. 'Married woman,' she reminded Bartholomew.

'Ah, yes. *Mrs* Farthington. Is that why you're here? To find out about the finer points of divorce? We won't mind helping you study if so...'

'Really! Are all law students as impudent as you?' Junie said, pretending to be shocked.

Only she wasn't pretending later on the ferry ride home, when that throwaway comment came and settled itself in for a long visit with her rabbit. Law was power, the one thing that had given Ernest the upper hand, but he wasn't the only one who could learn how to use it.

Maybe one day the cards would even out, one day when they had that power in common.

Thirty-two

'You're wondering why I'm not in uniform,' Bartholomew shouted above the music.

'No,' Dorn said, but Junie could tell she was lying.

'I've a hole in my heart. Had it since birth. Army won't take me.'

'Oh, that's so awful,' Dorn said, her face filled with sympathy.

Junie felt for him too. The poor man had received several cold stares since they'd arrived at the Trocadero and she almost wished she could ask the compere to announce his condition over the microphone so they'd leave him alone.

'Couldn't you do intelligence work like Harry?' Junie asked.

'Shh, the walls have ears.'

Dorn looked instantly worried and he laughed.

'It's all right. I doubt anyone could hear us over this racket. Yes, I am still trying for an angle there.'

'They took Harry, with his leg and everything…'

'Yes, but having a brain like Harry's makes up for any physical shortcoming by a long way. Speak of the devil…'

'Three deep at the bar,' Harry exclaimed, trying to land the tray without spilling its contents. 'Your drink madam,' Harry pushed a glass her way and Junie took it, drinking thirstily. 'What say we head out for a bite after this? I'm starving.'

'You're always starving,' Junie said.

'I'm a hungry man, what can I say?' he said, smiling at her a little too meaningfully and Junie lowered her gaze.

'I wouldn't mind some hot chips,' Bartholomew agreed. 'How about you Miss Dorn? Have you worked up an appetite?'

'Whatever everyone else wants is fine by me,' Dorn said, 'but I would like to visit the Ladies first.' She blushed a little as she stood and Junie joined her.

'Don't be too long,' Bartholomew called after them and Junie grabbed Dorn's arm as they neared the door, whispering in her ear.

'I think you have an admirer.'

'Don't be silly,' Dorn said, still blushing as they entered the bathroom. 'As if any man would look at me when you're around.'

She said it lightly but Junie sensed something else there and queried it after they visited the cubicles.

'What did you mean by that? About men always looking at me?'

'Nothing,' Dorn said, shrugging as she took out her hairbrush at the basins.

Junie opened her own purse thoughtfully. 'Do you...do you think I'm behaving...inappropriately?'

'Of course not.'

'Dorn...'

Dorn sighed, resting her brush. 'It's just that...well I understood about Michael. I know you loved him and wanted to be with him, and that your marriage to Ernest wasn't your choice and all, but...'

Junie waited. 'But what?'

Dorn hesitated before blurting it out. 'Why are you doing that to Harry?'

'Doing what?'

'You know – leading him on. He's too nice a fella Junie. He deserves better than that.'

'I'm not leading him on.'

'Dancing with him all night, letting him buy you drinks…'

'You're doing the same with Bartholomew.'

'That's different – I'm not married! Besides, like I said, he probably likes you too. Men always do.'

'That's just not true.'

'Yes it is!' Dorn said, shoving her brush back in her bag. 'Anyway, it doesn't matter.'

There was a strained silence as Junie considered which issue to address first.

'Dorn, I…I'm sorry if I've been leading Harry on. I didn't realise…' Dorn levelled a stare at her and she sighed. 'All right, maybe I did. It's just that, well it's nice. Having a man to talk to that's decent and… and kind. Not detesting every word that comes out of his mouth.'

Dorn sighed. 'You're making a mistake Junie. If Ernest gets wind that you're out flirting with these uni chums of yours…'

'Pfft, Ernest,' Junie said, turning to the mirror and straightening her yellow hat. 'As if he cares about anything but himself.'

'He'd care about this – it's all about appearances remember? You said so yourself.'

Junie lowered her hands, hearing some truth in that.

'Don't mess this up Junie – for all our sakes. I'd give anything to go to university, to have the opportunities you've been given…'

'You don't want my life, trust me.'

'I want that part. Toying with Harry will have a cost – and more than just the poor man's heart. It'll cost your reputation.'

'I don't care about…'

'…and it may cost your education. Don't tell me you don't care about *that* because I'll know you're lying.'

Dorn was right. She did care about that. She cared about Harry too, now that she thought about it.

'Let Harry alone Junie. Give him a chance to be happy and find someone he can actually be with.'

Junie nodded. 'I guess it just…it just reminds me a bit of what it was like being with our boys, you know?' Tears filled her eyes at the admission.

'Harry isn't Michael,' Dorn said softly.

'No…no, that he isn't.' Junie took out a handkerchief and dabbed her cheeks, trying to smile. 'When did you get to be such an expert on men?'

'Must be from watching you all these years,' Dorn said, shrugging. 'Although I'd hardly say I'm an expert.'

'Oh you're pretty close, well, except for one thing,' Junie said, wiping her eyes and picking up her bag.

'And what might that be?' Dorn said, as they made their way to the door.

'Bartholomew hasn't been looking at me, he's been looking at you all night.'

'He's just…he's probably just being polite,' Dorn stumbled.

But as they returned to the table Bartholomew *was* looking straight at Dorn and Junie figured even her modest little friend would have to admit that look was anything but polite.

⁂

If nothing else that girl always surprised him, Marlon thought, finishing off his whisky and watching her. Junie was the only woman in the room who'd been dancing with a crippled man. Mind you, the man had done a fair job of things and Marlon had to admire his efforts. Couldn't be an easy thing to dance with a metal frame on your leg.

Ordering another drink, Marlon noticed Junie return from the Ladies and settled in to look at her to pass the time, happy to observe life for now rather than engage. She had a friend with her and he was glad it wasn't Eliza – he'd had enough of adventures, especially of the female kind. In fact, Junie was the first woman he'd really taken much notice of since Darwin. He found himself wishing she wasn't wearing a yellow hat and took a deep gulp of his drink before resuming his watch.

Marlon could tell the man with the leg brace was attracted to Junie and he could also tell that Junie was fully aware of it. Weren't a husband and a lover enough for this woman? Apparently not, he decided as she made her way to the bar and finally made eye contact with him.

'Hello stranger,' she said, smiling. Wow. No wonder men were lining up in droves. 'Holding up the bar?'

'I don't know. Think they're making much money?'

'I think it's one of the few places on earth were the owners are happy there's a war on,' she said, ordering a drink.

'You're probably right,' he said, but felt bitter as the memory of a lone Japanese face without a helmet passed through his mind. 'Here with friends?' he asked, pointing his cigarette in the direction of her table.

'Yes, just celebrating the end of my first university exams, actually.'

'Boredom needs its pursuits,' he said with a shrug and she looked at him strangely.

'It isn't boring at all.'

'I wasn't talking about the studies.'

She was prevented from answering by the approach of the man with the brace.

'Care to dance?' she said instead, grabbing Marlon's hand before he could respond.

Marlon decided he couldn't really refuse but felt sorry for the man, whose disappointed expression was soon lost behind them in the crowd. Then he became aware of Junie's proximity and instantly forgot about anyone else.

'Something strangely familiar about this,' he said in her ear.

'Just don't get too familiar,' she warned.

He decided not to comment further, enjoying the feel of a woman's body despite himself. Junie was a perfect combination of lean and curvy and he had to admit holding her was getting him hot under the collar. And damn, did she smell good after months of only men for company.

'How's your husband?' he asked, trying to remember what he didn't like about her before his senses made him forget.

'Away.'

He watched her face, full lips and high cheekbones lit by shadows and light. 'And your lover?'

She looked hurt as she responded. 'I don't have a lover.'

'Sorry, I should say *lovers*, by the looks of things.'

Junie took a deep breath and he was surprised to see she was almost crying.

'I think this dance is over,' she said, walking away abruptly.

'Wait.' He ran after her and spun her around. 'Look, I'm sorry, all right? It just looked to me like you were trying to make someone jealous or using me to make a point. I don't know.'

'I was making a point,' she admitted, eyes still catching the sparkle of tears, 'and thank you for helping me make it.'

Marlon found himself almost feeling sorry for her and it annoyed him. 'Well, maybe we can make a better point than that.' He grabbed her before he really knew he was doing it, before he could remember he'd had enough of adventures. Maybe because of the dilution in his blood, maybe because of those lean curves, maybe because her face was just so beautiful at that moment, he just couldn't seem to stop the momentum that drew her mouth towards his.

And, oh, what a kiss it was. Her whole body was against him, soft as butter beneath whatever material she had on over that skin, and her mouth had no time to protest as an immediate chemistry erupted between them.

But then she pulled away, shock and outrage crossing those lovely features as she slapped his cheek. And then she was gone and he was left standing there, wondering what the hell was wrong with him that he'd done it. But try as he might, when he lay in his bed that night, Marlon Stone couldn't get to the point of regret. Not when something could fill his restless dreaming aside from planes and bombs and the screams of survivors.

And not when all he could think about was doing it again.

Thirty-three

July 1943
Bordubi Ridge, New Guinea

The mud made the climb almost impossible but such was everyday life here where they pushed their human forms to do superhuman things. Heaving themselves forwards on legs of lead, carrying their packs on corded, aching shoulders. Sleeping with faces exposed to the pouring rain.

Sliding on his boot, Michael caught at a branch to steady himself, kicking off the greasy stuff and wondering if he would ever feel clean again. It was a brief wondering, like when he wondered if he would ever feel full again or if he would ever sleep a whole night without the shakes that came and went from what he guessed was malaria. Or if he would ever feel this war was over – assuming he survived.

Jake gave Michael a glance of understanding, not bothering with words. Dirt and perspiration streaked his face and Michael knew he was reflecting a similar visage. The forest was seeping mud into their every pore, and he was glad they'd said good-bye to Father Patrick several miles back, leaving him to tend the wounded; at least the priest was spared this part of their journey. The part when hell had truly arrived for the Elite.

Being attached to the militia and the commandos had seemed a logical choice when the decision was made, but weeks later it seemed a suicide mission, so hazardous was each and every aspect of this battle. The Japanese fired from invisible positions and the Allies fired back, neither willing to give way and hand the other side the strategic advantage this ridge would give the victor.

Take the ridge and we can take Salamaua. Reminding himself of the basic plan usually reassured Michael. But sometimes it didn't work because sometimes they didn't seem real any more, this invisible enemy. Sometimes he felt the jungle itself was trying to kill him as sniper bullets whizzed past from a screen of continuous green. And then he would feel strangely abandoned and wonder where the bird of paradise had gone.

He didn't have time to further ponder things as they settled in for the scheduled artillery bombardment. Maybe today was the day they would dislodge those stubborn bastards from these hillsides.

The blasts commenced, shaking the ground and deafening them as they waited and watched to see what it would flush out. They didn't have to wait long: soon Cliffy was signalling and they all dropped to a crouch as Michael made his way forwards. Cliffy pointed and Michael saw it too. Movement. Uniforms. The Japanese.

They raised their guns, glimpsing the activity on the opposing ridge as the enemy continued to absorb heavy bombing, when someone was flushed out who they certainly hadn't expected. It was a native man and he was hurling himself down that ridge as fast as Michael had ever seen anyone take such a steep incline. And he was badly exposed.

Michael fired, giving the man cover, and the others did the same, but he had reached a rocky crevice and was stranded now, unable to move as machine guns peppered either side.

'Bloody hell, move 'round,' Michael called and they advanced, trying to take out the Japanese machine gunners.

The native man saw his chance and took off again, this time making it to a bushy copse but his sudden limp told Michael he was hit. And stranded once more.

'Okello,' said a strained voice alongside and Michael turned to see a desperate expression on Ovuru's face.

The Japanese were still firing and Michael pelted bullets back, making a quick decision as Okello looked set to run again, despite his leg.

'Take it,' he told Ovuru, who he'd been teaching to shoot. 'Cover me,' he called, rushing forwards.

'Shit, Mick,' Jake yelled before firing rapidly with the others.

Michael ran, dodging and weaving. Trying to remember to be a snake in long grass. It felt like a million bullets were trying to find him as he launched himself the last few yards towards Okello, heaving the man up and dragging him back.

Pain. Impossible. *Keep running.*

'Arrrgh!' he heard Cliffy yell as he fired his Owen Gun at the enemy with precision.

Michael was straining against a distortion of forest, mud and rocks and it tore, tripped and scraped at him as the pelt of machine guns and artillery filled his ears. *Almost there.*

Then he was on his back on the track and hands were hauling him forwards and the noise seemed white as it deafened his senses.

Then he realised that, somehow, they had made it.

'Okello,' wept Ovuru, pulling his brother into his arms as Semu checked the bullet wound on his leg.

'Ovuru,' Okello mouthed, staring at him in shock. They exchanged a few shouted words before Okello pointed at Michael and said something else.

'Sir,' Ovuru yelled, wiping at his tears.

Okello took Michael's hand and held it against his heaving chest.

'Sir,' he panted then nodded at him with wild eyes. Michael couldn't hear the word above yet another blast but he could read the man's lips as he said, '*Wantok.*'

❧

The radio was scratchy, as per usual, but the news was good. After a ferocious, climactic battle, the Japanese had retreated towards Salamaua at last and, even though the Australians could never really relax with snipers still around, they were in good spirits. Especially after being told they didn't have to advance – they were heading back to Port Moresby for a rest instead. Michael could already feel the warm, clean water from that long awaited shower and wondered if he would ever take such a thing for granted again. Looking at the numerous scratches on his legs and arms, it was just as well. This wasn't a place to invite infections.

Okello was doing well and they would take him to the medics in the morning but not before he entertained them all, it seemed. Propped up against a rock and drinking a cup of tea, he was rather enjoying himself, relating his escapades in a mixture of very broken English, native language and drawings in the dirt.

It seemed Okello had given up being a spy a few weeks ago and had kept himself busy as an assassin instead. His prized stash of collar insignias was proof of how many lives he'd taken, each patch cut from his victim's uniform and each with a story behind it.

'There's no private patches in here, though,' Cliffy observed.

'*Nitōhei,*' Mayflower said, translating 'private' into Japanese.

Okello said something in his language and Semu explained.

'Not important enough.'

'Ha! I'll remember that next time I save your arse from being mowed down by Jap fire!'

They all had a chuckle over that but Michael was a bit disturbed by the sinister collection that Okello was obviously rather proud of.

'That's a lot of killing,' he said, pointing at the pile on the ground.

Okello looked him straight in the eye and found enough English to say, 'Don't deserve live.'

Ovuru put his hand protectively on his brother's shoulder and Michael wondered at the depth of hatred he saw in their faces.

'Japs kill girl...daughter,' Semu explained quietly, nodding at Okello. 'Destroy village.'

'Don't deserve live,' Okello repeated, picking his collection back up and carefully putting it in his bag.

Michael couldn't judge him. Perhaps if he had a daughter himself he'd feel the same way.

That night the dream came again, only this time the log bridge was slippery with mud, not blood, and he was falling into a pit of torn little patches that called out for mercy in Japanese. The flash of crimson came and he woke in a sweat but there was no saviour here, just the black of night and a cold steady rain on a track on those bloody ridges. Where anything beautiful seemed far, far way.

Thirty-four

Z-Day – 5th September 1943
New Guinea

MacArthur was enjoying himself, Marlon observed, watching the man smile for the cameras and pat paratroopers on the back.

'All part of the glorious return,' muttered Major Hamlin in Marlon's ear.

'Long way from the Philippines yet,' he said quietly.

The general was followed by a throng of staff as well as reporters and Marlon frowned in vague recognition at one Australian officer.

'Where do we know him from? The one on the left.'

'Can't say I recognise him,' the major said, looking over.

'Hmm,' Marlon replied.

The man was definitely familiar and not in a good way. When had he ever argued with an Australian? Well, aside from Junie Farthington…wait – that's it! He's Junie's husband. Marlon hadn't liked Ernest that night he'd had to play decoy for Junie at the Trocadero and he wasn't feeling any warmer towards him now as he watched him hover around MacArthur and his staff like a teenage girl trying to get a movie star's autograph. Then the thought crossed his mind that this man slept with the woman who had occupied his fantasies since Sydney and he felt himself disliking him even more.

MacArthur was heading his way and Marlon cleared his thoughts, standing to attention and saluting the general as he passed, thinking there was certainly an air of triumph around the man today. Marlon just hoped they would pull it off.

༺✺༻

'Must be thousands,' Michael said as they watched the paratroopers board the planes.

Jake looked unconvinced. 'Bloody stupid idea, if you ask me.'

'Aw, come on. They wouldn't send that many if they thought they'd all plummet to their deaths.' Wally was grinning as he said it. Jake wasn't afraid of much.

'Need more than a petticoat to save you from gravity,' Jake asserted, looking at the planes with distrust.

'Nah, the Yanks do it all the time,' Cliffy assured him. 'We'll be up and down like a bride's nightie.'

Michael laughed with the others but truth was he wasn't too keen on jumping either. After this well-earned rest they were going to parachute into battle next week to join with the 2/6th commando squadron, a mixture of a few hundred seasoned Australian soldiers. This band, known as the Purple Devils, were well used to reconnaissance and long-range patrolling, something the Elite were getting quite used to themselves. But parachuting was a new skill altogether and the powers that be had decided to give the Elite the practice, just in case they'd need it at some stage further along.

Semu and Ovuru would remain as their carriers and Okello had managed to talk his way into joining them as a scout, but none of the locals would capitulate when Michael tried to encourage them to jump too. 'No, sir,' was the unanimous and emphatic reply. They were currently making their way by foot.

Michael felt the Elite had fit in well with the 2/6th. They were their kind of soldier – brash, daring and a bit unpredictable. They'd already found more than one larrikin among them in Port and Cliffy had been enjoying swapping his fair share of banter.

'Bets on, boys,' said one as he approached. Kieran 'Bevvy' Bolster was one of Cliffy's new mates and had a penchant for booze and betting.

'What's the gig?' Jake asked him, smoking a cigarette and watching the last of the paratroopers file past.

'The generals started it. Seems they've bet each other twenty cases of scotch their division will get to Lae first.'

'Who?'

'Wooten from the 9th and Vasey from the 7th.'

The 7th Division would land in the morning and the 9th had apparently landed on the coast last night so Michael figured either had a chance at it. The Australians would converge at Lae in a pincer movement so the timing would be close anyway. Depending on the weather.

'Windeyer is a brigadier in the 9th,' Mayflower reminded them.

Cliffy turned to him in exasperation. 'What is it with your family and that bloody professor?'

'Lenny says –'

'I think old Len might be a few sandwiches short of the picnic,' Cliffy said, tapping his head for emphasis.

They'd all met Mayflower's big cousin Lenny in Port. Now in his third year of service with the 20th Battalion, the man had talked incessantly about his commander, Windeyer, resulting in a colourful variety of comments, from Cliffy in particular.

'Hey, that's my cousin you're talking about.'

'Runs in the family obviously,' Cliffy said with a wicked grin. 'If brains were dynamite he wouldn't have enough to blow his nose.'

'Don't think you'd be saying that to his face,' Jake said.

'Yeah, that bloke's built –'

'Like a brick shithouse,' Liquorice and Allsorts agreed.

'Actually, I did say it to his noggin but I don't think he got it,' Cliffy replied, ducking as Mayflower threw a stick at him.

'He might be dim but that professor sure ain't,' Bevvy said. 'Don't underestimate him.'

'Even professors can't control the rain,' Michael said, flicking his map. 'That's a lot of men to get across from the beaches. I'm betting the 7th make it first.'

'Nah, y'got rocks in y'head. Think about the ungodly shit the 7th have to get through to make it to Lae,' Jake said.

'Same direction we're going,' Mayflower reminded him. 'Lucky bastards that we are.'

'Imagine trying to get an army up those bloody ridges. They look even worse than Bordubi,' Jake said, nodding at Michael's map. 'I'm backing the 9th.'

'Well, I'm not backing that flippin' professor,' Cliffy said. 'Bloody Len will brag about it till he's ninety! My money's on the 7th.'

Various opinions continued to flow and Bevvy looked pleased with the long list of bets he'd made in his book.

Then they heard the whirr of engines and stood back to watch the show as hundreds of aircraft began to roll forwards and take off. Whatever the outcome, Michael had to admit the Americans knew how to impress. Painted stars shone on steel in the morning sun and they went forth in perfect parade, loaded with men, ammunition and supplies. A heavenly sight to the Allies and sure to be a hellish one to the enemy. He could only imagine how the Japanese would feel when they saw them arrive, covering the sky like a plague of locusts.

'Glad I'm not a Jap on the ground about to see that,' he shouted to Jake.

'Yeah, well they can suffer in their jocks,' Jake returned.

One by one they took to the skies, then they were gone and the Elite wandered back to base.

'Who's up for a drink?' asked Nugget.

'Nah, think I'll stay home with a nice cup of tea,' Michael said, laughing as Cliffy began to sing loudly in response to that suggestion.

'Bollocks! was all the band could play.'

'Bollocks! they played it night and day,' Jake joined in as the others followed suit.

'Bollocks! yes, it was Bollocks! It was Bollocks! Bollocks! You could hear it two hundred miles away.'

Michael found himself singing too, thinking the Elite may have lost their battle innocence but they hadn't lost their sense of humour. Or each other. His father's training had kept them all alive in the jungle, and in his eyes that meant only one thing: so far, they were winning.

❦

Marlon flew in the giant aerial armada, trying to take in its scope: three hundred and two aircraft from eight different airfields; MacArthur himself on one of the B-17s. It was an ambitious plan, and sure to be a spectacular one for the film crew on board.

He watched in fascination as A-20 attack bombers began to peel off and lay down a smoke screen. It spread in a thick blanket, as if to cushion the paratroopers' fall. Then the men spilt out, seventeen hundred white parachutes automatically billowing into domes over the abandoned aerodrome. The sky filled with them, reminding Marlon of a massive bloom of jellyfish he'd seen in Hawaii one day as he flew over Pearl Harbor. Back before any of this mattered.

It was an incredible sight from the air and Marlon had to hand it to MacArthur and his staff: the footage would be invaluable to morale and make Z-Day an event to remember.

But he couldn't help but consider just what would happen once the white domes disappeared below those smokey blankets; wondering just what this war had in store for them on the ground.

'Just put it on,' Michael coaxed.

'Expecting us to jump out of a plane. It isn't natural,' Jake muttered, his hands shaking. Liquorice and Allsorts were looking slightly green too and Mayflower had already thrown up this morning. Cliffy had put a bet on it happening. For a so-called elite band of soldiers they weren't looking too flash today, Michael observed.

'What if it doesn't open?' Liquorice asked, eyes round.

'You impersonate jam,' Cliffy said cheerfully.

'Stop enjoying this,' Michael muttered, hiding a grin as he finally got the parachute onto Jake's shoulders.

Jake looked over at the plane, still protesting. 'That thing has definitely seen better days.'

'At least the radio works,' said an American voice and they turned to see a certain captain at the shed door. 'You look familiar for some reason.'

'Must be the uniform,' Michael suggested and he and Marlon clasped hands with a laugh. 'Good to see you, sir.'

'Likewise, Riley. Ready to fly, monkeys?' he called out to them all.

'They can't wait, sir,' Michael lied.

'Well, we've had some good news. The 7th and the 9th have taken Lae.'

'Who got there first?' asked Cliffy and Jake in unison.

'The 7th.'

'You beauty!' crowed Cliffy, dancing about while Jake muttered something about this not being his bloody day.

'Anyone would think some illegal betting has been going on,' Marlon observed dryly.

'Course not, sir. Just feeling very patriotic today,' Cliffy assured him.

'I'm sure. Now, what's all this doubt about the safety of my plane? I've even let young Harris here give her a makeover,' Marlon said, leading them outside and pointing at the painting of a sea princess that wrapped around the word *Liwa*.

'Could have given her a few more assets, sir,' Cliffy suggested, and Michael noticed that the woman's body was indeed obscured by the word.

'That's my grandmother you're talking about. Come on, get on board. I haven't got all day to discuss women's bodies with Australians – I'm pretty sure you've got about a hundred sayings that will scar me for life. Mind Harris there. He's going to give you a few pointers. You travelling all right there, Loadsman?'

'No, sir. Not fond of heights, sir,' Jake admitted.

'Just think about your wife back home,' Cliffy suggested. 'Name's Katie, Captain. Good sort, unlike his last girlfriend. Now she had legs on her like a pool table...'

By the time Marty Harris had given the instructions several times over, Michael felt pretty sick himself. It was cold with the doorway open and the idea of willingly jumping out of it seemed completely ridiculous.

'What if the 'chute doesn't open?' Allsorts asked, echoing his brother.

'You impersonate a peanut butter and jelly sandwich,' Harris responded and Cliffy clapped him on the back.

'You know, I'm beginning to rather like you.'

Marlon turned from the cockpit and yelled over the engine, 'Just heard from HQ. The 2/6th are all landed now and waiting for you. Up you get.'

'Don't see why they got out of jumping,' Mayflower complained, standing.

'Just add this to y'list of daring tales to impress the sheilas,' Cliffy suggested.

'They said it was a rough landing, if that makes you feel any better. Markham Valley airstrip's got more craters than the moon,' Marlon shouted.

'No, sir, that doesn't make me feel any better,' Mayflower said. 'We still have to get back out eventually.'

'One adventure at a time, buddy. Right, fellas, time to go. My shout when you get back.'

'See you on the other side, Captain,' Michael said, sending Marlon a salute and as much of a smile as he could muster.

'Nothing to it,' Marlon called back, grinning. 'Just click your heels and think about home.'

They lined up. Michael had volunteered to go first and looking at the empty miles of air, he was regretting his gallantry. Then Harris lifted his arm.

'Go!'

It took some doing for Michael to force his suddenly weak and heavy legs out the door and into nothingness but he did it, wanting to reassure the men. Then there was a moment of pure shock as he hurtled down before the parachute opened automatically and jerked him to safety. Breathing a very deep sigh of relief, he looked up to watch as each man's parachute also opened successfully, relaxing as he counted eleven white domes. Then he looked around him and felt a wave of exhilaration, the tension evaporating.

It was so beautiful. They were sailing with the clouds, like eagles. Far above people and conflict and war. Up here there was only silence, the world below just an artist's palette, a blur of colours; inviting, soft. More like heaven than earth. No-one could get to him here, order him to do things, make him order others. Force him to shoot, climb, outwit the enemy, save lives. Take lives. Leave his country, go to war. Watch the love of his life sell herself to an undeserving man. It was a stolen slice of unexpected reprieve, what Father Patrick would term a conversation with God. What Michael just considered peaceful.

Maybe this was what death was like, before you landed in the afterlife, he mused, wishing he could hold onto the feeling.

But earth was drawing close once more, and humanity with it. Shells sounded in the distance and men crawled across that beautiful palette like ants – killer ants about to invade the enemy's nests. It seemed mankind was intent on painting hell down here instead.

That stolen peace drifted away as his feet hit the ground maybe to find him again one day. But as he watched a truck filled with ammo thunder by, he couldn't help but feel that day was a very long way off.

Thirty-five

September 1943
Sydney, New South Wales, Australia

The azaleas were so thick their pink petals obscured the bush's leaves but Junie barely noticed them as she hurriedly gathered Francesca out of her new car and ran into the Rileys' house. She was late from studying too long at the library and hoped the girls wouldn't be disappointed with her, especially as they had gone to so much trouble for her daughter's first birthday party.

Junie knocked on the door and it was thrown open almost immediately by a very excited Katie.

'She's here!' she exclaimed happily to the room, grabbing Francesca and placing her on her hip before Junie had even walked in.

'Oh, isn't she looking lovely! Hello, Junie, how are you dear?' said Mrs Riley, kissing her cheek and smiling at Francesca. The baby smiled back and Junie thought the resemblance to Michael was so obvious she almost wanted to take her and head back home. How she hated this part of the ruse – denying her baby's grandparents the right to know this was their beloved son's child.

At least Beryl and Dorn knew Francesca was their niece and they held her chubby hands and cooed over her with the others, taking turns to be in raptures over her little outfit and fine golden curls.

'Come on, you lot, stop smothering her and give me a proper look,' ordered Rory as he sat down in his chair and patted his knee. The baby was duly handed over and he studied her closely. 'Her hair is so fair,' he remarked, patting it awkwardly with his large hand. 'Maybe she takes after your mother.'

'As long as she doesn't take after Ernest's mother, that's the main thing,' Katie said.

'Katie!' Mavis scolded, but she was hiding a chuckle.

Francesca kicked her dimpled legs and laughed her adorable baby laugh, grabbing Rory's nose.

'She's a beaut,' he declared with a grin, reclaiming his nose before handing her to Katie. 'Better give her back before she cries.'

But she didn't cry. Francesca spent the afternoon charming everyone with her sunny nature and Junie couldn't help but feel very proud of her daughter as she watched her interact with these much-loved people from home. Her true family.

She wished she had organised her parents to have attended this rather than the Farthingtons' official party, although there was sure to be plenty of entertainment on offer there too. Constance was coordinating what appeared to be some kind of baby debutante ball, knowing full well Eliza would be there with her baby girl, Marigold. Eliza was predicting their daughters would be 'frothed up like meringues' by the time Constance and Jane were done, calling it 'the society Nana duel of the season'.

'Here,' whispered Katie, tipping a little brandy in Junie's teacup and they giggled as they went into the garden and sipped the warm concoction.

'What are we drinking to now?'

'Tea?' Katie suggested.

Junie laughed. 'How about babies?'

Katie's smile fell away and Junie mentally berated herself.

'I'm sorry.'

'No, no, don't be. Happens all the time, doesn't it? Anyway, we can enjoy trying again.'

Junie nodded, wishing Katie's pregnancy hadn't come to such a sad, abrupt ending just before Easter.

'Any news about the boys?' She braced herself for any details about Michael as Katie shared the latest from Jake's letters.

'So it doesn't look as if they'll be out of New Guinea any time soon,' Katie finished. 'I thought he might get some leave when they went to Port Moresby, but no such luck.'

'Maybe he'll be home by Christmas,' Junie said.

'Here's hoping,' Katie said thoughtfully. They relaxed into silence as each sipped on their tea, thoughts of war hanging between them. The sweet scent of jasmine reached them from the fence and Junie tried to imagine the scenery where the men were now. This serene suburban garden seemed a universe away from the wild terrain the boys would likely be struggling through.

'I wish I could walk into a magic wardrobe, you know, like that one you used to read to me about. With the lion,' Katie said.

'*The Lion, the Witch and the Wardrobe*. I loved that book,' Junie said, smiling.

'That's it – with the secret passage to that other world.'

'Narnia.'

'Only when I go through it's always to where Jake is, you know? So I can talk to him whenever I want.'

'And what would you say?'

Katie considered for a moment. '"Stop buggerising about playing war and get yourself home to the cheese and kisses. Wifey needs a baby."'

'And you need someone to appreciate your lovely turns of phrase.'

'Exactly! "So get in that wardrobe, Jakey, and don't let the door hit you on the arse on the way out!"'

Junie laughed, spilling her tea. 'Oh, you really are too funny!'

'I'm here all week,' Katie said with a bow and a grin.

'Thank God for that. I think I've become a horrible bore with all this study. I've missed your corruption.'

'Some may say corrupt, others delightfully diverting,' Katie said in a posh voice.

'I just wish you would come to the Farthington party.'

'Oh, you'll have Eliza. You won't need the likes of me.'

Something in Katie's continued posh tone made Junie change the subject. 'She's been very spoilt today. It's lovely of the Rileys to do this.'

'Imagine if they knew the truth,' Katie said and Junie looked at the ground, suddenly quiet. The breeze was picking up and Katie turned to her, pushing her hair back as it whipped at her face. 'I know you can't say anything to them, of course, but I've been thinking…well, sooner or later someone is going to let it slip to Michael that you have a baby. Jake's the only one that knows over there and he won't say anything, and the girls and his parents are keeping it from him too – I know that much. But he will find out at some point Junie, you know that. Imagine how he's going to feel.'

'Might be worse if he knows the whole truth,' Junie whispered, shrugging.

'Maybe, but I think you should tell him. I know, I know,' she said, raising her hand. 'I've no right to say it. But you're my best friend, so I'm saying it anyway. Every day we hear more and more of our fellas are dying up there. This isn't something he should go to his grave never having known. God forbid.'

'God forbid,' Junie echoed automatically.

'It's a basic human right, surely? To know you're a parent.' She turned away, tears in her eyes. 'I just think he has that right too.'

Junie said nothing but moved her hand to squeeze Katie's and they stood silently until Mavis's voice called them in for birthday cake.

Watching her daughter's face illuminated by the candles as her unwitting grandparents looked on, something almost painful pulled in Junie's chest and she knew then that Katie was right. Just because she hadn't got to him in time the day the train pulled away didn't mean she should never try to tell him again. It wasn't a matter of her choosing either way any more. He had a basic right to know, it was true.

Later that night, Junie walked to the end of the street, her daughter asleep in the pram, and kissed the letter goodbye that said the words at last.

She knew she was doing what was right. This was all about equality, in the end.

And in her heart that really just came down to one thing: upholding her own common law.

Thirty-six

19th September 1943
Kaiapit, New Guinea

The water crossings had been treacherous, as per their expectations, but it had taken less than forty-eight hours to get to the cluster of three villages that constituted Kaiapit and Michael was grateful for that much. What he wasn't grateful for was the large number of Japanese they'd encountered and he wondered at the inaccurate estimation of enemy presence.

Captain Gordon King, their young commander, had ordered a three-pronged assault and they'd surprised the enemy with their bold aggression, resulting in dozens dead on the Japanese side to one Australian. The remainder had fled to the next village and Michael's squad was settling in for the night while Captain King sent Jaffa to ask for more ammo. Meanwhile Nige and Wally were trying to get the radio working, which was proving impossible, as usual.

'Nice night for a war,' Jake remarked, handing him a cuppa. He looked spent, as did most of the men. Despite their break in Port Moresby, the constant exhaustion was already back and their combat faces had returned, pallid from sweat and strain.

'Goddam animals,' Cliffy exploded, landing next to them.

'What now?' Michael asked.

'Japs set up a booby trap and two of the fuzzy wuzzies have been blown up turning over a corpse. Sick bastards. Semu knows one of them. He's pretty cut up.'

'Where is he?'

'Burying them.'

A Japanese voice could be heard nearby and it was silenced by the sound of an Owen Gun.

'Don't think there'll be much mercy now,' Michael said. 'Whatever was left of it.'

'Okello's right: don't deserve live,' Cliffy said savagely. 'Animals.'

But the sound of that merciless gunshot haunted Michael that night as they tried to rest before the next assault, and images of crimson feathers visited his dreams, each one wet with blood.

༺ঊঞঞ৯༻

It's always darkest before the dawn, Michael reminded himself, and it was very dark right now, in more ways than one. There'd been two counterattacks by the Japanese, both repelled by the Aussies, but they were now nearly out of ammo and the enemy seemed to have expanded. Captain King had turned out to be a courageous leader, moving among them and taking the front, despite an injured leg, but the enemy were attacking again and it was stronger this time. King had ordered bayonets to be drawn if need be and Michael prayed it wouldn't get that critical. Swords against bullets; a few hundred against possible thousands.

They've got nothing until they've actually got you. Until then you are free men. Fight for it, lads. Michael drew on his father's words from what seemed like years ago, spreading that strength out to the men.

'Conserve it,' he shouted, and they took to responding to the firepower sporadically, choosing carefully, not wasting a single shot.

Then King ordered a counterattack. So they ran and they shot and they lay like snakes in the grass until the blades on their guns were all they had left. Then Liquorice rose in the morning light and sprinted, bayonet forwards as a Japanese soldier pointed his gun at Allsorts who'd been suddenly exposed by a falling piece of wall.

'Get down!' Michael shouted.

It was about then that the shots were fired, Michael supposed later. Who could tell in the thick wall of sound? But it must have been exactly then. At the precise second he'd yelled his warning in the orange light of that dreaded dawn.

The brothers finished their lives as they'd lived them – together. Identical deaths at the end of bullets. Identical moments of falling to the earth. Identically, unbelievably gone.

'No,' Michael screamed, and it ripped at his throat.

And just then the Japanese began to retreat; the Australians had their victory. But Michael knew they were no longer really winning.

Not the Elite, anyway.

Liquorice and Allsorts were buried side by side in identical graves and Michael wanted to say a few words but they wouldn't seem to come. Cliffy seemed to understand and he sang instead, slowly.

'Bollocks! was all the band could play, Bollocks! they played it night and day.'

The jungle watched them through the green wall that was draining them still, now with two of their brothers forever in its grip.

'Yes, it was Bollocks!'

The drone of a plane sounded far above and Michael thought about the peace that floated above them. Just out of reach.

'You could hear it two hundred miles away.'

They were walking back from the burial when they heard it, a scraping sound. Something was moving away and it was on foot. Michael held up his hand and they took to the sides of the track. Placing his finger on his lips he signalled to Jake to check for tracks and he soon found one.

'One man. Injured – he's limping,' he whispered to Michael.

Michael pointed at Cliffy and Nugget and they took off silently to find him. Just let any Jap mess with the Elite today.

'Found him hiding behind a rock like a bloody coward,' Cliffy said, shoving the Japanese man forwards. 'Where's y'men, y'piece of chicken shit?'

Michael looked at the captain's insignia on his sleeve and sighed, shouldering his gun. 'Better bring him back with us. They'll want to interrogate him.'

The others didn't move.

'Thought our job was to kill him, not take him prisoner,' Cliffy said.

'He's an officer – he might know stuff,' Michael reminded them. 'Bring him along.'

Cliffy looked disgusted but did as he was asked. Reluctantly.

'Make sure you have his hands well tied,' Jake warned as Cliffy shoved the prisoner in front. 'Who knows what these suicidal bastards are capable of.'

'Won't give me much,' Mayflower said. 'Just some guff about how we are all damned to hell and have no honour.'

The Japanese captain rattled off some more and Mayflower translated. 'He says the fruits of our labour will come to nothing. Heaven will bear the righteous forwards, or something like that.'

Major Jim Horsely ran an exhausted hand over his face, flicking the perspiration away. Michael figured he was probably thinking he had enough to worry about, getting this mosquito-ridden village operational as an air base, without half-crazed Japanese officers showing up.

'HQ, sir,' Horsely's assistant said, handing him the line, and a minute later the problem had been taken off the major's hands.

'Corporal Riley, is it?' he addressed Michael.

'Yes, sir.'

'Seems they need a small force of infiltrators for the coastal push north. Get back to Port for briefing and you can move up to Windeyer.'

'Yes, sir,' Michael replied, wondering what Cliffy would have to say about that. 'And what do we, er, do with him?'

The major shrugged as the Japanese captain glared at them. 'Whatever you want. Take him with you, or not. But you didn't hear that from me.'

ॐ

'Gonna be a rough take off,' Harris warned. 'I nearly lost it on landing.'

'Just get us back,' Michael said, shoving food into his pack.

'But, sir, the weather –'

'What do you mean he's coming with us?' Cliffy demanded, approaching Michael in furious strides.

'Exactly what I said,' Michael responded, throwing in a few more supplies.

'He's a bloody lunatic. Look at him,' Cliffy said, pointing at the Japanese captain, who was muttering in fanatical undertones as he waited nearby.

'He's a danger, Mick,' Jake agreed. 'Just shoot him and be done with it. I'll do it, if you like.'

Michael turned and looked at the Japanese officer, who sent him a look of pure loathing in return. But his wrists were bleeding where the ropes cut against him and his bones showed above his collar. Filthy, emaciated, pathetic. Mad, certainly. But still an unarmed man.

'I'm not committing cold-blooded murder,' Michael said firmly. 'He's coming with us to Port. Let them deal with him.'

Cliffy lifted his gun and pointed it at the man. 'I'm dealing with it now.'

The prisoner ceased his muttering.

'Put the gun down, Cliffy.'

'Filthy bastard. He's probably the one who gave the order to booby trap one of his own dead men,' Cliffy said, a manic edge to his voice.

Michael slowly dropped the bag he was holding. 'You don't know that.'

'Just how many of us have you killed, eh?' Cliffy whispered as the Japanese captain stared back, fear and hatred running between them.

'This isn't your decision to make. I said put it down,' Michael ordered, moving to stand between them.

Cliffy blinked, staring at Michael, and his arm shook as he lowered his weapon away from his friend's heart. Looking past Michael to the prisoner, he spat on the ground before walking away. 'Don't deserve live.'

꧁꧂

The tension was palpable as they said goodbye to their native friends and made their way towards the plane, and it wasn't just because of the prisoner.

'How are we supposed to get back in that?' Jake said, staring at the almost green cloud front to the east.

'It's not very far,' Michael said, hauling himself on board. Smitty shoved the Japanese officer ahead of him. The man stumbled with his bound hands, unable to balance properly, and Michael considered having him untied but knew the men were angry enough as it was.

'I grabbed these from the hangar just in case,' Harris said, throwing a load of parachutes on board. That did little to reassure anyone and Harris said nothing else as they took off, the whirr of the engine droning against the growing rumble on the horizon.

About ten minutes later, Michael felt apprehension turn to fear.

'Like looking at the gates of hell,' said Jake in his ear as he crouched next to him near the cockpit. And so it was. The distant storm was now a massive cliff of flashing plumes, roiling and thundering alongside their thumbnail of a plane.

'Can we turn back?' Michael asked Harris, wishing he hadn't been so distracted when they boarded. He should have taken more notice.

'No. It's right in the way. I'll have to try to outrun it. Hold on.'

Jake yelled to the others to grab on and the plane veered hard, the terrifying storm fast on their heels, and the Japanese prisoner fell across the floor. Nugget shoved him back, holding his shirt to stop him from breaking his neck.

Michael noted the action but was too busy clinging on and trying not to be sick to comment. It was a race, and he felt the sweat pour down his back as Harris flew the plane as fast as it would go, the angry mass roaring behind them. Minutes passed, stretching into a long, tense hour as the storm grew ever closer. Harris veered again and again, trying to navigate a way to avoid it but it was no use.

'We're going to hit,' Harris shouted, white knuckled, shirt soaked from his efforts.

'Grab everything you've got. Nugget, just strap him down somehow,' yelled Michael. Nugget grabbed a parachute strap and tied the prisoner to the rail as the storm-front arrived, flashing white then black as the wind hit with force. Then it truly was hell.

Michael lost track of any sense of time as they were buffeted and thrown, the plane now a plaything for the monstrous storm as it toyed with them like a cat with a mouse. Anything not tied down became a missile and they grabbed and slid and threw arms across their faces, and all the while the lightning sporadically illumi-nated the turmoil like a demonic photographer. Michael couldn't see anything through the rain-splattered windscreen, except how blinding the flashes were up close. Nothing could survive this, he thought with a painfully beating heart as they entered a green-grey light that eclipsed all terror so far.

'Holy shit!' Cliffy yelled in pain, blood pouring down his face.

'Hold on! Just hold on!' screamed Michael.

But the plane was sideways, then upside down. Harris fell unconscious as his head hit the window and Michael lunged forwards to grip the controls, trying to recall anything he had observed about flying but guessing his only hope was to take his own advice and hold on, whatever that meant at this point. Grav-ity seemed non-existent and every direction seemed fleeting and unnatural.

His entire physical body was consumed with survival and Michael fought to remember his training, going back to that time in the cave, long ago. Go inside, he reminded himself. Find some-where safe. And so he retreated into that place in his mind where all the things that had ever offered him comfort resided. A girl walking out of the water on a clear summer's day. His father's pride when he was promoted to corporal. Cliffy and Jake running with him down a back street in Parramatta, laughing fit to burst.

A stolen piece of wonder when he floated down to the earth. Junie in a crimson crown. A single, beautiful bird of paradise.

It calmed him and he gripped the controls firmly as the storm became a fight between himself and fate; atonement for whatever choices he'd made up until now. This hell was the hell of losing the woman he loved. The hell of watching a brave captain die near a log bridge. The hell of twin souls falling to the earth. He'd survived everything life had thrown at him and he would survive this too. Not just for his own sake, but for the sake of every man in this plane. Even the bloody Jap.

He shut his eyes, the brilliant white flashes burning even that comfort red, and he thought of those crimson feathers, holding onto them as he opened his lids once more.

'Hold on,' he yelled again. It can't be forever.

Hell continued to assail them but Michael met it head on and slowly, eventually the flashes dimmed, the rain eased, the darkness became a paler grey. Then, incredibly, the blue sky returned and they were no longer creatures trapped in hell. Instead, they seemed forgiven as they sailed out into majestic cloud castles, orange and soft. Like heaven.

Harris came to and Michael checked the gash on his head.

'You all right?'

Harris nodded, looking dazedly at the dashboard. 'How long was I out?'

Michael looked at his watch. They'd been in the sky for less than two hours but it seemed like days.

'Shit,' Harris said before Michael could answer. 'We're gonna run out of fuel. Must have a leak.' He held his head as he began to switch the controls.

'Mick,' called Jake.

Michael went to the back to check on the others. Nugget had a bleeding shoulder, Cliffy a nasty cut on his cheek and Wally seemed concussed, but it was the Japanese officer who was the worst off. His already injured leg was now mutilated where it'd been smashed and blood covered most of his face.

'There's nowhere to land. We're gonna have to jump,' Harris yelled from the front.

'Where are we?' Michael moved to the cockpit and stared out.

'Not sure. West. It's pretty mountainous.'

'The whole bloody country is mountainous.'

'Yeah, but this is really remote. I think we're off the charts.'

'Not the best place to jump out of a plane,' Michael said, looking down at the impossible terrain.

'Better than crashing in one.'

'True.'

Michael turned to the back, making his decision. 'Righto, fellas, we'll have to get ready to jump. Put on your chutes. Nugget, put one on the prisoner and untie his hands.'

'What?' shouted Cliffy.

'Y'gotta be kidding me,' Jake said.

'Pushing a man out of a plane is no better than shooting him,' Michael said. 'Do it.'

No-one moved until Mayflower finally broke the standoff. 'Mick's right. There's a difference between killing and straight-out murder.' He walked over and began to untie the prisoner as the others watched.

'He'll kill you as soon as look at you,' Cliffy said.

'*C'est la vie.*'

Parachutes were put on but there was a mutinous silence behind the whine of the engine.

'Ready?' Michael called, standing at the open door. Mayflower moved forwards but no-one else would look him in the eye.

Michael paused. He wasn't jumping like this.

'Look, I'm sorry you don't agree with me – I'm just doing what I think is right,' he shouted. 'It just isn't who we are, is it? If we… if we lose our mercy then we may as well lose the war.'

'What mercy have they shown our boys?' Cliffy yelled back and there were nods of agreement.

'That's not the point. The point is we are fighting for what *we* believe in and last time I checked, Australians didn't believe cold-blooded murder was acceptable. Not the Australia I'm fighting for.'

No-one spoke and he tried again. 'One day you'll have to live with this decision.'

'So will you,' Cliffy warned, and they exchanged a long stare.

'I'm your leader, for better or worse, and I'm choosing not to kill an unarmed man.'

The whine of the engine increased as they began to lose altitude and he looked around at these men, his Elite brothers, reading their faces. Pulling rank was only alienating him further. Then for some reason he remembered Father Patrick's words – that perhaps moments like this were a test from God. A challenge of sorts. So he challenged them instead.

'Well, I'm going to jump out of a leaking plane into uncharted mountains with a wounded Japanese prisoner who hates our guts. Because I'm a crazy bloody Australian.' The wind tore at him as he backed up to jump. 'Who's with me?'

There was still silence, save the engine's wail, then Jake stepped forwards.

'I am, mate,' he said, pulling his parachute up higher in readiness. 'I'd follow you anywhere, stupid bastard that I am.'

'Me too,' said Mayflower, and one by one the squad gave him their support until it was just Cliffy left.

'You owe me beer for life,' he said.

That made Michael grin and he turned to jump, satisfied now his mates were with him, but he was stalled by a Japanese voice as the great open space spread before him.

'*Omae wa ikiru kachi wa nai!*'

'What did he say?' Mick cried out, but he never got his response.

Because with his hands now free the Japanese officer had reached into his pocket and was holding a grenade in one hand, its pin in the other. A booby trap not one of them had thought to check for.

As the plane exploded above the wilds of New Guinea, those Japanese words were the last the Elite would hear.

Omae wa ikiru kachi wa nai!

You don't deserve to live.

꧁꧂

But back home loved ones would weep in inconsolable grief as the opposite truth consumed them: The Elite did deserve to live – they deserved a whole life, these young men of war.

Katie wept for her Jake, who would never again laugh at her cussing or kiss her dimples. Or be able to give her the baby she so longed for as she faced life alone. Just another war widow, not yet twenty-one.

Mavis wept for the loss of her second, last remaining son, chain smoking in the yard as she listened for currawongs. She wore no coat, welcoming the cold, as she turned her back on God, once and for all.

Rory wept, tears soaking his shirt unchecked, because despite all he had done, in the end he couldn't save those brave young men. And he couldn't save their leader, his only boy.

And Beryl and Dorn wept for the loss of their friends, and for Michael. They had no brothers left to pray for now. Their parents no sons to welcome home from war.

But Junie sat dry-eyed, beyond the comfort of tears, filling her head with knowledge and facts about law. She stuffed them in until the rabbit in her mind was buried, unable to run and remind her again. Then she poured wine down the tunnels, just to make sure.

Because there was one fact she didn't want finding its way out – but it wouldn't stay buried, despite the study and wine. A fact so terrible it blanked out all others and filled her heart with a pain so cruel she could barely draw breath. To believe it meant there was nothing to hope for, nothing to dream about.

Nothing that mattered.

She took to walking on the beach, looking across the sea to where he should still be. But without him under that same sun, even the great southern lady was no comfort any more.

Not since the fact arrived that wouldn't stay buried.

Not since God took her Michael away.

Part Five

Thirty-seven

'Mrs June Farthington. Honours.'

She walked across the stage and accepted her degree to the enthusiastic applause of her supporters, trying to ignore her daughter calling out, 'That's my mum!'

'Mr Bartholomew Frewe.'

Bartholomew didn't receive honours but Junie was pretty sure he felt honoured enough, based on the look he sent his pregnant wife, Dorn. She held up their baby boy to wave at him and clap his little hands.

One by one they came, only about two-thirds of those who had started, and Junie wondered what had become of those who'd dropped out. She'd heard Brian Chester – the smirker, as she always thought of him – was working in a bank and hoping to be manager someday, although so far he hadn't made it past clerk. Bartholomew had particularly enjoyed relaying that piece of information.

The great hall was suitably magnificent on this sunny autumn day and she felt the weight of the paper in her fingers with deep gratitude. God had taken many things from her but He hadn't taken this and, for the first time in many years, she felt an old emotion move through her. Not pride, so much – her daughter gave her plenty of that – it was a different feeling, more like satisfaction.

They were all waiting for her outside and gave a mighty cheer as she approached in her cap and gown.

'Photos, photos!' called Katie happily and they posed. One with Ernest and Frankie (her daughter had long ago chosen the nickname for herself), one with her parents and brothers, one with the girls and one with Bartholomew and Harry, her long-standing uni chums. And one with Digger, of course, although he didn't like wearing the mortarboard. Eliza hadn't come at the last minute, something to do with a headache, she'd said on the phone, and Frankie was getting bored without Marigold to amuse her.

'Play with Stevie,' Junie suggested and Frankie immediately went over and began chatting to her little friend. Steven David Michael Frewe was besotted with his animated older cousin – even though he had no idea they were related – and began to laugh loudly as Frankie pulled faces and did cartwheels to amuse him.

'Francesca, really,' Lily scolded, trying to stop her granddaughter while her doting uncles laughed. Archie had two boys and Bill's wife was still expecting their first so the only girl in the family had them all wrapped around her bossy little finger.

'Now just you stop laughing,' Frankie said to Stevie, hands on hips, then immediately imitated a gorilla as soon as he did.

'Hahaha!' laughed Stevie, rolling back in his stroller as Digger joined in with a happy flurry of barking.

'Nonsense, Junie would be delighted,' Junie heard Ernest say as he walked towards her with Cecil Hayman.

'Look who I found watching his nephew graduate.'

'Welcome home, Cecil,' Junie said, trying to be polite as always. She knew the Haymans had recently returned from New

Guinea where Cecil had been the acting Australian ambassador. Eliza had said she could only imagine how much Eugenie would have to say about the weather there when the next dinner party rolled around, vowing to stand outside instead, rain, hail or shine.

'Thank you muchly, and I believe congratulations are in order, Mrs Farthington,' Cecil said in what she supposed he thought a charming manner, but as usual his kiss on the cheek lingered and she drew back her hand as soon as she could.

'Cecil and Eugenie have graciously accepted a dinner invitation for tomorrow night. I've promised them one of your finest roasts.'

'Oh dear, I'm afraid I will have to lift my game after all this study,' Junie replied, wondering if she could talk Eliza into coming or if she would make good her threat and stand outside in the garden.

'After the sub-standard roasts the natives had on offer up north, I'm sure it will be a meal fit for a king.'

Junie sobered as his words grated with their racist undertones.

'Junie! Class photo time,' called Harry and she excused herself gladly to join the others.

'You know, I really have to wonder if you did the degree part time just to graduate with us,' Junie teased him as they took their spot.

'Of course I did. Can't have the prettiest girl in Sydney University throw her cap in the air without the most dashing man on campus by her side.'

Junie patted his arm, glad to know he was only joking these days as his fiancée smiled at him from the crowd. Then they really did have that wonderful moment at last, throwing their caps high to the enthusiastic applause of their friends and family.

'I seem to remember you did that once before. Some hideous yellow creation as I recall,' Harry said.

'I'll have you know it was the height of fashion at the time.'

'Here's hoping you have better taste in law firms than fashion.'

Junie flicked some grass off her cap as they retrieved them. 'They're not exactly beating down my door.'

'Try one of the trendier firms. They may even find a place for your hat.'

꧁꧂

She was washing the dishes when he found her although she was slopping quite a lot of water on the ground.

'You're upset.'

'Of course I'm upset.' She paused to finish her drink, glaring at him.

'Junie, there's no question of me turning it down. It's a perfect opportunity. Think of what it means in terms of my career.'

'I'm not raising Frankie in the bloody jungle.'

There was a pause as the sound of Cecil's car driving away reached their kitchen and she slammed her drink down, fuming at the ambush that had taken place over dinner.

'Eliza says she can stay with Marigold at Queenwood. She's going there anyway, why not board?'

'She's only six years old!'

'Almost seven. Besides, it's only for two years and you'll be able to travel home every school holidays and Mother will be here –'

'That's hardly a selling point.'

Ernest ignored that, pushing what he knew she'd consider *was* a good selling point. 'Marigold loves boarding and you know Frankie has been begging to be allowed to be with her.' That much was true. Frankie was obsessed with Marigold's boarding life, which she seemed to think sounded just like one of Enid Blyton's novels, something else she was obsessed with – she was an early and avid reader, just like her mother.

'I won't allow it.'

Ernest grew angry then. 'You do not get to allow or disallow anything. We are going and that's final.'

She poured herself another wine. 'You've known this for weeks, haven't you? Plotting away with that Cecil…'

'You're drunk,' he said with disgust.

'So sue me,' she said.

'I *can* sue you and I will if you ever try to take matters in your own hands. Don't forget what you signed before we got married.'

'That doesn't mean you *own* me! Or my child.'

He grabbed her arm then, squeezing hard. 'Yes I bloody do, Junie, and you'll do well to remember it. We are leaving for Port Moresby on the twenty-fifth and Frankie will stay here and board with Marigold. Don't try to fight me on this, because you will not win.'

'Let go of me.'

He shoved her away. 'An ambassadorship is not something you turn down, Junie. Sort it out with the school.'

'Darling, you simply have to let her stay. It's paradise for little girls – look at them.'

Marigold and Frankie were running around the dorm and jumping on beds and Junie had to admit the entire place was very luxurious. She was impressed with the staff too, despite herself.

'But the idea of sending her to boarding school…'

'My daughter's at boarding school and I live in the same city. I actually don't know anyone who keeps their child at home.'

Junie was silent at that piece of information. In this set that was true.

'You know she will absolutely love it. It's you that you're really worried about. You're worried you'll miss her but, honestly, they have so many holidays…'

'I will miss her. I'll miss her every moment.'

'No, you won't, because you're going to have some company.'

'What do you mean?'

'Miles has been given a transfer.'

'To where?'

'Where do you think?'

Junie stared at her. 'Port Moresby? But you can't be serious.'

'District Commissioner, no less. Quite an achievement for a brainless man, but there you go.'

'But – but surely you don't want to go?'

'Actually, I think it might be a bit of fun – I know a few ex-pats who live up there. Anyway, God knows Sydney would be beyond ghastly with only Eugenie for company. And it's just for two years.'

'I suppose…'

'We can host marvellous dinner parties and go on tropical adventures.'

'You really think we should do this?'

'Darling, we *are* doing this. Now let's get these girls to the park before they destroy the place. Nanny said she'll watch them. I want to take you to lunch so we can start scheming.'

Junie called their daughters over and they descended the stairs, the girls chatting and running ahead.

'But what about my degree? I wanted to start on my career after all that work.'

'If I know you, you'll find plenty of hard-luck stories to occupy that legal brain of yours when we get there. I just hope you'll have enough time to play with me.' Eliza turned with a devilish grin. 'I wonder if they have any elephants in New Guinea?'

'You must be kidding. *Really*. You are, aren't you?' Beryl said.

'No, we're going on the twenty-fifth. It's all booked and organised,' Junie replied, trying to sound happy about it.

'You mean to tell me you're putting a *six-year-old child* into boarding school? I don't believe it,' Katie said, aghast.

'All our friends do it. It's quite the norm.'

The others gaped at her, but Katie exploded. 'Are you listening to yourself? My God, who the hell are you these days?'

'Katie...' said Dorn.

'No, she needs to hear it. It's getting beyond a joke.'

'What is?' Junie said, meeting her glare.

'The way you behave these days! You're turning into a – a bloody snob!'

Junie picked at her napkin, trying to hold her voice steady. 'I did have reservations but it's important Ernest takes this role for his career. You can't turn down an ambassadorship.'

'Of course you can! And since when do you care what Ernest wants?'

'Since he is my child's legal father.'

'Yes, *legal*.'

There was a very uncomfortable pause as Junie bit her lip against the pain of those words. 'I didn't have the luxury of being married to the man I loved. He's the only father she's got now.'

'He's a father who wants to put his child in boarding school when she's just a baby,' Beryl pointed out gently. 'That's not being a very good parent.'

'You don't understand the world I live in. *Everyone* boards their children. She'll be with Marigold and girls who will become her lifelong friends. That's how it operates, don't you see? We will be setting her up for an incredible life. Ernest might end up prime minister at the rate he's rising – don't you think she would want that?'

'I think she will want her mother,' Dorn said.

'Well, I can't change that fact!' Junie said, her voice breaking.

'What a load of crap,' said Katie. 'You just care about social climbing more.'

Junie was shaking now. 'How can you say that to me?'

'Because you need to stop this before it's too late!'

'I can't. Anyway, Eliza has organised everything and the house is rented and –'

'Yes, good old Eliza. What's she getting out of this?'

Junie sniffed against the unwanted tears that had begun to stream down her face. 'She's not *getting* anything; she just wants to help. In fact, she's coming too.'

'What do you mean? To New Guinea? Why?' Beryl said, confused.

'Miles has a job there. District Commissioner.'

'Who gave that bozo any power?' Katie exclaimed.

'Well, he –'

'No, I don't even want to hear any more of this. Go to New Guinea, go find another bunch of witless fools and drink your bloody expensive plonk. But don't bother contacting me when you come home to visit your lonely little kid. I'm over it.'

'Katie…'

'No, I mean it. Find yourself some friends who don't care about you, Junie. Fewer people will get hurt that way.'

Katie walked out of the café, slamming her chair as she went, and Junie flinched. Then there was a terrible silence and she mopped her face with a napkin, her hands trembling.

'She shouldn't have said that to you,' Beryl said, taking hold of one of those hands.

'No, she should have. I deserved every word, that's the whole problem.'

'Then don't go,' Dorn said, picking up her other hand and holding tight.

'I have to. Ernest has too much power. If I don't play along, if I try to divorce him, he'd get the best barrister in the country to ensure I never see Frankie again. I know he would.'

'You have your own legal connections now,' Beryl reminded her.

'Not ones like he does. Besides, I signed a contract, remember? I'd be bankrupt for a start – and my parents with me.'

'Your brothers could support you all now, surely?'

They'd offered of course but Junie knew it would be a good few years until all debts could be met. 'Support, yes; absolve, no.'

'So be poor,' Dorn said simply, running a hand across her own swollen stomach. 'Money isn't everything. Believe me, I know.'

'No. No, it isn't,' Junie said, trying to smile at her through her tears, 'but bankruptcy isn't very nice. Anyway, enough of all this. What's done is done. I'll go to New Guinea but I'll come home as much as I can and as soon as the two years is up, Ernest will score some cushy position back here and I can be with Frankie every day. It will all work out for the best.'

'Of course it will,' Beryl reassured her.

But as she drove home, Junie had to pull over to the side of the road to throw up. Seeing her world through her Braidwood friends' eyes was like holding up a mirror that showed the truth, an ugly reflection revealing the machinations behind the life of an aristocrat; what the cost truly was when you gave your child everything money could buy but couldn't give her what she needed most: your time.

Perhaps that was why she drove over the bridge to see Eliza instead.

The mirrors in her house would be far kinder.

Thirty-eight

1949
Port Moresby, New Guinea

'Thank you, Binta. You should be a hairdresser.'

The young maid smiled shyly. 'Yes, ma'am. You look beautiful, ma'am.'

Junie moved her head to view the back. 'Well, here's hoping I pass muster.'

Binta looked confused but smiled anyway before she left, leaving Junie to admire her handiwork. It was a sleek chignon and the perfect style for the dress. She stood and turned in front of the full-length mirror, swishing the skirts from her narrow waist and loving the feel of the multiple layers of fabric. Her shoulders were bare under narrow straps and with her hair up, there was quite a lot of golden skin on display; it bordered on too much perhaps, but this gown made Junie feel elegant, which helped her confidence. Tonight was her entrance into New Guinean society and she had an important role to play.

She tried to mentally prepare for the evening ahead but, running her hands across the fine material, she found herself remembering another party dress instead. It had been pink and silky and she'd yearned for Michael Riley to feel the way it glided over her skin. She imagined him here now, standing in the corner of her bedroom, watching her with the same expression he'd worn all those years ago at the Trocadero, and she felt a longing for him to materialise that was so strong it physically hurt. It came like that, quite often, just a sudden vision that he was there: alive, whole. She sometimes wondered if she was seeing his ghost.

Digger thumped his tail, watching her, and she sighed at her own foolishness.

'What do you think? Will I do?'

He wagged at her lovingly as always and she gave him a pat. Thank God she'd been able to bring him to their new home at least. He gave some small solace to her perpetually aching heart.

'Ready?' asked Ernest as he entered wearing his tuxedo, hair well-oiled as always.

'Almost,' she said, putting on the diamond drop earrings he had given her for her birthday. They were her only adornment. The spectacular dress was enough.

'Wow,' Ernest said, pausing to look at her. 'Well, I have to say you'll be the talk of the evening. The ambassador's wife,' he announced, pleased.

Junie followed him out of the room slowly, any pleasure in her appearance fading. Suddenly the dress felt more like a costume than a gown.

※

'Here she is,' Eliza called happily, floating towards them in dazzling gold. The style of her dress was similar to Junie's, although she had lace stretching across her shoulders in an intricate black and gold pattern. 'That gown was worth every cent,' she whispered.

'This old thing?' Junie said and they laughed. She had to admit that shopping for this move before they'd left had been a lot of fun – especially for glamorous evening wear.

'Come and meet the gang,' Eliza said, handing her a glass of champagne from a passing tray as they walked over. 'Allow me to introduce Philippe Rafel and his charming wife, Felicity. Philippe manages a mining company.'

'*Bonsoir*,' said Philippe, bowing politely. He was quite a handsome man with thinning dark hair and brown, almost black, eyes. His plump wife Felicity didn't seem very friendly, however, and was eyeing Junie's dress as she said hello.

There was an older Australian couple, Gertie and Paul Baker, two Englishmen who immediately made her laugh with their foppish witticisms and a middle-aged doctor from Canberra.

'Dr John Colgan,' he introduced himself. 'Welcome to the jungle.' There was a knowing amusement in his tone and Junie decided she liked him best so far.

A few others were arriving, including a local government official and his wife, and Junie soon found herself surrounded by conversation and aperitifs as the room swelled to twenty or so. It seemed meeting the new ambassador was quite an important social event and, as they took their places to dine, Junie felt grateful she had Eliza with her.

Their dining hall was modest by Sydney standards but the view was lovely, taking in some of the port waters that were silvery in the twilight. Junie sat at one end of the long table, Ernest at the other, and she was glad she wouldn't have to be near him and pretend to be happily married all evening. Instead she had Dr Colgan on her left and Miles on her right. Etiquette dictated the male/female seating arrangement but Eliza had assured Junie she would swap seats with her husband later. If Junie could bear Miles for that long.

'Perhaps Dr Colgan would be kind enough to say grace tonight,' Ernest said and the doctor stood, making the sign of the cross.

'Dear Lord, for what we are about to receive make us truly thankful. And we pray that our hosts have a safe and beneficial life in their new corner of the world, helping us to uphold what is just and fair for all. Amen.'

'Amen,' said the room.

The soup was served, a delicious seafood bisque, contrary to Cecil's damning reviews of New Guinean cooking, and Junie sipped at it, wondering at the tone of the doctor's prayer.

'How long have you worked here in Port Moresby, doctor?'

'Please, call me John. I'm not usually in Port, actually, just dropping by to welcome you, then I'm back inland.'

'Well, that's very kind of you, John. Where do you call home?'

'Wherever life takes me, which is anywhere, I suppose.'

Junie smiled. 'What a lovely sentiment.'

'Not a sentiment, my dear. A fact,' he replied.

'And where does life usually find you at the present time?'

'Wamena. It's a village up in the high country. Quite remote and therefore very fascinating. I'm with some aid workers from the United Nations and we've been forming a clinic.'

'How have the natives reacted so far?'

'They're very distrustful of white-man medicine, which makes things hard. Won't let us take blood, for example – they think we're stealing their spirit.'

'What an incredible life it must be.'

'Doctor to the darkies, eh?' Miles said, overhearing. 'Good Lord – I'd be more worried about them taking my blood than about taking samples of theirs.'

John flicked a glance his way then had another taste of his soup before replying. 'Their customs and beliefs are actually quite complex. I'm not trying to convert them to our ways overnight, merely trying to support what they can accept.' He broke off a piece of bread. 'And protect them.'

'Protect them from what?' Miles laughed. 'Hungry relatives?'

'Ignorance,' John replied.

Miles looked confused. 'How do you propose to make them less ignorant?'

'Who said I was talking about the natives?'

Junie cleared her throat as John calmly continued eating his soup.

Yes, this was one person in New Guinea she definitely liked.

※

'Thank God that's over,' Eliza said, landing next to Junie as Miles wandered off after the speeches. 'Who was that ghastly third man? Never heard a more boring selection of drivel in my life.'

'Shh,' Junie said as the man in question walked past.

'Do you think he heard?'

'Yes.'

'Good. Hopefully it will discourage him.'

'Behave yourself,' muttered Ernest near her ear as he passed and Eliza laughed.

'Oh pooh, go away. I want to gossip with your wife.' Ernest obliged and Eliza leant towards Junie. 'Now, what did I miss? How did you like the doctor?'

'Very interesting, I must say – works and lives with the natives. In the jungle.'

'Really? How positively primitive.'

'They've opened a medical clinic right up in the mountains.'

'Sounds horrid. However would you style your hair?'

Junie laughed, about to reply, but she was interrupted by an angry yell.

'Miles?' Eliza said.

They rushed into the next room to find Miles covered in coffee and shouting at a terrified Binta.

'Look what you've done, you stupid black bitch!' He swung his hand, striking her across her face and Junie rushed forwards, standing in front of her.

'How dare you hit my maid!'

'Arrrgh! It's burning!'

'Calm down, dear. You, get some cold water and towels,' Eliza ordered another maid who was standing nervously nearby. Other people had come to the door and Eliza moved quickly to close it. 'Just a little mishap. Nothing to worry about.'

'She threw it at me!'

'I'm sure it was just an accident,' Eliza soothed.

'What happened?' Junie asked the maid.

'He grabbed me,' Binta whispered, holding her hand to the nasty welt that was forming on her cheek.

'Come now, it was probably just a misunderstanding. Take her away, Junie, I'll look after Miles,' Eliza said, grabbing the towels as the other girl returned.

'But he –'

'Go. You're missing your own party.'

Junie decided getting Binta away probably was her highest priority but her tongue ached to hurl abuse at Miles. Later, she decided, taking Binta to a side door and leading her to the kitchen to get some ice. 'Wrap this and hold it to her face,' she told the second maid. 'Binta, take the rest of the night off. We'll deal with this in the morning.'

'Yes, ma'am. I – I didn't mean to –'

'It's all right. I'll take care of it,' Junie assured her before returning to the dining room, taking another wine and trying to compose herself.

'Everything all right?' John asked.

Junie was fuming but forced the lie. 'Yes, fine. Just some spilt coffee, I'm afraid.'

John studied her face. 'Some advice, Mrs Farthington, for what it's worth. Look out for that ignorance I mentioned. You'll find it a powerful enemy.'

❦

Junie awoke to the familiar throb of a hangover and blinked against the sun shining through the white curtains.

'Ugh, pull the drapes,' Ernest said, shielding his eyes. She got up and did so, the room immediately darkening, then went to the bathroom.

Ernest's eyes were on her as she returned.

'Come back to bed.'

'Not today, Ernest.'

'It's been weeks, Junie. You can't expect me to go without.'

'Why don't you just get a mistress like everyone else?' she said, bitter.

'Don't be ridiculous,' he returned, but she wondered if he had one already. Probably. The rate of intimacy between them was about once a month, at best. 'Besides, I still haven't given up on more children, even if you have.'

Junie felt an ache in her heart as Frankie's photo looked at her from the dressing table. 'Maybe God only wanted to send us one,' she said. In truth, she wondered if Ernest was infertile. She obviously wasn't.

'Maybe we should have more sex and give God a hand.'

He walked over and held her hands in his but they were clammy, as usual, and she felt the revulsion rise. She was saved by a knock at the door.

'Come in,' she said quickly.

'Good morning, ma'am,' said the second maid from last night, entering with a coffee tray.

'Good morning…I'm sorry, I didn't catch your name yesterday?'

'Delphine.'

'Good morning, Delphine. Where's Binta? Is she feeling all right?'

'Binta gone, ma'am,' the maid said, placing the tray very carefully.

'Where?'

'Not sure, ma'am.' She was staring at the floor. 'Maybe she run away.'

'But that's ridiculous. Where would she go?'

'Not sure, ma'am,' she said again. The maid looked very nervous and Junie walked over to her.

'Delphine,' she said, trying to catch her eye, 'what is it you're not telling me?'

'Nothing, ma'am. He said – nothing, ma'am.'

'Just let it go, Junie,' Ernest said, yawning as he poured a cup of coffee.

'Who said?' Junie insisted, ignoring him.

Delphine looked over at Ernest fearfully.

'It's all right. We won't be angry if you tell us the truth. This is our house, Delphine – we need to know what goes on in it.'

'Did she take off into the jungle?' Ernest asked, half amused.

'Police took her,' Delphine blurted.

'What?' Junie said, shocked.

'The police were at my door?' Ernest said, not amused any more, Junie noted. Scandal was Ernest's worst fear.

'Where did they take her?' Junie asked.

'Jail.'

'Why?'

'He say she threw coffee –'

'Bloody Miles! Well, we'll just see about that!'

'Slow down, Junie – Junie what are you doing?'

'Fighting ignorance!' she yelled, flinging her nightgown off and a dress on and searching for her shoes.

'What's that supposed to mean?'

'I'm going down to the jail!' she said, hopping on one foot as she put a shoe on.

'You can't just march in there –'

'Yes, I can! I'm a lawyer *and* the ambassador's wife, so I think I have every right to march in there and reclaim my poor maid. For God's sake, she's only a child!'

'I don't want a scene.'

She stood with one shoe on, hands on hips. 'Ernest, what do you think will be worse, everyone knowing our teenage maid was thrown in jail or everyone knowing we did nothing about it?'

Ernest had to capitulate then. 'All right. But be discreet. Just pay what they ask for and get her out.'

But she made no such promise as she found her other shoe.

It seemed she may just need to practise law sooner than expected.

෴

The life of an ambassador's wife was being rewritten, or such was the entertaining thought that crossed Marlon's mind as he watched Mrs June Farthington stand beneath the ceiling fan in the local jail in Port Moresby. He wasn't sure which part of the scene amused him the most: the reaction of the clearly flustered police sergeant or the presence of a large, rather fluffy black dog sitting protectively at Junie's side. Looking at her gorgeous face and figure, he decided he'd have to start attending some of these political dinners Philippe was always trying to drag him to. The photo in the newspaper announcing their arrival really hadn't done her justice. She looked even more beautiful than the last time he'd seen her, all those years ago, and the memory of that stolen kiss sprang to mind.

'I'm sorry, ma'am. She has to have a trial.'

'And you are being a trial for me. Just tell me how much the fine is and give me my maid back.'

'As I said, I cannot do that –'

'May I be of assistance?' Marlon enquired politely from behind.

'No, I'm quite –'

The sight of him halted her and he had to laugh when she found her words.

'Oh God, what fresh hell is this?'

'Now what kind of a way is that to greet an old friend?' Marlon reached down to let Digger sniff his hand then scratched his ears, receiving a wagging tail in response.

Junie gave him an exasperated look and turned back to the sergeant. 'Look, I really haven't got time for this –'

'Then you shouldn't be wasting it,' Marlon said, leaning over to murmur in her ear. 'You're barking up the wrong tree.'

'What do you mean?' she whispered back.

'You don't bribe the sergeant; you bribe the judge. Actually, with your connections, you may not even have to offer him a bribe.'

'How do you know?'

'It's not my first time here.'

'Why doesn't that surprise me?'

'Come on, I'll introduce you.'

An hour later they were helping a very shaken Binta into a taxi and Marlon's admiration for Junie was growing by the minute. Watching her take on that crooked Judge Mosley had been entertaining, to say the least, and Marlon felt his old interest in

Mrs Farthington return. He wanted to see her again, married woman or not. Years ago such things bothered him but then again, years ago, he'd been pretty naïve. The war had taken care of that affliction.

'Looks like you learnt a thing or two at that law school of yours,' he said. 'I might have to pick your brain regarding a friend of mine. Are you free for lunch this week at all?'

'I'm not sure that's a good idea,' she said, putting on a wide-brimmed hat and squinting up at the sun. 'Good lord, is it always this humid?'

'Constantly. There's a nice air-conditioned restaurant nearby if you'd like to have a drink before you go.' Damn, he was sounding too keen. Seems he forgot everything he knew about women around her.

'Not today. I have to get Binta to her family. Probably best to keep her away from certain gentlemen of our acquaintance for now.'

Not today. That wasn't a no.

'I'd say so,' Marlon agreed. 'Off you go then. Hopefully I'll see you soon.'

'Thank you for your help today,' she said before she got in. 'I never did ask you what you were doing there.'

'Oh, I often hang around police stations. You never know when a beautiful lady might walk in with her dog and need a crash course on bribery.'

He patted Digger, who licked his hand, and Junie laughed a little as she went, the sound of it staying with him as he headed back to the station. She really was the most distracting woman – he'd just left his mate to cool his heels in a jail cell for an unnecessary hour to help her out. Oh well, Joseph would just have to be patient. It's not every day a woman like that crosses your path, especially here.

Now all he had to do was figure out how to make it happen again.

❧

Eliza was on the verandah and Junie saw Ernest drop his hand from her arm before walking rapidly away. They looked as if they'd had an argument, Junie thought, surprised.

'Everything all right?' she asked.

'Oh, there you are. I was worried,' Eliza said, her frown disappearing as she glided towards Junie in a white tennis dress, cool and immaculate as always. 'How did everything go?'

Junie gave her hat to Delphine, not quite sure how to respond. 'Fine…in the end,' she said. 'Everything's all right now,' she said gently to the nervous maid. 'How about you fetch us some tea?'

'Where's the girl?' Eliza asked as Delphine headed off, looking relieved.

'With her family.'

'Oh. Well, I'm sure that's for the best.'

Junie went back indoors to sit on the lounge and Eliza did likewise, an awkward silence ensuing.

'It seems there really are elephants in New Guinea. One in this room anyway,' Eliza joked.

Junie didn't laugh. 'I want you to know I'm not letting Miles get away with this. He can't just walk into my house and treat my servants this way. I don't care who he is.'

'Come now, Junie, it's just the way things are here. When in Rome, and all that. You don't want to make waves,' she warned lightly, crossing her slim, bare legs.

'You mean *you* don't want me to make waves.'

'What are you cranky with me for? It's not my fault Miles is so horrid. Now let's just drop it and talk about more pleasant things. I'm meeting the tennis crowd today and thought you might like to join in –'

'What did you argue with Ernest about just then?' Junie interrupted.

Eliza looked taken aback. 'Don't be silly, we didn't argue. Ah, here's the tea.'

'He seemed angry.'

'Oh, you know what he's like – hates a scene. Speak of the devil…'

Ernest walked in and told Delphine to fetch the driver. 'Everything sorted is it?' he said tersely.

'Yes. She's gone home now.'

'I hope you told her to keep things quiet. Where's my blasted lighter?'

'In your pocket, usually,' Eliza said, sipping her tea.

Ernest found it and lit a cigarette. 'Right, I'm off,' he said, turning to look at Junie. 'Don't forget Philippe and his wife are coming for dinner Friday night. You might want to invite a few others if you like. Nothing too large. I want to hear more about these mining ventures of his.'

'All right,' Junie said.

He left without saying goodbye and silence stretched once more. Eliza was picking at a biscuit, something she rarely ate, and Junie was watching her.

'Was he angry with you about Miles?'

'Still on about Ernest? All right, yes, we argued,' she said, sighing, 'but I don't want you to worry about it. He just seems to think I should be able to control the bloody man but it's easier said than done, isn't it?'

'Yes, it is.'

'Come on, let's not talk about our boring husbands. Who are you inviting to this dinner party? Please say a dashing man for a change.'

'Actually I did find one at the jail,' Junie said, smiling as Eliza leapt forwards.

'Oh, do tell!' She held up her hand. 'No, better yet, let me figure it out. Was it a dangerous gangster, immediately in love with you?'

'We're not in Chicago,' Junie remarked, enjoying their old guessing game.

'A swashbuckling pirate?'

Junie shook her head. 'Not an eye patch in sight.'

'*Clark Gable.* Tell me it was Clark Gable.'

'If it was Clark Gable I would have committed a crime and stayed!'

Eliza laughed, pouring another tea. 'And I would have joined you. All right, tell me now. I've run out of ideas.'

'Well, you weren't too far off. He is American. Do you remember that pilot we met at Government House?'

'Marlon Stone!' Eliza's eyes were round.

'In the flesh.'

Eliza sat back with her tea and a knowing smile. 'Now there's a man I never forgot.'

Junie looked at her uneasily. 'Did the two of you...spend some time together?'

'Some quality time,' Eliza admitted.

'I'm sure it was,' Junie said, hiding an odd feeling of disappointment. 'Well, you'll have your chance to see him again on Friday night, if you like. I thought I might invite him along – he was very helpful today.'

'I do like! Whatever shall I wear?'

'That would get his attention,' Junie said, nodding at the short tennis outfit.

'Oh, that reminds me – I really do need you to take up tennis! Don't say no – I'm a horrible player and I need you to be horrible with me.'

'Not today – I've had a pretty trying morning, as you can imagine. How about next week?' Junie said, yawning.

'Of course. Actually, I really need to get a move on. I'll call you tonight,' Eliza said breezily, kissing her cheek as she left.

Junie went upstairs to lie on her bed beneath the fan, vaguely wondering who else she should invite to this dinner on Friday. Dr Colgan, if he was still in town. He'd be a welcome distraction while Eliza flirted with Marlon.

She was annoyed that their affair bothered her. It wasn't as if Junie'd ever had much of a connection with him. Then the Trocadero came to mind with its beating swing pulse and she was back in the moment when Michael and Ernest were approaching simultaneously and Marlon had come to her rescue. Then she remembered the next time she'd seen him, when he'd unexpectedly kissed her – and she'd slapped him for his efforts.

Thoughts of Michael took over then, flicking in various memories like a short for a movie. The expression on his face around the campfire on the beach that first night. The hurt in his eyes near that cold stone wall. A Christmas farewell that broke what was left of her youthful hope. Her secret given to the sea.

No, no more lovers. It wasn't worth the pain.

But as she gave in to the pull of sleep that tall American was dancing with her once more and that stolen kiss was visiting her dreams.

Thirty-nine

'They serve prawn cocktails at sunset. With champagne, of course,' Philippe added. The guests were relaxing after a four-course meal and, with Marlon present, the conversation at Junie's dinner party was centred around his tourist flight business.

'What a delicious idea,' Eliza said, her eyes on Marlon. 'How often do you take people there?'

'About once a month or so. Mostly ex-pats who want to head down to Salamaua to their holiday houses, although that bar Philippe enjoys is worth the trip on its own,' Marlon said, putting out his cigarette. 'I could make enquiries for you if you want to go for a weekend. Plenty of friends of mine would be willing to rent out their place.'

'Or you could just invite them to dinner and most men would offer these ladies a place for free, I'm sure,' Philippe added in his smooth French accent, lifting his glass towards Junie.

She smiled an acknowledgement, aware that his wife Felicity was beginning to detest her, and turned to John instead. 'I'd be interested in visiting you at the village, if that's allowed. Where was it again?'

'Wamena. I'm not sure if you'd enjoy it as a holiday destination, I'm afraid. It is very much a traditional life the locals lead – the

Dani, they're called – and the workers have few modern conveniences. You could come for the day though, I suppose. Marlon still runs the occasional joy flight up our way.'

'Isn't that where you go to see the Shangri-La Valley?' Felicity asked.

Junie's head snapped towards Marlon. '*The* Shangri-La Valley? Where the American plane crashed?'

She'd been obsessed when that story had hit the headlines in 1945 when a plane went down in the remote New Guinean highlands, killing several people and stranding a handful of survivors. It was an amazing enough story of rescue in itself, made even more poignant for Junie as she thought of the ill-fated Elite, but it was also a tale that fired her imagination. Somewhere called Shangri-La really existed – it wasn't just a fictional place in a book or a movie.

'Oh no, now you've done it,' Eliza said with a sigh. 'She'll never leave you alone until you take her there,' she told Marlon with a knowing smile.

'What is this Shangri-La place?' Philippe asked.

'You remember, I told you about it when it was in the news a few years back. Honestly you never listen to a word I say,' Felicity said, annoyed. 'The Americans lost in the jungles with the cannibals? The rescue?'

'*Cannibales*? Surely not,' Philippe said.

'No, no, apparently so. Something to do with appeasing the spirits after warfare, or so the people say in Wamena,' John told them. 'But no-one really knows all that much about the valley tribes, not even the Dani.'

'The Kurelu, they're called,' Marlon added. 'They're completely cut off from the western world, like a lost race.'

'How is that even possible in this day and age?' Eliza asked him, twisting her hair around her fingers.

'You'd understand better if you saw it from the air,' Marlon said, gesturing as he spoke. 'The whole valley has limestone cliffs protecting it, all the way down, and they're pretty much permanently enshrouded by cloud, so it really is hidden. A pilot came across it by accident in 1938, then of course came the plane crash and rescue mission in forty-five, and it was front-page news. Aside from that it is a complete mystery – no-one really knows what's down there.'

'It's a wonder no-one has organised an expedition,' Junie mused.

'You can't be serious! No-one in their right mind would approach such blood-thirsty cavemen,' Ernest said, scoffing.

Philippe drew on his cigar. 'Depends what's there.'

Marlon watched him and Junie wondered at his intense expression, but it was quickly masked.

'I wouldn't risk it,' Miles said, agreeing with Ernest. 'Bunch of savages, by the sounds of things.'

Junie shot him a look, resenting anything that came out of his mouth. It was only after quite a good deal of persuasion from Eliza – and martinis over lunch on Wednesday – that she'd agreed he could attend tonight.

'Don't forget they saved the survivors' lives and I'm told no-one got put in a boiling pot,' John pointed out.

'Not even the pretty girl,' Marlon added, rolling a cigarette and looking over at Junie. 'Most un-Hollywood, really.'

'The girl who was rescued was rather attractive, wasn't she?' Eliza said, clinking her glittering bracelets as she sipped her champagne. 'What was her name again?'

'Margaret Hastings…and the plane was called the *Gremlin Special*. I've saved the newspaper clippings,' Junie confessed with a self-conscious smile. '*Lost Horizon* is my favourite novel.'

'Really? I found it a bore,' said Felicity. 'Romantic, fairy-tale rubbish.'

Junie blushed but met the woman's gaze regardless. 'It was the notion of a Utopian society that captured my imagination, so I tend to fear accusations of political radicalism rather than romanticism.' She nodded politely. 'You'll forgive me if I take that as a compliment.'

Felicity gaped like a fish and Eliza appeared to have some trouble swallowing her wine.

'I am sure your *raisonnement politique* is anything but *radicale, madame*,' Philippe said smoothly, shooting a dark look at his wife. 'And long live the romantic in all of us.'

'*Bien dit!*' toasted Eliza and the rest were obliged to follow suit.

'Novels aside, I can assure you this lost horizon has a very real valley beneath it,' John stated.

'And the whole area is quite spectacular from the air, however "lost in time" it may be, as the romantics say,' Marlon said, with a meaningful look at Junie. 'I'd be happy to take you.'

'I'm not sure I should allow it,' Ernest said.

'Oh, don't be silly, Ernest. Marlon is an experienced pilot. I want to go too,' Eliza said. 'Honestly, what's the point in coming to New Guinea if we don't do something adventurous?'

'But this seems rather extreme,' Ernest said.

Junie plotted for a minute. 'Well, it does seem a nice photo opportunity for you. "Australian ambassador visits remote frontiers." Getting to know the natives and so forth.'

'With his beautiful wife,' Marlon added and Junie felt foolishly pleased by the compliment.

Ernest seemed to consider then. 'Well, I suppose it might be a bit of an adventure as you say...'

'Excellent, I'll contact Gus Peterson, my reporter friend. What day shall we go?' Eliza said.

'We are taking a trip to Hong Kong,' Philippe said, appearing disappointed, 'but please, you must go without us this time.'

'I could take you on Wednesday?' Marlon said, checking his small diary.

'Perfect,' Eliza exclaimed. 'It's all settled. To finding Shangri-La!'

Junie drank with the others, surprised to find herself so thrilled, a feeling that increased as Marlon smiled at her over his wine, his dark eyes holding hers.

'To next Wednesday,' he said, and she dropped her gaze.

Marlon finished his conversation and hung up the phone, pleased. Word had come through from John via radio: he'd managed to talk their mutual native friend Pukz into accommodating five tourists overnight in his village, and Marlon was grateful. Not just because he wanted to spend the extra time with a beautiful woman, although she was that. He wondered if Eliza had told Junie about their brief affair and hoped she hadn't. Junie Farthington was already enough of a challenge.

Pushing thoughts of women aside, he made for the door and hailed a taxi to take him to the jail.

Hopefully Pukz would have the answer he needed. It was the best shot they had for now.

Forty

In all her life, and for the rest of it to come, Junie knew she would never experience another day quite like this: the day she first saw the New Guinean Highlands from the air. Green, purple and blue, they rolled beneath the plane like the great southern lady rolled in her waves: misted, mystical and breathtakingly wild.

Marlon, Junie, Ernest and Eliza had set out early with Gus Peterson, the journalist, and the trip had been a pleasant one in the morning sunshine with the landscape becoming increasingly remote with each passing mile. The country had been unveiled from behind brief curtains of clouds, a heavenly vista in vast undulations, almost too beautiful to take in.

As much as she was looking forward to seeing the village, Junie didn't want to leave the air but they eventually began their descent to make a hair-raising landing in Wamena.

Junie's immediate impression was that she'd stepped into the pages of a *National Geographic* magazine as dark-skinned, almost naked people stared at her in wonder and a little fear. Women with bare breasts held babies with round tummies and the men came forwards adorned in paint and brightly coloured feathers with strange cylinders over their private parts. They were not a tall race, the visiting party towered above the villagers, but they were wiry and, Junie imagined, very strong.

A handful of men welcomed the group in a strange, halting language, managing to do so despite large bones through their noses, an adornment Junie imagined denoted seniority. They seemed quite friendly with John and Marlon, especially Pukz, who Junie found out was actually the chief's son, and soon they were being shown around while Gus took photos for his story. The villagers had experienced having their pictures taken by tourists a few times before, Marlon told them, and didn't seem to mind, standing proudly before the cameras.

'Over here, Junie,' Ernest instructed as he prepared a pose with Pukz and the chief, hissing in an undertone, 'For God's sake, what's going on with her hair? Fix it will you, Eliza.'

Eliza combed Junie's hair down and Junie stood and smiled obligingly for the camera, trying not to feel embarrassed by the look of disgust Marlon was directing towards Ernest.

Then they moved through the village and the sights soon overpowered any negative undercurrents. The huts were domed in grass, a design that undoubtedly protected them well from the rain, and the main house, the *honai*, was quite large. Native women were decorating the clearing in front of it with flowers and Junie was told it would be the location for a celebration tonight, something that had the villagers quite excited.

'They may not be into clothes but they're big on accessorising,' Eliza observed, and it was true. The women were using whatever the forest could provide and the result was a kaleidoscope of rich colour. Necklaces and headdresses in red, orange, yellow and green appeared brilliant against dark complexions and Junie felt it a shame the photos would appear only in black and white.

Large brown eyes followed her every move, but they weren't unfriendly. In fact, the villagers were going all out to impress, and not only with adornment – there would be quite a feast, judging by the mounds of food being prepared. Large baskets of fruits and yams were being cleaned and Junie was pretty sure pork would also be on the menu, based on the amount of pigs – *wam* – running around.

John's clinic was bigger than she'd expected and Junie was impressed by how well run it was. The United Nations had given them two staff from Port Moresby, local women with nursing training, and limited medical supplies, but it was still very basic. While the doctor was busy telling Ernest what they needed, Junie visited each patient, eavesdropping on the conversation for future reference.

'Smile, your worshipfulness,' Eliza said, as Gus clicked away with his camera.

Junie obliged, stroking the cheek of the little girl lying in the bed, who stared at her with apprehension. She looked to be only Frankie's age and was suffering from a fever.

'Don't be afraid, little one. I won't hurt you,' Junie whispered softly and the girl slowly returned her smile.

Junie reached to pour her some water but Marlon was there, handing her the glass. 'Allow me.'

'Goodness, is it hot in here?' Eliza asked no-one in particular.

After their village visit it was time for the scenic flight, although Junie couldn't imagine anything superseding what she'd seen so far. Pukz was coming as a guide and they were told he was the only person in his village ever to have flown in a plane. He was also the only one who had much knowledge of English, although it was very limited, but John said he was slowly picking it up as he worked alongside him in the clinic. Likewise, John was trying to learn Dani, hoping to get as fluent as Marlon.

The other villagers seemed impressed with Pukz's bravery as he climbed on board and Junie sensed he was something of the village daredevil. It was his third time in the air, Marlon told her, which Pukz confirmed by grinning beneath thick, cracking face paint and holding up three fingers. Then muddling things by proclaiming, 'Turd!'

Marlon laughed loudly at that and turned on the engine. 'Ready to fly, monkeys?'

'Why monkeys?' Gus asked, buckling in.

'Because we're apes and we're about to fly. Haven't you ever seen *The Wizard of Oz*?'

'I was made to endure it once.'

'Made to? It's the best story ever told, isn't it, Junie?'

Eliza looked at Junie's face, amused. 'You won't get a yes there, especially today. *Lost Horizon* is her favourite, remember?'

'Ah, that's right. *Elle est une romantique*. But *The Wizard of Oz* is romantic too,' Marlon protested.

'In what possible way? Unless you're suggesting something about the witch and her harem of monkeys?' Eliza said, laughing.

'You're disgraceful,' Ernest told her with a shake of his head.

'I don't know. Think about it from the poor witch's point of view...up in her castle, all alone...' Eliza continued as Junie giggled.

Marlon turned towards her. 'What's so funny? I thought you were the soft-hearted romantic?'

'And an animal lover,' Eliza added.

'Yes, but not a lover of animals,' Junie said, trying to keep a straight face.

Marlon chuckled, breaking into 'We're Off to See the Wizard' as he turned the plane around for take-off.

'Oh Lord, now he's singing. Make a note of that in your story, Gus. Tell the world how we perished from bleeding ears,' Eliza instructed.

They rose above the village and out towards the valleys in good spirits and Pukz began to point out various sights as they flew along: rivers and ravines; a lone, majestic eagle; a shimmering waterfall. Marlon was doing his best to translate what he could, then Pukz rattled something very fast and Marlon strained to listen above the engines.

'This is the lost valley coming up now. Beyond those clouds along the ridges. Pukz is saying that he has been down there, but only a few times. Most are too afraid to go.'

The passengers couldn't see anything as they moved through the white mist, but then it cleared in feathery strips and there it was. Steep, wild hills protected hidden depths that were green and thick with vegetation, darkening to indigo in places, and a great river cut through it like a golden, twisting snake in the sunlight.

'My God, it looks like the river really is filled with gold. Like in the book,' Junie exclaimed, and for some reason she wanted to laugh or cry. She did a bit of both as goose bumps rose on her arms. 'It's – it's incredible.'

'Like a yellow brick road?' Marlon teased.

'Far better than Oz,' she said in awe. 'It's Shangri-La.'

The valley truly did look like paradise from up here; a vision hidden by the gods, a secret utopia teeming with brilliant life that clung to its edges and burst out of gullies and hillsides. Every inch seemed covered in unique, abundant foliage unchanged by time; a landscape from a primitive era. The way the world must have been before man grew advanced enough to destroy it. Strange-looking birds glided through patches of low fog and gigantic ferns shadowed unknown depths.

'Amazing,' said Gus, clicking his camera. 'Has Pukz ever seen any of the natives up close?' he asked Marlon, taking a photo of Ernest, who immediately put his arm around Junie.

Pukz nodded. 'Kurelu.'

'He's got some guts,' Gus said. 'Takes a brave man to wander into that.'

'Bah, he's stone age himself. Probably cracked a few skulls with them over a fire,' Ernest said, laughing at his own joke, and Junie moved away from him, revolted.

Fortunately, Pukz didn't seem to take much notice and pointed out something else to Marlon.

'Kuji,' Pukz said, pointing to the western side.

'What is Kuji?' Eliza asked.

'Who is Kuji, you mean. He's like a spirit man – a white ghost who walks with the Kurelu tribes. I've heard him mentioned before; I think he may be a legend in these parts,' Marlon told them.

'Sounds like a *Phantom* comic,' Gus commented, writing it down. 'Fascinating.'

'A ghost? God, they really are primitive aren't they?' Ernest said.

Marlon shrugged. 'Maybe my translation is poor.'

'You – Kuji,' Pukz repeated, pointing at Ernest.

He laughed again, a little nervously this time. 'Well, here's hoping. I won't be too pleased if I'm about to become a ghost.'

'It'd do wonders for my story,' Gus muttered.

Eliza slapped his arm. 'Behave.'

They sailed along for another ten minutes or so, marvelling at prehistoric-looking forests and becoming excited at the only sign of mankind: a smoke trail wafting from what appeared to be a cluster of huts. Junie leant her forehead against the window, wishing desperately for a closer look but knowing it was impossible.

'Time to leave, people. Take your final photos, Gus,' Marlon called.

They made their way to the rim of the valley, the white encompassing them once more and blocking a full view of the exterior walls as they climbed out. Junie was grateful for Marlon's skills as she observed the sharpness of the stone in fleeting glimpses, conceding the valley really was extremely well protected from the rest of the world. Suddenly she felt very privileged to have seen it, one of very few westerners ever to have done so. It was so different to the earth she knew, almost like it wasn't really a part of it, so removed had it seemed.

And now obscured once more, like it had never existed.

'The Lost Horizon,' she said out loud.

Marlon looked over at her and his expression was difficult to read. 'Maybe it should stay that way.'

They turned in a slow circle and began their journey back, leaving the mysteries behind in their deep folds, and Junie hoped to return again one day. It was too much to take in on one viewing.

By the time they landed back on the rough strip at Wamena, Eliza was pleading a headache and lay down on the floor of the *honai*, seemingly uncaring of the little tribe of children staring at her from the entrance. Gus was making notes as Ernest sat and conversed with the leaders, John assisting, which left Marlon with Junie.

'Tea?'

'My, very sophisticated,' she said as he produced a thermos from the plane, whistling a tune as some villagers watched in fascination.

'You get used to it,' he said with a nod at them.

'Yes, I suppose you have to. I must look very peculiar to them.'

They sipped their tea in companionable silence as the locals began to wander off, returning to everyday mountain life.

'I must thank you for that incredible flight today. It was far beyond anything I could have imagined.'

He looked over at her, a glad smile spreading. 'Like you went inside your book at last?'

'Almost,' she said.

'Sometimes, when I'm flying over, it feels like I'm sailing somewhere between heaven and earth. Like it isn't quite real.' He flushed a little and she couldn't help but feel drawn to him. 'Guess I'm the romantic now.'

'I guess you are,' she said, liking the fact.

They fell to silence again and she noticed that he seemed very preoccupied.

'Is something wrong?' she asked.

'Yes,' he said, sighing as he took out his cigarettes. 'I'm afraid I have a favour to ask you and I hope you don't mind, but it's legal in nature.'

'What have you done?' she asked, immediately concerned.

'No, not me,' he was quick to reassure her, 'my friend. He's a native fella I've worked with for years, Joseph. Got into a bit of trouble over a poker game and – well, basically Judge Mosley is accusing him of stealing from white people.'

'Did he?'

'No, definitely not. Joseph is no thief, I assure you.'

'What does he allege Joseph stole?'

'Based on the contents on the table, there was a watch and a fair bit of cash. I gave him the watch so he certainly shouldn't be accused of stealing that, and I pay him well, so the cash is justifiable too. I think I could get him off but there is one item he had I didn't know about and I can't prove where he got it.'

'Why not?'

'He says he got it from Pukz, traded it for some supplies, and of course we can't really ask Pukz to testify or they'll just throw *him* in jail instead.'

Junie nodded, absorbing that fact. 'What's the item?'

'A silver lighter.'

'Where on earth would Pukz have got that from? Perhaps someone on a joy flight?'

Marlon shrugged. 'Probably. That's what we need to find out while we're up here.'

'Without making it sound like an accusation of any kind.'

'Of course.'

Junie considered his predicament. 'Why don't you just bribe the judge?'

'It'd be a hefty bribe. Did I mention he's not very good at poker?'

She nodded slowly, understanding the situation now. 'So if he keeps Joseph in jail, he keeps the booty from the game.'

'Exactly.'

Junie sipped on her tea thoughtfully. 'How can you prove it's the same lighter Pukz gave him anyway?'

'It's engraved.'

⁕

Ernest was taking a while and Junie wondered if he'd gotten lost. It seemed he wasn't keen on using the part of the bush the locals favoured as a toilet. Eliza was only just coming back and Junie had to laugh at the look on her face.

'How did you get on with your little spade?'

'I think the least said about the matter the better,' she replied, sitting down. 'Pass my bag would you?'

'God, what's in this? A brick?' Junie wondered, handing it over. 'How's your headache?'

'Mostly gone. I think it must have been Marlon's singing that caused it. By the way, I've decided to give up on him – he obviously fancies you.'

'Don't be ridiculous. I'm…I'm married….'

Eliza seemed to find that funny. 'Good Lord, even more reason to play the game. Shh, here they come.'

Ernest had found his way back and Marlon was helping the women carry drinks. They passed them around, fresh juice of some kind, and Eliza added some vodka she produced from her bag. *That explains the brick*, Junie thought.

'Can't leave all the comforts of home at home,' Eliza said, winking at her as she poured.

Gus set up his camera and they watched with interest as a dance began. It was filled with strange yelps and noises and Junie soon realised it was an imitation of war. The paint on their faces was elaborate, filled with markings and dots, and feathers framed the eyes of some, with long quills bobbing up and down on the foreheads of others. Large bark masks were held in front or hung from behind to symbolise both spirit and man, or so Marlon tried to explain.

Eliza seemed more interested in refilling glasses but Junie was captivated.

The meal came next, lots of pork as expected, and a variety of forest fare. Junie thought it all rather delicious and they ate hungrily, filling their stomachs at the villagers' encouragement and thanking them continually for their generosity. The women smiled at her shyly and one pointed at her diamond bracelet, repeating something that Junie guessed was a request for a closer look. She took it off and they all had turns holding it and admiring it before returning it to her.

'Nice rocks,' Marlon said.

'Ernest likes me to wear it,' she said with a shrug.

'You make it sound like a chore,' Ernest said. 'Never grateful for anything, are you?'

Junie was embarrassed but was saved from commenting as Ernest lit his cigarette with his gold lighter. The villagers became very animated and they pointed at it, chatting excitedly.

'Litter,' said Pukz immediately.

Ernest, Gus and Eliza were engaged in showing the villagers the further contents of their pockets and Marlon seized his opportunity while they were diverted.

'Have you seen one before?' he asked Pukz, then quickly tried to translate as Junie leant forwards in anticipation.

'Yes, thank you,' Pukz said.

'Yours?' Marlon asked.

'Pukz,' he said proudly.

'And did you give it away?' Marlon moved his hands in giving and receiving motions and Pukz seemed to understand.

'Joseph.'

Junie and Marlon exchanged relieved glances and Marlon asked where he originally got the lighter from, translating awkwardly when Pukz didn't understand the question in English. Pukz went into a long, rapid-fire explanation. Well, that was easy, thought Junie as he spoke, but Marlon looked pale.

'What is it?'

'Seems Pukz did trade the silver lighter for some food with Joseph. He said he didn't want it any more because the magic didn't like him. Must have run out of fuel. Then he said Joseph didn't want me to know because he's not supposed to do deals on the side when we're working, which all rings true.'

'So where did Pukz get it from? Was it someone on a joy flight we can track down?'

'No, that's the weirdest part – he says he got it from someone down in the valley.'

'*These* valleys? But who on earth…?'

'That's just it, he said it's not someone from earth,' Marlon told her. 'He said he got it from Kuji.'

❧

Marlon was deep in conversation with Pukz when Junie approached the plane next morning.

'Goodnight,' Pukz said, nodding as he left them.

'Hey, it's a greeting,' Marlon said, shrugging at her confusion.

Junie had to smile. 'What were you just talking about? Did he tell you anything else?'

Marlon nodded. 'Among other things. Sometimes it's hard to bridge the gap.'

'You mean you don't understand the language or the culture?'

'Half versed in both, I'm afraid.'

Junie leant against the plane, shielding her eyes to read his expression, her lawyer senses on alert. 'Is something else going on?'

Marlon sighed. 'Let's just say that the day is coming when we may need a very big bridge.'

Junie cocked her head to one side, trying to understand. 'So what's next?'

'With Joseph? There's nothing else for it. I'll have to bribe Mosley.' He checked his watch.

'Yes, it seems like it. You can't exactly get a testimony from a ghost. How much do you think he'll want?'

'At least a thousand pounds, I'd say. Bloody old crook.'

Junie was shocked. 'So much! Have you got the money?'

'Just,' he said, loading their bags and helping her into the plane. She took her seat and an awkward silence followed.

'It's none of my business is it?' she said quietly. 'I'm sorry.'

'No, it's all right. I, uh, got into a bit of trouble after the war, hitting the bottle too hard...and I don't mind a gamble myself,' he admitted. 'Had a month's pay on the table in the same game actually.'

'But you seem to be doing all right, with your plane and all.'

'Oh, I'm getting back on my feet now and look to get a pretty nice contract signed with Philippe by the end of the year, ferrying mining staff back and forth. Except for a bit of poker and whisky when the mood takes me, I'm right back on track,' he said. 'This will clean me out, though.'

'And you can't make a call to the States?'

Marlon looked out the window with a frown and she wished she hadn't asked, annoyed with herself for prying a second time.

'My parents basically washed their hands of me after the first few years when I really went off the rails,' he told her, 'and my grandmother died in forty-six, so...yeah. Not many options there.'

He went quiet and Junie suspected that memory was a painful one.

The village children were waving and they waved back.

'Do you miss it? Your home?' she asked, looking around them at what must seem a million miles away from America.

'San Francisco? Not really. I miss Sausalito though. Have to get out of Moresby and into the wilderness sometimes – especially the open coast. It's in my blood.'

'I think it's in mine too,' she said. 'Society life isn't really my thing – despite appearances. I much prefer just being by the ocean or in the countryside. Or the jungle,' she added, looking around them. 'Just feels right for some reason. More natural.'

'I remember thinking that about you the first time we met. That there was something a bit untamed about you.'

'Just a wild colonial girl at heart,' she said lightly, but she was blushing.

'I'm a bit wild at heart myself,' he said.

She gave him a teasing smile. 'You don't say?'

'More than you know actually,' he confessed. 'I'm part Native American – Coast Miwok. My grandmother Liwa was full blood.'

Junie stared at him, intrigued. 'Wow, well, that explains a few things.'

'Such as?'

'Well...such as why you seem so at home up here. And why you have so much compassion for native peoples...like your friend Joseph.'

'You have compassion for native people too and it isn't in your blood. Look at what you did to protect that maid of yours.'

'Maybe it's an Irish throwback. Maybe I've got some ancient fisher woman in me.'

'Now that's a delicious thought – you throwing your nets to the ocean on a wild Irish coast,' he said, observing her closely now. 'Your eyes are the colour of the sea.'

'Are they?' she said, trying to act as though the words didn't affect her. 'I do miss it, I must admit. The beaches are different back home.'

'And what else do you miss about Australia, Junie?'

She frowned, the admission hurting. 'My daughter, Frankie.'

'I didn't know you had a child.' He looked surprised. 'How old is she?'

'Nearly seven.'

'Seven! That doesn't seem possible – you look too young.'

'I was only nineteen when she was born.'

'Oh,' he said thoughtfully. 'I suppose that makes sense then. Where is she staying?'

'She's at boarding school.'

Marlon digested that fact. 'I went to boarding school but not quite so young.'

'Yes, her father insisted – anyway, she wanted to go.' Junie hated how weak it sounded when she said it out loud.

'I detested it. Then again, I was a teenager and it was an all-boys school. I missed seeing girls…especially pretty ones like you.'

Her heart began to hammer. 'Stop trying to charm me, Captain Stone.'

'Stop being so charming and I will.'

The few feet between them suddenly seemed like inches and she was aware of his physicality in intoxicating detail: that he was slightly unshaven; that his shirt held faint traces of petrol; that his hair needed cutting where it touched his collar.

'I think I need to remind you that I'm a married woman.'

'Not much of a marriage, from where I sit.'

She went to protest but couldn't deny it. 'It's complicated.'

'Like I said, not much of a marriage then.'

The charged energy between them was broken by the sound of approaching voices and Marlon held her eyes just a second longer before getting out to assist the others on board. Ernest and Eliza fell in amid much laughter, carrying an assortment of objects she had bartered for.

'Had to do some shopping,' she explained and Junie observed the phallic statue in her arms with amusement. Then Gus arrived and they loaded the last of the equipment on board.

'Ready to fly, monkeys?' called Marlon as the engine whirred into life and he began to whistle.

It seemed the whole village had come to watch the plane take off and they waved until it found the sky once more. The mountains and valleys melted away beneath them, shrouded in mist one minute, brilliant in the sun the next, and Junie watched the patterns cross them thoughtfully. Looking back to the hidden valley, she decided again that it truly was like the place in *Lost Horizon*: hidden, timeless, beautiful. A paradise where man could take his fill from nature's bounty. But in other ways it was as secretive and dangerous as anywhere on the planet. A place where men ate the flesh of other men and believed that a white ghost walked among the living, somewhere in those shadowed gorges.

She wondered about the spirit man, this Kuji, and what kind of life he led, if he existed at all. Then she shook her head at her own folly. Even down there, man couldn't cheat death, because it wasn't a true paradise. Life wasn't eternal in the Shangri-La Valley any more than it could be in the great cities of the world; babies were born, people grew old and died like everywhere else.

And the dead remained dead. That much, sadly, she knew.

Forty-one

'How much?'

'You heard me.'

Marlon stared at Judge Mosley, stunned. 'You can't be serious.'

'He is a thief, Captain Stone, with no witnesses to say otherwise. Find me five thousand or he can rot, for all I care.'

They argued for a while until they were interrupted by a knock on the door.

'Sorry, Your Honour. She wouldn't wait,' the assistant said as Junie breezed in.

'Good afternoon,' she said. 'I do apologise for being late but I was caught up in discussing this case with some witnesses. Have I missed any progress regarding my client?'

Marlon and the judge stared as she sat down, taking off her gloves.

'*Your* client?' the judge said.

'Yes, Joseph is a friend of mine and I do like to look after my friends. Goodness, it's awfully stuffy in here. I must ask my husband to look into some better ventilation. The budget is coming up, I understand,' she added, fanning her face with her notebook.

'That won't be necessary, Mrs Farthington, and I fail to see why you feel the need to offer your legal services to a native, especially in this case. It is quite black and white, I assure you.'

The judge seemed displeased with her presence and Junie seemed pleased in the knowledge.

'Oh, I'm well aware of the black and the white issue…and the *red* as I understand. Poker can be rather addictive, can it not? Red may be quite the colour your wife turns if she finds out about your gambling habits, Your *Honour*.'

Marlon had to smile at the expression on the judge's face. Junie had gotten the better of the man before and she was in her element again now. He sat back and let her talk, preparing himself to enjoy the show.

'I have no idea what you mean.'

'It's a curious thing that, in high society, the men seem to think the women are oblivious to what goes on behind closed doors, but the truth of the matter is we know everything. Boredom leads to gossip, you must understand, and I'm afraid I've been hearing some rather dreadful gossip about you today. It seems you've been spending some time down at the Jungle Club? In the back room…?'

The judge had turned a very bright pink. 'Rumours mean nothing to me.'

'Yes, but rumours ruin reputations, I'm afraid, and I know your wife is rather protective of hers, which by unfortunate association depends on yours of course.'

'Come to your point, Mrs Farthington,' the judge said darkly.

'Let my client go free and return his winnings and I may invite you and your lovely family to luncheon at our home. That should silence this terrible gossip, don't you think?'

The judge laughed. 'You seriously overestimate the value of your invitation, Mrs Farthington. The law overrides petty politicians in this part of the world.'

'The politicians make the laws, Judge Mosley.'

The judge gave a shake of his head. 'The winnings belong to the crown, as does the fine, which still stands. Five thousand and not a penny less.'

'Two thousand and you return the items that belong to my client. And no mention of this on his record.'

Marlon moved forwards at those words. 'Junie, can I speak to you –'

'Three thousand,' said the judge.

'Two and a half,' Junie said, putting up a hand to stop Marlon interrupting again.

The judge tapped his fingers together as they waited in the airless room.

'I hope you have cash.'

༄

They were laughing as they sat in the hotel bar and Marlon ordered celebratory drinks.

'You were brilliant, I must say.'

'So grateful, missus. To think that you would go to so much trouble without even knowing me. I can't thank you enough. I can't…' Joseph had been wiping at tears since they brought him out of the cell and led him into the fresh air. A storm that would relieve the heat had been brewing – almost as if the afternoon itself knew the tension was breaking.

An older New Guinean, Joseph was quite articulate in English, based on the rambling thanks he kept offering, and he had a sincere, open face that further confirmed Junie's confidence in his innocence.

'Justice prevails,' she said happily as the drinks arrived. This man's expression was all the recompense she wanted but Marlon was having none of that.

'We'll pay you back. Every penny. As soon as the contract comes through from Philippe.'

'No, justice is enough reward for me.'

'Nevertheless –'

'Don't be silly. I have plenty of money. Eliza always talks Ernest into giving me ridiculous amounts for shopping.'

'I would have thought he was careful with money.'

'He is. But he also knows that my appearance is an investment in his career, or so Eliza tells him.' She leant forwards and said in a conspiratorial whisper, 'I've been a bit cheeky over the years and tucked a fair bit of it aside. You never know when you might need it for a rainy day, and today it's pouring.' She pointed outside to where the rain was now bucketing down.

'Still, I feel uncomfortable using another man's money.'

'It's *my* money and, believe me, I earn it. Come on, enough talk of that. What shall we drink to?'

'Rainy days,' Marlon proposed, and they clinked their glasses and drank.

'Oh,' said Joseph with a deep, satisfied sigh. 'That's really good.' They laughed and he reached into his pocket, taking out the small bag they'd handed him. 'Can't believe you even got my watch back.'

'Just as well. Cost me a bloody fortune,' Marlon said.

'You said it was an old one of yours that didn't work properly,' Joseph replied and Junie giggled as he added, 'he tells lies. Lucky he wasn't on trial.' He shook the other item out and held it. 'I know you say justice is enough reward, miss, but I will repay you somehow, one day – and with more than money. Whenever you need me, I will help you. This I vow,' he said, and she was moved by his sincerity. 'Meanwhile, please take this silver lighter as a seal to this promise. It's yours now.'

She took it, knowing she could hardly refuse, and thanked him. 'That is very kind Joseph, thank you. I –' She paused, feeling the inscription on the back and turning it over to read it before continuing.

Then the world stopped around her, fading to grey. The faces, the tables, the room. Nothing existed except the sound of the rain that beat with her heart as she read the words that were etched in the silver. For it was her own hidden truth that lay in those tiny grooves, echoing a moment long gone. The moment that had haunted every day of her life since. Her own words, brought back by a ghost and placed in her hands as the heavens opened.

Burning Palms, December 1941.

Forty-two

Marlon and Joseph had been concerned but Junie had to get out of that room. She had to run. She had to think.

Kuji. A ghost had owned Michael's lighter. The only gift she'd ever given him had survived. Whoever he was, wherever he found it, this Kuji knew something about that plane wreck and she had to know what it was. Any tiny clue. Anything. Even to have a crash site to lay a plaque with his name. All of their names. Those beautiful Elite boys, stolen from them in a single blow.

The moment returned in familiar, terrible replay when her gentle mother said the most violent words of her life:

'It never arrived and they are missing…presumed killed.'

'…all of them?'

'All of them, my darling. They're saying it's impossible for them to have survived – there's nowhere they could have landed.'

'But they…they could have used parachutes…?'

'They weren't wearing any when they boarded.'

Nowhere to land. No parachutes. Junie remembered her head swimming in desperate circles as her mother continued.

'I'm so, so sorry…I know they were your friends…Michael was like a brother, really, wasn't he?'

'*Missing?*' she'd whispered the terrible word.

'Yes. It seems too cruel. Such a devastating thing to carry for their families.'

Missing. Until now.

Junie desperately needed to talk to someone from home and she longed for Katie but settled for Eliza. Today, more than ever before in her life, she needed a friend.

It was time at last for Eliza to know the truth.

༺❀༻

Junie rushed in the room and flung her wet jacket on the chair. 'I need to speak to you,' she said, her breathing in great rasps.

'Good Lord, calm down,' Eliza said, startled from her magazine. 'Anna, fetch a glass of water. And some gin. Hurry, girl.'

The maid ran and Eliza drew Junie to the couch, holding her hand.

'What on earth's wrong?'

'It's something we should have spoken of long ago...secrets between friends,' she began, taking out a handkerchief with shaking hands.

'Shh, it's all right. Have a drink,' Eliza soothed, as the tray arrived and she poured a generous amount of gin over ice.

Junie took a gulp and several deep breaths.

'Now, start from the beginning.'

She looked to the ceiling, tears brimming. 'The beginning? When was that? When I agreed to this sham of a marriage?'

'Marriages like ours are arranged, not welcomed.'

Junie nodded, sniffing. 'I guess that's why we – we can't resist when someone else offers what we really want...'

'I think that's exactly why,' Eliza said softly, patting her hand. 'You're being so good about this.'

'Am I? Well it's hard to know how to explain it after all this time.'

Eliza shrugged. 'I guess we just have to put it down to chemistry.'

'Yes. Chemistry. And when the drug is right there in front of you, what choice do you really have?' Junie said, taking another drink and wiping at the tears that were sliding down her cheeks. 'We're just flesh and blood really, aren't we?'

'I'm glad you understand that. I've been hoping you would.'

Junie looked puzzled. 'Of course I do...I know exactly why I did it.'

Eliza paused mid-drink, a fleeting look of realisation passing over her face. 'Why you had an affair?'

'No, it was much more than just an affair. It was *love*,' Junie said, crying now. 'It was love.'

Eliza refilled their glasses. 'Why on earth didn't you tell me?'

'It was early days. I guess I didn't know you well enough and then...'

'And then what? He went to war and you figured why bring it up?'

'Exactly.'

Eliza stood and began to pace the room. 'And now what's happened? Is he in New Guinea? Does he want you back?' She stopped, clicking her fingers. 'It's Marlon, isn't it? I knew there was something between you two.'

'No,' Junie said, tears clogging her words. 'No, Marlon's just a friend. This man can't want me back. He – he died.'

'Oh,' Eliza said. 'Oh, I'm so sorry, Junie.' She sat, taking her hand again. 'He...he was one of those country boys, wasn't he? In that Elite squad that went missing?'

'Yes.' Junie whispered. 'His name was Michael. Michael Riley. You know, my friends' brother.'

'And...was today the anniversary of his death or something?' Eliza said.

'No...today I found out a clue about him. I might be able to find out where they crashed. Or...I don't know – anything about what happened. That ghost man in the Shangri-La Valley. The Kuji. Pukz said he traded this with him.'

Junie took out the lighter and Eliza traced the inscription.

'It was Michael's. It was a gift...from me.'

'1941,' Eliza said in wonder. 'However did it get down there?'

Junie sniffed. 'That's what I need to find out.'

Eliza nodded thoughtfully. 'Well, one thing's for sure. The ambassador's wife can't very well traipse herself off into a valley full of cannibals to visit a ghost, now, can she?'

'No. And being the ambassador's wife won't help me organise a search party, because I can't very well show this to Ernest. The engraving – that was when I was with Michael at the beach.'

'Burning Palms. Lord, that sounds raunchy. Was it a place or a physical state?'

Junie couldn't help but smile. 'Both,' she admitted. 'Ernest knows I was there on a holiday with the girls but he doesn't know the boys met up with us. He'd make the connection. He'd know I was with another man when we were engaged.'

Eliza shrugged. 'And that matters now because...?'

'Because I need his help.'

'And this would hardly motivate him. I see.' Eliza thought for a moment. 'Does it really matter that much to you? To know where they ended up?'

'It matters to all of us,' Junie whispered, holding the lighter once more.

'Yes, I suppose so,' Eliza said. 'There's a lot of people left in the dark, isn't there? Let me ponder on it for a little while and see what I can come up with. And don't worry about Ernest. I can handle him for you when the time comes,' Eliza said.

Junie nodded, exhausted now as her head fell on Eliza's shoulder. 'You always do.'

⁘

'I'm sorry to barge in but you've had me worried sick. What happened? Why did you leave like that?'

Junie looked like she'd been crying all afternoon and Marlon's concern increased as she gestured vaguely towards the couch.

'I'm so sorry, Marlon. Please, have a seat. Coffee? Tea? Wine?'

'Anything. What happened?' he repeated, sitting opposite her.

'I just…had a bit of a shock,' she said, pouring from the half-empty bottle of chardonnay. She was shaking.

'I could see that much,' he said, waiting.

Junie sipped her drink and he wondered how much she'd had. Then she took the lighter out of her pocket and handed it to him. 'I recognised it,' she said simply.

'From where?'

'It belonged to a – a friend of mine. I gave it to him – that's my inscription.'

Marlon stared at the lighter, incredulous. 'Was he…did he serve over here?'

'Yes. He died here. No-one knows where exactly. The whole squad never came back – they say it was a plane crash…'

'They lost contact during a freak storm.'

'Yes.'

'And there was an American pilot called Harris?' Marlon asked slowly.

Junie froze. 'Yes, that's the name. You knew him?'

'I knew all of them. The Elite were with me. In Wau.'

Neither said a word as they stared at each other in shock, digesting this link they hadn't known they shared. A painful memory that had sent them individually into dark places in the years that followed that tragic day.

'Which one did you give this to?' he asked, tracing the words on the lighter.

'Michael Riley,' she whispered.

Marlon closed his eyes briefly, seeing him clearly when she said his name. 'I remember him well,' he said, his voice breaking. 'Very well indeed.'

Junie nodded and her anguish was evident as she took the lighter back and held it against her chest.

'He was the one, wasn't he? That night at the Trocadero?' Marlon said, remembering now. The look on her face. The young man he recognised when they met in Wau. *Must be the uniform.*

Junie nodded.

'The man you actually loved?' he added, seeing it plainly now.

'Yes,' she said, beginning to cry and Marlon took her in his arms as she dissolved into sobs, sharing the grief with her, comforting what could never really be comforted.

'I need to know where it happened...I need to know why.'

Marlon held her and stroked her back, the bloodshed of war once again fresh in his mind. 'Yes,' he said softly. 'I think we'd all like to know that.'

'It was...like a needle in a haystack but now...' Junie wiped at her eyes as she pulled back and they sat together in silence.

'Maybe it's better we don't know,' Marlon said. 'It would be a difficult thing to see.'

Junie wrung her handkerchief through her hands. 'What we've imagined already couldn't be any worse.'

'True.' He'd been down that dark path in his mind many times over the years.

'For me it's not a matter of *if* we should find this Kuji and ask him where he found it, but...but when and how we can organise a group to go down there.' Junie had found her practical voice again, although it was somewhat muffled by tears.

'Being married to the ambassador should help things along.'

'I can't exactly show him this,' Junie said, pointing at the inscription.

'Burning Palms,' he read quietly. 'Sounds exotic.'

'It was.'

A twinge of jealousy spiked in Marlon, despite the circumstances. 'Lucky man.'

'No, he wasn't. Quite the opposite in the end.'

Maybe it was the sorrow that flooded her face, or maybe it was the way she managed to sound guilty and innocent at the same time that moved him to say his next words, but whatever the reasons, he couldn't take them back once they were out.

'What if there was another purpose for going down there?'

'Such as?'

Marlon stood, picking his hat up from the table and making up his mind. 'Have you told anyone about this?'

'Only Eliza.'

'Good. Don't say anything to anyone else for now, all right?'

'All right,' she said, watching him in confusion. 'What do you plan to do?'

'I've got an idea, but you're going to have to trust me. Can you do that?'

Junie nodded, and it was easy to read her complete confidence in him. 'I do trust you.'

Marlon tipped his hat and left, thinking that when she sent him a look like that maybe she really shouldn't.

It was dark when Marlon returned to his apartment and he turned on the light and rummaged in the back of the cupboard, pulling out the box and unlocking it. Picking up the gourd, he stared at the black gold inside it.

Philippe would want in, that much he knew.

He moved to the window, opening it wide to the lights of the port, thinking of the dangers involved, the power in his hands.

Yes, there was more than one form of treasure that had found its way out of Shangri-La. But what price would be paid if they went in for more?

Forty-three

Junie tapped her pen, wondering if she should tell Katie and the girls but knowing Marlon was right. She shouldn't tell anyone else for now. It was too explosive on its own – just a missing piece of the needle from within what was, still, a very large haystack. Better to wait until he came back with whatever plan he seemed to be devising.

Sighing, she picked up the letter that had arrived yesterday, trying not to feel hurt by the last few paragraphs but failing.

Frankie had a wonderful long weekend with us all at Braidwood. I've never seen a child more fascinated with 'secret adventures' before – we really need to get her off those Enid Blyton books. I must have watched her explore your dad's old desk for an hour!

Your mum and dad both dote on her and I really don't understand why you haven't taken her back home more often but then again I don't really understand what you're doing in New Guinea away from her. I know if I'd had a baby to the man I loved, I could never bear to be parted from them. Especially when it's all you have left.

Anyway, I'm done preaching to you, Genie-Junie, if you are still that girl (and I guess you are). I wish you'd come home and prove it to me. Maybe Frankie will convince you better than I can that boarding school was a bad idea.

Love regardless,
Katie

Junie picked up her little girl's letter, unable to keep from crying over it again.

Dear Mummy

I am well eggsept I have hurt my finger when it got betten by a cow on the farm but Katie says cows don't have propa teeth but I got bit so they do have gums that hurt any way. Marigold says you are in a house but I think you are in a casel because you are a famous pursen in new gini. I think it has hiden passige ways and you can run from baddies if they try to steal your treasure. I wish I culd find a passsige to you because I am sad at night and cry in my pillo but the teachers don't know becus I turn it over so they don't know its wet next day.

I miss you Mummy. Tell Daddy to let you come home now but don't tell him I cry becus it's a secret.

Love Frankie xxxxxxxxxxooooooooooo
PS don't get aten by any corocdiles becus I love you.

Holding the letter against her heart, Junie ached with a wrenching, maternal longing. Only six more weeks and she could go home for holidays, she reminded herself. It isn't that long. *Yes, it is,* her mother's heart screamed back. *It's an eternity.*

Maybe she couldn't do this. Maybe she should go home for good and let Ernest take her to court and be done with it – but not before she exhausted this lead on Michael's final resting place. She was too close to the possible answer here and a clue presenting itself almost like a miracle surely had to mean something. Perhaps it was a sign from him somehow, if she could believe in such things.

She owed Michael this; she owed it to them all. Maybe it would be the final part of the puzzle she could share with their child one day: who her father really was; why she couldn't be with him; how he served his country. Where he died.

It would be the kindest way to tell Frankie the truth, if Junie ever decided she could. That he was safe in Shangri-La forever now. Laid to rest in paradise.

Forty-four

Philippe's house was extravagant, as expected, and Felicity was certainly in her element tonight as she sat next to her husband at the end of the table. Her hair was heavily lacquered and she wore a new dress she'd had made in Hong Kong – which had cost a small fortune, she had no hesitation in sharing. The blue silk did look expensive but it was an unfortunate style for her large frame, her exposed arms white and jelly-like as she sawed at her steak. Junie could almost feel sorry for her if it weren't for the snide put-downs that Felicity directed her way. She reminded her too much of Constance then for any real pity.

'And how did you enjoy your adventures with the *cannibales*?' Philippe asked Junie.

'I don't even know where to begin, really. The village had domed huts and it was so colourful – the people decorated everything. Even the ground. And they did a performance for us wearing giant masks and feathers up to here.' She gestured above her head. 'And the way they painted their faces –'

'Savages,' mumbled Miles.

'No, they weren't savage at all,' she said. 'They were gentle and welcoming and the men seemed…well, very proud.'

'And what of this clinic they have set up?' Philippe asked, looking to Ernest.

'Needs more funding, of course. I think that's why I was invited,' he said. 'It certainly got some attention in the press, though, have you seen it yet?'

They hadn't and he clicked his fingers. 'Junie, hand that paper over.'

'I hate to think what they did without it,' Junie said, taking the newspaper out of her purse and passing it down. 'Some of the children would certainly have died without modern medicine. John is teaching what he knows to the chief's son, Pukz, who's also trying to learn English, which is quite hilarious at times,' she said with a giggle, looking at Marlon. 'It was just…amazing, the whole thing. And I haven't even mentioned the flight! That was like nothing you can even describe.'

'I'm sure you'll give it a try…at great length too,' Felicity remarked. 'I'm just joking, of course. What did you make of it, Eliza?'

'Let's just say they gave me a little spade when I asked for directions to the ladies' bathroom.'

'How disgusting,' Felicity said as the others laughed.

'Here it is,' Ernest announced. '*The Sydney Morning Herald* no less.' The inside page spread was passed around to the impressed table.

'Listen to this: "Ambassador to all: Farthington extends his hand to primitive man". I say, that reads well,' said Miles, squinting at the caption below the photograph of Ernest and Junie with Pukz and the chief.

'Oh, you look lovely in that one. Like a movie star!' exclaimed Eliza at the photograph of Junie with the sick little girl. '"Mrs Farthington was moved to tears by the brave children in the mountains who fight illness that western drugs can prevent. She has vowed to continue to support the clinic in the future and this journalist sees a beautiful patroness in the making,"' she read. 'Honestly, darling, you're a modern Florence Nightingale!'

'You'd think they would have done your hair and make-up,' said Felicity, appearing bored as she glanced over.

'It has served its purpose well, no?' said Philippe, ignoring her. 'The handsome young diplomat and his lovely wife caring for the native peoples. Perfection for the publicity machines.'

Ernest looked pleased.

'I would like to go back,' Junie admitted. 'There is so much to be done.'

'You mean money to be spent,' said Ernest, folding the paper back up.

Felicity agreed. 'The poor always cry poor. They have two nurses and this doctor of yours building a nice little bamboo hospital. How much more do they really need?' That made a few at the table laugh but Junie was unimpressed.

'For a start, they need more equipment.'

'Enough for now, ladies,' Ernest said. 'Let's talk of something more pleasant than sick natives, shall we? Who has any other topics for discussion?'

Junie opened her mouth to argue but Marlon intercepted.

'Actually, I do.'

'As long as it doesn't involve government funding, talk away,' Ernest said, pouring more wine.

'Actually it's an opportunity to make money. Potentially a great deal,' Marlon said and the table turned towards him.

'We are all the ears,' said Philippe.

Marlon reached under the table and picked up his bag. 'As you know, our friend Pukz is a curious lad, and he found something a few months back. Something he has shared with me. I have hesitated to act on it until now but I can't think of a better time, especially as I need each of you involved if this is to succeed. A mining expert, a government official and perhaps a financial backer,' he added, nodding at Philippe, Ernest and Miles in turn.

'If what is to succeed?' asked Felicity.

'An expedition.' Marlon took the clay gourd out of his bag and placed it on the table, opening the lid. 'It seems there truly are riches to be found in Shangri-La.'

They stared into the gourd as Marlon's meaning began to descend.

'Is that...?'

'Oil,' Marlon confirmed.

That had the group's full attention, especially Philippe's.

'Where did he find it?'

'About three days' walk into uncharted parts, he said, deep into the valley. His party were afraid of it,' Marlon told them, nodding at the gourd, 'said it looked like the earth was bleeding black blood – but Pukz collected some and brought it back anyway. Then when he saw me checking the oil in the engine one day, he ran and got this to show me.'

That explained those ambiguous comments near the plane, Junie realised.

'Any idea how much?' Felicity asked, her excitement palpable as Marlon handed Philippe the sample.

'No, just that it sits in a flat area near a bend in the river. Like a wound, Pukz said, or that was the best translation I could figure out.'

'Seems the valley holds more than a few secrets,' Eliza said, looking at Junie while Philippe passed the sample along to Ernest.

'Well, if there is potential for mining, then I owe it to the people of New Guinea and Australia to investigate,' he announced. 'Who knows? Could have a positive effect on the economy. My duties would prevent me from actually going myself but I'm sure I can get government approval for an expedition.'

'I would be willing to help form a party. Of course we'll need a geologist,' Philippe said.

'I feel I must remind you before we go any further that this part of the country is untouched and unmapped, and the natives reputedly very war-like. I have no idea how they may react to us.'

There was silence as the others reflected on Marlon's words.

'Can you get help from your contacts at Wamena?' Philippe asked.

'Some,' Marlon said. 'I'm confident Pukz will oblige – that man has no fear. My friend Joseph will be invaluable too – he's an excellent tracker and grew up in the jungle. Who else? A few carriers, I suppose, and a medic –'

'An armed escort?' Felicity suggested.

'I don't think it would do well to appear like we're invading, but we will need to be armed, yes.'

Miles nodded at the gourd, making up his mind. 'Well I, for one, won't be going on this bloody expedition of yours, however I would be willing to finance it,' he said. 'But top secret all right? Not a word of this outside this room. And we'll need a contract drawn up.'

'Of course.'

'I can help with that,' Junie said.

'No, we'll get a barrister,' Miles said, dismissing her offer.

Ernest nodded. 'I'll get Smythe down at the embassy to take care of it.'

'So is it official? Are we in?' Philippe asked, hand in the air, and one by one, each man raised his.

'An expedition into the jungles of New Guinea to search for black gold,' Eliza announced dramatically. 'You know, boys, I think I'm actually excited for you.'

'I'm excited for all of us,' said Felicity, giggling.

'To treasure hunting!' said Philippe.

Marlon toasted but he was watching Junie. *Yes, to treasure hunting*, she said to him silently. In whatever form that took down in the valleys of Shangri-La.

❧

Perhaps it was the wine wearing off, or more likely the number of issues playing on her mind, but Junie couldn't sleep. What she wouldn't give to be able to go on that expedition herself, but of course it was out of the question. She wondered if Marlon would have revealed his secret today if it was his only motivation for going down the valley, or if he would have waited. She knew something was bothering him about this trip, more than just the dangers.

Tossing aside the sheets she gave up on sleep and went in search of some hot milk in the kitchen.

'Stay,' she said to Digger, patting his sleepy head as he looked at her questioningly.

The clock chimed one and she realised she had forgotten to tell Ernest he'd had a call from the embassy to say that his meeting time had changed for tomorrow. Damn, she thought, chances were she'd sleep in and forget to tell him in the morning. She headed to his office, where he'd likely be asleep in his chair.

'It may all work in our favour,' she heard a voice say from inside the room and she was surprised to hear it was Eliza's. At one in the morning? she thought, confused, but for some reason Junie didn't push the slightly ajar door and enter. She looked through the crack instead.

'Overnight as a one-off was all right but this seems extreme. She could be there for weeks.'

'Only one week, by the sounds of things, and John is there and his staff. And with the men heading up there anyway it is a perfect opportunity for her to visit the clinic,' Eliza said, '*and* the publicity continues. A win-win, I'd say.'

Ernest stood and walked over to the window. 'I suppose I could send a bodyguard or something.'

'I doubt that's necessary. You've met them – they're a friendly people.'

'It's not only the natives I worry about,' he grunted into his scotch.

'Don't be jealous, darling. It doesn't suit you,' Eliza said, lighting a cigarette. 'Besides the men will be off in the jungle most of the time. Focus on what I'm saying. It's good for your image: caring ambassador's wife continues her work with the natives and all that rot.'

Junie smiled. Eliza was getting her as close as she could to that expedition, which was something at least. She was a true friend.

'And what exactly are you getting out of this, vixen?' Ernest asked, his words freezing Junie's hand as she went to push open the door.

She watched in shock as Eliza slipped onto the desk and pulled Ernest in between her legs.

'You to myself, of course.'

'Always the bad girl,' he said, unbuttoning his shirt.

'Guess that's why I can't resist such a bad man.'

Junie walked the halls in a daze, finding her way back to the bedroom and laying on the coverlet. Some part of her wondered if they used her bed when they had their trysts. At least someone was having sex in it, she thought, then began to cry.

She sobbed for a long time, hugging her legs like a child, the grief wrenching from her. Not for her marriage or Ernest. Not even for the betrayal. She cried because Katie had been right all along. Eliza had never been Junie's friend; it had always been about what she could get out of her. Keeping the enemy close so you could blind her from the truth. Offering her friendship because it made it easier to keep her lover – they were always in the same place.

She'd been used.

And it hurt the most because she loved this friend who had never been a friend at all.

John had been right that night at the first dinner party. Ignorance was a cruel enemy, indeed.

Forty-five

It had been a long few weeks, made longer by the fact that he'd barely seen Junie, and when he had, she was very quiet and withdrawn. Marlon suspected it was due to that obnoxious husband of hers and he wondered how a woman like that, smart and confident in so many ways, could put up with such an unworthy marriage. And be torn away from her child. Something didn't add up.

Anyway, he'd see her today, and without that bastard Ernest in tow. Somehow Junie had talked her way into returning to the clinic while they went on the expedition and the thought cheered him until he went to pack the gourd and paused to consider what he was about to do. The whole country was slowly being scouted by mining companies – sooner or later someone was bound to find oil in that valley he reasoned to himself yet again. And it was better for him to control the claim and protect the natives than most westerners – he wouldn't let them be exploited in the ways other tribes had. But thinking about any destruction of such a mysterious, ancient place sickened him, and it didn't help that he'd tied himself to such dubious partners. It also didn't help that they might all end up dead at the end of a spear.

Despite these misgivings, he was also excited. There was money in it, of course – potentially – but that was small motivation in comparison to setting foot in territory that had long fascinated him, a part of the world completely cut off from the rest of mankind. Even Pukz had only seen a fraction. Marlon's fascination with Indigenous peoples had come full circle, and first thing tomorrow he would be Miwok once more, at one with the earth, if not the sea. His home would be the forest floor, the tribes he met interwoven into nature in every respect with culture and customs unknown.

He and his party would be explorers in a modern age discovering secrets time forgot. The concept was a thrilling one. And there was more. Somewhere in that lost land roamed a soul that held the only clue to a mystery that had never been solved, one that had nearly destroyed what was left of Captain Stone, the broken man he'd become back during the war.

He opened the top drawer of his dresser and took out an envelope he rarely touched, filled with memories he feared to visit: a newspaper clipping of a missing squad of men; a photo of himself and Marty Harris, standing in front of a plane with a sea goddess painted on the side. The mass tragedy that had split the cracks within him wide open.

Memories came like an armada then: Pearl Harbor and a swarm of iron sharks; Darwin and the limp form of a girl in a yellow dress; New Guinea and a band of men on an ill-fated plane. A war that just wouldn't end despite an ever-starving enemy whose planes were held together with cardboard. Then the terrible finale that finally came; the atomic obliteration of mass populations – the devastating price of victory.

Marlon fell too then. Long hours in bars. Gambling, women, booze. Nights in the lock-up. A scattered end to a scattered war. Without Major Hamlin, he supposed he would have ended up in jail, but that man had turned out to be a true friend. His latest letter had said he'd divorced and remarried to a very nice teacher named Ellen and Marlon was glad. The major deserved a lot more respect than his first wife, Samantha, had ever given him.

But Hamlin couldn't save Marlon from himself, and it had taken years to conquer his demons and piece his life back together. Joseph had been a large part of that: waking him when he slept in; keeping him in the sky. Eventually time slowly wound the horrors down and offered him sleep once more. Purpose. Goals. And now this one last kindness: the possibility of an answer.

Yes, he did want to know what happened to that group of young men, boys who'd landed in the jungle green as the hills around them, yet couldn't wait to fight. Killed in a plane flown by a pilot he had trained himself. He did want to know where they finally lay – but unlike Junie, he didn't need to know; Marlon had already made his peace with that tragedy. It had been hard won over the years but finally he'd accepted that the dead would want the survivors to live, and live well. That was what he could truly give them – a more important tribute than a grave or a monument.

Yes, an answer would be nice, but it wasn't essential. It was for Junie Farthington he would seek it out, then maybe she could make her peace with the past too. Because until she did that she was lost – more lost than those missing bodies. More lost than anyone he'd ever met.

Placing the envelope back in the drawer, he picked up his bags and swung open the door to begin his journey. Whatever secrets lay in that valley he suddenly couldn't wait to seek them out. Then he could get on with his life.

And maybe Junie could begin to live hers.

'You know, it took some doing to get Ernest to agree to this,' Eliza reminded her.

'I'm sure it did.' Junie slapped the case shut and went to make up a toiletries bag.

Eliza tapped her foot, smoking near the window. 'Tell me what's wrong. I know you're upset with me although God knows why. I got you your clinic holiday and now you'll be right there if any news comes out –'

'Yes, I'm very grateful. Thank you. Is that the car?'

Eliza parted the curtain. 'Yes.'

'Then I'd best get a move on. See you soon,' Junie said, putting on her hat and gloves.

'Just like that. No "I'll miss you, Eliza, I don't know what I'll do without you, Eliza"? You know, I'm beginning to wonder if my friendship means anything to you any more.' She picked at the curtain and Junie thought she saw water gathering in her eyes.

She put her bags down, deciding the time had come. 'Did we ever have a real friendship, Eliza?'

Eliza looked at her in surprised hurt. 'How can you say something like that? You're my best friend in the world. I…I followed you to New Guinea, for God's sake.'

'We both know it wasn't me you followed.'

The silence was heavy with the truth and a tear traced its way down Eliza's perfectly powdered cheek. 'How long have you known?'

'Since the dinner party at the Rafels'. I saw you in the middle of the night. In his study. On his desk.'

Eliza drew on her cigarette, her hand shaking. 'I see. Rather a long time to wait to tell me.'

'I had to sort out my own feelings first,' Junie said.

Eliza nodded and her eyes shimmered. It was the first time Junie had ever seen her cry. 'And what did you find?'

'That I couldn't really care less what Ernest has done.' Junie picked up her bags, the words trailing behind her as she walked out. 'He wasn't the one who broke my heart.'

The curtain was still parted as Junie looked up from the car window and she knew the woman standing there was about to learn just how lonely life can be without a true friend in the world.

❦

Marlon was whistling as she walked across the tarmac and he paused in his last-minute inspection of the engine to chuckle at her and wipe his hands.

'Did I really agree to that?' he said, nodding at a wagging Digger.

'Yes.'

'Hmm,' he said, walking over and scratching Digger's ears before straightening. 'Well, are you ready to fly, monkey?'

'That depends, where are we headed again?'

'Somewhere over the rainbow.'

'Ah, that's right. Perhaps I should have worn my ruby slippers,' she said.

He feigned offence. 'Anyone would think you don't trust my plane to get you back home again.'

Junie had to smile, her mood lifting. He looked ridiculously handsome standing there with his shirtsleeves rolled up and grease on his arms; even on his cheek as he grinned at her. 'I told you before, I do trust you,' she said.

'Maybe you shouldn't,' he said and she felt a warm secret unfold between them.

'Hey!' he called to Philippe, who was arriving with Carl Spillane, his geologist colleague from Canada. 'Welcome, fellas. Mind your heads.'

There was a cough from behind and she turned to greet Joseph warmly.

'Looking forward to treasure hunting?' she asked.

'In all its forms.' He winked, and she knew Marlon had told him.

Soon the whole party was in the air: Joseph, Carl, Philippe, Marlon, a young doctor from Hong Kong called Felix Yu and Junie. And Digger, much to Philippe's distress. He confessed that he was terrified of dogs.

'How can you be scared of this big sook?' Junie asked, holding Digger's adoring face in her hands.

'He is like the wolf!' Philippe shuddered, moving as far away from Digger as possible. That arrangement suited Junie just fine.

By the time they'd arrived, she had almost forgotten all the complications associated with getting to this place once more. The simplicity of it was immediately palpable with the sounds of the forest the only background noise behind the rhythm of village life. The natives were as curious as before, watching the westerners alight and unpack with wide stares and occasional conversation. Then the elders arrived and Junie was touched by their formal welcome, appreciating the paint, feathers and mask adornments. She knew enough now to know they were being honoured.

John was pleased to see them once more and even more pleased to meet Dr Felix Yu. He showed them around the clinic almost immediately and the young doctor seemed to share his enthusiasm for the work being done, marvelling at how much they had achieved already and offering suggestions that were carefully recorded in John's diary.

'Don't forget he's coming with us tomorrow,' Marlon reminded John.

'Yes, yes, of course. I was thinking of introducing a laboratory...' John said as he led Felix away.

'I doubt they'll get much sleep,' Junie said.

Marlon stretched, yawning himself. 'Rested or not, he needs to be ready to go at seven.'

'You look ready to go to bed now.'

'Not likely,' he said, his brown eyes following her. 'I don't believe in taking afternoon naps on my own.'

Joseph cleared his throat, but it set off a coughing fit and John returned, listening to it with concern.

'That sounds nasty. How long have you had it?'

'Got worse...overnight,' Joseph told him, recovering his breath. 'I'm all right.'

But he wasn't, and by dinner time he was the newest patient in the clinic, tossing and turning with a fever.

'What will you do if he isn't ready in the morning?' asked Carl of Philippe, who turned to Marlon.

'It is your expedition. Should we delay?'

'Let's see how he is in the morning. He could always follow with one of the guides a day later, if need be.'

'But no longer than that or he'll never catch up?' Carl guessed.

'Yes, no longer a gap than that. Even an experienced man like Joseph doesn't want to hit unknown areas without the group.' Marlon sounded calm but Junie knew he was worried.

'Everything looks better in the light of day,' she said cheerfully, handing around the roasted pork as it arrived, 'and on a full stomach.'

'Ah, *merci*, *madame*,' Philippe said, leaning back to smile at her. 'But where is the wine?'

'Eliza isn't here so I guess we're not drinking,' Junie said, feeling pained as she said the name.

'I, uh, thought to put this in the bag,' said Carl, taking out some white rum.

'Good man,' said Marlon and they added it to their juice. 'We may as well enjoy our last night in civilisation.'

'This is civilisation?' Carl laughed as the dancing rituals began.

'It is, compared to where we're going.'

By the time the new visitors had sat agog at the tribal rituals and the rum bottle had been emptied of its contents, Junie was ready for bed. Unfortunately Philippe was well in his cups and seemingly intent on trying to persuade her into his.

'Surely you must have been a fashion model in Australia?' he said. 'This face and this figure...*tu es la femme la plus belle au monde, il n'y a pas des mots pour le dire.*'

'As I said, I don't speak French,' Junie said, moving ever closer to Digger, who watched the man warily.

'He said you're the most beautiful woman in the world,' Marlon translated, overhearing as he returned from checking on Joseph.

'*Parlez vous Français?*' Philippe slurred in surprise.

'Only phrases like that. Come on, let's call it a night, eh?'

'No, no, we stay up to watch the stars...' Philippe said, leaning towards Junie as Digger gave a low growl.

'You'll be seeing stars at this rate. Come on,' said Carl, helping him to his feet. 'How is Joseph?'

'Fever hasn't broken. Felix is monitoring him for now, so we'll see in the morning. Careful there,' he observed.

'Right you are,' Carl said, a little unsteadily as he propped up a muttering Philippe who was saying something about 'the wolf'. 'Well, good night all. See you in the morning.'

'Good night,' said Junie as she stood as well. 'I might head off too.'

'I'll walk you,' Marlon said, and she didn't argue.

The jungle was filled with mysterious noises and Junie half wondered what made them as each one arrived from the dark edges of the village. Scuttering ran across the insect song and she thought she identified both flapping and slithering too. It made her worry for the men.

'I'm afraid of what you might find out there.'

'So am I,' Marlon admitted. 'Especially considering what impact it could have.'

'Which discovery?'

'Oil,' he said, sighing. 'A crash site has already had its impact years ago.'

'If it's there. Even looking for this Kuji might be a waste of time.'

'Nah, he's just a ghost running around in paradise! How hard can it be?' He grinned at her.

'You think it's impossible.'

'No, I think we may well find him,' he said, sobering. 'Pukz told me tonight that he lives not far from where he found the sample. *Lives.* That got my attention. Not a wandering holy man like I was thinking he probably was.'

Junie felt hope rise a little more. 'So, not completely a missing needle?'

'No. Mind you, I'm starting to wonder –' He paused, his expression difficult to read in the moonlight. 'Does it really matter to you so much – knowing where they crashed? Now that you've had time to think about it?'

She considered that. 'At first – when I saw the lighter, I got such a shock. Like Michael was contacting me somehow from beyond the grave but now...I guess I just want to close that chapter once and for all. It would be nice to be able to do that.'

'You can close it without that knowledge, you know.'

'I know. Still...it would help, I think. I wish I was going,' she said wistfully. 'I wish I could see this man for myself.'

He stopped and looked down at her. 'You know it's out of the question, but if I find out anything at all, I'll tell you. You believe me, don't you?'

Junie nodded. 'I know the information isn't going to be easy to hear whatever it turns out to be...but I know you'll tell me the truth. I really do trust you.'

He moved closer then. 'I thought I told you maybe you shouldn't.'

The night was cool and when Marlon ran his hands along her arms, she shivered. He said nothing as he pulled her closer and Junie couldn't resist as his mouth brushed against hers, asking if she wanted more. Then his arms went around her back and he pulled her body against his, kissing her in a sudden rush, and the chemistry they found fleetingly years ago instantly reignited. It had been so long since she felt passion in her veins she drank him in at first, but then the shame arrived.

'I – I shouldn't. Oh God, I'm such a hypocrite,' Junie said, drawing back.

'Why do you say that?' he asked, mouth against her ear, his breathing uneven. 'Because of a lover from years ago? I think you've let enough water flow under that bridge, don't you?'

'No, it's not that. Well not entirely,' she admitted, guilty at the thought of Michael. 'It's because of Eliza…I found out she has been having an affair with Ernest. All those years of betrayal and I never knew.'

Marlon absorbed that then kissed her forehead softly, as if to draw the hurt away. 'The betrayal by Eliza you mean, because you thought there was true friendship there.'

'Exactly.'

'So this is completely different,' he said, stroking back her hair. 'Because you don't have any real relationship with Ernest, do you? Not even friendship.'

'No.'

'So you're betraying no-one. You're no hypocrite, Junie.'

'Then what am I?'

He held her chin then, meeting her eyes. 'Lost.'

The simple answer was so true, tears formed. She let him kiss her again and there was sweet longing there but it was tainted. *Oh God, I'm lost. I'm so lost. Where did it go so wrong?*

Marlon paused and brushed her lips with his thumb.

'How do I find my way out?' she whispered against it.

'That's something we're going to have to figure out, isn't it? It helps to know what you want.' He paused. 'What do you want, Junie?'

She rested her head against his chest, her eyes closing against the force of an old, familiar ache. 'I just want to be happy. It's all I ever wanted, but it always slipped away from me somehow.'

Marlon kissed the top of her head in the moonlight and she felt comfort envelope her for the first time in a long while as he wrapped his arms around her.

'To hold on to happiness,' he summarised. 'Well, that's a start.'

Forty-six

It wasn't until near dark next day that Joseph turned the corner and Junie helped him sit up to eat, smiling her relief.

'Not a very good trick to get sick as soon as we arrived, now, was it?'

'Sorry about that, ma'am. I'm a bloody nuisance, excuse the French.'

'Yes, we've had enough French around here,' she agreed, thinking of the very irritable Philippe who had left with the party earlier. 'Pukz's friend Tooh says he can take you down tomorrow, if you're up to it.'

'I'm sure I will be,' he said, eating the yams and pork hungrily. 'This is good.'

'Appetite is back I see,' John said, walking in.

'Takes a lot to stop me eating,' Joseph said between mouthfuls. 'Could you let Tooh know I'll be ready in the morning at sunrise?'

'Are you sure?' Junie asked, checking his forehead again, but the fever really was gone.

'Feel like a new man.'

'I don't need a new man, I need you. I'll let Tooh know,' she said, patting his arm as she went.

Tooh lived not far from the clinic and she walked over, avoid-ing several pigs being chased by some children with sticks as she went. Digger ran with them and the children kept their hands on his back as much as they could, pushing against each other to have the honour of being connected to him. Feared at first, her big dog was now quite the village celebrity, winning them over with his friendliness and charm, especially when he rolled on his back and shook hands for treats.

'Hello?' she called into the empty hut, then saw Tooh on the ground nearby. He'd been sharpening a spear and stood to greet her.

'Missus,' he said with a nod.

She knew Pukz had been teaching him a smattering of English but she wasn't sure how much he would understand, so she tried some gesturing as she spoke. 'Joseph go tomorrow to valley,' she said, pointing at the clinic then in the direction of the expedition. 'At sunrise.' She frowned, trying to think how to visually explain dawn.

'Sun,' he said, pointing at the sky, then holding his fist behind his arm and raising it slowly.

'Yes. Very good,' she added.

He smiled with a mouthful of uneven teeth and continued to sharpen his spear. Junie wasn't sure whether she should go, but curiosity kept her there.

'Hunt *wam*?' she asked, remembering the word for pig.

He nodded. 'And sef.'

'Sef?' she repeated.

'Sef,' he said again, holding the spear out away from her as if to shield her from harm.

'Safe!' she said, understanding. 'To stay safe.'

He nodded, his crooked smile on display again. 'Sef.'

'From who?' she asked, not really expecting an answer.

'Kurelu.' He shrugged. 'Kuji.'

Mary-Anne O'Connor

Junie locked on the word. 'Kuji? You have seen him too? You... see?' She pointed at her own eyes.

He nodded again. 'Pukz, Tooh see. Litter.'

'Yes, that's right, the lighter. I have it,' she told him, taking it out of her belt bag. 'See?'

Tooh was excited to see it again and spoke rapidly in his native language. 'Kuji,' he said. He held his hand high above his head then pointed at her arm.

'I don't understand.'

Then he pointed at her beige shorts and back at her arm. 'Kuji.'

Something began to whirr in the back of Junie's mind. 'Tooh,' she said, trying to remain calm. 'Come with me.'

He followed her in confusion as she almost ran back to the clinic.

'John,' she panted. '*John!*'

'Yes, my dear. What's wrong?' he asked, coming out from the back.

'Tooh said...Tooh, say it again. About the Kuji.'

Tooh looked reluctant and she encouraged him.

'About the lighter.'

'Oh yes, the story of the lighter. Pukz told me about that,' John said. 'Can't imagine where they found it down there but I suppose it was a trade with some wandering villager.'

'They say Kuji gave it to them.'

'Kuji?' John laughed. 'But that's absurd. He's a mythical character – a ghost or something, not a man. What's all this, Tooh?'

Tooh looked worried and didn't seem to want to speak so John conversed gently with him in his limited Dani, persuading him.

'I think he is trying to say they were concerned I would be insulted that they have met a god and I have not, me being a healer or magic man,' he explained, then listened further. 'So they didn't tell me that Kuji gave it to them.'

'Ask him what Kuji looks like,' Junie said, her pulse racing.

He did so and Tooh chatted and pointed once again to Junie's shorts and then their arms and faces, then held his hand high above his head.

'He says Kuji's skin is white, like he has died, and that he is tall, so he can reach the spirits above,' John said the words slowly, sitting down. 'How peculiar.'

Tooh continued and the doctor stared at him, stunned.

'What is it? What did he say?'

'He…he says he is afraid of him – that he will steal his spirit. He says we are *like* Kuji too but he's not afraid of us – we're not the same.' His eyes held Junie's as the last words fell. 'This Kuji floated on a white cloud from the sky. This white man came from the gods.'

꧁꧂

'He – he could be a *survivor*, don't you see that? From the war.'

'It's impossible,' John said.

'It's not. People survive plane crashes every day. Look at those people on the *Gremlin Special*. That Margaret What's-her-name… Hastings. They were wrecked in the same place!' Junie held his shoulders, imploring him. 'John, he floated down on a cloud from the sky –'

'Native language is difficult to translate.'

'He is white!'

John sighed, running his hand over his grey hair. 'Even if some poor fellow ended up in the valley during the war, why didn't he ever try to come out? He could have gone with Pukz and Tooh. He could have left any time he wanted.'

'Maybe he isn't right in the head. Maybe he's traumatised – I don't know.'

'Maybe he doesn't want to leave,' Joseph said, who'd been listening intently. Thoughts of *Lost Horizon* leapt to mind and she shoved them aside.

'There's something else going on here isn't there?' John guessed.

'Tell him, Junie. You may as well.'

Junie held the lighter in her pocket tight in her hand, debating how much to reveal, then figured she had nothing left to lose any more anyway.

'I know who owned it,' she said, handing it to John.

'You…you know this man?'

'Yes. He and his friends disappeared in a plane crash during a storm in 1943. Somewhere in the central inlands of New Guinea. They think. That's all we ever knew – until now.'

'And you're saying…one of them survived?'

'Well it's possible! I mean they said at the time they weren't wearing parachutes but what if there were some on the plane? We don't know for sure.'

'You think one of them jumped and now he lives with the Kurelu? Come now, Junie…'

'It's not what I think, it's what I know: someone in the Shan-gri-La Valley owned this lighter and he is no ghost.'

John tapped the lighter on his knee.

'You're going down tomorrow anyway, Joseph. Why don't you see what Marlon reckons and have a scout around while you're there?'

'Marlon was already going to try to find this Kuji,' Joseph said, looking to Junie.

'Marlon knew the men in the plane too,' she admitted.

John frowned. 'Well, you kept that pretty damn quiet. Do the others know he is hoping to find this Kuji while he's down there?'

'No,' she said. 'He is supposed to live near the oil sighting anyway and, well, we were just thinking it was a Kurelu who might know something about the crash site,' Junie explained, 'no-one else's concern, really. Besides, we never even imagined…but now –'

'Now what he's looking for may have different criteria,' the doctor said, 'and that may make him harder to find.'

'Some people want to stay lost,' Joseph warned.

The words haunted Junie as she lay down that night, knowing sleep would be unlikely as the magnitude of this new possibility washed through her. It was almost too much to consider, let alone predict, but a single thought stayed. Her only verdict for now, because she didn't quite agree with Joseph – she just couldn't bring herself to. Surely no-one wanted to stay lost, not really. They probably just didn't know how to get back.

In the blush of dawn the pair made their way down, walking fast to make up time and catch the others. But in their path stood a woman, her skin the colour of the new sky, a large black dog by her side.

'You vowed you would repay me one day…that I could ask you for anything…'

'No,' he said adamantly. 'Not this.'

'You didn't put terms on that promise Joseph.'

Forty-seven

1949
The Shangri-La Valley, New Guinea

Thick, corded roots blocked their way and they wrapped themselves like vines at the base, making the going slow and arduous, but that was only one of their problems. The animals were joining in with the vegetation in trying to block their access to this hidden valley – insects stung whatever flesh they could find and spiders the size of a human palm alternated their visits with venomous snakes. If that wasn't enough to put them on edge, the sighting of a crocodile on the other side of the river earlier in the day had put Philippe, in particular, in a constant state of agitation. He said it made Junie's 'wolf' look like a kitten in comparative threat.

They were following the Baliem River mostly, no longer a welcoming yellow brick road as it had appeared from the sky. Up close it was a raging, dangerous beast that roared through this part of the valley in loud denial of permission to cross. Above it rose protective limestone cliffs that looked like skyscrapers from the valley floor, the only sign of man in the occasional plateaus at their base. Some had been tiered by human hands, although they were not currently tended and Pukz informed Marlon they had about two more days walk to reach the 'black blood'.

A canopy of leaves gave them sporadic shield but it was hot now that the sun had burnt off the clouds, and Marlon called for a break, taking out his canteen.

Pukz said something to Dexjo, one of the village carriers, and the man immediately climbed a nearby tree to scout their position, bare feet running up the trunk with skill. Marlon's eyes moved across the foliage as he waited, taking in a giant rhododendron whose white blooms were the largest he had ever seen, and the thick stands of wood ferns that surrounded them among the moss and lichen. Birds called constantly to each other, mostly parrots, he recognised, and Marlon felt the rich abundance of life here engulf him. It permeated everything, like it couldn't draw enough into itself, filling every crevice and exploiting any opportunity to claim ownership of sunshine. In all it was certainly beautiful, when it wasn't trying to kill you.

It reminded him of other paradises he'd witnessed, places where only those whose blood ran with it truly understood it. The Miwok, the Hawaiians, the Larrakia. And now these native people: the Kurelu. There was something very comforting about being in the wild once more for Marlon, like it welcomed him somehow.

Not so for Philippe, it seemed.

'*Merde!*' he exclaimed, peeling off his socks to view the blisters on his feet.

Felix crouched down to examine them, grimacing at the sight. 'You really should wear thicker protection. Perhaps two pairs of these,' he advised, looking at Philippe's expensive business socks doubtfully.

'How is it you wear nothing and I have this?' Philippe said, pointing at the feet of Pukz and the carriers, who looked to their bare soles and grinned. They were interrupted by an excited Dexjo.

'What's he saying?' Marlon asked as the man pointed north and called out something in rapid Dani.

Pukz yelled something back and turned to Marlon. 'Kurelu.'

'How many days?'

Pukz climbed the tree to find out and returned with his verdict. 'One. Mebbe.'

'What can you see?'

'Fire.'

Marlon nodded, taking that into consideration. It could mean many things of course: hunting, a village, a meeting; a call to war. One thing was for sure, they'd soon be encountering this ancient man. And he had no idea what would happen when they did.

'Damn,' John swore, slamming his diary shut where Junie had scrawled her note, knowing he always wrote in it over lunch. When she hadn't risen from what she'd said would be a long sleep-in, he'd begun to worry – and his concern had proven well justified. Looking at his watch, he figured she was already a good six hours into the jungle and probably only a few hours from Marlon's team. What good would it do to chase after her now? By the time he got a search party assembled it would be several more hours and by then she'd almost have caught up with the others.

John turned on the radio, trying to make contact with the port, figuring Junie's husband should at least be told where she was, as cold as he suspected the man to be. Junie Farthington was the ambassador's most valuable asset, even a fool could see that, and the man she'd married had a right to know she'd just walked straight off the map, into a world where no western woman should ever dare to go.

What was concealed from the air was now upon her very skin as the forest engulfed her, swallowing her into its giant, pulsating heart. Every detail fed off the other; every tree, vine, flower and fern, every insect, animal, bird and fish. Humans were just another part of the whole that strove to not only survive but flourish in this rich environment. Despite her fatigue, her fear and her churning mind, Junie was entranced by this place and its trillions of secrets: flowers like lettuces, birds so brilliant no dressmaker could ever match them, trees covered in berries and fruits and chestnuts. Bountiful and abundant, the forest beckoned to her like Eden called to Eve, and she was connecting to its rhythm with each step, extending into it like it was her primal home.

It had a familiar echo, like the purple hills in Braidwood where the eagles soared, or the crashing waves at Burning Palms where the great southern lady hurled her skirts. Yet it was different too, like nothing she'd ever experienced, and it both frightened and calmed her; forbidding her entry even as it embraced her. It was almost hypnotic.

Joseph held up his hand, signalling them to wait as he crouched to read the tracks then, looking ahead, he pointed at the largest bird Junie had ever seen. She put a warning hand on Digger and paused in wonder. It was tall and perhaps heavier than a man, its back thick with silky black plumage, and it walked along the forest floor on strange legs, like those of a giant fowl. Junie gasped as it raised its brilliant blue and red neck to peer at them from a paler blue face beneath a gold crown.

'Cassowary,' whispered Joseph.

The bird cocked its head from side to side and Junie watched in fascination as it made its slow way off the track, as strange and peculiar an animal as she'd ever seen, fittingly prehistoric in this ancient world.

It wasn't the only remarkable sighting of the day. When they broke for lunch, Joseph saw tree kangaroo tracks among those of Marlon's party and Tooh was able to spot the shy animal in the branches above. It was a soft, brown-red ball of fur, more like a teddy bear than a marsupial, sitting not too far away from a bril-liant green and yellow tree python that had wound itself tightly around a branch like a glorious hose.

The exertion of the trek had rendered them mostly quiet until now, but Joseph found his voice as they rested and was pleading with her yet again to let them return.

'It's too dangerous. We don't really know anything about the tribes down here and if anything was to happen to you…'

'We are a big party. I'm sure Marlon would never have come here if he didn't believe we would be walking back out.'

'He may well believe it but he doesn't *know* it. No-one can guarantee your safety, not even Marlon. He's going to be very angry when he sees you.'

Junie knew Joseph was right, and certainly she was sure if she'd thought about it more and been in a rational state of mind she never would have come, but she was sick of being told what to do, of being the ambassador's wife: restrained and cautious and fear-ful. Those were the things that had kept her in a loveless marriage with false friendships, in a sham of a life where money and booze gave the only comfort. Where she feared the loss of the daughter she loved so much she had become lost herself.

'It's no place for a woman like you.'

'Other women live here, have done for centuries.'

'You know what I mean,' said Joseph, frustrated.

'You mean I'm not strong enough? Smart enough?'

'I know you're both those things. That's why I owe you this debt! But please, Miss Junie, don't make me pay it this way.' Joseph watched her, his expression strained.

'You don't understand. I can't turn back.' And it was true. There was too much pain unanswered, too many other people who needed this too. She was doing this for Katie, for Beryl and Dorn, for the Rileys and all the other parents. For the Elite themselves.

And for Frankie.

But, yes, most of all – for herself.

The answer was close now, too close to resist. A white man lived down here. A man who had floated from the sky and kept a piece of Michael with him for a very long time. He knew something – maybe even enough for Junie to put the past, with all of its injustices and grief, behind her. To end the war at last.

At twenty-six years of age she would walk out of this valley with some kind of answer, whatever that may be, and take her first step towards some kind of happiness.

And as Marlon said himself, that was a start.

The night was filled with the discordant song of animal and insect noises, as expected, but that wasn't what unnerved the party as they sat, listening.

Hoo-ahh, hoo-ahh, hoo-ahh.

It sounded like a large multitude of voices and no-one was sure what it meant, but they were all thinking the same thing: war.

Pukz had climbed the tallest tree he could find and his expression did nothing to comfort Marlon as he undertook a less nimble climb to join him. Then he saw what had given Pukz such consternation: a wide, flat part of the valley covered, not in vegetation, but in human bodies. Men in their thousands, naked but covered in elaborate headdresses, feathers, furs and paint, doing tribal dances with spears and other weapons, back and forth around an enormous fire. They looked like ripples on the sea as they bobbed up and down, terrifying in their numbers, breath-taking in their vibrancy and sequence. They danced much as their people would have done for thousands of years, unchanged, in repetition of their ancestors; sacred parts of earth adorning their bodies as they prepared to return to it, or send others into these valley floors.

Hoo-ahh, hoo-ahh, hoo-ahh.

Marlon had to pinch himself to make sure he hadn't been transported in time, so primitive did it feel, so powerful in its raw energy and swell.

'How long will it last?' he asked Pukz.

Pukz held up two fingers, then three.

'Couple of days, huh? Where?'

He shrugged, but pointed at the field where the dancing was taking place as a guess. Marlon was still churning it over when Philippe hissed up at them.

They climbed back down to see everyone crouched and on alert.

'Company,' Carl whispered.

What now? Marlon wondered, frightened at the thought of being captured and led towards that massive throng.

Marlon gestured for Pukz and Dexjo to investigate and soon their fears abated as Joseph was led into the clearing, followed by Tooh.

Marlon laughed, clasping his hand. 'You made it.'

'Yes,' Joseph said, looking nervous.

'What's wrong? Did anything happen on the way?'

'I, er, had to pay a debt,' he said and stood back as someone else joined their group – the person Marlon wished to see more than anyone on earth but the last person he wanted to see here. Tonight.

'Junie?' said Philippe in disbelief.

'What the hell are you doing here?' Marlon said, furious.

'I have to tell you something,' she said, appearing infuriatingly calm.

He stared back. 'And I suppose it couldn't wait until I got out of the stone age?'

'No,' she said. 'It couldn't.'

Everyone was still gaping and Marlon grabbed her arm, moving her away. 'A word, then.' He walked a good twenty feet then spun her around. 'Do you have any idea what you've walked into?'

'Shangri-La?'

'No, not right now. In fact, quite the opposite. Hear that? That's war, Junie. Tribal, spear-throwing, eat-your-enemy kind of war. What in God's name did you have to tell me that couldn't wait, because it better be good.'

'Someone survived.'

'Survived what?'

'The war – I think.'

'Half their luck. I hope we do the same.'

'Kuji is a white man. Not a ghost or healer or whatever people believe. He's a man, flesh and blood with white skin. Tooh told me. He met him with Pukz.'

Marlon considered that new information. 'Why didn't Pukz mention that?'

'Maybe he enjoys being the village daredevil on his own.'

'No, not that Tooh was with him, I mean, why didn't he tell us Kuji is a white man?'

'Maybe he did.'

'Lost in translation,' Marlon said, remembering Pukz pointing at Ernest on the plane. *You. Kuji.*

He began to pace. 'It could be anyone…a missionary, a lost soldier…'

'Tooh said he fell in a cloud from the sky. Sent by the gods. That's why they fear him.'

Flashbacks of parachutes assailed him, thousands of them. Like angels.

'He had Michael's lighter…'

Marlon looked into her eyes, into the pain that had lived there for so long, now at the surface. 'You can't keep hanging onto his ghost, Junie.'

'Someone else did,' she said, holding the lighter up. 'Someone held on to it down here – and I have to know why.'

'You can't be here! How am I supposed to protect a woman on top of everything else?'

'For God's sake, I'm not made out of glass. I've walked this far and I'm perfectly fine. And I've got Digger –'

'And you've got legs and breasts and a beautiful face! And there are thousands of head-hunters over there having a big old war party who may just think you'd make a pretty gorgeous sacrifice – or a meal!'

She looked momentarily unnerved then flicked back her hair and regarded him coolly. 'Well, don't you think it might be an idea to move around them while they're preoccupied?'

As he strode away, he wasn't sure what annoyed him the most: the fact that she was right or the fact she was here because she still loved a dead man. Either way, this expedition was steadily deteriorating into the worst idea of his life.

❦

It was cold and exhausting travelling on that night, but it was their best shot, Marlon had to agree. Moving around right now was their only chance of pulling this off, as Junie had so frustratingly pointed out. The ritual would actually be a perfect diversion, keeping most of the men away from the area they needed to get to – but time mattered more now. They could sleep when they got home, because by forgoing it, they would hopefully get to the site by tomorrow afternoon, find out everything they could, then get the hell out of here.

Who knew when or if they would ever take this chance again? Privately Marlon was hoping there wasn't any potential for drilling. Only a mass development would be plausible now considering the dangers the area posed and, seeing this valley first-hand, he definitely didn't want it being invaded by the twentieth century. It had been a mistake to show the others that canister.

But he couldn't undo that fact now. They knew the site was there, and sooner or later someone would have come to investigate – probably Philippe, with a lot more ammunition and men. Best to do it now when he could do everything he could to discourage progress and protect this untouched world and the hidden race of people that belonged here. Western culture would be like a drop of poison that spread through it, infecting it like a plague, much as it had for many other native peoples of the world, including his own. Marlon's Miwok blood ran cold at the thought.

Yes, completing the expedition now was in the Kurelu's best interest. He only hoped it was in theirs too. Sympathetic to this ancient race he may well be, but that didn't mean he wasn't also terrified of being caught in the middle of whatever it was that sea of warriors were up to. And it wasn't as though he could put the image of thousands of armed cannibals out of his mind.

The drums beat through the thick night in continuous, dark threat, the already dangerous forest now alive with the call of war, warning them to go back with every step they took forwards. It thumped in their chests and leapt through their veins, reminding Marlon of similar fearful moments during the war. The pound of shells through woolly mountains. The whirr of engines from black dots carrying shiny pencils. The only thing keeping his focus away from it was the woman in front.

Junie was climbing a slippery slope and he held her hand to help. She was doing well to keep up, her figure silver in the moonlight, but he walked near her protectively at all times, Digger nearby. The others had been aggressive in their questioning of why she had come and how to get rid of her, but Marlon had reasoned that there was nothing else for it: she had to come with them, and in the end no-one could argue that piece of logic. And there had been no time to stand around and do so.

But that was two hours ago and exhaustion was now taking its toll. Even with the jungle pulsing at their fear their bodies were heavy with fatigue and it was Philippe who finally called for a break. They took one reluctantly, falling to the ground and pulling out water and assorted pieces of food.

Marlon passed Junie a canteen and she drank, her features pale.

'You all right?'

She nodded and he knew she would say she was even if she were dying, perhaps just out of pure damn stubbornness.

'Still angry?' she whispered back as the others conversed in murmurs nearby.

'Yes.'

She drank again, watching him, then ventured something else. 'I have to know, Marlon. For all of the people who loved them. I'm here on their behalf too.'

'I thought you said you trusted me.'

'You told me not to, remember? Besides, you didn't have all the facts.'

'Joseph would have filled me in.'

'But I –'

'Cut the bullshit, Junie. You came because you're sick of being told no.'

She studied the canteen. 'I guess that's true. It's the first time I've done something rash in a very long time, you know.'

'And how does that make you feel? Happy now?' he said, unable to stop the sarcasm from creeping into his voice.

'No,' she replied. 'But maybe it's a start.' She took his hand behind a tree trunk and he looked down at it, surprised.

'You know, I really hate it when women throw my words back at me.'

'Maybe you should stop being so charming,' she said. She leant against the tree then, resting her eyes, but she didn't let his fingers go. And somehow all the anger he felt simply slipped away with that tender little act, leaving her words to echo in his mind as he stared out at the menacing forest. Whatever charm he had couldn't compete with the perfect memories she had of her lost lover.

'It's no use, you know,' he said, more gently now. 'Loving a ghost.'

Her eyes remained closed but she answered him at least. 'I know.'

Marlon held her hand just a little tighter before letting it go, knowing that if they made it through to tomorrow it would bring that ghost as close as he would ever be. He could almost smile at the irony of it as they sat among the drums of war, trying to find a way to bury a soldier from battles past.

But like Junie had said, it was just something she had to know – what happened in the end – and if she needed Marlon to walk with her through the last hours of Michael's life, then so be it. Because the only way she would ever find new love was if she let the old one go.

Forty-eight

'There.' Pukz pointed and they moved down the hillside with excitement. Two full days and a night of walking had depleted them all, but the drumming had finally faded mid-morning. And now it seemed they'd actually made it to the site where the sample had been taken.

Philippe moved over to where Pukz now stood, smacking the damp area near the water with his stick, and sure enough, the black oil oozed from the ground, thick like blood, as the natives had termed it. An apt description, all things considered, Marlon thought. Carl knelt down and the men began to converse excitedly as Pukz moved away.

'Mission accomplished,' said Felix, sitting down on a fallen tree trunk and fanning his face with his hat. 'How long till we can get out?'

'They'll want to investigate for a while – I'd say a few hours or so. Meanwhile I have something I need to check out with Junie. I'll take Tooh and Joseph, if that's okay. And Digger,' he said, patting the dog as he sat by his side. They were good friends now, probably because he sensed Marlon's protectiveness over Junie. Dogs were experts on loyalty.

'How long will you be gone?'

'Not sure, maybe till nightfall.'

'All right,' said Felix, a little uneasily.

'Tooh,' he called and the man made his way over, Joseph and Junie following. 'Let's go.'

They said their goodbyes and Tooh walked them towards the river, which was quite shallow at this juncture but Marlon still held Junie's hand tightly as they crossed. He hadn't come this far for her to float off down the Baliem.

They walked for about two hours then paused at the sound of human activity, hiding behind some bushes as a village came into view. It was quite small and looked innocent enough with its quaint mushroom shaped roofs and elderly women chatting in the sunshine. No men were visible, although plenty of children ran around.

Tooh pointed to a hut perhaps a hundred feet away, isolated from the rest, with its own garden plot in front, and Marlon nodded. He made his way towards it stealthily, only to return ten minutes later with a shake of his head.

They couldn't very well search every abandoned hut in the area, nor every piece of forest nearby where the man might have gone, so Marlon took the chance.

'Ready?'

Junie was so filled with nerves by now she couldn't speak, so she gave him the thumbs up instead. They stood, walking in single file into the village to make contact with this lost race of people at last.

One by one, the inhabitants came out to stare.

'Kuji,' said one, pointing, and another came closer, an older woman, and touched Junie's arm. She said something then, peering at Junie's eyes, and they all came closer to investigate. The old woman was pointing at the sky and Marlon wasn't sure if they thought Junie was a spirit or just that her eyes were the same shade of blue, or something else entirely.

Marlon nodded at Tooh and the man did his best to talk, although it was a different language down here. A few words got through when Junie produced the lighter and they pointed at the hut, chatting rapidly.

'What is it?' Junie asked and Joseph took her shoulder, already guessing.

Tooh looked sad as he delivered the news, making a moving motion with his arm and pointing back.

'The river?' said Joseph.

'Yes,' Tooh confirmed.

The old woman held Junie's blue eyes with her own dark brown, understanding there as Tooh said the words.

'Kuji dead.'

༺❀༻

There'd been no evidence to collect in the hut, nothing to tell them about the man in the end, only the bare essentials of village life. Nothing to say he was Australian or even white. Only that he was very tall for these parts, judging by the way he slept.

Junie felt as if Michael had died a second time, so strong was her disappointment. It was with heavy feet that she followed the others along the path with Digger, who seemed to sense her sadness, licking her hand every now and then.

She had believed so blindly she would find answers that she could scarcely fathom she'd been wrong. She'd even dared hope that it was Michael, of course. So foolish. Junie wished she'd never heard of this false Shangri-La, feeling worse than just lost – now she was devoid of any emotion, save the need to be with Frankie; at least there she'd find Michael's smile. Still in the world. Real.

Marlon was watching her, she could feel his kindness and concern, and she wanted to thank him for trying but even those words couldn't be found as they reached the river once more. She was too heartsick to speak. There had been a surge in tides and the water ran faster now. Maybe that was how it happened. Maybe the current had caught him by surprise, whoever the man had been.

'Hey,' called Joseph, waving over at Philippe and the others across the water. They waved back but then something made them freeze. Then panic and run.

Hoo-ahh, hoo-ahh, hoo-ahh.

Junie watched in shock as men rose from the forest, rushing towards the party on the opposite side of the river, throwing spears as they crowed for war.

Hoo-ahh, hoo-ahh, hoo-ahh.

'Shit,' she heard Marlon say as he and Joseph took out their guns and began shooting in the air. Junie realised she was still standing and went to crouch when fire ripped through her shoulder and she fell instead, straight into the cold water where her head found a rock and everything turned black.

The last thing she heard was a man call her name, but it wasn't Marlon. It wasn't his voice at all.

❦

'Come on – wake up, please wake up.'

That was Marlon's voice, she realised as she opened her eyes.

'Oh, thank God. Come on, we have to get out of here. Can you walk, Philippe?'

'*Oui*,' he grunted, holding his side as Felix strapped a wound.

'Digger?' she asked as he shook his wet fur over her.

'He must have pulled you out,' Marlon said. 'We found you around the bend on the shore.' He ripped the material away from her shoulder as Felix finished with Philippe and rushed over to check her head then bandage her wound.

'We'll have to watch out for concussion but this isn't too deep,' he said, running water over her shoulder wound. 'Hold on.' He bandaged her shoulder quickly and precisely but it hurt like hell and she gritted her teeth.

'Where are…?'

'They ran off when we fired the guns, but they could come back. Nearly done there, Felix?'

The doctor fastened the last of it. 'Finished.'

'Let's go,' Marlon said, half carrying Junie away from the area the men had come from. 'Which direction should we take?' he called to Joseph, who was staring at tracks in the sand.

'This way,' he said suddenly and they found themselves moving down an obscured path, Joseph leading them at a run.

Green, Junie found herself thinking as it passed by in mottled shades around her. So much green.

'Stay awake,' Marlon warned, lifting her closer against his side as they went.

It's like a tunnel…a chlorophyll tunnel, Junie mused, drowsy with the patterns. I'm going to be hunted and killed here. Then the tunnel will turn white and lead me to Michael.

'Stay with me.'

Stay with Marlon.

Junie focused on him as hard as she could, holding on with what strength she could summon as he propelled her forwards.

'It's all right, Junie. I've got you now.'

It seemed endless, this flight through the green, but they finally stopped and Marlon let them collapse and rest. It was deep forest now. The tunnel had turned shadowy and mysterious, the sun struggling to break through, and Junie blinked, trying to halt the fall of her eyelids into total darkness.

'Do you think they followed?' Philippe panted as they tried to get their breath.

'No, I think they ran off,' Marlon replied. 'Might track us, though. Speaking of which, why did you choose this way?' he asked Joseph.

'Big footprints,' Joseph explained, wide eyed as he saw the source. 'I was following him,' he said, pointing.

'Who?' Junie asked, lifting her aching head off the tree she was leaning on, but Tooh answered for him.

'Kuji.'

She blinked through the shadows towards a rock not twenty feet away and there, in what remained of his Australian corporal's uniform, sat the ghost at last. His hair was matted in a long tangle, his beard obscured most of his face, and his arms and legs appeared so tanned he was more brown than white. But his eyes held a familiar man's soul and it was very real, indeed.

'Michael,' she breathed.

Then for the second time that day, Junie's world turned black.

Forty-nine

'Still nothing?' Joseph asked, returning from filling the canteens.

'Not one word,' Marlon told him, trying again. 'I said the uniform is familiar. Remember? Up in Wau?'

Michael was hungrily eating the biscuits they'd given him but was seemingly disinterested in anything else and Junie was watching everything he did in stunned shock, reaching out every now and then to touch him, but dropping her hand when he flinched. There was a nasty scar running from his temple to his neck and Marlon wondered when it had occurred. He was wondering a lot of things, as were they all, but one thing was for certain: something was deeply, terribly wrong.

'Did you walk in here or is this where you landed?' Philippe asked.

Marlon pressed too. 'Michael, where's the wreck? Did anyone else survive?'

But there was no response. Marlon asked Felix his opinion.

'He seems to have some kind of head injuries from the fall, presuming that's how he got here. Maybe combined with shell shock,' he guessed, watching Michael intently as he rummaged for more food. 'It's hard to say. I've seen plenty of similar patients at the veteran's hospital in Hong Kong. They just can't cope, so they retreat into silence. He's probably worse because he's had no-one to talk to for so long.'

'Can…can he be treated?' Junie asked, fear evident as she stared at this faded version of the man they once knew.

Felix hesitated. 'Possibly.'

'What do you mean?'

'Well, he doesn't seem to recognise either of you, for a start… and, he doesn't respond to basic questions – hell, he probably doesn't even realise the war is over,' he said, handing Michael the canteen, which he looked at blankly. 'John has some experience in the field so he might know more, and we'll run some tests, but I can tell you right now, this is…well, it's going to be a very long road.'

'He hasn't spoken yet,' Marlon reminded her.

'He…he said my name when I fell in the river. I'm sure of it.'

'Well, that's a start,' Marlon said softly and she looked at him with tears in her eyes.

'Yes,' she said, 'it is.'

༚༝ཊྛༀ

They walked into the night, making as rapid progress as they could, fearing more attacks, but none came, and Marlon finally called for them to stop.

'We'll have to rest,' he said, and despite the dangers, no-one argued, falling to the ground and most asleep within minutes.

Michael had followed them willingly enough and now he curled into a ball in the dirt and went instantly to sleep too as Junie watched him through drugged eyes. Her head and shoulder were throbbing and she wanted to sleep so badly that her body already felt like it was, but still her mind resisted. The shock washed over her in waves of residual adrenalin. *Michael is alive. Michael is alive.*

'Come here,' Marlon whispered as he lay nearby, reaching out his arm in understanding, and she fell against his chest, clinging to the man who would let her touch him.

'Not dead,' was all she could manage to say.

'No,' Marlon said, smoothing her hair. 'Kuji is real all right.'

She fell asleep as well then, feeling Marlon cover her tenderly with his jacket as she did so and move a respectable distance away.

The moon rose over Shangri-La and the magic of the place filled her dreams. Michael floating here with the gods to live by a river of gold, where the forest fed him and the people revered him and no white man's war could touch him. Shangri-La saving his life, after all.

When morning came she felt stronger as the shock slowly began to fade. Yes, Michael was alive. The miracle she'd longed for all these years had come to pass.

He lived right here, in paradise.

Now all he had to do was leave.

৽৽৽

All the following day they walked until again they paused for sleep at night and throughout the journey, Junie fought for a sign of the man she knew. Marlon helped when he could. They used every trigger they could think of to pull something out from beyond whatever walls now surrounded Michael – photos, stories, even songs – but nothing registered, nothing except Digger. The dog wouldn't leave Michael's side and it was the only thing that made him smile; a small, vague little smile, but a smile just the same. And, as Marlon mumbled just before they fell into an exhausted sleep once more, that was a start...and it was better than a poke in the eye with a blunt stick. That gave Junie a small, vague smile too.

Next morning was thick with fog and Junie watched Michael as he flicked a brilliant feather around with his fingers. It was the only object he seemed to carry with him, apart from a crude sort of knife that he used at meal times, and she felt emptied of ideas as she observed him.

'Wonder why he does that?' Marlon said, watching him too.

'Repetition can be very soothing to a disturbed mind,' Felix told them. 'They're starting to use it as a kind of therapy. Meditation especially.'

A disturbed mind, Junie repeated to herself. Is that what the doctors would term it? They were higher up now, nearly back to Wamena, and she watched the fog swirl its way across the valley, obscuring what lay there, blinding the viewer from any answers as to the mysteries of this place. Michael's mind was likewise filled, she reflected, a thick fog lay across it she couldn't dispel. Maybe no-one could, came the realisation and it frightened her.

The confronting thought remained that afternoon as they finally arrived at Wamena and walked into the relieved arms of John, whose reaction soon turned to incredulity when he saw Michael.

'The man you knew?'

'The man we *know*,' Junie corrected him.

'Yes, of course, of course,' John said, still staring. 'Come, son, how about we get you some fresh clothes, eh? These look...worn.'

He led Michael gently to the clinic, speaking to him in soft, calming tones as his patient looked about him in confusion. By Shangri-La standards, Wamena truly was civilisation. Junie took advantage of the simple indulgence of warm water, soap and clean towels as she washed up out the back. Then she ate a hot, welcome dinner at Marlon's insistence, giving John time to examine Michael.

'And how does he respond to photographs? Is there any sign he – oh, there she is.' John paused, interrupting his discussion with

Felix. 'Your, uh, husband wants you to call him on the radio,' he told her, pointing at it.

'All right,' she said, dreading the idea. Sooner or later she would have to face Ernest and Eliza and that whole farcical world, but right now the only thing that mattered was the injured man in front of her. And the man he used to be.

'Can I have a word first, Junie?'

She moved outside with John as the jungle prepared for night, the now familiar sounds of the nocturnal forest rising.

'When did you say the plane went missing?' he began, lighting his pipe.

'Six years ago – 1943.'

'Six years, eh?' He puffed, nodding. 'That's a long time to be lost.'

'Long time to grieve too,' she told him.

'I well believe it. Close friend, is he?'

'Yes.' She had forgotten momentarily that the doctor had no idea of her history with Michael. 'His family will be completely beside themselves when they hear the news. When do you think he will be able to travel?'

The doctor cleared his throat and resumed his pipe. 'I think we should hold off on anything like that just yet – let him acclimatise himself first. Felix has agreed to stay on.'

'I – I was hoping to take him home...'

John looked at her with soft concern. 'It's probably better for you to go and break it to his family rather than stay here for now. It's going to be bittersweet for them and it's better coming from you.'

'Of course. I can go to Port Moresby and be back in a few days.'

'Make it a few weeks – in fact, why don't you go home and tell them in person? Get that shoulder healed. See that daughter you're missing so much.'

'But what if...what if he needs me?'

He sighed before answering. 'Junie, this could take years…if, well, if we can help him at all. You do understand that, don't you?'

She didn't, but she was trying to.

'The best we can do for him is take things slowly here for a while. After that…' He paused and she felt dread begin to build. '…I'm sorry but the only option is a hospital of some kind.'

'No, I'll take him to his home,' she said, shaking her head firmly. 'His family will want to look after him.' *As will I.*

'His family won't be able to treat him. He's nothing more than –' he cleared his throat, '– he's nothing more than a shell of a man, Junie. This is going to be painful for all of you.'

'He can't just be locked away like an animal.' The image of a mighty elephant near a concrete pool passed through her mind.

'I'll make sure he is cared for kindly. I promise you.'

'I know you will,' Junie said. They all would. But nothing would change the fact that Michael would still be imprisoned in a room as well as his mind. Staring out at the jungle, she wondered if taking him from the valley was a mistake. At least there he had been free, in his own way.

'Why don't you say goodnight to him now?' John said, patting her arm and packing his tobacco and pipe away. 'He seems exhausted and so do you.'

She nodded and waited until he left to compose herself for what she had to say. How much to reveal. If he would take anything in anyway. Probably not.

'Hello, Michael,' she said, walking into the clinic and sitting next to him as he stared out the window. She tried to take his hands but he pulled away. The same hands that once couldn't wait for her touch, she reflected brokenly.

'I…I thought it might be time to talk about your lighter.'

There was no moment of recognition. He didn't even look at it as she placed it between them on the bed, but she felt he was listening. Well, hoped.

'The inscription was there to remind you…of me.' She touched it, an old, wrenching pain twisting at her heart. 'Do you recall that night on the beach at Burning Palms? When we went down to the shore, just the two of us? I still had a silly crown on, I think.' She smiled a little. 'And you and I…we made love for the first time.'

He didn't move; no expression, no flicker of memory. Just stillness.

Junie felt her strength begin to fail her as the pain fell to despair and the wretchedness of the lonely years she'd spent longing to share these words with him was unleashed.

'Michael, I loved you so much,' she said, her voice breaking, 'please…just show me some sign that you are still in there somewhere. Just something, anything…' The tears flowed now, choking her. 'You used to love me too once, but I – I had to marry Ernest instead. There was no choice because my parents were in so much debt. You *must* remember?'

His once kind eyes were blank and that emptiness tore at her. That and the tragic truth that came with it. He didn't remember. Burning Palms, the sacred night they shared, the stolen moments that followed that summer before life drove them apart. Those precious memories now belonged only to her, and that terrible knowledge twisted into the loneliest corners of her heart.

Her voice was barely a whisper now against it.

'I'm so, so sorry you've been through so much but please come back to me. Please. I need you.'

But he remained silent, so she grasped his hands, desperate now.

'Our daughter needs you. Michael, you're a father – that night we made a baby. We have a child.' The tears ran unchecked, the truth freed at last. 'A beautiful little girl. I named her Francesca, but she prefers Frankie.' Junie struggled to finish as their daughter's face filled her mind. 'She has your smile.'

He pulled against her hands but she held on this time.

'Ernest doesn't know but I wanted you to...I tried to tell you before you went to war and I sent you a letter but I was too late. I'm *sorry*...I'm so, so sorry. Please tell me you can hear me now. Please!'

She searched for any glimpse of the man she knew but there was only the mask-like visage of a broken soul, a deceptive facade that cruelly looked like the man she had loved but was strangely vacant inside. Michael back from the dead but not with the living.

He pulled his hands harder now and they slipped from her grasp. And she had no choice but to let them go.

'All right,' she said, her mouth trembling. 'It's all right.' She struggled to stand, fatigue overtaking her. 'You just...you just have a nice sleep. I'll be back in the morning and we'll talk some more, okay?'

He said nothing as she straightened her clothes, her body unsteady as she made one final plea. 'If you are in there somewhere, I hope you can hear this at least: Michael, you don't have to stay lost. Someone taught me that recently. You just have to know what you want.'

But as she left she knew whatever that was, it was something Michael couldn't share. And it wouldn't be what she wanted to hear, even if he could.

∞≈≋≈∞

Outside the clinic, Marlon leant his head against the wall, his chest aching as he understood at last what drove Junie Farthington; what life had done to make her fight so hard for others. Why she loved her child so desperately – it wasn't Ernest's child at all, it was Michael's, and she'd had to live with the lie, all these years. Forced to marry the wrong man for her family's sake and watch the other march off to war, never to return.

But mostly his chest ached because she loved that soldier still, a man who no longer existed in his own white skin. The Kuji. Not really of this world. Unable to love her back.

No wonder Junie couldn't find happiness – what she wanted was impossible.

And happiness was denied him now too because he loved that lost girl. Which meant he had nowhere to start.

Fifty

Kuji watched the woman leave, the one they called Junie. A name he knew somehow. She had a dog, a big soft one that he thought he might have seen once as a pup. They knew him, the woman and the dog. And the big man with the sad eyes.

He knew them too. They were part of the bad dreams. They lived under a bridge in the forest with the others. Where people screamed that name: Michael.

He reached into his pocket and took out the crimson feather, its colour as brilliant as the day he'd found it on the forest floor.

The woman should have it, he decided, placing it on his pillow before leaving.

For some reason he thought she might like it.

Fifty-one

'No!' she cried. 'We have to go after him. We have to find him!'

'We'll never find him, Junie.'

'We found him before!'

Marlon caught her trembling hand in his. 'He found us, remember? We can't hope to go back in there and hunt him down. You've seen how thick the jungle is, and how dangerous. It's impossible.'

'The only way we will ever see him again is if he wants it,' Felix told her. 'If he walks out of that forest one day, remembering who he is and looking for help.'

'It could happen,' Joseph said, but they all knew it never would.

'I drove him away,' she sobbed. 'I said too much.'

'No, Junie. He wasn't hearing anything you said; there was no comprehension.'

Junie looked at John, her face stricken. 'But now I...I've lost him twice.'

The doctor shook his head sadly. 'Michael was lost a long time ago. Let him live out his days in the way he can deal with them – simply, with the Kurelu. Not in some asylum or veteran's home. You know that's no kind of life for him, Junie.'

'Life,' she repeated, her eyes drawn to the forest once more. 'Is that what he's doing? *Living* down there?'

'It would be no life at all in our world,' Marlon said gently.

'But his family – his mum and his dad and Dorn and Beryl. You don't understand. They thought they lost both their boys in the war. They…they should get to see him again.'

'You can go to them and tell them what you saw. You can give them that much,' John reminded her.

'Maybe they'll come looking for him, maybe they'll see there's no point – either way, you'll be giving them more than most ever get. You'll be giving them an answer,' Joseph said.

'And a son, somewhere on this earth still,' Marlon told her, opening her hand and placing the feather inside it. 'Let him live there on his own terms, Junie. I think he was trying to tell us that in his own way. Let him go.'

'Some people want to stay lost,' Joseph reminded her and she knew now that it was true.

Fifty-two

The plane engine droned as they flew towards Port Moresby and Junie looked out as the wilderness gave way to civilisation, thinking Michael had fulfilled one dream for her at least: he had stayed in the pages of her favourite book; he had remained in Shangri-La.

'What are you pondering over there?' Marlon asked, and she turned to find him observing her.

'I was just thinking about Shangri-La, how it feels surreal down there really. Like it doesn't actually exist at all.'

He waited while she gathered her thoughts closer.

'That Kurelu woman…she said Kuji was already dead. Strange really. Maybe her meaning was lost in translation.'

'Maybe it was her way of explaining the way he is.'

'I guess so. I'm realising now they've been very good to him. Perhaps they're not afraid of him at all; perhaps they're actually trying to protect him.'

'Not all of the Kurelu are trying to kill people, you mean?'

'Exactly.'

'I know Philippe likes to say we barely escaped with our lives from savage head-hunters –'

'And don't think he won't be dining out on that story for a few years,' she predicted.

Marlon smiled wryly. 'But the truth is we walked into their war ceremonies, their conflict. How do you think it would have been if a Kurelu had walked into one of our wars? I can't imagine everyone putting down their weapons to let them march on through. In fact, I saw what happened to the villages that got in the way up in the ridges.'

Junie thought about that for a moment. 'I wonder what it is that drives them to help Michael survive?'

'Maybe they think they have to look after him because he came from the gods, like a ghost,' Marlon said, gesturing at the sky.

'Or maybe they're just very kind.' She stared out the window to the clouds below. 'I feel like I did only see his ghost,' she said sadly, touching the glass. 'Like I visited him in some sort of after-life. It didn't feel like earth, but then again, it certainly didn't feel like heaven, just that place in between, like you said to me once. The only place he can belong now, I suppose.' She shrugged. 'It's just such cruel irony to find only pieces of him, not the whole man.'

'Does it make it easier or harder to let him go? Or are you still holding onto those pieces?'

Junie looked over at Marlon and she saw something in his expression that made her think carefully before answering. 'I'll always hold onto pieces of Michael Riley, Marlon. He owns part of my heart and nothing can ever change that. What we shared can't be erased and – I don't want it to be. I will love him forever,' she admitted. 'Always.'

'The Michael that was or the Michael that is?'

'The Michael in here,' she said, pointing at her heart. 'I guess it's hard for you to understand –'

Marlon shook his head. 'I understand that a lot more than you know.'

Junie was curious but she didn't pry into whatever pieces of love still clung to Marlon's heart. They flew on in thoughtful silence, watching the mountains below. She was sad to leave this beautiful place, she realised, despite everything.

'I'm glad they've decided not to drill for oil,' she said after a while, thinking about the beauty of the valley in the late morning sun, the mists still clinging to the outer rims in ethereal protection.

'I think Philippe couldn't get out of there fast enough. Besides, it looked like there wasn't really that much there.'

'Good,' she said. 'It should stay the way it is.'

'Sure you haven't got any Indigenous blood?' he asked, but there was approval in the jest.

'Nah, I'm just a wild colonial girl, remember, with some Irish fishing wench thrown in.'

Digger woke up as the plane dipped slightly and she patted him back to sleep, glad he was the only other passenger. The rest of the team had been picked up a day earlier by a charter who'd flown in to deliver some medical equipment, courtesy of a few phone calls Junie had made on her last return. She and Marlon had stayed under the guise of helping out, but in truth it was because Junie wasn't quite ready to give up on Michael returning. And because she didn't want to face going home.

'I have a confession to make,' Marlon said as she absently twirled the feather she'd had resting in her palm. 'I overheard you that last night. Talking to Michael.'

Junie flushed. 'That was a private conversation.'

'I know, and I'm so sorry. I didn't mean to eavesdrop at first but then I had to know.'

'Had to know what? My sordid past?'

'The truth. You've been a mystery from day one, and I guess I just had to know why you chose the life you did. Why you still do.'

'I told you, it's complicated.'

'Yes, I heard.'

She felt her temper rising then as she tapped the feather. 'You know, it's so easy for a man to judge a woman. We don't have the same tools you have. We don't get to bully our way through and get what we want through sheer force.'

'You have tools. Good ones, as I recall.'

She glanced at him, looking for innuendo. 'I imagine you are referring to my skills as a lawyer.'

'Of course.'

'Ernest would get the best barrister in the country. You don't know him. He won't let his child go – or his perfect image as a family man.'

'But she isn't his child.'

'No.'

'Why haven't you ever told him?'

'There didn't seem much point. Better for Frankie to think she's legitimate, I suppose.'

'Better how? So she has to live the life he chooses for her instead of what you would choose? What Michael's family could share with her? Seems to me it might be the perfect way out – telling him the truth then threatening you'll tell the press.'

'I could never do that! I couldn't make her the subject of gossip or scandal –'

'Better to be called a bastard than have no family life at all. I think Frankie would choose to see you every day over name calling, if she had the choice. I know I would.'

'Hah!' she said derisively. 'What do you know about it?'

'Native American, remember? I've been called every name in the book but it was worth it a million times over to grow up with my Miwok grandmother.'

Junie heard the truth in his words but was too angry with him to comment.

'You know what I really think? I think you want to stay lost too.'

There was a pause before she responded. 'How can you say that?' she said, deeply hurt.

'Because you don't think there's any other life on offer, maybe? Because it's safer? Because you're too scared to take on the power Ernest holds? I don't know. Maybe because you're happy to fight for everyone else but not for yourself.'

'I've fought. I fought for an education –'

'That you don't use.'

'I've fought for my child –'

'Who you don't see.'

She went silent, frustrated to find herself crying.

'There's only one thing worth fighting for, Junie, and that's happiness. That's what you really want – you told me so yourself.'

'Nothing can make me happy any more,' she said, rubbing her cheeks.

'I've called you on it before and I'll say it again – bullshit,' Marlon said as the plane began to descend towards the runway. 'You just keep thinking happiness lies in all the things you can't have. You can't *have* the 1941 version of Michael. I'm sorry to sound so harsh, but you just can't have him, Junie. He's gone.'

'I know that!'

'Do you?'

Junie paused, wondering if she truly did. 'It's just…I used to imagine over and over that he would come back – every day, the same dream – and now that miracle has finally arrived but it's been distorted.'

'Maybe it's time to stop dreaming. Pull that heart of yours into reality, into right *now*. You can't have him, but you can have... other things. Don't tell me what you want that you *can't* have, tell me what you want that you can.'

She frowned, confused. 'Such as?'

'You're a smart girl – you tell me.'

He left her to think as he landed the plane and got out to unload her luggage.

'Got a list yet?'

'I – I'm not sure.'

'Well, if you do figure it out in time, I'm refuelling then I'm off to stretch my wings. It's a free ticket in one hour, if you want it.'

'To where?'

'Wherever this tells you to be,' he said, pointing at his heart.

'Your heart?'

'No, yours, you goose. I already know where mine wants to be – with a damn stubborn woman. Problem is, she won't settle down in here.' He tapped his chest again and shrugged. 'Keeps getting lost.'

Fifty-three

'About bloody time. I've been waiting half an hour.' Ernest was angry as he flicked his cigarette into the bin and pointed at his chauffeur, William, to take the luggage. 'Can't even imagine what kind of explanation you have for such ridiculous behaviour,' he said in a low voice as he steered her through the airport by the elbow.

'I had my reasons,' Junie replied, trying to remain composed.

'Whatever they were they couldn't possibly warrant you taking off into the jungle searching for a hermit. The whole of Port Moresby is talking about it, although fortunately it didn't make the papers. You're a complete embarrassment.'

'And what of your ridiculous behaviour? Anyone writing about that yet?' she returned coolly, although her heartrate was beginning to build.

He paused as William opened the door. 'Don't be coarse, Junie.'

'No, heaven forbid I embarrass *you* further.'

He sat opposite her and she felt his scrutiny as she looked away, disgusted by the sight of him. 'Let's not do this now, all right? Fix yourself up. Eliza's having some surprise dinner party for you and you can't go looking like Jungle Jane.'

'Eliza?' she said, snapping her gaze back to stare at him.

'Yes, Eliza.' Digger jumped into the car and Ernest screwed up his nose. 'God, he smells like the jungle too. Better give him a bath tomorrow.'

She said nothing, waiting.

The car took off and Ernest tapped at his leg, scowling in the silence before smoothing back his hair in typical fashion. 'Do you really want this out in the open between us?'

'Yes.'

He sighed. 'Fine. Eliza and I have an understanding, all right? You don't have to be a baby about it. Everyone has affairs; it's not a big deal.'

'How long has it been going on?'

'I don't see why that matters.'

'How long?'

'From before we were married,' he said dispassionately.

Junie nodded, swallowing that slowly. 'So she decided to marry a wealthier man but befriended your second-choice wife — just to keep you close, is that it?'

'Oh for God's sake! It's not as if you didn't enjoy her company and vice versa. I actually think it works rather well — and you do too, if you'd only admit it. Affairs take the bedroom duties away from the wives and we both know you'll be happy about that.'

'I see...so does that mean I can have one?'

He gave a short laugh. 'Who with? The idiot version of Michael Riley? Philippe said he doesn't even speak, let alone bathe.' He poured a drink from the console. 'Not much more than an animal by the sounds of things. Or does the idea of being with Tarzan turn you on?'

Her eyes flickered at the cruel streak that ran inside the man she married.

'What are you going to do, run off into the jungle when the mood takes you? I don't think so, Junie.' He poured her a drink as well then, her first in many days. 'Come on now, be a grown-up. You live in the real world – a *civilised* world – and it's not like we don't have a good arrangement. Your family have their farm and their money, your daughter goes to the finest school…who knows? You may end up in Kirribilli House.'

Junie placed her untouched drink back in the holder and took her compact from her handbag, applying her lipstick as her rabbit began to run.

'I'm even happy for you to practise law, if that's what you want. You can't say I've been unreasonable to you, Junie – most men I know wouldn't allow their wives an education, let alone a career.' He nodded at her hair as they neared their house. 'Better fix that too.'

Junie closed the compact as the rabbit paused. 'Tell me, Ernest, have you heard of the Magna Carta?'

'Of course,' he said, distractedly, looking down the drive. 'Even a first-year law student is familiar with that.'

'Refresh my memory, would you?' she asked as they drove towards their friends, who were waving from the front porch, Eliza holding balloons and champagne. 'Or have you forgotten what it means yourself?'

'Don't be ridiculous. It means every man, even the king, is bound by common law,' he said in a bored voice as they slowed down.

'Quite like our current constitution really, only with one small amendment,' she said, closing her purse.

'That being?' The car stopped and an excited Eliza blew Junie a kiss.

'In Australia, the law protects the just, whether that be a man *or* a woman,' she stated as he got out and waited for her, impatience etched on his face. 'I want a divorce, Ernest. See you in court.'

Junie closed the door and tapped on the chauffeur's window.

'Where to, Mrs Farthington?' William responded.

And, as she named her destination, she had the satisfaction of seeing every snobby face on that porch watch her leave.

Then Eliza's gloves lost their grip and the balloons slipped away, far above them all.

⚜

Junie stood at the water's edge, barefoot and scrunching her toes into the sand, as she contemplated Marlon's words. She'd spent so long wishing for what she couldn't have that the very idea of wanting something she could have felt peculiar.

The sea air picked up her hair and she revelled in the feel of it, realising how much she'd missed the great southern lady since she'd been in New Guinea. She regretted that she hadn't thought to visit more often as the water eddied about her ankles.

Tell me what I really want, she begged as the waves rolled lazily towards her. I'm as lost as ever.

You're a smart girl. You tell me, Marlon's words echoed.

Maybe it would be easier to think of what she didn't want.

Pain.

The image of Michael the last moment she'd seen him, staring into space, trapped somewhere she couldn't go, appeared in her mind. I don't want to torture myself, or him, any more. I don't want either of us to suffer.

She supposed that was a pretty good start. What else?

I don't want to live in the past.

Did that mean she'd finally let him go?

Never the love, but...yes. I'm letting go of wanting to be with him as he is now. Even if I could find him again, he can't love me like he did, and I can't watch him sit in a cage in his mind, unable to do so.

Junie blinked against the glitter of sun on water. The grief was still there but she was slightly amazed at that new truth too. So what now?

I don't want to be married to Ernest any more, at least I've decided that. But I don't want to be lonely now that I've left his world and Eliza behind.

The water lapped at her feet and she started to feel some kind of purpose evolve as she faced the original question once more. What *did* she want?

I do want to go home. I do want to raise my daughter. I do want my family and friends back in my everyday life.

Something was bubbling now that felt oddly like excitement.

I do want Michael's family to know Frankie is his child. I do want them to help me raise her.

Now she was almost smiling. The sound of a plane droned in the distance and another thing she wanted exploded.

Junie took off at a run, back to the car, yelling to William to start the engine. Yes, she definitely wanted something else she could actually have. She just hoped she wasn't too late.

'Any room for Dorothy and Toto?'

Marlon turned from checking the engine and a flash of black fur ran past as Digger jumped into the back seat, wagging his tail expectantly. Then he grinned that long, slow grin of his and she hoped he wouldn't wipe that grease smudge off his cheek as he cleaned his hands on the towel.

'You're three minutes late, Mrs Farthington,' he said, checking his watch.

'Wallace,' she informed him. 'The name is Junie Wallace.' Because she wasn't Junie Farthington at all, she never really had been, and from this day forward she would be true to that girl from Braidwood; true to following her own common law. No longer lost, not any more.

They climbed on board and he turned to her, their faces close.

'Ready to fly, monkey?'

'Yes,' she said smiling slowly. 'I finally am.'

He kissed her then, and it was neither hesitant nor questioning; it was one of those kisses that intoxicated with its mixture of craving and love. She felt the sheer thrill of him opening up to her with all the passion and possibilities that entailed as he held her close, the places where their skin touched suffusing in a sudden, wonderful warmth. There was no pulling back to slap him this time, no turning away with guilt. She placed a hand on his grease-smeared face instead, allowing herself to love again at last with this man, the one who had shown her where to start – and that place was right here and now, with him.

'Where to, Miss Wallace?' he said, catching her hand and kissing it.

'There's no place like home.'

'Figured out what really matters, did you?'

'It's actually a very short list.'

And with that the plane took to the skies, heading south to the land that held the rest of the people she loved, the people who were capable of love in return, and she figured that happiness was something you could not only find but hold on to – if you chose what you could actually have.

And what you wanted the most.

Her rabbit lay down, resting at last, and she looked out to where the great southern lady shone in the afternoon light, leading her home.

It had taken a while, but she'd found Shangri-La in the end.

After all, Junie Wallace was a smart girl.

Acknowledgements

I am a very fortunate woman in that I have a colourful, extensive family to draw inspiration from for story-telling, as evident in my first novel *Gallipoli Street*. In *Worth Fighting For* I was able to include the first-hand experience of my parents, as well as my twenty-one aunts and uncles, in order to paint a picture of Australia during WWII and I'd like to share a few facts behind the fiction with you here.

To me they are forever the 'the Golden Generation'. I suppose this is in part due to the fact that they were youthful during the Golden Years of Hollywood, an era that produced many of my favourite movies, but it is also a fitting title because they all shone somehow. Each and every one – in unique and extraordinary ways.

The character of Junie is completely fictional however I wanted my heroine to have a strong name so I chose my auntie June's uncommon, special one for the role. I must humbly thank her husband, my Uncle John, for giving his kind permission to do so.

The story of Michael Riley is inspired by my Uncle Jack Clancy, who passed away in December 2014 at the age of ninety-one. He too tried to join up under-age and was caught out, then sent to train with other young would-be soldiers at Liverpool under the instruction of his father, my 'Da' James Clancy. Jack's face always lit up when he talked about that training period – a merry old time spent with his dad and his mates. As the months wore on the self-named 'Elite' grew as tight as brothers and by the time they left a strong bond had been formed, the kind of bond I imagine only soldiers leaving for war truly understand.

They formed part of the 2/31st Battalion and experienced harrowing months of combat against an aggressive enemy in some of the places mentioned in this novel, including the Markham Valley and Lae. By then Jack had become great mates with a soldier called Hughie Kilpatrick who was quite a bit older than the others, possibly even in his thirties. One day they were walking along a road that the Japanese had mined with booby traps and a bomb ignited, killing many of Jack's mates. He and Hughie survived – although Jack was lucky to do so. He was the closest one to the

Jack Clancy, 1941

The Elite, circa 1942. (Jack Clancy far left.)

bomb which apparently exploded upwards then out, sparing his life, although he was injured.

By the time Jack made it back the war was drawing to a close and his mate Hughie was involved in one of the last patrols the battalion would ever make. They were approaching some other Australians in the dead of night, and accidentally surprised a soldier on duty who had fallen asleep. The terrified man opened fire and Jack's mate Hughie was killed.

The war ended not long after and I know Jack found that a painful irony to live with – to lose Hughie to friendly fire only weeks before the whole nightmare came to a close. All I know is Hughie Kilpatrick must have been an awesome person to have been our Jack's best mate. You can't help but wonder what life he could have led if it wasn't cut so cruelly short in a foreign jungle.

Even though Jack had to live with the grief of losing Hughie and many of his brothers in the Elite you wouldn't have known, for a kinder, more cheerful soul you'd never meet. For the record, Jack did get to marry his sweetheart, Beryl, and had many children and grandchildren to bless him through life.

Marlon's character is also fictional, although the exploration of the Shangri-La Valley in New Guinea is part of my family history. Mum's other adored brother, Des Clancy, was an adventurous soul who played a pivotal role in the region's discovery and exploration. A pilot during the war, he went to New Guinea afterwards and became a patrol officer. There he soon gained the reputation as a brave explorer, often leading patrols into crocodile-ridden, uncharted territory, including Shangri-La, where real-life cannibals came face-to-face with their first Caucasian/ westerner – my uncle. And yes, they did call him 'ghost'.

I always think of the expression 'larger than life' when I remember Uncle Des. He was a wonderful gentleman and a celebrated humanitarian who became the much-revered District Commissioner of the Southern Highlands.

A former kiap who worked under Des, Peter Barber of Melbourne, wrote these words for his eulogy: 'The indigenous people of the Southern Highlands respected him, indeed loved him. (Des) ensured that their new world was harmonious, progressive and the least traumatic he could programme. He built significant relationships with the Southern Highland leaders; he was a bridge across the cultures.'

I grew up hearing his fascinating tales and New Guinea was a place much discussed in my family. I hope I have managed to capture some of Uncle Des's compassion for native peoples in Marlon and have given readers a glimpse into the wondrous Shangri-La Valley, one of the last, lost pieces of paradise on earth.

Des Clancy, Papua New Guinea, early 1950's

Dorn Riley is inspired by my gentle mother who in her small role herein reminds us that education is a wonderful privilege and not to be taken lightly if you have the opportunity to gain it. She had to leave school at the age of fourteen and always ached to learn once more, and so she did in her fifties, earning her degree at Sydney University beneath those wonderful Gothic spires. There is much of my mother Dorn's compassion and understanding in this character and I thank her for being such a beautiful influence in my life.

Beryl is so-named for yet another Clancy sister – my fabulous, fun Aunty Beryl Colgan. I also named Dr John Colgan after the real-life Beryl's husband who wasn't a doctor at all (but was smart enough to be one if he'd cared to). Uncle John was very dear to me and I'm glad I've been able to include his full name in the novel. Beryl and John were part of the gang that holidayed down in the

Kevin Best (my father) and Beryl Colgan (my aunt) dressing up at one of many parties with the Burning Palms crowd

'Fibro Majestic' at Burning Palms, a real-life shack that sat at the bottom of a rugged, thickly vegetated hill. Many of the Clancy sisters and their friends frequented the shack and fun dress-up parties and fishing were part of the agenda. I always loved hearing about Burning Palms and hope I captured some of its magic here.

My father's brother Jim and his darling sisters have also been an inspiration, especially when it came to fashion with the girls. It wasn't hard to paint images of the Trocadero with these fabulous women in mind.

I have managed to include all twenty-one of my aunts' and uncles' first names in the novel as a kind of thank you/tribute to them for all they gave me in life; all the memories, advice, love and oh-so-much laughter. You are a precious generation to all of us and I never want to let any of you go, but I guess I'm not really. I'm holding you right here, in little black sentences, for as long as people read my work.

I would also like to make mention of a final name inclusion, not part of this generation; not even a relative, but a young man who was very special to many, many people: Jake Loadsman.

Jake was the adored nephew of my close friend Zoe, and, as such, was like a nephew to me too. Like the fictional Jake in the novel he was witty, funny, loving and an incredibly loyal person. And he loved his country. In fact, he had just been accepted into the army when he passed away tragically one week after his twenty-first birthday. I was writing about loss in the novel at the time and some of that grief is reflected here.

I thank his mother Sarah for allowing me to include her son's precious name for my very Australian character. A truly 'good bloke' and mate; a kind and generous young man.

And finally just a few more thank yous before I go:

To my friends and family who always so patiently support me and read my endless drafts I thank you so very much, especially Mum, Gen, Linda, Benison, Thuy and Theresa. And to my neighbours with whom I spent one particular, most hilarious night on 'research'. You have forever enriched my knowledge of colourful Australian colloquialisms, even beyond my father's wealth of sayings. Well played Chris Naysmith, in particular. My notebook remains full.

To my wonderful editor Jo Mackay and the team at Harlequin, I can't thank you enough for your wonderful company and hard work. You always put in above and beyond the call of duty and your expertise continues to inform my writing. Thank you for believing in me.

To my husband Anthony who makes this journey with me with much humour and good grace and my sons who have complete belief in their mum – bless their beautiful hearts. And to my adorable dog Saxon, the inspiration behind 'Digger'. Humanity can learn a great deal about love from our precious canine friends.

To the people of Australia during World War II who fought so hard to protect our way of life under terrifying circumstances and the Americans and Allies who fought alongside: we have everything to thank you for. I only hope we can strive to do your sacrifice justice and remain compassionate – above all things. Always.

And finally to my beautiful dad Kevin Best, always with me. I'm following that star for you, as promised. Rest in golden peace.

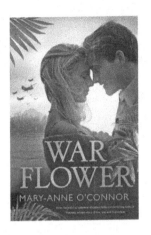

Turn over for a sneak peek.

WAR
FLOWER

by

MARY-ANNE O'CONNOR

OUT OCTOBER 2017

One

'Might snow.'

Poppy Flannery gave him a nod, finding an expression that she hoped neither patronised nor encouraged the drunk as he huddled in his blanket on the ground, slurping from something in a brown paper bag.

She would have liked to inform him that she was studying geography as part of her leaving certificate and there was no evidence of it *ever* having snowed in Hornsby, at least as far as she was aware. Then she imagined what it might be like to spend the winter on a railway station and emptied her purse into his beggar's hat instead.

'Don't encourage 'im,' the station master warned her as he passed by, but he didn't try to evict the man and she was glad. Perhaps the company of constant, random strangers gave him comfort.

The drunk burst into a merry rendition of 'Let it Snow! Let it Snow! Let it Snow!' and the words followed her as she moved along. She half wished it would – at least they'd have something miraculous to cheer them up on this dreary day; it was so cold her fingers were icy little sausages that curled up inside her jumper sleeves. To make matters worse the train was late and now pulling in slowly, clanking and straining in crimson steel which had long earned these models the moniker of 'red rattlers'.

Poppy dragged her things on board, the smells of dank uniforms and forgotten lunches at the bottom of school cases filling her nostrils as she collapsed on the vinyl bench seat. It was wet but she was grateful for it, regardless. Most afternoons she was forced to stand, crowded as the carriages always were during the earlier school rush.

Pushing damp strands of blonde from her eyes and under her hat Poppy steadied her cello case as the train lurched forward, trying not to lose control of her other belongings lest they slide across the floor. That achieved, she relaxed somewhat, free now to take in the other passengers. Her eyes passed over the young boy picking at a scab on his hand and the elderly lady reading her book to keep scanning, spying familiar figures chatting beyond the doors: Barbara Rowntree, Judith Bentley and Raeleen Montgomery, three particularly vicious 'cool chicks' who were probably going home late due to detention. Poppy's twin sister Rosemary had dubbed them 'the Dogsquad' years ago when they first began to bully everyone outside the in-crowd.

The trio had taken off their hats and were now shaking their long, wet plaits free, a calculated risk considering Sister Ignatius often patrolled the trains to ensure uniform rules were being obeyed. Poppy suspected they did it mostly for the benefit of the boy who stood near the door and turned to investigate him herself.

He was quite attractive, tall and fair in his camouflage fatigues with a cadet beret thrown casually on his school bag. Watching him almost with the whites of her eyes lest he notice her stare, she observed that he was unwrapping something bound in milk bar paper. Something that smelt very, very good in the fetid air. This was what the police should use to torture the bad guys into talking, she thought to herself as the scent arrived in force. Then she couldn't think much further because her salivary glands exploded, flooding her mouth until she almost drooled onto her jumper.

Oh dear God, they've added vinegar.

Poppy forgot to hide her stare now as the boy lifted one fried, salty potato scallop in the air and took a big bite, ripping the crispy coating from its white, soft innards. The air around his mouth fogged from the sudden heat in the cold carriage air and his lips were shiny as he chewed, mouth half open, probably from burning his tongue, but he didn't seem to care. Suddenly she wanted to kiss that mouth even more than she wanted to eat those delicious golden discs, so sensual was his pleasure, so eager his hunger as his mouth devoured that flesh.

Then he did notice her and she felt herself blush as he paused mid-chew. A slightly teasing smile spread across his face, transforming him from 'quite attractive' to 'bloody gorgeous'.

Licking his fingers, he offered her the wafting pile. 'Want some?'

There was something so suggestive about it she could almost imagine he was asking her to share in carnal adventures rather than fried potatoes and her cheeks flamed as the old lady looked up with a disapproving frown, sliding her gaze from the boy to Poppy.

'I do,' said a voice heavy with flirtation.

The Dogsquad were on the prowl and Poppy could only watch as they approached, swinging their hair about and grabbing onto poles in predatory fashion. Rosemary predicted they would seduce the richest men they could find after graduation and have more money than any of the 'dags', the group she and Poppy were usually considered part of. Unless they got themselves pregnant over summer and stuffed up their North Shore housewife careers, Rosemary had added hopefully.

The train paused at Warrawee Station, sighing into inactivity, and the boy let them take a scallop which the prowlers divided and ate with exaggerated rapture.

'Mmm,' Barbara said, smiling at him as she licked her lips. The boy continued to eat, watching them almost expectantly, like he was used to this kind of attack. Then he shifted his gaze back towards Poppy and to her shock gave her a wink.

Contempt soured Barbara's otherwise pretty face and Poppy tensed, knowing retaliation would be swift and sharp.

'What are you doing coming home so late, *Ploppy*? Are you in an oompa loompa band or something?' she sneered, nodding at the cello. The other two girls laughed and all eyes in the carriage turned Poppy's way.

'Just the school band,' she mumbled, wishing she had the courage to tell Barbara such Bavarian groups were made up of brass musicians, not string, but of course that would just prolong the ridicule and scrutiny. Truth was she loved her cello and was majoring in music, hoping it would be her ticket to ride, as the Beatles would say, straight into university.

'Maybe she had to go to pirate class,' Raeleen suggested and Barbara let out a short laugh.

'Yes, where is that eye-patch these days, freak-show, or is Mummy changing the pattern?' Poppy felt every part of her body tense up at the mention of her most embarrassing teenage moment: the day her mother covered half her glasses with orange floral wallpaper to hide the gauze and bandaging beneath. Having an eye operation at thirteen was bad enough, having every person she passed stare and laugh at her mother's attempt to pretty the situation up was social suicide. The eye healed eventually, so well she no longer even had to wear glasses, but the stigma had long remained.

Fortunately the boy didn't ask any questions, seemingly more intent on finishing his feast, and Barbara moved closer, flirtatious facade back in place.

'And why are *you* home late? Or is this your normal time to catch the train?'

Poppy let out a relieved breath, glad to have the focus shifted from her, and listened to the answer. She had been wondering that herself; Poppy knew most of the boys on this train-line after six years of high school – by sight only, for the most part. Staring at his beret and fatigues she figured he probably had cadet training after school.

'Drills on Thursdays.' He shrugged. 'We moved recently. I used to live in Adelaide.'

'Lucky Adelaide,' Barbara observed.

The elderly lady made a noise of disgust and Poppy couldn't have agreed more. Looking at Judith and Raeleen she wondered how they felt about always being in Barbara's shadow while she did her thing as Queen Bee. Rosemary liked to say they all knew what the 'B' stood for.

The boy was starting to look uncomfortable and put on his beret to hide it, something that made Poppy like him even more.

'My station,' he said, moving towards the door as the train pulled into Wahroonga.

'What's your name?' Barbara called out as he alighted.

'Ben,' he called back, walking off with his back hunched against the rain.

Ben. The name echoed in Poppy's head as the Dogsquad ran back to their double seats, no doubt to dissect the whole scene and scheme about a way to run into him again. With their aptitude for earning detention, Poppy figured that wouldn't take long.

The train arrived at Waitara and she clutched both school case and umbrella in one hand, dragging her cello with the other, but the umbrella's fine material was flimsy defence against this particular afternoon. The wind whipped at her little arc, turning it inside out and flipping her about with it as the rain tapped at her face like a typewriter. Poppy struggled against it almost instinctively, her mind still reeling from the previous assault on her senses.

Ben. Each tiny shock of rain in her eyes reinforced the shock of his impact.

'Pass,' the ticket officer ordered and she wriggled to retrieve it from her bag and show it to him. She wished the dratted man would stop asking her every day – surely he recognised her by now. It was difficult to remain inconspicuous carrying a massive instrument. But she forgave him as music wafted from the little transistor he always carried, the sound of the Ronettes following her down the stairs in a freezing draught of winter. Their voices were filled with longing and she knew that song had just become the soundtrack to many hours of daydreaming about a boy on a train. A boy called Ben who wore camouflage fatigues and tempted her with salt and vinegar.

Then she lost her battle with the wind and watched her umbrella take flight and sail down the street, realising right at that moment that any attempt to ignore the force of that boy would be as futile as fighting the elements this day. The day that he became, to one rain-soaked girl clutching a cello case on the side of a road, her one and only baby.

'For what we are about to receive may the Lord make us truly thankful. Amen.'

It was quiet as they commenced eating. Robert Flannery didn't believe in having the radio on during dinner, let alone the television. He said it distracted them from appreciating how fortunate they were to have a good, solid meal in front of them every night. Besides, it was also an opportunity for everyone to share their news. The girls hated doing that. It was almost as bad as going to Confession, although Father John was far easier to appease than their parents. A few Hail Marys and all spots on the soul were dissolved in that little cubicle. Here in the Flannerys' kitchen nothing less than lives lived in perfect Catholic schoolgirl servitude would suffice and spots on the soul were considered grave stains.

'How was school today, Rosemary?' their mother, Lois, asked, looking at her expectantly.

'Very satisfying. I managed to get eighty-seven in that Chemistry exam which wasn't too bad considering the average was only seventy-two.'

It was a good pitch but Poppy knew her father wouldn't be satisfied.

'Thirteen marks short of what you're capable of though, isn't it, young lady?'

Rosemary sighed. 'Yes, sir,' she mumbled, picking at her peas.

'And what of you, Poppy?'

She raised her eyes heavenward, looking for inspiration. 'The recital went down well at practice although it kept me late and the train was –' filled with the aroma of delicious scallops and an even more delicious boy called Ben, '– delayed too.' Her father looked about to comment and she rushed to add something that would please him. 'I saw a homeless man drinking from a brown paper bag on the station. He looked so cold, he even said it was going to snow so I…er…gave him my pocket money.'

'Is that wise, considering what he will most likely spend it on?' her mother asked, fork pausing mid-air.

'No, well…perhaps not.'

'It's a better idea to give a man like that some food or clothing,' Robert advised between mouthfuls.

'Rosemary gave him her sandwich last week,' Poppy informed them, thinking that might put her sister in the good books.

'Did you? And why are you giving away my expensive ham?' her mother asked, unimpressed.

Rosemary's mouth dropped open as she looked from one parent to the other, like those clown heads at the Easter Show, Poppy observed, waiting for a ping pong ball. 'Well…he just…he looked hungrier than me.'

Their father sat back, observing the twins as they awaited his verdict. 'Matthew 25:40.'

Both girls quoted at once: 'Jesus said, "Whatever you did for one of the least of these brothers and sisters of mine, you did for me."'

'Quite so,' he said, nodding slowly. 'Charity should be your way of life, every day. But charity also begins at home. Is it charitable to give away your mother's ham after her hard work making your nutritious lunches each day?' He looked to them both and they knew he expected no answer. Robert Flannery enjoyed his dinner sermons far too much to tolerate interruption. 'Then again, if we walk past the least of our brothers without compassion we let the Lord down, do we not?' He tapped his knife thoughtfully on the tablecloth. 'You need to appreciate the hard work that comes with true charity as opposed to giving what you already easily have. Tomorrow you will both make your own lunches and this man's as well. To give truly is to put *all* others first.'

'And no messing up my kitchen,' Lois added, frowning, probably at the thought of a single starched tea towel out of place.

'Yes Mum,' they agreed.

Later that night Poppy stretched herself away from the table where she and Rosemary were studying and walked over to the window to see if the rain had eased.

'Well would you look at that...'

'What is it? Saints alive – Mum! Dad!' Rosemary called, rushing to open the front door, a sudden gust of ice invading the heated room.

The family joined her on the porch, each mesmerised by the sight of what appeared to be some kind of miracle. Snow had fallen on their Sydney yard, cloaking gum trees and sleeping hibiscus, transforming the lawn into a silver carpet in the moonlight. It was a wonderland. Like the pictures they'd seen in storybooks from Europe and America, where Santa arrived on a sleigh and children built snowmen that came to life.

The twins rushed out, picking up the powdery stuff and hurling snowballs across the drive, their laughter on the freezing air.

'Careful now,' Lois called, but their parents didn't try to stop them having fun for a change and the girls enjoyed that miracle too, pausing in their game to build their very own man of snow.

'What shall we call him?' Rosemary said breathlessly as they added two pebbles for eyes and a short stick for a nose.

'Ben,' Poppy replied, giggling at her sister's confused expression. 'I'll tell you later,' she promised.

It was quite late by the time Poppy shared her secret with her sister, in an excited whispering that had them looking forward to their dreams, and, as she clutched her pillow and gazed out at the beautiful night, she knew with certainty that her life had changed on this miraculous day.

Yes, let it snow, and let it be a sign that the beautiful night promised her the beautiful boy. That the magic wouldn't melt away, come tomorrow.

Two

'Come on, give us a look,' Graham 'Chappy' Chapman complained, trying to peer at the grainy faces over the rest of the group's shoulders. 'Is that Barbara Rowntree in the netball photo? Man, she is smoking.'

'One and the same. I remember she had a bra in sixth class,' Chris Plumpton said with authority. 'My mum plays tennis with hers. Nice family genes, if you know what I mean.'

'You're a sick puppy,' John Hawkens said with a shake of his head, but peered harder through his glasses just the same. They had gathered in the library with a few others to look through the convent school yearbook and research possible hook-ups at the school dance come Friday.

'Wait till you see her, Ben,' Chris said, pointing Barbara out. 'Bet you've got nothing like that in Adelaide.'

Ben studied the face and shrugged. 'Not in Adelaide but I think I met this girl on the train last week. Had some friends with her…a redhead and brunette?'

'Judith Bentley and Raeleen Montgomery.' Chris sighed. 'Divinity comes in threes.'

'Did you talk to her?' Chappy asked, half joking.

'Yeah, a bit. She came up and asked me for a scallop.'

'*She* came up to *you*?' The others were staring, impressed.

'Well, yeah. They were good scallops.'

'Let me explain something here,' Chris said, enunciating carefully, 'a girl like Barbara Rowntree doesn't approach *anyone,* even to get a free bit of potato. Guys approach *her.*'

'If they have the guts,' Chappy added, still slightly incredulous. 'What else did she say?'

'Just asked me why I was travelling home late and stuff.'

'Yep, she's definitely after him,' John said, looking to a thoughtful Chris for confirmation.

'Let me ask you something...did she swish her hair around like this?' Chris made quite a show of flicking his imaginary locks and the others laughed.

'She did do that a bit, actually,' Ben admitted.

'In like Flynn,' Chris declared. 'You have to make the most of this, my friend. An opportunity to score with Barbara is a rare and precious gift.'

'I don't know,' Ben said, shrugging. 'Maybe...'

'You're not thinking straight, man. Look at her!' Chris said, pointing back at the photo. 'There is no "maybe" here. You need to strike while the iron's hot.'

'...and the girl's hot,' Chappy agreed.

'We'll see,' Ben said, moving away as the bell sounded.

'*We'll see*...geez, you've got rocks in your head,' Chris told him as they made their way down the stairs. 'She obviously likes you.'

Guess she did make that obvious, Ben thought to himself as they lined up for assembly, wondering why that didn't excite him more. Then the national anthem began to play and he shut down any further thoughts of girls. There really wasn't that much point.

'It's hopeless,' Poppy said as she stared in dismay at the mirror. 'She won't let us wear anything that dates past nineteen-fifty. It's like she's trying to repel boys from us.'

'Of course she is,' Rosemary told her, frowning at the brown velvet and tugging at the hem. 'Maybe if we roll up the waistband...'

'Maybe if we just don't go...'

'Oh no you don't. You can't go telling me about some dreamy boy on the train then not go to his school dance.'

'Maybe he won't go.'

'Everyone goes. Try this,' Rosemary ordered, throwing a twin-set and skirt her way.

'Twins in twin-sets? We'll look stupid!'

'Pfft, guys don't know what they're called,' Rosemary said, turning up the radio. 'Ohh, maybe we could wear these.' Poppy had to laugh as her sister pulled out the fancy dress box, putting on their mother's long evening gloves and pointing dramatically as she sang along to the opening verse of 'My Guy'. Poppy sang back, giggling and dancing too. Clothes and costumes were held up and discarded in comical fashion now as both girls tried to outdo the other for bad taste; not a difficult challenge considering the contents of the box.

'Stop in the Name of Love' came next and well-practised routines took over as they mirrored each other, imitating Motown stars they'd seen on *The Ed Sullivan Show*.

'It's no use,' Poppy said finally, breathless with laughter as the song ended, and she fell on her bed. 'We'll have to be hideous.'

'Hmm,' Rosemary said thoughtfully, stroking the long gloves. 'You know, there may just be a way to make this work.'

'Unless you find a magic wand or a fairy godmother in that box I fail to see how.'

Rosemary turned to her and grinned. 'Not quite…but I think I may have just had the most magical idea of my entire life.'

talk about it

Let's talk about books.

Join the conversation:

 on facebook.com/harlequinaustralia

 on Twitter @harlequinaus

www.harlequinbooks.com.au

If you love reading and want to know about our authors and titles, then let's talk about it.